Also by Dana Mentink

A SPRINKLE IN TIME

A SHAKE SHOP MYSTERY

DANA MENTINK

Poisoned Pen
PRESS

Published by Poisoned Pen Press, an imprint of Sourcebooks
P.O. Box 4410, Naperville, Illinois 60567-4410
(630) 961-3900
sourcebooks.com

Library of Congress Cataloging-in-Publication Data

Names: Mentink, Dana, author.
Title: A sprinkle in time / Dana Mentink.
Description: Naperville, Illinois : Poisoned Pen Press, [2022] | Series: A
shake shop mystery ; book 2
Identifiers: LCCN 2021042283 (print) | LCCN
2021042284 (ebook) | (paperback) | (epub)
Subjects: LCGFT: Novels.
Classification: LCC PS3613.E496 S67 2022 (print) | LCC PS3613.E496
(ebook) | DDC 813/.6—dc23
LC record available at https://lccn.loc.gov/2021042283
LC ebook record available at https://lccn.loc.gov/2021042284

Printed and bound in Canada.
MBP 10 9 8 7 6 5 4 3 2 1

To Laurie, editor-in-chief and head of sprinkle operations. You add sparkle to my life.

Chapter One

TRINIDAD JONES HAD NEVER BEFORE realized how much her senior dog, Noodles, appreciated yodeling. Some primal instinct prompted her failed service-dog rescue to chime in with abandon when the bearded visitor took the stage. Not a proper stage, but the small wooden platform adjacent to the charming train car bed-and-breakfast. A couple dozen visitors sat grouped around on folding chairs, tapping fingers and toes along with the music. Was it actually music? Trinidad was not convinced.

Music or not, Alpenfest activities were bringing people to Eastern Oregon in droves and, if a yodelfest was a crowd-pleaser, that was fine by her. A parade, a freebie tasting and concert, a 10K run, and a genuine Alpenfeast were among the other events clustered around two weekends. The tiny town of Upper Sprocket was finally poised to rake in a share of the much-needed tourist money, and Bonnie's recently finished bed-and-breakfast would be a draw as well. Trinidad intended to scoop up her own portion of the visitors with the

Shimmy and Shake Shop, home of her massive Freakshake creations that would become famous if she had anything to say about it. There was no other choice. Start bringing in some money or lose her hard-earned dream. She'd spent the last few months in preparation, inventing creamy fall flavors. How could she fail?

Upper Sprocket couldn't compete with neighboring Josef for the number of amenities to offer tourists, of course, but when the hotels and lodges were booked up, the over-flow yodelers had come to stay in Sprocket. Bonnie had barely finished preparations in time to offer them rooms. The assembled group had decided a small outdoor concert would be the perfect warm-up for the Alpenfest Yodeling Contest set to begin the following day in Josef. Storm clouds were gathering in the sky, and Trinidad hoped the rain would hold off for another hour or two to accommodate.

She noticed the mayor of Upper Sprocket, Ramona Hardwick, sporting a smile that looked suspiciously like a grimace as she gazed at the yodeler. How did the mayor manage to appear so youthful when she had to be knock-ing at her mid-fifties? Trinidad would love to try some of Ramona's skin cream on her own thirty-six-year-old face. The Miami sunshine had not been kind to Trinidad when she lived there with Papa Luis and her parents prior to her marriage to Gabe.

Ramona looked disapprovingly in the direction of Trinidad's dog and put a finger to her lips. The sun-speckled skin on her hand looked every bit her age, which made Trinidad feel both better and worse about herself.

Trinidad again shushed Noodles. He made a valiant effort, but whines and howls kept spurting out of his lips like a teakettle venting steam. Every canine inch quivered to join in the yodel fest.

"He's a natural," Quinn Logan said, striding up to grab a stack of the promotional flyers he'd volunteered to distribute. "You gotta get him signed up with the troupe."

Quinn's blue eyes were framed by adorable little crow's-feet. Why did everything that handsome hazelnut farmer say warm something deep down in her belly? One would think that, after her disastrous marriage to a liar and felon, she would be more on guard. Still, she found herself tucking her frizzy dark curls behind her ears and remembering her mother's admonition to stand up straight. Silly. Trinidad was a generously pear-shaped woman with a sweet tooth and little regard for fashion. No amount of straightening or tucking was going to make her any more glamorous.

She let the rain-scented wind blow the thought away as she took in the view. Glorious. It still stunned her to think that all of Gabe Bigley's former wives were now collected in this one tiny spot on the globe: number one, Bonnie and her daughter, Felice; number two, Juliette; and now Trinidad herself, running her very own ice cream shop. She clutched her stack of flyers tight, calculating how many milkshakes the average yodeler might consume during the two weekends of Alpenfest.

It was hard to keep her mind on business with such scenery pulling at her attention. This piece of land that Gabe had deeded Bonnie was exquisite, the perfect place for a quaint train-car bed-and-breakfast. Bonnie's Sprocket Station exuded charm year-round, but it shone like a jewel in autumn. Tall trees and a thicket of succulent blueberries created a lush backdrop for the four brightly painted railroad cars that now served as rooms.

Bonnie's beautiful piece of land might have made her envious were it not for the fact that Gabe had deeded Trinidad a storefront, which had given her a new lease on life. That storefront was now the Shimmy and Shake Shop, her own piece of paradise...if she could manage to hold on to it.

"Don't miss anyone," Trinidad said to Quinn, handing him more flyers to disperse to the spectators in between yodeling numbers. The inn's dining hall was still partially unfinished, and there was the slightest scent of fresh paint underlying the pine, but at least the first paying customers had arrived. Those new guests would surely meander into town to partake in artisan ice cream during their stay, wouldn't they?

Her insides quivered with the combination of terror and titillation. The bare-bones truth was the Shimmy and Shake Shop needed an infusion of income desperately, since her store had to be rebuilt after a criminal tried to destroy it, and her, two months earlier. So much for quiet small-town life. Murder, mayhem, and milkshakes. Who'd a thunk it?

Quinn's pleasant expression suddenly turned to stone. "Uh oh. We've got competition, headed our way."

A short, red-bearded barrel of a man, Forge Emberly, was thrusting his flyers into the hands of anyone in the vicinity of the yodel fest. His metal wheeled rail bikes were a hit with tourists who happily pedaled along unused train tracks to take in the sights.

"Come experience the rails on the Forge Railriders pedal-powered adventure," he said. "It's a three-hour excursion following the tracks as they pass through timbered canyons and some of the loveliest farmland you'll ever see. Definitely worth the price."

"Not in my book," Quinn muttered savagely.

Trinidad was caught by his uncharacteristic anger. He'd been opposed to Forge's various plans to expand his business, since his ideas usually impacted creeks and forested areas, but she didn't realize the depth of Quinn's distaste for the man.

"If you come back this summer," Forge said to the crowd, as he pressed flyers into more hands, "we'll have a second route that will take you right along the river with views of the Wallowa Mountains."

That last comment brought Mayor Hardwick to her elegantly booted feet. She cinched her knitted sweater against the late September chill and marched over, stopping inches away from Forge. Her blond hair flashed in the sunlight peeking through the gathering storm clouds. "You will stop touting that second route right now," she muttered through clenched teeth. "There is no way the council and I will approve that project. We're not cutting the trees just to suit your sight lines."

Forge's latest proposed trail would connect the existing rail line with another set of unused tracks that swooped much closer to the grand Wallowas, Trinidad knew.

Forge's eyebrows formed a grizzled row. "Maybe you won't be the mayor in November anyway."

Ramona went pallid, lips unhealthily red against the white. "You're not going to win the mayor's seat. People know you're just in it to serve yourself."

He laughed. "Me? Talk about a hypocrite. Think people can't see through your 'Betty the Beaver' scam?"

Trinidad was a relatively new arrival in Sprocket, but even she had heard the accusations. Mayor Hardwick was hanging on to her seat by the skin of her teeth. Rumor had it that she "suggested" to organizations negotiating deals with the city that they purchase supplies of her children's book, *Betty the Beaver Brushes Her Teeth*. The local dentist bought 3,000 copies and suddenly found the sidewalks outside his office repoured. The hospital board, upon which Hardwick served, ordered 50,000 copies while applying to the town for expansion of their facility.

Now Hardwick's complexion turned cranberry. She poked a finger at his chest. "There is nothing illegal about any of my actions. You're not going to get that second route approved."

Forge shrugged. "Already got Quinn here to agree to sell me the two acres I needed as a cut-through. I'll get the approval for the rest in time."

Trinidad gaped at Quinn.

Quinn's gaze was firmly fixed on his boots. No angry retort at Forge's outlandish statement? Several beats later, she began to have a sickening feeling that Forge was telling the truth. But that was lunacy. Why would Quinn have agreed to such a thing, this man who was passionate about his privacy, his land, and his environmental principles? He'd fought Forge at every turn. She was stunned and overwhelmed by a growing sense that she'd missed something important. How? She and Quinn had spent time together almost every weekend for the past two months, in addition to daily texts, phone chats, and what Trinidad had tremulously started to consider "dates." Why had he not mentioned something this momentous?

Hardwick looked to Quinn. She appeared similarly thunderstruck. "Is this true?"

Quinn raised his head but didn't quite meet the mayor's eyes. "Yes."

A one-word reply? No explanation? A cold clamminess took hold of her stomach. *He's been keeping things from you…like Gabe.* Just like that, memories of Gabe's betrayal made her doubt herself all over again. No, there had to be an explanation. She wanted to pepper Quinn with questions, but Forge started in.

"I'm going to unseat you for mayor in November because you're crooked." Forge raised his voice. "And everyone in town knows it."

At that moment, the mayor lunged forward and, with one determined palm, knocked Forge Emberly onto his solid derriere. His flyers floated to the ground like lazy fall leaves in the quickening breeze.

Noodles broke off from his yowling to eye the action with concern.

"You saw it," Forge cried from his position on the ground.

Was he speaking to the crowd or Trinidad? "You saw her assault me. Did someone get that on video?"

Someone did.

Bonnie approached, towering over them. At six foot eight, Bonnie, the former professional basketball player, towered over pretty much everyone, and with an almost-six-year-old child perched on her shoulders and a cell phone in her hand, she loomed even larger. Bonnie's hair was pulled into a ponytail, which Felice held in one small hand, but plenty of it frizzed around her face, the same pale color as her skin.

Felice waved at Trinidad. Trinidad's heart always skipped a beat when she saw Felice. Of the three wives—Bonnie, Juliette, and Trinidad—Bonnie was the only one with a child. Trinidad's friendship with Bonnie was still in its infancy, yet she felt a strong connection, like she had to Juliette. It was that odd "sisterhood of exes" thing, she figured.

"I was recording the yodeling," Bonnie said as Felice twirled her mother's ponytail like a propeller.

Quinn was already helping Forge to his feet, dropping the man's hand quickly afterward, as if the touch was disgusting to him.

"I'll need that video," Forge said.

Bonnie smiled. She always smiled. "No."

Forge frowned. "I'll call Chief Bigley, and she'll force you to turn it over."

Bonnie's smile didn't diminish. "Sorry, but the video will be deleted before she gets here."

"You better not do that."

Bonnie still smiled. "It's my land, Mr. Emberly. I want people to love being here. This isn't a place for politics or arguments. I don't want that around my girl." She held on to Felice's little shin with one hand and toggled it playfully. Felice's hair was caught up in a knit cap with a massive pink pom-pom on the top. Her luminous blue eyes were wide, taking it all in. Each tiny fingernail was stained purple from picking the blueberries Bonnie had generously offered to share with Trinidad.

"Pollyanna," Forge spat.

Still the smile. "Not the worst I've been called. So let's just listen to the yodeling, okay? This isn't a place for name-calling either."

"You should be helping me," Forge said to her. "A second railway will be a win for your business."

Bonnie shrugged. "Some things are more important than winning." She turned her back on the two bickering people and gestured for the yodeling to recommence. "I'm sorry," she called out. "Let's hear that again, okay? Verse two? Or are they stanzas? There's a storm coming, and I don't want us to get rained out."

Now two yodelers took their places and began a complicated choral jousting. Noodles wagged his tail and joined once again in hysterical accompaniment. Forge resumed his flyer delivery. No sign of Mayor Hardwick, who had slipped away after the confrontation.

The collected crowd, an even mix of locals and visitors, did not seem too concerned about what had happened. Most were still seated in the chairs and occupied themselves with friendly chatter and sips of the free hot cider Bonnie had provided. The yodelers were equally calm as they finished one song and plunged into another. They looked straight out of a postcard in their poufy red skirts and gold-laced black blouses. Trinidad was disappointed the men wore long pants with their snappy vests instead of lederhosen.

The chief yodeler cued them up for another song. Though Trinidad sported a smile, her insides were twisted up. She desperately wanted to have a private moment with Quinn, but he was already passing out Shimmy and Shake flyers during the pause, a smidge too focused, she thought. When the yodeling was done and the flyers all distributed, she couldn't spot him at all. She looked at Bonnie, who was now chatting with her newly hired cook, Gretchen Torpine.

"Where did Quinn go?" she asked.

"Didn't notice." Gretchen adjusted the comb that caught her mane of white hair.

Bonnie hoisted Felice down. "Felice and I packaged the blueberries. They're all boxed up for Papa Luis. He said he's coming by later."

Papa Luis, her dear grandpa, newly transplanted from Miami to the rescue. He'd made a bit of a business for himself, schlepping people and property around in his gorgeous 1951 Chevy Bel Air. For Bonnie, she knew, he'd do it for nothing. And that was another issue whirling through her brain. Was Papa intending to take up permanent residency in Sprocket? She knew it was not what her mother wanted, which probably explained the phone call she'd received but not returned.

Thoughts of blueberries made her mouth water. Trinidad didn't know yet what she would concoct with them, but the fragrant jewels were too precious to pass up. Gretchen could only use so many for the scones she was going to bake for the guests. "Papa said he'll pick them up when he delivers the last of your overnighters."

Bonnie turned pink with pleasure. "Guests. I keep pinching myself. This is going to be the most wonderful place for people to visit. They can let go of their troubles and just…be."

Trinidad found Bonnie's sanguine nature a puzzle. After all, this was a woman who'd earned the nickname Bruiser as a power forward for the Oregon Pistons. She'd broken plenty of noses in her heyday. It still amazed Trinidad that she'd shown up after the Shimmy and Shake Shop had been destroyed, shovel in hand, with Felice decked out in tiny overalls, and announced, "You're family. We're helping." And she'd drawn the standoffish Trinidad right into her circle without a moment's hesitation. Trinidad would be forever grateful. Not biologically related, just the former spouses of the same nefarious man. Family, nonetheless.

At the moment, Quinn's strange behavior and the altercation between Ramona and Forge left no room in her psyche for her to ponder Bonnie's quirks. The flyers were gone, there were shakes to be invented, and a pair of eager teen twins running the shop. The boys were incredible, but she dare not leave them too long, especially since their first official Alpenfest event, the freebie tasting at the gazebo, was scheduled to kick off the next day.

Time to get back to business. When she could finally

tear Noodles away from the yodeling, she packed up her Pinto and returned to the shop, keeping thoughts of Quinn shoved firmly away. Their "dates" had been simply casual encounters. He was just a friend, after all.

Liar, her heart whispered.

He was merely a friend the way a Ming vase was just an old pot.

So why was he keeping secrets from her?

———

Back aching and hands tired from scooping, Trinidad finally locked the door of the Shimmy and Shake a half hour before sunset. Noodles settled himself in the passenger seat of the Pinto. When they reached Main Street, the first sprinkles of rain appeared on the windshield, and the dog activated the wiper with his left paw.

"Thank you, Noodles." She'd adopted Noodles after her divorce from Gabe, unable to resist the old Labrador who had been surrendered so his family could acquire a newer model. She could relate, since Gabe had started up with the younger Juliette while still married to Trinidad.

Ugh, stop it, Trinidad. Don't go there again, she ordered herself. Somehow the past was clinging close to the present once more.

Noodles flapped his ears. He had so many hidden talents he revealed at the most surprising moments. The driving assistance was a fairly new development. She stroked his satiny head as they drove out of town.

"Love you, sweetie," she said.

He answered with a lick to her wrist.

They headed toward her rented home. Along the way, she passed the tree-studded turnoff onto Linger Longer Road, the steep route up to Bonnie's property, thinking again of the unpleasant scene with Forge and the bizarre deal Quinn had made with the man. Her hands were cold, gripping the wheel. After a long, sizzling summer, it was a treat to activate the car heater. She hoped she would feel as cheerful when the winter snow hit. She'd lived in Oregon with Gabe during their marriage, but Portland apartment-living was not the same as riding out the wild winters in the eastern part of the state.

She could not suppress a sigh. Winter meant the end of summer tourists, and she still had not caught up financially after repairing the wreck of her store. The weight of her loans sparked a wave of panic, bathing her forehead in sweat and contorting her stomach. *In with the good air, out with the bad*, she repeated to herself to quash the feeling. It was enough to reduce her fears while she completed the drive. Alpenfest would go a long way toward ensuring her financial recovery.

The storm swept in as Trinidad pulled up with Noodles to the tiny house they shared. "Tiny" was the appropriate word for the structure. When her grandfather abruptly arrived from Miami two months earlier, bunking on the sofa, the house had gotten even tinier. But Papa's perpetual good cheer, uniquely Cuban outlook on life, and his near-genius brain had swept away some of the grief she'd experienced over Gabe's departure and the ruination of her store.

Like a phoenix, the Shimmy was rising again, in large part thanks to the efforts of Papa Luis and Quinn. Thinking about Quinn chafed at the sore spot in her heart.

Quinn had actually agreed to clear-cut some of his property at Forge Emberly's urging. Forge was certainly a wheeler and dealer in town, the loudest voice at town council meetings, and a go-getter. There had never been any rumors that he was untrustworthy, but his blunt aggression did not seem to be the kind of personality to win people over. She still could not wrap her mind around their surprising agreement. Was Quinn financially strapped, and had Forge offered a deal? She knew hazelnut farming was not a massive moneymaker, and Quinn was the sole provider for his younger brother, Doug, who had special needs. But he'd never so much as hinted that he'd been desperate for money.

She and Noodles scurried into the house through a curtain of steady rain. She set about warming up a pot of beans and rice Papa had made in his newest efforts at batch cooking. The fragrance of garlic and black beans made her mouth water. *Congri* was so simple, yet so comforting. She added a few slices of cold pork and a plate of biscuits to the table to round out the meal. Headlights from Papa Luis's Bel Air shone through the front window as he rolled up the drive.

"You stay here, okay Noo?" she said. The dog wagged his tail from his spot on the fuzzy beanbag he used as a cushion. He was getting old, she thought with a stab. Silver washed his muzzle, and his back legs were stiff. Impulsively, she draped him with a blanket to keep off the chill that would inevitably reach him when the front door opened.

Papa pushed inside as he always did, in a cloud of barely contained energy. "Those train cars, so amazing, don't you think?" he said, his Cuban accent thick as ever. "Bonnie has done such a fine job, excellent judgment in such an endeavor, which unfortunately did not kick in when she chose the Hooligan."

Papa would only refer to Gabe as the Hooligan. She was happy Papa had become close with Bonnie in the past two months, but then, he had never met a stranger. He'd been making friends with everyone from the pastor to the postman since he arrived in Sprocket. Did she feel it again? That insidious pinprick of jealousy that her beloved Papa had grown an affection for Bonnie? And the other ex-wife Juliette for that matter? Wasn't Papa's love supposed to be exclusively hers? Wasn't *something*? She shook off the feeling. If they were her sisters, then Papa was their grandpa too.

She kissed him. "Raining hard?"

"A real palmetto pounder." He shivered. "And so cold here. This rain is not the same water that falls on Miami."

She laughed. "Wait until the snow comes."

He groaned. "I will have to fortify."

Did that mean he was planning to stay in Sprocket? She was afraid to ask, fearful he'd say what? Yes? No? She wasn't sure which was best, but every day he stayed would make it so much harder to watch him leave.

"That supper smells good, if I do say so," he said. "Let me bring in the blueberry box before we eat."

"Why don't you wait until the storm passes?"

He gave her that look. The one that meant, *you can't*

possibly suggest I leave that untidy box in my impeccable and precious machine known to others as a car?

"Need help?"

He waved his hand airily. "Of course not. You spoon up the meal. And make me a café, will you? Such cold."

She began work on the strong, sugared coffee Papa could somehow swill even into the wee hours of the night. Of course, the man only required four hours of sleep. Another blast of chill air sent Noodles burrowing deeper into the blanket until he noticed that Papa had reentered but left the door ajar.

The dog crept out and nosed the door shut and sat looking at Papa, puzzled.

Now Trinidad looked closer too.

Papa stood with an indescribable expression on his face, his thick thatch of black hair speckled with raindrops.

"Trina?"

"Yes?"

"There is something…unexpected in my trunk."

"Like what?"

"Perhaps you should come and see."

Something in his tone made her hustle to grab her raincoat and follow him out. The porch light illuminated the shining sides of the pristine Chevy. Papa had closed the trunk but not all the way. He opened it again, and they looked inside.

Next to the blueberry box was a rug.

Under the rug was a bundle.

To the side of the bundle, something white protruded.

The white thing had five fingers and a palm.

Before she could get out a sound, Papa took the tire iron and poked vigorously at the hand and then the bundle. It didn't move. He reached in and gently applied two fingers to the wrist.

"What…what is it?" Trinidad asked stupidly.

Papa shook his head and withdrew his fingers. "A dead person."

"Dead?"

"Thoroughly."

Her stomach clenched. "Who?"

Papa reached in again to sweep away the rug when a rumble of thunder roared across the sky followed by a spray of lightning.

The electricity failed, and the porch light was extinguished.

Trinidad's common sense kicked in. "Don't touch anything else, Papa. We have to get inside and call the police and an ambulance in case…I mean…to help."

He nodded, closing the trunk lid with his elbow, but not fully, to shield the occupant from the pouring rain. "We should stay inside with the coffee," he said practically, leading her back to the porch where Noodles waited.

She stumbled as if in a dream.

But this wasn't a dream.

It was a real dead body…in Papa's trunk.

Chapter Two

CHIEF CYNTHIA BIGLEY ARRIVED WITH Officer Alvin Chang in tow approximately thirty minutes later. Her tall, slender physique always made Trinidad feel like sucking in her own stomach. The only relief to the "all business" demeanor was the glimpse of an unusual necklace when her top uniform button came undone. Was it a pearl? An opal? A tooth? Trinidad had never had the courage to ask her.

Though she'd already dealt with the chief thanks to previous criminal activity in Upper Sprocket, her brown-eyed gaze, so reminiscent of her baby brother Gabe's, still made Trinidad uneasy. The chief might always see Trinidad as the ex-wife who had cooperated in the investigation that sent Gabe to prison for embezzlement. Certainly Bonnie, Juliette, and Trinidad had plenty of grievances against the philandering Gabe. *Enough,* she told herself. That ice cream had already been churned. Sprocket had only one police chief, and, when a body turns up, who else was she supposed to call?

Officer Chang stayed inside, his raincoat dripping on the floor as he jotted down their comments in a soggy notebook. Every so often, his dark eyes would skim longingly over the stove, where the dinner was still warming.

"Any idea how the body got into your trunk, sir?" he said to Papa.

Papa raised his palms toward the ceiling. "I was at Sprocket Station, Bonnie's new place. I loaded the blueberries. Felice wanted to show me something she found in the trees, a bunch of wildflowers. Such a sweet little girl. Kids are so full of life and curiosity, aren't they?"

Chang heaved out a weary paternal sigh. "I'll say."

Papa continued. "She was so eager, I left the trunk open. I returned around twenty minutes later and drove here. It did not occur to me that someone had closed the trunk."

"We'll check that out," Bigley said.

Trinidad bridled. Did she mean to say Papa was a suspect?

Chang looked at Trinidad. "Any idea of the unwanted trunk passenger's identity?"

She would have smiled if he hadn't appeared to be dead serious. "No. I only saw the…" she swallowed, "hand of the trunk passenger."

Chang shot another glance at the food on the stove. The man had four hungry boys at home, including two seven-year-old twins, and as far as she could tell, he lived on crumbs because he was forever famished, his belt cinched to the tightest hole to keep the pants clinging to his skinny frame.

"Let me get you a bowl of beans and rice," Trinidad said.

"Oh, no, I couldn't possibly," he said, but the hope in his tone did not match the words. While she was dishing up a bowl, the chief joined them. Surreptitiously, she slid the bowl back on the counter. The chief did not appreciate her officers eating on duty. Noodles wagged a friendly tail. Papa stood politely and pulled a chair out for the chief at the miniscule table.

"Sit, please. A café…to warm you." Without waiting for her approval, he started to pour her one.

"No, thank you, Mr. Jones." she said firmly.

"Please call me Luis," he said gallantly.

The chief was not immune to Papa's charms. Trinidad saw the quickly concealed smile. "The last time I drank one of your cafés, I couldn't sleep for two days," she said.

"Ah. Well maybe some juice, then?"

Officer Chang declined as well, admiring the rice and beans from afar.

"We have a small problem," Chief Bigley said.

"Yes, we do." Trinidad figured that was an understatement for a dead body in a person's vehicle. "Do you know who it is?" she forced herself to say.

"No." Bigley's tone was flat.

"A stranger?" Papa said. "So many people in town for Alpenfest."

She shook her head.

So, it was a local? Puzzling, since she figured the chief knew pretty much everybody in Upper Sprocket. "But…?" she started.

"This is going to be easier if we do it together," the chief sighed. She eyed her ravenous officer. "Alvin, can you hold the light?"

Chang readied his high-powered flashlight.

They all zipped their rain jackets and pulled up the hoods. Trinidad did not want to go look at that dead body again, but the chief's tone brooked no disagreement. In the pelting rain, they watched as she opened the trunk. She held her breath. Chang shined his light inside, and they bent over to see the…

Blueberries.

Trinidad scanned the trunk, mouth open in shock, but all she saw in the pristine interior was the container of blueberries. No rug, no hand, and certainly no body. She looked under the car, next to the porch step, scanning wildly.

She stared again into the trunk, then goggled some more. Papa stood with his head cocked to one side. "Imagine that," he said.

"Well, how would…?" Trinidad sputtered. "I mean, maybe it revived and climbed out." She whirled around. There was the long, dark drive—empty. Fields of slick wet grass that vanished into the wooded acres behind her rented property and up into the mountains. "Or someone stole the body?" They would have heard a vehicle approach, surely. Was the body-snatcher on foot? Where would someone dispose of a body if they did steal it? "Maybe the murderer snatched the corpse to dump in the lake?" Even she realized that sounded like fodder for a bad TV movie.

The chief closed the trunk lid with a gloved finger until it nearly latched. "We'll look for fibers and prints in the morning. I'll get an easy-up tent over the scene and post Officer Chang here to keep watch tonight. No one drives the car until I say so."

Papa's jaw went slack, but he bore it with stoicism.

But the chief wasn't done. "I have to ask… Are you positive you actually saw a body? Maybe it was a trick of the light?" She paused. "You haven't been drinking, have you?"

Now Papa straightened, wrapping a beefy arm around Trinidad's shoulders and squeezing. "Madam," he said, probably the only living man to still use that word. "If my daughter and I tell you there was a body in the trunk, it is the truth. You can take it to the bank."

Chief Bigley sighed. "Right. We'll do a more thorough search for your missing corpse in the morning. Until then, let's keep it quiet, okay? We've finally gotten things straightened out after the last go-round with criminals. This town doesn't need any more murder rumors, especially with Alpenfest in full swing."

Trinidad heartily agreed. She was thoroughly chilled by the time she reentered the tiny house. Officer Chang wrestled up the canopy and trudged to his squad car to begin the long watch until morning. In between downpours, Trinidad delivered him a bowl of rice and beans with a biscuit, a couple slices of cold pork, a fork, and knife.

"Thank you, ma'am," he said in hushed tones, as if the departed chief might somehow catch wind of his illicit meal.

"Come on in when you need to use the bathroom," she added, "and there'll be breakfast before I head to the shop."

He beamed, declining her additional offer of a blanket.

"Can I…?" she said. "Is it okay for me to go to the Shimmy while…during the investigation?"

"Don't see why not," he said, brushing raindrops from

his glasses with his sleeve. "It might suppress the inevitable murder rumors if you kept to business as usual. Not for long, though. Anyone listening to the police scanner knows there's something afoot." He grinned. "Did you hear how I used the word 'afoot'? I've been listening to all the Sherlock Holmes books on audio while I rock the baby."

Rumors. In the eyes of many Sprocketerians, she was already "that ex-wife" or "the one who got wrapped up in the Popcorn King's murder investigation." Could her business and her reputation withstand being the subject of more sizzling gossip? She forced a smile and bid him good night.

She and Papa returned to the table, but neither was in much of a mood to eat. Papa assured her he would stay at the tiny house and supervise while she went to work the next day. And he would be watching to see that his precious vehicle was treated with the utmost care, that was certain.

Papa sipped his coffee. "Life is funny. There you are one moment, packing up blueberries, and the next you've found and lost a corpse—all in the same day."

She swallowed. "I wouldn't say funny, but it's definitely not what I'd planned."

Papa swigged more coffee. "There's your plan and God's plan, and your plan…"

"Doesn't count," Trinidad finished with a laugh. "I remember."

She cleaned up and left Papa listening to Lawrence Welk music on an old cassette player she'd found at the flea market. Briefly, she considered rounding up some Sherlock Holmes tapes for him, but Papa was a man whose brain made no time for fiction. He was more likely to be mentally sketching out designs for the greenhouse he'd decided to build with the landlord's permission and Quinn's construction expertise. She was happy about the greenhouse plans. If they followed through with building it, Papa would surely stay in Sprocket.

Noodles did not howl an accompaniment to Lawrence Welk, at least. She fed him his dinner and took him out for one last reconnoitering, staying well away from Papa's trunk.

When at last they were settled in for the night, she climbed the steep ladder to the loft and laid down to chase sleep that did not come. She wished she could talk to Quinn about the corpse playing hide-and-seek, but something kept her from calling him. Distrust? No, she refused to let doubt creep in. She'd worked too long to overcome the wariness that she had developed after she'd learned how Gabe had deceived her. Whatever Quinn had cooked up with Forge must have a reasonable explanation. Tomorrow, she vowed. She'd tell him tomorrow and ask him about the Forge deal. Much better than speaking on the phone.

Questions and corpses chased each other in her mind until she finally fell into a troubled sleep.

The next morning Trinidad let herself and Noodles into the Shimmy and Shake Shop and allowed the peace of her miniature world wash over her. After the divorce, the doctor told her that meditation might ease her anxiety, but it had only made her more anxious to realize she was terrible at medi-tation. The Shimmy had eased her spirit in a way no pills or practices ever could. She intended to put the Shimmy's best foot forward at the Alpen freebie tasting that afternoon… the first official event where the Shimmy would provide services. She'd offer six flavor choices, which were sure to please almost everyone.

Pristinely clean aluminum machines, repaired walls returned to their glorious state of pink with pearl accents, and tubs for her freshly made ice cream awaited. Wasting not a moment, she tied the apron around her middle while Noodles installed himself on the cushion at the other side of the front counter. She'd turned on some cheerful music to which Noodles could yodel to his heart's content if he wished.

Apple Pie and Caramel Crunch were the two flavors featured this week, and she'd need enough to supply the store and the event. Either flavor could be made into a fab-ulous Freakshake. Apple Pie would be transformed into an Autumn Apple Avalanche shake that had already proven popular since a fall chill had replaced the hot summer weather. That monster dessert would include generous scoops of freshly churned ice cream blended with pieces of cinnamon piecrust, doused with a pecan sauce and topped with a hefty chunk of browned butter apple bar and swirls of whipped cream. Since it was featured on the flyers they'd passed out the day before at the yodel fest, she figured it would be a good place to start.

Just before nine a.m., the ice cream was churning, and the apple bars were in the oven. The whole space was redolent with fall aromas. Twins Diego and Carlos barreled into the shop, ready to start their shifts, taking advantage of a week of no school for parent conferences and teacher training. All arms and legs and dark eyes, the twins were finally distinguishable, without too much trouble. She noted that they'd grown a few inches lately. There was a hole in the toe of the athletic shoes Diego had gotten for summer sports. How did their mother keep them in clothes?

Amid the exasperation and the bills, there must be a deep satisfaction in being called "Mother." It was a title she'd assumed she'd earn with Gabe as parents to the three children she'd always imagined them having. But, no, that was another goal she had never achieved. She refocused on doling out work instructions until she noticed all wasn't sanguine in the teenage world.

Diego was not his usual imperturbable self. He shoved up his glasses, tied his apron, and glumly started in on chopping the day's supply of walnuts. She feared for his fingertips.

"Don't mind him," Carlos said. "He's in a funk because the school newspaper turned down his latest article."

Diego whacked the cutting board with the handle of the knife. "Ridiculous. It's an excellent piece explaining how exotic hadrons fit into the Standard Model, which, as you know, is an incomplete explanation of how the smallest particles of matter..."

"Puh-leeze," Carlos said. "No one knows that, or cares about it, except for you and a couple of other dozen eggheads. I keep telling you. Normal high school kids, heavy emphasis on normal, don't want to read about that. They want articles about computer games, cell phone hacks, dating tips. Or maybe a gritty true crime story." His eyes lit up. "Murder and mayhem. That's the stuff people want to read about. Right, Miss Jones?"

"Uh, I don't know. I am out of touch with what teens want these days." There was no way she was opening up the body-in-the-trunk topic for the twins' eager examination.

The door's bell tinkled as a man stepped into the store. His shoulder-length black hair was held away from his face in a sort of knot on the top of his head. There were streaks of gray in his small, pointed beard that mirrored the gray in his thin mustache. Baggy clothes and a knapsack slung over one shoulder completed his casual look.

Trinidad put on her business smile and eyed the clock. It was barely a quarter past nine. "Good morning, sir. I'm sorry, but we're not quite open yet. I must have forgotten to lock the door. If you come back in a few hours, we'll be all set for you. Wonderful ice cream selection and hand-crafted milkshakes of epic proportions. We call them Freakshakes."

He stuck a hand in the baggy pockets of his trousers and pulled out a crumpled business card. "Not here for ice cream. I'm a writer. Doing an article. Thought you could help me."

"I'm a writer too," Diego piped up. "What's your beat?"

The man blinked. "Covering the Alpenfest."

"Why'd you come to Sprocket, then?" Carlos asked. "Josef's the place where everything happens. It's about twenty minutes from here."

The twins had no clue how precarious their jobs were, she thought. "But Sprocket is an up-and-coming destination location," Trinidad piped up. "I'm sure that's why he's here. What paper do you write for?"

"Not a paper, a magazine called *Go West*. Travel and leisure type things."

Trinidad realized her face was getting sore from smiling so hard. She turned it down a notch. "We'd be happy to help you in any way, Mr....?"

"Orwell. T. J. Orwell. I'm thinking about hitting several different angles in my article. A local business slant as well as some prominent figures. Maybe the mayor. Ramona Hardwick, right?"

Trinidad was fixated on the "local business" mention. The chance of publicity made her nearly salivate. "Yes, she's the mayor of Upper Sprocket."

"But not for long, my mom says," Carlos sang out. "Forge Emberly might bump her out because she's misusing her office."

Trinidad shot him a "let's not air our dirty laundry at this moment" look, but he was oblivious.

Orwell frowned. "Oh, is there a problem with the mayor?"

Diego nodded. "Mom says she's as crooked as a dog's hind leg."

"Crooked?" Orwell arched an eyebrow. "I used to write the local crime beat. What's she accused of?"

"Nothing," Trinidad said, a jot too quickly. "No formal accusations of any kind. She's running for reelection, and you know how dirty politics can be."

"Uh huh, so what did she—?"

"Anyway," Trinidad spoke over his question. "I'd be

happy to give you my thoughts on local business. I've just reopened my shop, as a matter of fact."

She realized her slip when he asked, "Reopened?"

"Yeah," Carlos said, before she could give him a warning poke with her spatula. "The Shimmy got flattened by a murderer. Can you believe it? He—"

"Carlos," Trinidad said firmly, "Mr. Orwell wants to talk about small business, not…"

But Orwell was clearly fascinated.

"We churn the ice cream fresh every morning," she hurried on. "It's not ripened yet, but would you like to try some?" He appeared ready to decline when Juliette Carpenter, Gabe's third ex-wife, burst through the door, blond hair cut into a chic bob that complemented her dewy skin. Juliette was even thinner, since her time in jail had left her with an unrecovered appetite. Noodles gave her ankle a lick, and she patted him.

"Trinidad, I heard the absolute zaniest rumor about Papa Luis's…"

She tried to both silence Juliette and wave her behind the counter. "Uh, you're really early. I don't need your help until 2:30 for the freebie tasting."

Her compulsively early friend waved off the remark. "I know…but I couldn't wait after I heard that…"

The bell on the door clanged at just the right moment. The next person merely popped his head in. Mechanic Zane Apperton, nicknamed Zap, flashed a smile from beneath the lush gray mustache that was at odds with his shiny bald head. "Dropped off Lyds at the Inn to practice for the performance today, and I figured I'd check in. Free stuff yet?" He wiggled eyebrows that looked like two fuzzy caterpillars hopping on his brow.

Lydia, his wife, was a frequent customer. Zap and Lyds. Only in Sprocket. "Not until three, at the gazebo," she called, wondering if she had the guts to order Carlos to lock the door before anyone else barged in. She wasn't rich in nerve when she'd come to Sprocket, but recent events had emboldened her.

"This is T. J. Orwell," Diego was saying to Juliette. "He's a reporter."

"A reporter?" Juliette's mouth gaped. "How did you find out already?"

"Find out about what?" Orwell said.

Trinidad was scrambling for an answer when gas station owner Mr. Mavis shoved in, pink-cheeked from his morning bike ride up and down Main. His face was unhealthily white due to the layer of sunscreen Mrs. Mavis insisted he apply. She was a cleaning lady who worked for both the police station and the health clinic, so she was up on all the health and safety tips. "I heard you're gonna give out freebies," he said.

"At the gazebo," she repeated, relieved that at least he wasn't in on the missing corpse gossip. "That starts at three. We're doing a free tasting during the concert," she explained to Orwell with her most winning smile cemented into place. At last she'd gotten them back to the topic of business and stopped Juliette's announcement. Home free, she thought, until Mr. Mavis added, "So Papa Luis found a corpse in his trunk, eh?" He paused, frowning into the ice cream case. "Will there be free banana ice cream?"

With a groan, the smile crumbled from her lips.

Noodles, ever-attuned to her mood, struggled up from his cushion, meandered to the entrance, where he stood on his hind legs, and bolted the door with his teeth.

Thanks, Noo, but you're too late, she thought as everyone turned to stare at her.

Chapter Three

"WE'RE GOING TO HAVE TO work on your timing, Noodles," she muttered to the dog, as she unlocked the door and shooed away everyone but the twins, promising to fill Juliette in as soon as she arrived for her shift. Orwell had agreed to phone her for an interview, ostensibly to learn more about the ice cream biz, but she had her doubts.

As soon as the bolt turned, the twins immediately let her have it.

"A body?" Carlos goggled.

"In Papa's trunk?" Diego finished.

Diego found his power of speech. "Do they suspect Papa? Like maybe he called the cops to throw off suspicion?"

"Of course not," she snapped. She would not disclose how relieved she'd been when the chief phoned to say that Ernst, the chief yodeler, confirmed seeing Papa walk away from his open trunk with Felice as the yodeler was leaving for town. "Plus," she'd added, "I knew, if your grandfather had killed someone, he would never have put the body in his vehicle." The chief had chuckled. Trinidad hadn't.

Carlos was practically quivering with excitement. "Like an authentic dead person? Who?"

But she answered only that she had no idea who, where, what, or how and that the police would straighten it all out in good time. That was like stuffing in a sock to plug a fire hose. The boys could barely contain themselves, but, since the list of to-dos was enormous, she sent them quickly to work. The adorable clock with the ice cream scoop hours ticked relentlessly away. The prep work was barely finished when she officially opened for business at eleven. The thrill of seeing four actual patrons waiting to enter blasted away the earlier rough morning. "Welcome to the Shimmy and Shake," she pronounced like a Disneyland tour guide as she ushered them in.

Then it was all scoopers in motion as she and the twins delivered the creamy bounty. Her mouth watered as she prepared two plump scoops of caramel crunch in a crispy waffle cone. She'd heard people suggest she must be heartily sick of ice cream, but, so far, she was as ravenous for it as ever, even enjoying a quick breakfast milkshake upon occasion. She didn't have the money to buy herself larger-sized pants since her last used-clothing upgrade at Lydia's Off the Rack store, so she was trying to keep that indulgence to a minimum.

Business was brisk as the lunch hour approached. She was thrilled that a quartet of brave tourists had ordered Freakshakes and set about in twos demolishing them. Their excited comments and giggles drew the attention of everyone from the tiny pink tables, and she heard several additional patrons vowing to return the next day to get their own Freakshakes. Word of mouth really was the best advertisement. Perhaps that was the plus side of wagging tongues.

The business continued, and they kept up a steady pace until it was time to load the food truck. Carlos was the one to accompany her while Diego stayed back with Juliette. It was a risk, of course, handing out free cups of ice cream, but Papa always said generosity was never wasted, and she hoped showcasing her flavors might garner some more action for the Shimmy. If nothing else, it would provide a nice counterpoint to the sausage sandwiches handed out by the local Rotary Club to folks listening to the various performers.

Trinidad could see the questions churning through Juliette's mind as she tied on a Shimmy and Shake apron and took her place behind the counter while the twins were packing ice cream cups into insulated boxes to be transferred to the food truck.

"Okay. I waited, and I'm done being patient. A dead guy?" she whispered. "Are you serious?"

"How did you hear about it?"

"Mr. Mavis's wife was at the police station for the nighttime cleaning, and she heard Officer Chang on the phone with his wife, explaining that he wouldn't be home since there'd been a body discovered at the home of one Trinidad Jones."

"Officer Chang could use a few lessons in discretion, along with Mr. Mavis's wife."

Juliette waved a palm. "That's a small point. I want to know whose body was in Papa's trunk."

"You and me both. I only saw the hand." She was trying to keep her voice down, but the twins were shamelessly eavesdropping anyway.

"Well can you at least guess an age? Gender?" Juliette pressed.

"Yeah, like was it a wrinkly, busted-up old hand or a fresh, young one?" Carlos called out.

"That's insensitive to people with wrinkly, busted-up hands," Diego said.

Trinidad sighed. "Male, I think. Not young, but what do I know? Maybe he was a twentysomething with aged hands. The important thing is he isn't there anymore—in the trunk, I mean—so I am praying Papa was wrong about the lack of pulse and whoever it was climbed out and went on his merry way."

Juliette dropped the ice cream scooper on the floor. "Sorry, that gave me the creeps. Like a zombie movie in real life."

Trinidad picked the scoop up and put it in the dishwasher, fetching another of the pink-handled devices. She hoped Juliette's focus would improve. "Maybe it's one of those weird small-town happenings."

"A body in your trunk isn't a happening, it's a horror movie," Juliette said.

Trinidad found three pairs of unblinking eyes staring at her. *This is what a mouse must feel like in an owl's nest.* "That's all I know, really. Honest."

"A trunk body. Cool," Diego and Carlos said at once.

"A vanished trunk body is even cooler," Carlos said.

Juliette pursed her lips. "If it was an actual dead person, how can they disappear without anyone noticing?"

"I saw this in a movie once," Carlos said. "This alien would come and infiltrate someone's body and lay down these spore things, and then, when it was finished—"

"Listen, everyone," Trinidad interrupted. "This is a police matter, and none of you are to spread this information around. Got it?"

Three heads nodded. Juliette, she knew, would keep the knowledge to herself. After what they'd gone through, their trust was a bond that would withstand the juiciest gossip. As far as the teen boys went… Hopefully the problem would be all sorted out by the time they could disperse the news.

"No," she snapped, as Carlos surreptitiously tried to slide his cell phone from his back pocket. "You're too busy to text anyone right now. I'm paying you to work, not to text." She shoved a cardboard carton filled with small paper containers in his arms. "We have to get to the gazebo."

"And you," she said with a stern glance at Diego. "You must not write about this for your school paper or anywhere else until we have all the facts." It was a stalling tactic at best.

Diego raised his chin and gave her a haughty look. "I have journalistic integrity, you know."

That sent Carlos into gales of laughter. He was still chuckling as they climbed into the behemoth truck, painted a snappy teal with "Shimmy and Shake—home of the world-famous Freakshake" emblazoned on the side in bold letters. She'd thought the slogan too grandiose at first, but Quinn's advice was "go big or go home." The unwieldy vehicle had once sold oatmeal, but they'd long since removed the fiberglass anomaly on the top that was supposed to represent a bowl of the mushy stuff. Food-truck oatmeal…a recipe for failure if there ever was one.

But the truck itself was a blessing. She'd all but decided to go home after her shop was destroyed, back to Miami with her mother and brother and Papa Luis. But she'd changed her mind, and the truck had kept her afloat while repairs were made. Quinn was a large part of her decision to stay. The sick feeling ripped through her again.

The partnership with Forge that would mean Quinn's trees would be cut was still unfathomable. She and Quinn had attended a town meeting together once to support an initiative to save one of Sprocket's oldest trees from being felled for a truck stop. Dozens of residents with "Trees Not Trucks" T-shirts had turned out, and Quinn had worn his proudly. And Quinn had told her he'd spoken out against Forge's initial proposal to add another railriders route the previous fall. She could not understand his seeming about-face…unless he had an ulterior motive. Again, the unsettling wave of self-doubt returned. Had she been hasty to trust another man? Or stupid?

The fact that he hadn't stopped by or texted since the revelation sent fresh alarm bells ringing in her mind. What was going on with him? She could ignore it, sit quietly by and wait for developments, but, scared as she was, she wasn't going to take that route. Trinidad Jones might be a lost cause as far as love was concerned, but she wasn't going to allow herself to be lied to, not again. It was the next item on her agenda to find out the truth after the freebie event.

Noodles wagged his tail from his cushioned spot in the passenger seat. He was an ice cream ambassador, to be sure. Everyone in town knew and loved her old pooch. She'd left the truck windows open so Noodles could shove his head out and feel the breeze ruffle his ears.

They pulled up to the parking lot, which dumped out into a wide swath of green grass. She could still hear the tiniest burble of Messabout Creek that backed the lush area and trickled through the fields beyond. The six-sided white gazebo with the shingled roof was already surrounded by families on picnic blankets, ready for a concert and, hopefully, ice cream. The late-afternoon temperatures had hit the eighties and would stay warm for another couple of hours. Not as conducive to ice cream as the sizzling summer but plenty respectable.

The recurring shiver of fear hit her again. Soon the mercury would plunge into the freezing range as winter snow swept the gorgeous mountain town. And what then? With Alpenfest done and summer long gone, how would she keep an ice cream shop in business? She still had not fully nailed down her off-season business plan.

Maybe you don't have the stuff to be an entrepreneur.

Trinidad had never been terribly brave, an identity forged partly from her nature that sunk in more deeply due to Gabe's betrayal three years before, which left her reeling. Yet here she was, running a business, an ice cream business no less, in a place with rugged winters and yodeling and two newly rediscovered sisters of the soul.

Papa reassured her that he'd be happy to return with her to Miami anytime and help her establish a business there. What better place for an ice cream shop than Miami? But there was something about standing on her own two feet in this quirky town of apple orchards, goat tenders, and likeable busybodies that made her feel as if she could draw in a full breath and live her life instead of just pass the time. Did courage and fear go hand in hand for everyone else or just her?

Her musings were cut short when Carlos unfolded the chalkboard easel next to the truck, which outlined the free offerings: half-scoop portions of Caramel Crunch and Apple Pie as well as Mr. Mavis's favorite banana and a few other options. Each freebie would be offered with a coupon for 50 percent off a Fall Freakshake.

They weren't the only food choices at the event, she noted. Paper-covered tables held sausage sandwiches hosted by the local Rotary Club. Another booth boasted samples of salty soft pretzels, the scent of which made her mouth water, accompanied by condiment cups brimming with mustard. All served on compostable products instead of plastic, since Sprocketerians were concerned with sustainability matters, largely thanks to Mayor Hardwick.

The line outside the truck formed instantaneously. She and Carlos scooped for all they were worth until a mournful honk split the air. They jerked a look at the gazebo, where Zap's wife, Lydia, was standing at the mouthpiece of a ridiculously long horn, the end of which rested on the ground. It was sculpted from some sort of wood and spanned a good twelve feet. Her cheeks puffed into pouches as she blew and produced a sound not unlike the trombone Trinidad's brother, Yolo, had taken up for a day and a half. Noodles was on his feet and out of the truck instantly, dancing on excited paws as the horn-blowing continued.

Carlos took a picture with his cell phone. "What is that thing used for anyway?"

"Calling the sheep from the fields," said a man in a red vest and shiny black pants who materialized at the truck's ordering window. It was Ernst from Bonnie's outdoor concert.

"Wouldn't a whistle be easier?" Carlos asked, giving him a scoop of caramel crunch.

"The Alps are vast. If you want your sound to spread out from peak to peak, you need a big horn," he said. He eyed Noodles, then Trinidad. "Didn't I see you and the dog at the Yodelfest at the B and B? The gentleman who drove me from the airport in his amazing car told me he was your grandfather, I think."

"Yes, sir," Trinidad said, "Sorry about the dog accompaniment. The bed-and-breakfast belongs to my friend Bonnie and her daughter."

"Ah. This town is fantastic, for sure. Police interviewed me and some other guests about what happened. Shame about the body. Bad press for the inn. And your relative being involved and all."

Her stomach plunged like a downhill skier. What should she say? Thank you for getting Papa off the chief's list of suspects? Sprocket is usually not a hotbed for corpses?

He continued before she could decide. "The police chief is still checking the area around the Station looking for this missing dead person. Can't help thinking, in a town this size, you'd be able to figure out who hasn't shown up where they were supposed to. Not like this is New York City or something." He touched his cap. "Catch you later."

Trinidad watched in dismay as he left. Bad, bad, bad. Of course the cops would start their search with the last place Papa and his trunk had stopped. Bonnie's Station. Why hadn't she reached out to her friend, knowing how traumatized the woman might be? Because, truth be told, she felt a buzz of uncertainty around Bonnie. Bonnie was the alpha wife, Gabe's first, the one who'd given birth, which Trinidad's confused mind translated to legitimacy.

You're beyond ridiculous, she thought. She resolved to go over as soon as the freebie fest was over. Besides, she needed to firm up a few plans for Felice's upcoming birthday party to be held at the Shimmy on Sunday night.

Ernst sidled up his mega horn next to Lydia's, and they began a mooing duet. Noodles could not hold back his yowling.

"I've got to move him away a bit," she told Carlos. "I guess horns have the same effect on him that yodeling does. I'll be gone until the song's ended, okay?"

Carlos yawned. "Sure thing. Looks like there's no line right now."

She gave him a sharp look. "No texting your friends, right?"

He raised innocent brows. "Just gonna fill in Diego, the

hard-bitten investigative journalist. Tell him what the yodeling guy said."

She eased Noodles away toward the trees. Her heart beat faster when she spotted Quinn and his brother, Doug, pouring ice into the pitchers of water at the beverage table. *Run away*, her heart said. *March right over*, her brain demanded. She settled on an awkward stroll in Quinn's direction, but a man at the sausage table stopped her before she got to him.

"Trinidad?" It was Judge Alexander Torpine. Tall and elegant, aging into his mid-fifties in that annoyingly attractive way men did. The judge was always well-dressed, clean-shaven, and smelling of Old Spice. Today, though, his eyes were shadowed with fatigue.

"Oh, hi, Judge."

"Would you like a free sausage sandwich?" He smiled. "My role is to lure in the customers with my charm and salesmanship. How am I doing?"

"Very charming," she said, "but no thank you on the sandwich."

Gretchen, wearing a plastic apron, shook her head. "I told my brother we should toast the buns, but you can't tell a man anything. They need to be led about by the nose like sheep."

There was a good-natured fondness in her scolding, which Judge Torpine didn't seem to mind.

Out of the corner of her eye, Trinidad was tracking Quinn, who was adding another bag of ice to the water. His brother, Doug, stood at the ready with a roll of paper towels.

Doug avoided doing anything that resulted in him getting wet, dirty, or sticky.

She was easing away when Judge Torpine stopped her, leaning confidentially closer as Gretchen delivered a foil-wrapped sausage to a visitor. Noodles leaned in, too, in case there might be a meaty mishap with which he could assist.

"I understand there was some unpleasantness yesterday," the Judge said.

Was there anyone in town who *hadn't* heard? "Yes, but I really can't talk about it. The police…"

His elegant eyebrows arched. "I wasn't aware there was police involvement." He flicked a glance at his sister, but she was turned away to retrieve another sausage. "Did Forge press charges?"

Forge? She exhaled. He meant the altercation between Mayor Hardwick and Forge at Bonnie's inn. "Oh, that. No, no police involved. That was a small disagreement, as far as I could tell."

He frowned. "I understood that Forge accused Mayor Hardwick of impropriety."

Of course, Gretchen, Bonnie's new cook, would have filled in her brother, she realized. Wait until he got wind of the other problem that apparently started at Bonnie's property. Gretchen's sausage duties must have kept her away long enough that she hadn't heard.

"I guess that's what happened," Trinidad said. "Why did you, er, I mean, why are you curious about it?"

He flashed her a chagrined look and put a hand over his chest. "Ah you're right. What is that from Proverbs?

Whoever guards his mouth preserves his life." Another smile. "I should work on my own predilection to gossip."

His sister nodded in agreement. "Yep. A man on the brink of an appointment to an appellate court should be more discreet."

Again, the judge offered a humble shrug. "My sister is my keeper, apparently."

"Well someone's gotta do it." She whipped off the apron. "You're on your own now. I have to get back for the evening cookies and cocoa service at the inn." Pride suffused her face. "My chocolate crinkle cookies are a hit with the yodelers."

"They sound wonderful. I'd love to get that recipe sometime. I'm going to do a Chocolate Chipperoonie Freakshake next summer."

Gretchen cocked her head. "Since you are Bonnie's friend, I will share, but not unless I get credit on your menu."

Trinidad realized the woman was serious. Family recipes must be a big deal to some people. Papa Luis handed them out to anyone who asked, but his were usually a running record of "toss in this" and "add a handful of that."

"Oh, right. Of course. Well…" She noticed Quinn had accepted a paper towel from Doug as he finished his duties.

"I've got to run now, Judge." He waved her away, and she hurried over to Quinn, pulse pounding. It might have been her imagination, but she thought she saw Quinn gulp when she approached. But his smile was as warm as ever, wasn't it? Exasperating. When exactly had she turned back into a middle-school girl, measuring every male behavior as a reflection of her own attractiveness? Ludicrous. Purposely, she resisted the desire to fold her stray curl into the elastic holding back the rest of the bunch.

"Hi, Trinidad," Quinn said.

His blue "I'm Nuts for Hazelnuts" shirt was the same color as his eyes. A hole showed a glimpse of pale skin above his belly button. "Hi, Quinn. Hello, Doug."

Doug nodded but did not speak. Trinidad had learned in the eight months she'd lived in Sprocket that Doug rarely spoke and generally stayed away from any and all social interaction if he could help it. Quinn cared for him tenderly, in a way that both encouraged and protected him. Another "Quinnism" that warmed something inside her. But that was before the suspicion began to creep in.

He shoved his hands in his pockets. "I…uh…wanted to come talk to you yesterday, but, uh, things got busy."

Did they ever. Apparently, he, too, had not heard about the body in Papa's trunk. Not surprising, since he was usually on top of a tractor tending his hazelnut orchard or trying to coax an old sorting machine back to life using his Army mechanic skills. The silence begged to be broken. She did so after a full breath for courage. "I was surprised when Forge said you were going to sell some of your land." There. It was out in the world. Courage wrapped in fright.

Quinn's mouth firmed into a tight line. "It's not optimal, but it's necessary."

She wanted to ask why, but he filled in. He folded his arms across his chest and looked at the ground. "We can use the money." And that seemed to be all he wanted to say on the subject.

"I understand, but, I mean, I didn't think you had much respect for Forge. You spoke out against his plans to expand the railriders route when he first proposed it."

"I have zero respect for the man," he snapped. "I think he's a poisonous snake, and I'd like to chop him in two."

The hard tone made both her and Doug startle. Trinidad realized the judge had looked in their direction too.

Doug stayed quiet, dropping to his knees to scratch Noodles. Trinidad did not know how Noodles understood that Doug's sensory difficulties required that he should not be licked, but, somehow, Noodles never applied his slobbery tongue to any part of Doug.

Trinidad summoned another supply of courage and edged closer and spoke in a quieter tone. "Then why would you sell to him? Surely there are other people who might be interested in buying some of your acreage. A couple of months ago, you said it was your best harvest ever."

"It's a done deal, Trinidad," he said. His tone was harsh, and she recoiled.

"I'm sorry for prying."

"No," he said, blowing out a breath and taking her hand. "I'm the one who's sorry. I'm down in the dumps at having to give up that land. The trees are old ones, and owls nest there. My mom used to tote us to that grove to bird-watch when we were young. Still, that's no reason to take it out on you. Forgive me."

Selling the grove that meant the world to his late mother? Quinn looked so downcast that she let go of her doubt long enough to squeeze his hand. "Don't worry about it." Maybe he was right not to tell her. They were what? Friends? Good friends, she'd thought or imagined. Maybe something more? Could be he didn't feel the same way. In spite of her words, his tone still stung.

The financial concerns that made him partner with a man he obviously couldn't stand were not her business. She considered the rest of the Judge's Proverbs quote: "He who opens wide his lips comes to ruin."

She closed her mouth and let go of his hand.

Trinidad saw Ramona Hardwick approaching the sausage table. She looked charming and youthful in a printed peasant top and jeans that hugged her toned legs. Sidling up to the table, she pushed her hair behind her ear.

Trinidad's romance radar activated. Hair fiddling? And wasn't that a coating of freshly applied lipstick on the mayor's mouth? She couldn't catch what Ramona said, but it got an answering chuckle from the judge. And wasn't the judge standing up a smidge straighter? Was he interested in the mayor for something other than her leadership skills?

And that was the moment she caught sight of Chief Bigley strolling across the grass. No, it wasn't strolling, exactly. Her booted feet were cutting across the ground at a much faster pace than the mellow alpenhorn music seemed to encourage. Trinidad experienced an unpleasant flashback to July, when she'd stumbled across the body of an unfortunate local, murdered and tossed in his enormous popcorn kettle.

She swallowed the nonsense. This was a small idyllic town, the "Swiss Alps" of Oregon, for goodness' sake. That murder had been a bizarre one-of-a-kind situation, and lightning didn't strike twice in the same spot. As she closed in, Trinidad could no longer ignore the chief's steely expression.

From across the lawn, the alpenhorns joined together in a sound like the low rumble of thunder.

Trinidad braced herself for the lightning.

Chapter Four

QUINN MUST HAVE READ CHIEF Bigley's expression as well, because he took a step toward Trinidad and put his big palm on her shoulder.

"Hey, Chief. What's up? You look real serious."

Her expression remained grim. "Murder is a serious business."

Murder? Now the imaginary rumble of thunder turned into a full-on crash. She noticed Judge Torpine and Ramona had turned in unison as if magnetically drawn by the ugly word. *Here comes the lightning,* she thought.

"Did you say 'murder'?" Ramona asked, striding over with the judge right behind her.

"Yes, ma'am, I did."

Trinidad waited in terror. "So the body we found in Papa's trunk…?"

"A body?" Ramona said, after two exaggerated blinks. Trinidad had seen her use the same almost comical expression at town council meetings. "What body?"

"I dunno. We only saw the hand," Trinidad said, realizing she sounded like an idiot.

"How is that possible, exactly?" Ramona demanded.

"Anyway," the chief continued in a more strident tone. "This morning we found some evidence that indicated your corpse…"

"It's not my corpse," Trinidad wanted to say, but she didn't dare interrupt.

"…was removed from the trunk and carried to the road, probably loaded into another vehicle."

"Someone stole a corpse?" the judge asked. "And whose corpse are we talking about, by the way?"

"That's the interesting part," Chief Bigley said. "Too early to tell the cause of death, of course, but he had a head injury, which probably did him in. There's some other evidence I'm not going to discuss right now. The crux is we found the body in the deepest part of Big Egg where the body-snatcher dumped it."

"That's pretty unbelievable," Gretchen said.

Trinidad's ears buzzed. The Big Egg…the largest of the three connected bodies of water at Three Egg Lake. Trinidad's gulp was audible. It was the exact location she'd suggested to the chief in their earlier interview. "I…uh…I was a stenographer, so, before, when I mentioned it, I was just postulating that would be a good place to, you know, dispose of, uh, a dead person. Lakes are so popular for that kind of thing."

Uggh. Why must I continue to babble? Trinidad thought.

"I can see the fear in your face, Trinidad, but you couldn't have snatched the corpse from the trunk and lugged it to the lake while we were en route. That'd be a trick even for Houdini. And, if the phone call was a ruse and you'd done it earlier…well, why would you?" Bigley said.

Trinidad could hardly keep up. "I haven't the foggiest notion."

Bigley continued. "The corpse was wrapped in a tarp and weighed down. Probably wouldn't have found him at all except the tarp tore and he bobbed to the surface like an ice cube in a soda pop. Normally, I'd keep that to myself, but there were tourists out for a lakeshore stroll today when we brought him to shore, and, naturally, every last one of them whipped out a cell phone to take a picture."

"Disgusting," Ramona said. "Cell phones are the scourge of humanity."

Cell phones, not murderers? But Trinidad noticed with some part of her brain that Ramona had the newest iPhone model herself. Never mind that, her brain scolded as a buzzing started up in her ears causing Noodles to bump her knee with a concerned nose.

Trinidad hardly felt it. The body was found exactly where she'd suggested. And after they'd found it in Papa's trunk in the first place? Would anyone in town believe she had nothing to do with it? Or Papa? But there was still one important question to ask. Quinn, Ramona, and the Judge beat her to it by spouting out at the same moment, "Who was it?"

The chief looked closely at them all before she answered. "Forge Emberly."

"Forge?" Ramona's face read interested, if not exactly regretful. "Huh."

Trinidad glanced at Quinn but saw only shock in his expression.

"Okay. I admit I didn't see that coming," Ramona said. "And I know what's next." She waved a manicured hand, the nails bloodred. "Yes, I despised the guy and I shoved him at Bonnie's, but I didn't kill him."

Bigley cocked her head. "I didn't accuse you of it."

"Yet," Ramona said. "But I know how these things work. He was running for mayor against me, so I've got a motive, yada, yada."

The judge was shifting from foot to foot. "Uh…"

Bigley skewered him with a look. "Did you want to say something, Judge?"

"Well, nothing like a clue or anything like that. People say things, you know, in the heat of the moment. I've heard all kinds of things in court, believe me. Threats that were never acted upon…"

"Spit it out, Judge," Bigley said. "I'm on the clock, and I've got an investigation to work."

The judge's gaze flicked to Quinn almost apologetically.

Quinn stepped forward. "I think what he's trying not to tell you is that he heard me say a few minutes ago that I would like to chop Forge Emberly in two."

The judge relaxed. "Yes, I figured it was best to get that out into the open."

Bigley fixed Quinn with a look that made Trinidad think it might not exactly be the best thing for Quinn. "Interesting." She paused. "I'd like to talk to you and Ramona at the station, if you don't mind."

Quinn's face went pale. "Do I…need a lawyer?"

"I don't know, Quinn, do you?" The chief's stare was cold.

No, Trinidad wanted to shout, until the niggle of doubt bottled up the words. Quinn wasn't a killer, it was not possible. But he was a liar…

"Of course you don't need a lawyer," Ramona said. "This is fact-finding only, but I intend to have my attorney there as a precautionary measure. I have Alpenfest duties the rest of today, but I can fit you in tomorrow morning at ten, if that suits, Chief."

"All right," Bigley said, shifting to Quinn. "I'm busy with the coroner and the interviews at the lake anyway. Does eleven tomorrow work for you, Quinn?"

He nodded.

"I'm going to get out of here before we attract any more attention," the chief said.

Indeed Trinidad saw local busybody theater manager Cora Fieri and her long-ago ex Warren Wheaton eyeing the proceedings. A police presence was much more interesting than the alpenhorn concert.

Quinn shot a desperate look at Trinidad, and that old feeling took over, the one full of trust and loyalty. "I'll ask Stan to sit in, okay?" she said, touching his wrist. Stan Lawper, former butler, current lawyer, and proprietor of the Full of Beans coffee shop, had provided legal help when Juliette was accused of murder. She felt sure he would pitch in again now. "Why don't you take Doug back to the farm and get him settled? He looks upset."

Doug was standing stiffly with his hands balled into fists, mashing them against his upper thighs. Noodles was pawing at his knees, trying to forestall a meltdown as she'd seen her dog do before with Doug. To her knowledge, Noodles had never worked as a therapy dog, having flunked out of the program before entering civilian life, but the dog had a deep well of instinctual knowledge that amazed her on a regular basis. When a small sound of distress came through Doug's parted lips, Noodles bumped him right in the stomach until Doug began to pet him.

"Thanks, Trinidad," Quinn said. "And I'm real sorry I spoke harshly to you before."

"Don't give it another thought," she said.

But, as she returned to the food truck, her own thoughts were definitely spinning around their earlier exchange. She believed Quinn was innocent of harming Forge Emberly, but she still wondered at the source of Quinn's deep hatred for the man.

I'd like to chop him in two.

Was the sale of Quinn's land canceled now that Forge was dead?

The chief would be certain to ask such probing questions, and Quinn was not skilled at the poker face. Or was he?

When Gabe told her that his boss all but accused him of embezzling, she'd shared in his apparent indignation, believing 100 percent that her husband could not be guilty of any such behavior. Hook, line, and sinker.

And the topper was Gabe had been courting Juliette at the time, never mentioning to Juliette that he was actually married. He'd embezzled money without arousing the suspicion of any of the three women he'd married. Gabe, the handsome, ebullient, generous accountant, had been too good to be true, and Papa Luis was the only one who saw it.

Was Quinn also too good to be true? Noodles trotted at her heels as they returned to the food truck.

"You're back?" Diego said. "I don't think Zap's wife is finished honking that horn yet."

"Doesn't matter." She ordered Diego to roll down the shutters and fold up the chalkboard. "We're done here."

He gaped. "Was it about whatever Chief Bigley was saying? Did they find the corpse?"

She exhaled long and slow. "Let's go to the shop, and I'll tell you all at once before I go see Bonnie. Most of the action is petering out here. Leave a bunch of our coupons under a rock on the table, okay?"

"Yes, ma'am," Diego said, snapping into action. "I can't wait to hear this story."

It was one for the ages, that was certain. She steered the massive truck toward the shop, coasting onto Main Street only having ground into two curbs this time. Her truck-driving skills were improving. Diego was too preoccupied even to tease her about it.

She waved at Mr. Mavis, who was, by that time, back at his post at the gas station, readying himself for his afternoon bicycle ride up and down the road. Mr. Mavis was more reliable than an atomic clock. Rumbling into the parking place behind the shop, she parked, almost in the designated spot, and trailed Diego into the store.

She'd already called Stan Lawper at Full of Beans. The impeccable silver-haired gentleman greeted her at the Shimmy by pulling out a chair for her at one of the pink tables where Juliette and the twins were seated. Noodles found his comfy cushion for a nap. Stan took a seat opposite her and pronounced in his British accent, "Good afternoon, Trinidad. How kind of you to send for me."

"It wasn't kindness, Stan. You're an amazing lawyer."

Juliette joined them, sliding glasses of water onto the table and bobbing her head in agreement. "I'm walking proof."

"Perhaps I should remind you that I'm a coffee store owner, at the present. Litigation is not my current trade."

"It's okay," Trinidad said. "Quinn isn't charged with anything. He wants you there for moral support." She related the events, or most of them, before the twins had to leave for a robotics club challenge.

"Remember..." she called out to their departing backs.

"We know," Diego said. "No newspaper articles yet, but that guy from *Go West* Magazine said he'll be here at nine tomorrow."

She slumped. By then word would have flooded Upper Sprocket about the body in the lake, by way of Papa's trunk. She'd be lucky to get him to print anything about the Shimmy with that tasty morsel in his sights. The twins left, and Stan cleared his throat.

"It would appear to me that you have more to say, without the presence of the teenage ears."

She nodded. "I'm...er...worried that Quinn was somehow involved with Forge beyond the sale of his land."

"Involved?" Juliette said. "How?"

"I don't know. I am certain he didn't kill Forge, but there may be something he wants to keep a lid on."

"Something illegal?" Stan said.

She could not even bring herself to say it, so she offered a tiny nod instead.

"All right. Thank you for your insight. I will look into the matter when I meet with him before our appointment with the chief."

Trinidad thanked him profusely.

With a polite wave, Stan left the store.

Juliette went behind the counter without a word and fixed them both an ice cream sundae with a scoop of French vanilla custard ice cream and caramel sauce. As they dug in, Juliette said, "To quote Stan, it would appear to me that you have something else you need to say. Tell me what's on your heart."

"I'm concerned about Quinn, is all…"

She waved a dismissive spoon. "I said your heart, not your head. You can hide from everyone else, but not from me. You're worried that he's not the man you thought he was, right?"

"I…" She deflated in the face of her friend's scrutiny. "Yes. I trusted…I mean, I trust him."

"And you're scared he's a deep-down Bozo the Clown, like Gabe turned out to be."

"No." She felt her face heat up. "I do trust him. He's never lied to me before…that I know of."

"At the risk of sounding like Dr. Phil, this isn't a matter of trusting Quinn. The question is, do you trust yourself?"

And that was the crux of it. She'd made wonderful friends in Sprocket by trusting her instincts where her ex-sisters-in-law were concerned. But men… Well that was different barrel of monkeys altogether. Was it *hook, line, and sinker* time again with Quinn?

"I thought I could, but now…"

Juliette's smile was tender. "I know how you feel. I've loved two men who didn't love me back—not on the same level, anyway. Both of them were two-timers, so I figure, maybe, that's what I attract."

"You're worth so much more, Juliette."

"So are you. I like Quinn. I want to believe him for your sake. My only advice is, if your gut is whispering something, you need to listen, okay? I didn't, and I paid for it. I don't want that for you."

Trinidad nodded and accepted Juliette's tight hug.

"I owe you, remember?" Juliette said, prodding her with an elbow. "You got me out of the slammer and put away a murderer. Maybe you can repeat the performance now that we've got another dead body around town."

"I hung up my sleuth hat. I'm never doing that again."

"Never say never," Juliette said with a wink, giving Noodles a goodbye pat as she left.

The afternoon had given way to dusk by the time she'd finished puttering around at the Shimmy, and fatigue clung to every limb. Tomorrow would have to do for a visit to Bonnie at the Sprocket Station, and she called and left a message with Gretchen that she'd be over in the morning to discuss plans for Felice's upcoming birthday.

She drove home thinking about Three Egg Lake. If the chief was right, the murderer had tried unsuccessfully to submerge Forge's body. It wasn't a terrible plan, she thought. The lake was more than twelve hundred feet at its deepest, and there were always unattended boats on the dock the killer could have borrowed in the wee hours to transport Forge. The tourist activities, mostly jet skiing, paddleboating, and swimming in a roped-off area, would not get started until later. The killer might have run into an early-morning fisherman, but most of them clustered along the less rocky end of the lake, the far "egg," so to speak, so they would not have noticed a small speedboat or rowboat.

A local, Trinidad thought with a start. It must have been someone who knew where to get a boat, and when. Someone strong, she decided. A dead body, particularly Forge's dead body, would not be easy to lug. So maybe not Ramona Hardwick, though she could have paid someone to do it.

Quinn was strong and athletic, but he wasn't a killer. Her temples pounded a painful rumba. There was only one way to answer Juliette's question... Could she trust herself? She would have to figure out what Quinn was trying to hide. But what if she found out he'd fooled her like Gabe? Worry thrummed her nerves as she completed the drive.

At the tiny house, she found Papa Luis pacing like a caged lion. Noodles followed him back and forth for a while until he grew tired and decided to supervise from the comfort of his cushion.

"It's an abomination," Papa said, followed by a rapid burst of Spanish. "Incomprehensible."

"I feel the same way. Someone clobbered Forge Emberly and hid him in your trunk before they retrieved him and dumped him in the lake. Or do you think the killer had an accomplice?"

Papa came to roost next to the coffee machine. "I have not given it much thought. My car, Trina. The police have impounded my car."

His Chevy. She could only imagine how Bigley had tried to explain that travesty to Papa. "Oh dear."

Papa gave her an affronted look. "We are well beyond the 'oh dear' stage. I am an honest, law-abiding, tax-paying citizen, and see how I am treated?" He launched into a rant from which she was able to pick out the words "scratched" and "properly vacuumed" and "pistons."

"Papa, I'm sure they will take extra good care of the car. They have to process it for evidence. Did they say how long they'd need to keep it?"

"Possibly a *week*," he said with a groan.

He said the word "week" with all the emotion of someone being sent to the gallows. "Raul and I spoke of our cars every time we talked. Imagine if he was still alive and I had to tell him my car was impounded. He would never let me forget it."

Papa's brother Raul had owned a classic 1957 Cadillac convertible in Cuba, but after the revolution, it became impossible to find replacement materials. He'd had to make do with scavenged parts and jerry-rigged repairs. Even so, the car was the pride of his heart.

"And to add the insult to the injury," Papa said. "Officer Chang has provided me with a loaner vehicle."

"Well that was thoughtful."

"A Pontiac." Papa pronounced all the three syllables as though they caused sores in his mouth. "I told him to park it out of sight of the windows. It is too painful to look at."

She tried to calm him down by telling him everything she had learned about the Forge Emberly case. He listened, sort of, but his spirit was grievously wounded. As she moved around the kitchen to make them some sandwiches, an idea formed in her mind. A busy Papa was a happy one.

"Papa, why don't you give your greenhouse plans to Quinn so you two can start building? Winter will be here soon, and I'm going to need the mint you promised."

"But, Trina…" he wailed, flopping onto the armchair. She thought she heard the trill of tears choking his throat. "My car…left in an impound yard for anyone to abuse. It might as well be abandoned on the curb with a MUTILATE ME sign."

"And what about your magnum opus?" she continued doggedly. His grand scheme that topped all the others was to one day produce a substantial crop of pods from the notoriously finicky vanilla orchid, in "captivity," as he put it.

"I…" Something like purpose returned to her grandfather's eyes. He sat up. "I've been giving that some attention. The vanilla vines will require trellising, but I have thought of a design that might work. In the jungle, you see, they would climb up the trees and such before they send down roots into the soil. The material must be loose, because they are sort of a terrestrial orchid, if you will."

"Right."

"And there's the watering… We must keep the support and the medium wet so the air roots stay moist."

"Yep…those air roots."

"And the self-pollination. I've done this with toothpicks, but an electric toothbrush was much more effective, if you remember."

"Yes, I do." He had purchased half a dozen electric toothbrushes before he found just the right model.

Papa got up and fetched a notepad to scribble down ideas. "When will Quinn be here?"

"Oh, uh, I haven't asked him yet, but I'm sure he wouldn't mind if you called him."

Papa scampered off to the ancient rotary phone.

He was back in fifteen minutes, which was remarkable for a man of Papa's lengthy conversational tendencies. "He will be here tomorrow after he settles that nonsense at the police station."

Good. She'd have more opportunity to figure out if Quinn was the man she'd thought him to be. Trinidad searched her grandfather's face for any sign of distrust or uncertainty about Quinn. She saw none. And Papa had disliked "the Hooligan" Gabe from the beginning, hadn't he?

Trinidad decided she would put the nonsense out of her mind as well. But, as darkness crept across grass behind their property, borrowing shadows from the trees, she remembered that Forge was dead, murdered.

And whoever had done it probably lived in charming little Sprocket. That was not nonsense; it was stone-cold murder.

Chapter Five

TRINIDAD GOT UP BEFORE THE sun, easing down the creaky loft ladder so as not to awaken Papa or Noodles. It was a wasted effort.

Papa was already sitting at the sliver of a table, papers spread out before him, a ruler behind one ear, a protractor behind the other, staring through the glasses that had slid down his nose. Noodles watched from his cushion, wagging a tail in greeting at Trinidad.

"Do you need help for the Alpenfest things today?" Papa asked.

"No, thanks. The Shimmy's services are not required. Probably good since I've got a ton to do at the store, including an interview."

Papa declined breakfast, which he often did when engrossed in a project. She was relieved that the greenhouse was taking his focus off the Bel Air. A greenhouse was a symbol of his intent to stay in Sprocket, wasn't it? Plus, she admitted, she would like having Quinn on the premises, trust issues aside. Maybe he and Doug would be around for dinner. She mentally reviewed the contents of the weensy refrigerator and determined to fetch some groceries before she returned from the shop.

A half hour later, she was showered, dressed, and caffeinated. Due to her interview with T. J. Orwell, she'd taken extreme measures: pinning her hair back in a hefty clip and swiping on some lip gloss. Her mother, who was well-dressed and always smelled of French perfume, would have said, "Don't you have something more womanly in your closet, honey? How about that silk blouse I gave you for your birthday?" Jeans and a Shimmy and Shake T-shirt were as womanly as she could achieve at the moment.

Papa was still frowning and muttering over his papers when she kissed his cheek and hurried with Noodles to her Pinto. Another sunny fall day was on tap, and Fridays and warm weather always stimulated the ice cream appetites, so she intended to hurry straight to the Shimmy as soon as she'd checked on Bonnie. Orwell would no doubt be impressed with her machines whirling and churning in the background while he interviewed her.

The air was crisp as they piled into the Pinto. She noticed that Noodles had begun to shiver a bit in the mornings during his early constitutionals. The time was ripe to invest in a sporty dog vest, but she didn't have much extra money to spend, so she decided to stop by Lydia's Off the Rack store when she had a break. She hadn't been inside often, except to snag some necessaries, such as her inspired purchase of earmuffs to protect Quinn, Doug, and Noodles from the

Fourth of July fireworks. Quinn had PTSD from his military duties, but Doug and Noodles were also terrorized by the explosions. Lydia had everything from muffs to moccasins in her treasure trove.

"Don't worry, sweets," she said to Noodles as they drove to Bonnie's. "We'll make it through this winter." Come to think of it, she'd need some winter clothes herself. Living with Gabe, she had not acquired much of a snow wardrobe. Gabe's idea of an outdoor adventure was hustling to a cab on the way to a trendy restaurant.

This was Sprocket, a wee town lying at the feet of the massive Wallowas, which she'd been told made their own weather. But neighboring Josef seemed to hang steady with only a foot or two of snow at a crack, though Mr. Mavis had told her a harrowing story of one Fourth of July when the town received a few inches after a freak storm. That didn't seem so bad…unless one peddled frozen dessert for a living. Picturing snow-covered roofs and icy sidewalks caused an odd mixture of excitement and anxiety. *You sell ice cream. Who's gonna buy that when we're knee-deep in snow*? Quinn had suggested a frozen hot chocolate bar as a possible moneymaker. Was there a way she could offer such a product via her food truck? Could she navigate over icy roads? The date pressed down upon her…almost October, and she still hadn't finalized her winter plans.

Because she was on autopilot, she found herself guiding the Pinto toward town. After an illegal U-turn, she drove north, leaving the more settled parts of Sprocket behind. Then she turned on the aptly named Linger Longer Road.

The route was hemmed in on both sides by brilliant green hills and clumps of lodgepole pines, graceful against the perfect autumn morning. The scenery still floored her, and it would not have surprised her to see Julie Andrews twirling along, belting out a song. She rolled down the window to welcome in the fresh breezes that blew down from the Wallowas. In the middle of an off-key rendition of "Oh What a Beautiful Morning," she remembered with a start that Forge Emberly was dead—murdered, in fact—and her mission was one partially of consolation and support, not celebration. Chastened, she stopped singing but kept the window open, since Noodles seemed to be enjoying the fresh air.

When an elk stepped from behind a cluster of pines, she braked to a stop, to marvel. Honestly, the town could have been a postcard, except for the murder stuff. Resolutely, she drove the last steeply pitched part of the road and parked the Pinto at Bonnie's Station. The four yellow train cars appeared quiet, but the long green dining car was belching out the tantalizing scent of bacon. She and Noodles followed their noses. She told Noodles to sit outside, and she climbed up the metal steps.

The inside of the old dining car was unfinished, but Bonnie had put up folding screens to partition off a section with six small tables and a skinnier one along the wall that housed the buffet. The gracefully arched ceiling was not painted yet, but the pendant lights spoke of the elegance of years gone by and the ornate floor rug added warmth. Best of all, the patrons could see out the wide windows, which offered gorgeous wooded hills and a slice of the mountains beyond the treetops. The glorious view made up for the unfinished dining car.

The patrons were eagerly devouring blueberry pancakes, scrambled eggs, bacon, and toast with what appeared to be freshly made jelly. A typed flyer displayed in an ornate frame proclaimed the offerings in all caps. Gretchen's doing. Trinidad knew better than to ask for the jelly recipe. She was surprised to see Judge Torpine and Ramona Hardwick occupying the table farthest to the rear, set apart from the others. Had it been positioned that way, or did they do some covert scooting to afford themselves some privacy? Ramona's creamy complexion was offset perfectly by her soft blue sweater. The judge sipped coffee, seemingly devouring her every word.

Bonnie interrupted her thoughts, ducking under the low threshold, entering with a fresh tray of pancakes. Trinidad spoke softly to her while she off-loaded her burden. "I'm so sorry. I should have come earlier. How are you doing with… you know…the police attention?"

Bonnie shot her a look, smile fading. "Just incredible, right? That he would be killed on my property?" Her whisper was sharp-edged, and Trinidad realized how upset she must be.

"To think there is someone around here, so close, who would actually murder another person." She nervously arranged the bowls of cut berries and granola.

Felice came in, toting a glass jug of syrup. She wore a smaller version of her mother's pink rosebud print apron.

"Hi, Felice."

"Hi, Auntie," Felice said.

Trinidad felt that strange lurch in her heart whenever she heard Felice call her "Auntie." She smiled at the girl. "You're a good helper."

"Uh-huh," Felice said.

"Excited about your birthday party on Sunday?"

"Uh-huh."

"I wanted to ask what kind of ice cream you'd like."

"Pink."

"Ah. Pink." Strawberry? Cotton candy? Cherry cheesecake? "I have an idea. Would you like to make your own ice cream?"

"Uh-huh. Can Auntie Juliette and Quinn and Doug and Noodles and Mommy and Papa Luis make their own too?"

"Uh, yes, of course." She'd have to come up with a plan for that. "It can be a party activity."

Felice looked up at her and showed her the syrup jug and the napkins folded into her pocket. "I'm helping. May I get you a napkin?"

Trinidad laughed. "You are a super helper, but I am here for talking, not eating." Felice nodded and went around to ask the other guests.

Bonnie checked on the diners, who were all in good spirits.

"An excellent repast," Ernst, the lead yodeler, said, grandly holding up his coffee cup. He and his fellow diners saluted Bonnie with an impromptu yodel, which sent Noodles howling outside. Trinidad hastily excused herself to quiet the dog.

Gretchen exited the small cabin that served as a kitchen, separate from the one that housed Bonnie and Felice. Gretchen held wads of paper napkins.

"Hello," Gretchen said, stopping a moment. "Gorgeous morning."

Trinidad agreed.

Bonnie and Felice exited the car to join them. Noodles came over immediately to offer licks and wags to Felice. Her giggle made Trinidad want to giggle too.

"Everyone loves the breakfast, Gretchen," Bonnie said, beaming at her cook. "You are a whiz."

Gretchen's smile was humble, but Trinidad could see her cheeks take on a rosy tint at the compliment. "Tomorrow will be currant scones and sausage made right here in town. They're going to love that." Her gaze narrowed as she looked through the dining car windows. "Is that my brother?"

Bonnie nodded. "He and Ramona came after we started service and said they'd pay for breakfast even though they're not staying here. They didn't want to eat in town, I guess." She grinned. "Who am I to turn down paying customers?"

Gretchen's mouth pinched. "Are the police done with whatever they've been doing? I told them Forge was only here for the yodel fest, not as a guest. No more than an hour and then he left, as far as I know, but they're behaving as if he was hosting clandestine meetings here with his killer or something."

Bonnie's ever-present smile dimmed a notch, and she touched her daughter's pink fuzzy hat. "Why don't you go get your workbook, okay? Gotta practice our capital letters today." Clearly Bonnie did not want talk of the murder around Felice. Trinidad concurred. Life was scary enough when you were a grown-up. No need to add murder and mayhem to a child-sized plate. She recalled that it was Friday. She was about to ask why Felice was not on her way to Sprocket Elementary School when the child interrupted her thoughts.

"The man was choosing his favorites." Felice's high-pitched voice made them all look down.

"What man, honey?" Bonnie sank down on her knee to be closer to Felice's altitude.

"The man with the red hair."

Trinidad's pulse did the two-step. Forge? "What was he doing, exactly, Fee?"

"Picking. Like when you say I can choose my favorites for my jar while we're out exploring."

Favorites? Trinidad scanned Bonnie's face, figuring maybe she had some sort of Mommy Rosetta Stone that deciphered kindergarten talk.

"Felice has a collection jar," Bonnie explained, "with rocks and pebbles and pine cones and such, but we had to pare down when we moved into the cabin. So we just choose our favorites, now, to add to the jar."

Felice nodded soberly.

"So what do you mean, he picked his favorites?" Bonnie asked her daughter.

Felice put a finger in her mouth to wiggle her remaining front tooth. "He went for a walk and picked which trees he liked best. I saw him."

Trinidad exchanged a puzzled look with Gretchen while Bonnie bent closer to her daughter. "You saw Mr. Emberly walking around here? In the trees?"

She nodded. "At playtime, after the yodeling concert. I was pulling my wagon. You said to stop at the sphere rock by the bridge."

"The sphere rock? That's very precise, Felice," Trinidad said.

"We're trying to learn our shape words. I figured it was more educational than calling it the basketball rock."

Bonnie's smile did not erase the worried crimp between her brows. "That's great, Fee. Mommy is proud of you for following the rules. But...you said while you were out there you saw Mr. Emberly? The man with the red hair and beard?"

She nodded.

"Can you show us where?" Bonnie said.

"Uh-huh."

Gretchen's expression was pained. "I would love to see this play out, but I have to drop off these napkins. I'll tend to the service until you get back."

Trinidad could see that Ernst was already rising from the table. "If we don't want a bunch of curious yodelers after us, we better get going quick."

Bonnie took Felice's hand. "Thanks, Gretchen. Okay, Fee. Show us."

Felice led Bonnie, Trinidad, and Noodles along a narrow trail cut into the grass. Birds skittered in and out of the greenery, stuffing their beaks with seeds and bugs. Noodles gave them a glance, but, at his age, he put no pursuit plans in action. Trinidad looked back. The breakfast crowd had spilled out into the courtyard and flowed toward cars and one motorcycle. She'd heard talk that several would be taking the Wallowa Lake Tramway, which would carry them 3,700 feet to the top of Mount Howard.

The judge was getting into his sleek Mercedes. His other car was a beautiful classic Mustang, she knew. A far cry from a beat-up Pinto and a secondhand food truck. Was that the outline of Ramona next to him in the passenger seat? Those two were definitely talking about something important.

They came to the "sphere rock" as Felice called it. Felice stopped and tapped it with her forefinger. Another fifty feet away was an old wooden footbridge that spanned a shallow creek. Trinidad could see why Felice had been given strict instructions not to pass the point. The water was not deep, but it ran swiftly over the rocky bottom.

"The creek divides my property from Quinn's," Bonnie said. "He's been working on shoring up the other end of the bridge since the footing has come loose. We figured we could come up with a walking tour of the nut orchards or something along those lines when it was repaired. Well, that was our plan before he sold to Forge, anyway."

The bridge exited into a towering cluster of pines, some ponderosas, some lodgepoles, and a wide white oak.

Bonnie pointed. "Forge's second route would bring in people, for sure. The view would be spectacular, but I was surprised Quinn agreed to do it." She cut a look to Trinidad. "Weren't you?"

The current railriders' route was a fairly straight shot from where it originated at Forge's station behind Messabout Creek to the shores of Three Egg Lake. Forge shared the profits with the town of Sprocket and a small portion with the Apple of My Eye Orchard over which the old train rails crossed. This new route would certainly provide eye-popping views once the cut-through was complete. Quinn would presumably have been given a portion of the proceeds as well as the payment for the land. What would happen to Forge's business now? Did he have a partner? Or someone named in a will or trust who would take over? Might that be a motive for murder?

Felice pointed to the biggest of the trees. "He liked that one. He made a mark on it. See?"

"A mark?" Trinidad squinted.

"Felice," Bonnie said, "you stay here with Noodles while Auntie and I go see the mark, okay?"

Felice nodded and hunkered down next to Noodles, picking wildflowers from the grasses along the fence. She retrieved her red wagon she'd parked there and tossed the flowers inside. Bonnie and Trinidad walked over the bridge. The wood felt strong under Trinidad's feet until they got to the far end where it grew spongy. As they stepped off, she could see where the post had been partially unearthed.

"He hadn't gotten around to pouring the cement yet," Bonnie explained.

The dense shade of the trees chilled Trinidad, and she pulled her sweater tighter around her body. The branches overhead seemed to swallow up the sun. Grasses had given way to ferns and clusters of mushrooms that thrived in the dim light. The tallest of the trees was the regal-looking ponderosa pine, flanked by two smaller pines. An oak was set off to the side, enabling the canopy to absorb plenty of sunlight.

"I wonder what she meant by 'he picked his favorites,'" Bonnie mused. "I know he stuck around after the yodeling concert, wanted to take a walk, I think. To be honest, I figured, like Gretchen did, that he'd left at some point. That's what I told the chief, anyway. Embarrassing when she pointed out that his car was still in the lot. From now on, I'm having the guests give me their license plate numbers when they check in."

Trinidad drew close to the pines, trailing her fingertips over the bark. The scent of pitch was heady. She stopped. "Look at this, Bonnie."

Bonnie hurried over.

Trinidad pointed to an "x" carved into the trunk. "Recent. The bark hasn't healed yet. Forge must have marked this one for cutting."

"Never would have seen that if Felice hadn't told us to look. And here's two more," Bonnie added as they discovered the mark on the two other nearby trees.

"Makes sense. They'd all have to be cut for Forge's second railway."

They went silent for a moment. "Felice was right, then," Trinidad said. "Forge wandered on his own out here after the yodeling contest and marked the trees, probably trying to decide which to cut to maximize the views. Did the police search this area?"

"I don't think so. They primarily focused on the inn and immediate grounds."

They examined the oak and found another "x."

Trinidad tried to think it through. After the yodelfest, Forge had walked the property looking for which trees to cut, and someone had killed him, dragged him back to the station, and left him in Papa's trunk. That seemed like a lot of risk, though the growing darkness would have provided some cover.

They did not find any more marks carved into the trunks. Bonnie put out a palm and caressed a branch of the oak tree. "Maybe you've been spared the chopping block," she said.

And who would benefit from that? Trinidad could think of no one except some of the tree-loving townspeople.

Bonnie sighed. "This is not the kind of thing I envisioned happening on my land."

They had returned to the bridge when Trinidad noticed something glinting below the water. She stopped, peering over the railing, skin suddenly cold. Concealed by the deep shadow cast by the bridge, she could just make it out. "There's a shovel in the creek." A shovel. Was it the weapon used to clobber Forge over the head before he was stuffed into Papa's trunk?

"That's weird. Why would there be a...?" Bonnie stopped. "Oh man. The murder weapon?" Bonnie peered into the bubbling water. "Has the shovel got a blue stripe on the handle?"

Trinidad leaned on the railing to take a closer look. Something creaked. The wood split with a vigorous crack where Trinidad was braced against it. She tumbled stomach first, belly flopping into the ankle-deep creek with a splash. The cold hit her like a slap as she sat up, sputtering.

Bonnie's face loomed from the bridge; mouth open. "Trinidad, are you okay?"

"Yes," she said after a cough. She was trying to get some purchase against the slippery rocks to climb out when Noodles appeared at the bank. "No, Noodles, I'm okay. I don't need…"

But Noodles had already rushed into the water, taken Trinidad's sleeve in his teeth, and yanked her, standing, toward the shore.

"Awww honey," she said, feet sinking into the muddy bank. "Now we're both wet and muddy, and I wasn't really in danger of drowning in six inches of water."

Undeterred, Noodles set about licking her all over. "You would have made an excellent rescue dog," she said. Bonnie was hurrying to the bank to reach her.

"I'm so sorry, Trinidad. The wood was more rotted than I thought. Are you sure you aren't hurt?"

"Just my pride." As she was squelching out of the mud with Noodles, she was able to clearly see the shovel, its reflection dappled by the movement of the water. "I can positively state that there is indeed a blue stripe on the handle of the shovel. Do you recognize it?"

She grimaced. "Yes, unfortunately."

Trinidad braced herself for the bad news she knew was coming.

"It's Quinn's," Bonnie said.

Chapter Six

"WE'LL HAVE TO CALL CHIEF Bigley." Bonnie worried her lower lip between her teeth. Worry was unusual for Bonnie, but finding out from her young daughter where Forge had likely been murdered was not promoting peace of mind.

Should Trinidad offer comfort in some way? She wasn't sure. "Yes. Let's do that."

They made their way back to Felice, who scanned her up and down. "Ooooh, look at the mud. Did you fall in, Auntie?"

"Yes, but I'm okay."

"'Cuz Noodles saved you, right?"

"Er, yes. Yes, he did."

Noodles wagged his tail as if accepting the mantle of hero.

"Can we go to the forest and look for more treasures?" Felice asked Bonnie.

Bonnie sighed. "Not right now, Fee."

The child took the answer in good stride and followed Noodles, wagon in tow, outpacing the two adults. Bonnie watched her regretfully. "Quinn let her play in the 'forest,' as she calls it. She loves that old oak tree in particular, the one Forge was going to cut down. Every acorn and bit of sparkly white stone is a treasure to that kiddo." Bonnie sighed. "I can't believe Forge was actually killed there."

Trinidad tried not to squelch too loudly, but her shoes were full of mud. "I've gotta go. I have spare clothes at the store. If you can call Chief Bigley, I'll phone Quinn. He'll…want to know."

Bonnie stopped her with a touch on her damp shoulder. She bent a little to bring herself closer to eye level. "Trinidad, you know that Quinn had nothing to do with this. He's a good man."

She tried to sound cheerful. "Yes, of course."

Bonnie got that dreamy smile again. "You two have a nice relationship started."

"We're friends, good friends, is all." Her cheeks grew hot.

"It's risky to trust someone again after Gabe, isn't it?"

"My track record isn't great, Bonnie."

She laughed. "Mine neither, but you know what? I had a basketball coach who used to say, 'The only important statistic is the final score.' Don't take yourself out of the game because you lost with Gabe."

"I'm not sure I want to play the game," she said, trying for a joke. "I'm way too short for that."

Bonnie's smile only widened. "No, you're not, sis. And there were good things about Gabe, believe it or not. Those were real qualities that attracted you in spite of all the bad stuff that cropped up later." She leaned over and kissed a clean spot on Trinidad's forehead.

The gesture touched Trinidad.

"Now I'm gonna get you some towels so you and Noodles don't muddy up your car. We can talk birthday details real quick before you go. I'm determined the kiddo is going to have some sort of celebration if it kills me." She rolled her eyes. "Scratch that last remark."

While Bonnie loped off, Trinidad swallowed the lump in her throat.

Sis. Out of Gabe's betrayal, she'd become a sister to two ladies, and an auntie to boot. Maybe Bonnie was right about the score. There must have been some things about Gabe that were honest and true. Feeling sticky, but better, Trinidad wiped Noodles off as best she could with Bonnie's towels. They firmed up plans for the rail ride, which would be Felice's birthday outing and the follow-up ice cream extravaganza, and she drove back to the shop. On the way she thought about Felice and her fondness for jars to gather her treasures. The perfect idea sparked. Pickle-jar ice cream, a low-tech way of making ice cream that would surely enchant Felice. She and Yolo had loved to shake up their own personal flavors.

It wasn't until the moment she squelched through the door of the Shimmy that she remembered the nine o'clock interview.

T. J. Orwell was sitting at a table, eating a bowl of rocky road ice cream. Breakfast for the calorie-oblivious. Carlos and Diego each held a notebook and a cell phone. "Uh-oh," she muttered. While the cat was away, the mice had a chance to conspire.

Orwell's nostrils flared as he took in her mucky hair and sodden jeans. "Business casual day?"

"What happened to you?" Diego asked. "You look like you had a run in with the Swamp Creature."

"I fell in a creek, and Noodles rescued me."

They turned appreciative looks on Noodles, who accepted the praise along with a dog biscuit before he trotted to his beanbag.

"We found out something you'll never believe," Diego said.

Trinidad groaned. "Mr. Orwell, I'm sorry I'm late for my interview, but…"

"That's okay," he said. "The twins here are giving me all kinds of material."

Was he serious or joking? She didn't know him well enough to tell.

"We have news," Diego said. "Big news."

She shifted her weight from one soggy sneaker to the other. "Can it at least wait until I'm changed?"

Reluctantly they agreed. She went to the back room, grumbling all the way. Rough morning. She'd forgotten all about the interview and arrived looking like a half-drowned squirrel. In her absence, the twins had hijacked her reporter and, to top it all off, they'd given Orwell a scoop of ice cream from the emergency supply she kept in the freezer, instead of the fresh-churned variety. All her hopes of making a great first impression had dissolved in one squelchy swoop.

Grateful she'd insisted on installing a shower in the miniscule back bathroom for those all-nighters she occasionally pulled, she emerged ten minutes later, scrubbed and in clean clothes and shoes, determined to get the interview back on track.

Carlos gave her no time to launch her plan.

"We figured we could help try and prove Quinn innocent of Forge's murder," Diego said.

"Unless he's not," Carlos added. "I mean we like the guy and everything, but Ted Bundy was a cool dude too. What if—"

"Wait," Trinidad said. "Stop right there. No one has been charged with anything, especially not Quinn. Just because the police questioned him…"

"And Mayor Hardwick," the reporter added.

"That doesn't mean either is going to be accused of murder," she said.

"Sure, sure," Diego said, "but look what we turned up. Did you know there was a local woman named Cherry Lighter who disappeared thirty years ago from this very town?" His glee was almost uncontainable as he continued. "The police investigated and concluded that she'd run away, but her mother never believed it."

"Okay." She sat with a sigh. "You've dug up a cold case. I get it. What does that have to do with Forge Emberly's murder?"

"No clue," Diego said, "but it's super interesting that Cherry Lighter had connections to the same two people who were just questioned about Forge's murder."

Trinidad blinked. "What?"

Carlos nodded. "Uh-huh. Cherry Lighter worked at

Ramona Hardwick's real estate office on the weekends for a couple of months."

"And Quinn?"

"He was ten at the time she disappeared. According to our sources, Cherry Lighter used to babysit Doug while Quinn was at school."

She breathed a sigh of relief. "Well you can't possibly think a ten-year-old had anything to do with a woman gone missing."

"Sure I can." Diego waggled a finger. "I was listening to a podcast called *The Bad Seed* about this terrible child who freaked out and..."

"All right," she said. "I stand corrected. Ten-year-olds can be super villains, but the connections are coincidental. Sprocket is a small town. Of course this Cherry Lighter would have had relationships with the locals. I am sure Mr. Orwell isn't buying into your conspiracy theories."

Orwell shrugged, but he didn't exactly display the skepticism Trinidad felt was due.

He tapped his pen on the table. "Interesting, is all. The police concluded that there had been no foul play and that Cherry left of her own accord. A letter was received purportedly written from her." He leaned in. "And guess who she was dating?" He sat back, gloating.

"Who?" she finally said.

"Judge Torpine. He's the guy she sent the letter to."

Trinidad's head was whirling. "But, boys, it's a..."

"We know, we know," Carlos said, "It's a small town where people know each other, but I'm just reading between the lines in these old news stories, and there was some sort of disagreement between Cherry and Ramona. Ramona would have been in her early twenties at the time; Cherry was close in age. See the pictures here?"

He turned his cell phone to show her the photo of a newspaper clipping entitled, "Locals interviewed about missing woman." There was a professional picture of Ramona Hardwick in a suit with wide lapels and a scarlet blouse. Below the caption read, "Local real estate agent employed Cherry Lighter for six months before the woman's disappearance."

She shrugged. "It's coincidental for sure, but this has no bearing on the Forge Emberly case."

Diego leaned on his elbows. "What if Forge found something out about Ramona? He was going to expose her for the murder of Cherry Lighter, and she killed him to keep him quiet. Plus she'd be running for mayor unopposed. She'd be happy if someone else like Quinn got stuck with the blame."

Trinidad implored Orwell. "Mr. Orwell, you're a seasoned journalist. Surely, you're not buying into this bizarre theory, are you?"

Orwell eased back his chair and got to his feet. "Rule number one: reporters never turn their backs on a story idea, even if it's outside their purview."

"But…the interview…" she said.

"Sorry. I've got an appointment for another interview right now."

"With whom?" Diego asked.

Orwell grinned. "Mayor Hardwick."

Diego grinned back. "Will you tell us if you sniff out any intel?"

"No," Orwell said. "Rule number two: reporters don't share." With that parting shot, he left.

Diego shook his head. "We shouldn't have told him."

"Don't sweat it," Carlos said to his brother. "You can write your own story. This time, the school newspaper's gonna put you on the front page."

That was all she needed. A regrouping was called for, so she set them to their work. "We're going to create a new Freakshake," she announced. "It will be unveiled tomorrow to coincide with the parade and nighttime Burning of the Burger."

"Yeah, I still don't get that whole burger thing," Carlos said.

"Me neither, but it has something to do with welcoming winter. Anyhoo, back to the Freakshake." She noticed Ernst strolling along the avenue and into Full of Beans. Inspiration struck. "It's going to be called the Yodelayheechew."

"Ha ha," Diego said. "Good one, Miss Jones."

Trinidad brightened, as she always did when dreaming up another decadent creation. "I'm thinking we'll churn some fudge chunk ice cream with the cherries I've got in the freezer. We'll blend it up with milk and add some marshmallow cream and a chewy toffee topping. We can rim it with a pretty ganache with chocolate sprinkles and those little square caramels stuck around. Maybe some cherry gumdrops to up the chew factor and add color. What do you think?"

"We're ready to rock and roll on the Yodelayheechew," Carlos said.

She sent him to the freezer to retrieve the fruit she'd packed away in June. Diego hopped onto his computer to create a flyer to which he'd add a photo to be used in the window and on the Shimmy and Shake's website. At least they could do something helpful with their technology besides dredging up wild theories about missing persons.

Still, something about the story set her curiosity aflame. Tying on an apron, she dismissed it from her mind. With only a few hours until opening, she'd have to work quickly to add the new Freakshake offering. The twins would be have to trained on how to make it while she was representing at the fields where the Saturday parade, craft fair, and burger burning would take place.

Ernst was no longer in sight from where she stood behind the counter, but she hoped he and his fellow yodelers would feel the love for her new creation. The yodeler did indeed appear at lunchtime, joined by Lydia Apperton, his alpen-horn partner.

Lydia was dressed in overalls, her long hair threaded with strands of gray braided into a fat plait that hung almost to her waist. She eyed the Yodelayheechew flyer with longing. "That looks incredible, but I'm saving room for a bratwurst later. So I'll just have a scoop of caramel crunch for now."

"Not me," Ernst said, "I'll take one with the works." They waited for Trinidad and the twins to whip up their orders.

Lydia carried a bag with "Alpenfest is best" emblazoned on the front.

"How did you two practice for your concert?" Trinidad asked as she prepared their order.

"Lots of video calls," Lydia said. "I can't exactly carry my Alpenhorn places, and Ernst is from Washington."

"I usually stay in Josef, but I dillydallied until there were no rooms available. So I ended up here. Very entertaining place." Ernst watched the sticky milkshake marvel being constructed. "I saw you at the Station this morning before all the cops arrived," he said to Trinidad.

"Cops? What now?" Lydia's long-lashed eyes went wide. "Oh wait. Is this about Forge's murder?" She looked slightly chagrined. "I'm not into gossip, but Forge is family, so I have a right to know."

"Family?" Trinidad slid the Freakshake across the counter and rang up the bill. "I didn't know you were related."

"Forge is Zap's cousin. They weren't close, but Zap was the only family Forge had left, I think. They didn't spend time together or anything, because Forge was into business stuff and Zap is more of an outdoorsman." She lowered her voice. "Plus, if you ask me, Forge was the type who enjoyed arguing, and my husband is a live-and-let-live kinda guy. He'd be happy with fenders and taillights for company rather than people. Still, kin is kin, so what's going on at the Station? Did they arrest someone for Forge's murder?"

Ernst carefully hefted his shake. Trinidad was pleased to note the glossy sheen on the ice cream, studded with chewy fudgy bits. "Scuttlebutt is," Ernst said, "the cops found a shovel, which was the murder weapon, and maybe a spot under the trees where he was killed before the attacker dragged him to the parking lot and stuck him in the open trunk of the Chevy."

"Papa Luis's car?" Lydia said. "That's what I heard too."

"Ummm, so it would seem," Trinidad said.

"And then someone swiped the body? So bizarre, right?" Lydia shook her head. "Zap says maybe someone killed him by accident and dumped him in the lake in a panic."

Ernst placed the shake with care on the nearest table. "It's no accident when you brain someone with a shovel."

Lydia shrugged and sat down to scoop up some ice cream.

Trinidad noticed that her twin assistants were in the corner whispering and had likely taken in every word of the conversation.

"What I want to know is…" Ernst said, considering where to tackle his monster milkshake. "What did this Forge guy do that made someone want to kill him?"

Trinidad had a flashback to Quinn's comment about cutting Forge in two.

Ramona, too, couldn't stand him.

She wondered how many others in town were glad Forge was dead?

———

Trinidad closed up promptly at five. The ice cream–loving crowds had departed in favor of the Sausage Fest gearing up in Josef that evening so there was no need to stick around. Alpenfest lovers, God bless them, appreciated their food.

She was happy to load Noodles and hurry home, since she'd heard from Papa that Quinn and Doug were at work on the greenhouse. The clouds were thick with the promise of rain, which might cut short their efforts.

With the workday done, random imaginings assailed her as she drove: Forge getting brained with a shovel, a young woman, vanished. The twins were no doubt concocting a messy conspiracy theory and dragging a story-hungry reporter in for the feast, but still... It wouldn't hurt to ask a few questions about Cherry, maybe see if Quinn had any memories of her. With a bit of luck, she'd uncover a fact or two that would put the whole zany notion to rest.

Thinking about Quinn started up that uncomfortable dance of nerves in her stomach. She'd rounded the corner from Main past Little Bit Road, which ultimately led to Juliette's storage facility, when she heard a pop, and her Pinto bucked and shimmied. Holding the steering wheel in a death grip, she guided the car to the shoulder, only to realize that there was a shallow drop-off paralleling the road. Slamming on the brakes was too little, too late. The Pinto slid with a crunch into a shallow ditch, meant to catch the runoff water. They came to a bumpy stop.

Noodles had slid off the seat onto the floor but was otherwise unharmed. They climbed out to inspect the damage. If the day could possibly go from bad to worse, it certainly had.

Chapter Seven

HER WORN BACK TIRE WAS now a strip of tattered rubber where it had blown out. That wasn't as concerning at the angle at which her trusty Pinto was wedged into the collected leaves and rocks piled up in the depression. There was something askew with the axle, she was pretty certain. Dollar signs cha-chinged in her ears.

No way was she going to drive out of that ditch. A helpful Sprocketerian neighbor passing by would be hard-pressed to drag it clear, and they couldn't assist her with an axle repair, anyway. There was no help for it. Cell phone out, she dialed Marco's Mechanics, where Marco promised to dispatch Zap and his tow truck immediately. As she stood waiting in the breeze, sprinkles began to fall.

"Of course," she thought. "What else?"

Noodles licked a raindrop from his nose. She retrieved a polka-dotted umbrella from the trunk. It gave her a moment's pause, as if there somehow might be a body in her trunk too. "Ninny," she chided herself, and she and Noodles huddled together.

The light droplets had morphed into a chilling drizzle
by the time Zap arrived. He hopped out of his grumbly tow
truck and left the engine running. "Hey, Trinidad," he said.
"Looks like you crumpled it pretty good."

"Yes," she said, through chattering teeth. "I guess I did.
Go big or go home, that's my motto."

He chuckled, took off his cap, and shook off the water
before cramming it on again. "I can haul it out for you, no
problem. Tow you to Marco's to repair that axle and the
tires. Marco won't gouge you too much, since he likes your
ice cream." He flashed a grin that revealed a tiny chip out of
his front tooth. "You two look cold. Why don't you sit up in
the cab while I get this squared away?"

Gratefully, she climbed up, and Zap helped Noodles
with the steep step. Noodles set about sniffing every interesting inch of the cab, which included a napkin-wrapped
slice of pizza from Pizza Heaven. The local shop now had
a new owner who was partial to fancy toppings like spin-
ach and prosciutto and even offered a gluten-free crust.
Zap appeared to be a purist—pepperoni on a regular crust.
She kept a watchful eye on that slice of goodness since her
Labrador was nothing if not resourceful. A clump of key
chains hung from the rearview mirror, everything from a
fuzzy pair of dice to a pewter half-circle with an "A" carved
on it. Romantic, she thought. It gave her an unexpected
pang. There had been a "G" to her "T" once upon a time,
and she'd thought it would last forever.

Silly woman. A cloud of self-pity rolled over her. Her
recent feelings for Quinn, the trust she'd had for him, might

have been one-sided. She'd made a mistake—again. "No harm, no foul this time," she told herself. It wasn't like they'd changed their Facebook status; they'd just had a few dates, plenty of heartfelt chatter, some lovely moments where she'd begun to believe in a future that he obviously hadn't. She didn't need a key chain, just a friend, and she figured Quinn still qualified for that…if his cagey behavior wasn't concealing something more devious. How was he involved with a murdered man?

Guiding Noodles's nose away from the pizza, she considered Lydia's revelation that Zap was Forge's closest relative. They looked nothing alike, but neither did she and her own brother, Yudel Luis, nicknamed Yolo. They couldn't be more opposite in temperament either. Yolo never met a business scheme he didn't love, and, usually, he charmed his way into making somewhat of a success out of it. She admired his unshakable self-confidence.

She didn't have much social finesse, maybe, and, at the moment, there was no one to share a lovey-dovey heart key chain with…so what? It shouldn't bother her in light of all the other relationships she'd cemented since arriving in Sprocket. Yet something under her breastbone contracted when she thought of how withdrawn Quinn had been. He hadn't even called her to relate how things had gone with Chief Bigley. Was their friendship a fantasy too? Juliette urged caution, and Bonnie believed she should risk it. What was a girl to do?

The battered Pinto was hoisted up onto the truck after twenty minutes or so, and Zap climbed into the driver's seat, windbreaker beaded with moisture. He toweled off with a bandana tied to the rearview mirror.

"Locked and loaded," he said, easing them into a turn that would take them back to the mechanic's shop in town.

"Thank you so much, Zap. Thus far I've kept Noodles from eating your pizza."

"Oh, sweet. Lydia is not exactly a chef type, so this is my dinner. She's on her way to the sausage fest to play her horn, but I told her to slide a few brats into her pockets for me."

She saw her opportunity to fish for information. "I talked to her at the Shimmy today. She mentioned you and Forge are cousins."

He laughed. "You wouldn't have guessed, right? I mean he was a wheeler and dealer, and I'm a guy who fixes other people's wheels. He got the smart genes, I guess, but it didn't really make him happy, appears to me." Zap's smile dimmed. "Bad way to go, huh?"

"Do you have any guesses about who might have killed him and dumped him in the lake?"

Zap pulled a piece of gum from a pack stuck in his truck visor and offered one to her, which she declined. "Someone who disagreed with his plans to expand the railway, probably." He waggled his eyebrows. "Or maybe a woman scorned? Nothing more ferocious than that, except maybe a lady protecting her kinfolk. I've seen some mother bears who would rip a person apart for messing with the family."

Trinidad figured that might extend to dogs too. Anyone bent on injuring Noodles would receive a hefty dose of Trinidad's wrath.

"Anyway," he said, as they pulled into the mechanic's shop. "I'm done with my shift. Want me to drop you home?"

"Oh, I couldn't ask you to do that."

He shrugged. "Like I said, Lyds is eating sausage, so I'm alone anyway." He pointed a finger at Noodles. "Besides, your dog needs his supper. Busted," he said, as the dog's tongue made contact with the napkin around his pizza.

She left her Pinto in Marco's care and rode in Zap's truck through the pelting rain. Zap kept up a cheerful banter, which was a relief to Trinidad. She wasn't a natural conversationalist. She favored her nearly silent plumber father who had passed away three years before, after her wedding to Gabe. Maybe, if she hung around people like Zap, she'd improve in the chitchat department. The rain ebbed, and Zap opened his window.

"Man," he said after a deep breath. "Nothing like the fresh air after it rains, huh?" He turned onto the long drive to the house and whistled at the neatly stacked two-by-fours in the distance. "I wondered about that when I was here earlier. Construction project?"

"Greenhouse."

"Super." Zap's reaction to everything seemed to be "super." She realized what he'd said. "You were here earlier?"

Papa and Quinn were standing in deep consultation in the failing sunlight when he cut the engine.

"Yeah, I was, Thursday before sunup. The chief called me." Zap said, frowning for the first time since he'd arrived in his tow truck. "Ummm, last time I was here, your grandpa looked like he wanted to kill me. I probably should have left you back at the end of the drive. Didn't figure your gramps would be outside in this kind of weather."

"Oh, dear," she said, realization sinking in. "You were the one who towed his Bel Air?"

Zap offered a shrug. "Wasn't my idea. Chief's orders." He looked nervously at Papa as he stopped the car. She climbed out, and, after a moment, Zap did too.

"I had a car problem, so my Pinto's at the shop," she explained. "Zap was so kind as to offer me a ride home."

"See?" Zap said, wary eyes on Papa. "I really am a good guy, more or less."

Papa Luis stood blinking as if torn. Finally, he offered a handshake. "Though you confiscated my vehicle, it was under orders of a tyrant. Thank you for bringing my granddaughter home."

Trinidad snaked a look at Quinn, who stood with his hands on his hips. His smile was back in place, to a degree. Doug stood under the porch cover, slicker zipped as far as it would go, glasses glinting in the glare of a work light Quinn had activated.

Zap's phone trilled, and he fished it out of his sweat jacket pocket. "'Scuse me one minute." He stepped away.

"How's the project going?" she asked as Noodles went to stand with Doug. Did she sound cheerful? Carefree?

"We didn't get too far before it started to rain."

Papa went to examine the stacked wood.

"Did things go all right with the chief?" she asked Quinn softly.

"I think so. Hard to tell with her. She would be a great

poker player." He looked from Doug to Trinidad to his boots. "There's something I should…"

"Super! This is like something from a movie." Zap's exclamation interrupted their conversation. "Thanks, I mean, thanks a lot." He disconnected. "Aww man. You're not going to believe this. I can't even believe it. I hardly even knew my cousin, and I sure didn't ever think he'd leave me a dime but guess what?" Zap didn't wait for an answer. "Forge left me the Railriders business, can you believe that? The whole operation."

"Wow," Trinidad said. "That's something. Are you… going to run it?"

He blinked. "Me? Running a business like that?" He shook his head. "I don't think I'd be any good at it, would I?" He paused. "But Lyds is sharp about that kind of thing. I'm going to have to talk it over with her." He jogged to his car and then stopped short. "Do you think I would make a good business owner?"

It seemed to be a rhetorical question, which was good since Trinidad had no idea how to answer.

Zap's face clouded for a moment. "Man, and all this time I thought Forge was a real clod. Wish I would have known." He waved. "I gotta go home and talk to Lyds. See ya."

He bounced down the graveled drive. Trinidad watched him go and then switched her attention to Quinn. He was staring after the car, mouth pursed in thought.

"In light of Forge's murder, is the sale of your land still going through?" she asked. Standing close to him she caught the whiff of nicotine. Smoking? Had he returned to the habit he'd fought so hard to break?

"Stan is looking over the contract. It's unclear if it was notarized and formalized before Forge died."

"So you might still get the money."

Quinn didn't seem to hear. "I was hoping that maybe the plans to cut through my property died along with Forge. If the check was already issued, I could return it, forget the whole thing."

"I thought you needed the money, Quinn. Wasn't that the reason you agreed to Forge's plan?"

Quinn didn't answer.

He's keeping secrets. Alarming. Her thoughts continued on their bumpy track. If the contract had been finalized and Zap took over Forge Railriders, would he carry on the plans to cut the second route? Trinidad was beginning to believe the motive for Forge's death was linked to that second train track.

Papa was leading them into the house to avoid the rain that had started up again. "We will have coffee and some soup. It's simmering on the stove."

Inside the cozy house, she turned on the gas stove and prepared a crustless grilled cheese sandwich for Doug, who would not consume anything with a soupy texture.

The soup was one of Papa's specialties, more stew-like than anything and including pork, beef, plantains, pumpkin, and all manner of ingredients he somehow procured in Upper Sprocket. She suspected the numerous boxes he received from his friends in Miami might be padding his supply. Papa was a treasure, she thought, as she tasted the hearty, golden soup. It dawned on her that there had to be a reason keeping him here in Sprocket. Did he feel it his duty to care for her? Or was he beginning to fall in love with the place, like she had?

"Do you know the name Cherry Lighter?" she said to Quinn once they were settled at the table, several bites in.

Quinn frowned. "I don't think so. Should I?"

"Babysitter," Doug said.

He was so quiet, his statement startled her.

"That's right," Quinn said. "I remember now. She was Doug's babysitter. I was around ten, so you'd have been…"

"Almost three," he said. "Cherry was nice."

Quinn's face relaxed. "Doug's memory is incredible. I recall her now. Petite, long hair, she'd help Mom watch Doug while I had after-school sports. Why?"

"There was some talk that she disappeared."

"I don't remember. I was too young, I guess. Do you remember, Doug?"

He shook his head and began to cut his grilled cheese sandwich into neat squares before spearing them onto his fork and eating them one at a time.

"The twins have some nutty idea that Cherry's disappearance might be linked to Forge Emberly's murder."

That got everyone's attention. A lively inquisition erupted for which she had very little answer except, "I know that it's a wild notion."

Quinn shook his head. "I can't see Forge having anything to do with Cherry. I don't even think he moved here until maybe fifteen years ago? But I guess I'd go along with any theory that didn't put me as the killer." He swallowed and wiped his mouth with a napkin. "The chief came today to talk to us about my shovel." He shot a worried glance at Doug. "It was…upsetting. Doug had to go lie down for a while after."

Doug rearranged the grilled cheese squares on his plate with his fork.

"All I could tell her was the truth. I left that shovel at the footbridge. I forgot about it, to be honest. If the shovel was used to conk Emberly on the head, I had absolutely nothing to do with that."

She searched his face for any tells but read only honest confusion there. A sharp rap on the door made her jump. She'd not yet pushed away from the table when Noodles ambled over and opened it. Soon she'd have to try to undo that habit with a murderer on the loose.

Chief Bigley looked down at Noodles and solemnly shook his paw. "Good evening," she said.

Trinidad invited her to join them at the table.

"No, thanks. This is a quick visit because I saw your truck here, Quinn."

He balled up the napkin, fingers white as he gripped it. "More bad news?"

Trinidad braced herself on the table.

"Neutral, I'd say."

Quinn's tension did not diminish. He sat, clutching the napkin wad while Doug reorganized his plate again.

"Surely, a café, with this rainy weather," Papa said, waving his small cup at her.

"No, thank you. I have good news for you, though, Mr. Jones. Your car will be released tomorrow."

Papa's face split into a brilliant smile. "Music to my ears." He paused. "And I trust there has been no damage?"

"Not a bit. We examined the trunk and found hairs to confirm that Forge was really your passenger, so to speak. No blood, which is consistent with what the coroner said. He believes the blow caused a catastrophic brain injury."

Trinidad's stomach heaved. "Horrible."

"I'll say it again," Quinn said. "I did not hit Forge, nor did Doug. Someone used our shovel, that's all."

The chief cocked her head and gave Quinn a long look that made Trinidad's stomach add a flip-flop to the heaving.

"Chief," she said. "Do you know anything about a woman named Cherry Lighter? I heard a rumor that she disappeared from Sprocket thirty years ago."

The chief did some serious eye squinching before she answered. "That was before my tenure. Might I inquire why you are asking?"

"Oh…umm…just curious."

Her eyebrows drew together in a formidable vee. "The only reason I will not cut you off at the knees for entertaining gossip is that you were key in solving that crime last summer, and I owe you. But…" She sighed. "Is this gonna turn into a snipe hunt that sucks up all my life juices and takes me away from my real work?"

"No, no. I'll help," Trinidad said. "I can…"

"Don't help," she said, palm outward. "That sucks up even more of my life juices." She tapped a note into her phone. "That doesn't pertain to the issue at hand…the shovel."

Quinn gulped. "I told you… I didn't kill him, and neither did Doug." His face took on a stony facade that Trinidad hadn't seen often since she'd come to know him.

"There's no reason to spin wheels here," Quinn said. "I don't have an alibi except for Doug during the time you mentioned, and neither does he. We were both on the farm, doing our nut farmer thing." He spoke softer, as if he wanted to keep Doug from hearing the words. "If you're gonna arrest me, can we go outside?"

Doug squeaked, as if someone had trod on his foot. His eyes went wide with fear, and he shoved the chair away from the table, backed into the corner and began to moan.

"It's okay," Quinn said. "It's gonna be okay."

Noodles raced over to Doug, who bent awkwardly to clutch the dog around his neck.

"Doug, listen to me," the chief said, in a voice that was firm, but not unkind. "I am not here to arrest you or your brother."

Doug didn't acknowledge the remark, continuing to stroke the dog.

"You…aren't?" Quinn said.

"No, because, oddly enough, your prints aren't on the shovel."

He sighed in relief and then frowned. "But I use that shovel all the time."

"Hence the adjective 'odd.' There weren't any readable prints, as a matter of fact. The handle was wiped clean."

He blew out a breath. "Finally. Something works in my favor."

The chief continued to stare at him. "This time."

"What do you mean?"

"I'll avoid the spinning wheels, as you put it. Quinn, I've known you for a long time. You're a forthright, honest person, or so I thought. But there's something you're not telling me, maybe about your real reason for selling the land to Forge."

Trinidad heard Quinn gulp, and it tore at her heart. He was lying. He knew it, she knew it, and, worst of all, Chief Bigley knew it.

The chief stared at Quinn and waited a beat. "Is there something you wanted to say?"

Quinn was silent.

"About your relationship with Forge? That sale wasn't about the money, was it?" she pressed. "Whatever you're keeping quiet could help solve his murder. That is what you want, right?"

Quinn forced his chin up, but he did not exactly meet the chief's eye. "All I am going to say is that I did not harm Forge in any way. That's everything you need to know."

There was something bordering on ferocious in Quinn's expression. Whatever he was hiding, was something enormously important to him. The chief finally nodded.

"Okay. You know where to find me when you're ready to talk, but, if your prints had been on that shovel, we'd be having this conversation downtown." She said goodbye and let herself out before Noodles could break away from Doug to close the door.

Trinidad stopped her on the porch. "Chief, I'm not

butting in, but it seems to me that Zap has a motive in all this."

She zipped up her jacket. "Yes, he inherited the business from Forge. We're looking into that, and Ramona's alibi as well." She raised a brow. "Plenty of suspects to go around."

Quinn left shortly after. "Gotta get Doug back home. Thank you for the meal."

She hurried to slide Doug's sandwich cubes into a plastic bag, more to give herself something to do than because he'd be likely to eat it. When they were gone, she sat in the armchair, watching Papa working on the greenhouse plans.

What could be so important that Quinn would lie to the chief?

Or was it whom? Who was the one person Quinn would put everything on the line to protect?

That answer was an easy one. His brother, Doug.

Had Doug done something to Forge? Doug was certainly prone to outbursts from time to time, but she had never known him to be violent. She could not make herself believe that Doug would harm anyone. But Quinn had to be protecting someone.

She remembered what Zap had said. "Nothing is more ferocious…except a woman protecting her kinfolk." But he was wrong about the pronoun. Men, in particular Quinn, she was certain, would do anything to protect their family too.

Did it make her feel better to know the motivation for his subterfuge might be to shield his brother? It did, but her heart was not completely eased. It wouldn't be, until she knew the truth.

Later that evening, Trinidad settled into bed with a tattered cookbook Papa had found for her at the consignment shop. Old cookbooks held precious slices of history and culture. Last week she'd pored over a volume of Jell-O recipes from the '70s that featured some of the most elaborate wiggly constructions imaginable. This one was a "sips and sweets" collection with a whole section on "what nots," which were apparently recipes that didn't fit into any of the other categories. A recipe for cakelets topped with ice cream caught her eye. What if she could winterize it? With peppermint or something else? A possible new idea around which she could build a whole new line of products? She studied the pages for hours, lost in thought until she was tired enough to try turning out the light. No sense burning up any more electricity planning for the future when the "now" was staring her in the face.

Electricity! She sat up, realizing she'd forgotten to plug the food truck into the outside outlet, which meant the freezer would not be cold enough to peddle the treats for Saturday's Alpenfest pageant and craft fair. It was to be the lead-in to the first weekend's main event, the Burning of the Burger. The clock read eleven fifteen. She could hurry over now, and it would still have a good twelve hours before she'd need to roll out.

Easing down the ladder, she found Papa dozing on his cot with his plans draped over his face. The man slept so little that she made sure not to rouse him, padding toward the front door in her pajamas, a worn set of pants, and a T-shirt printed with flying ice cream cones. Her feet stuffed into slippers, she was easing the keys to the borrowed Pontiac off the counter when Noodles popped up like a lawn sprinkler from his cushion. He might be getting old, but his hearing was as sharp as ever.

Happy for the company, she let them both out. The air was chilly, so fresh it almost hurt to breathe it in. For all Papa's disdain, the Pontiac's heater worked well, and the car had been painted, so the police decals no longer showed. The light bar and internal works had been stripped too. Might as well use the loaner before it was returned, since her Pinto was languishing at Marco's.

Noodles found nothing worth sniffing, so he settled onto the seat, shivering until she got the heat up to par. She made it to the store in twenty minutes. For some reason, the unnatural stillness of the deserted street made her breath hitch. "It's the same friendly place where you come to work every day," she scolded herself. But it wasn't since the moment she'd seen Forge's body in the trunk of Papa's Bel Air. The first time she'd encountered a corpse back in July had been purely wrong place, wrong time. On this occasion the someone, no doubt the killer, had stuffed the body squarely into their lives. She left the Pontiac running, headlights on, sprinted to plug in the food truck, and leapt back into the car.

"We did it, Noo," she said. "No bogeymen or killers."

Noodles licked her wrist, and they headed for home. Embarrassed about her silly fears, she took the drive more leisurely. At the junction to Linger Longer Road, she saw a gleam of yellow eyes peering at her from the side of the road. A closer look revealed it was Ramona's Chihuahua, Frank.

"Oh Frank. Did you get out again?" She turned onto the road. Linger Longer really lived up to its name, even lit only by moonlight. Opening the window, she called to the dog.

"Come here Frank."

Without a backward glance, the dog continued on his merry way, sniffing at the shrubbery.

"You are a stinker." Trying to keep him in view, she drove past the Hardwick property, a neat bungalow with nicely tended shrubbery and a fountain in the front yard. One window glowed through the closed curtains. Ramona must be a night owl. She wondered if Orwell had pried anything out of her regarding Cherry Lighter. That would be some kind of matchup between the savvy stubborn mayor and the reporter, whom Trinidad suspected could be equally determined behind his slouched and rumpled facade. Should she stop and tell Ramona that Frank was AWOL? But then she might lose track of him. On she puttered, muttering complaints against Frank's deficient character.

Several acres of wooded ground separated the Hardwick home from the two-story cabin that Judge Torpine and his sister occupied. "Now that is more my style," she said to Noodles, as if they were on a luxurious house-hunting adventure instead of driving a stripped-down Pontiac toward their tiny rented home chasing someone else's naughty pet. Torpine's place was constructed of rustic logs, but the place was top drawer, with vaulted windows that probably had views of Three Egg Lake from the upper level. The front porch was a huge wraparound affair complete with rockers poised to catch the evening breeze or a gorgeous wintry wonderland in a matter of months. Baskets of hanging plants softened the porch outlines.

What would it be like to live in a place where the coffee table did not double as a seat? Surrounded by woods and acres of your own property to explore? It obviously paid to be a judge. Yet, as a court stenographer for years, she'd learned that judges had to endure their share of aggravation and pain. She recalled the nastiest cases of parents tearing each other to shreds in order to secure custody and divorce situations where love had turned to bitter hatred.

She'd wondered how she herself had come across in court, the clueless ex-wife who hadn't known about her husband's cheating or his cooking of his clients' books. Had the judge thought her stupid? Naive? What about Juliette and Bonnie? Trinidad hadn't known them at all back then, but she was sure their guarded expressions probably matched her own. After taking a punch to the gut, people tended to keep their fists up.

Was she doing that with Quinn? Guarding herself now that she knew he was lying about something, though it probably had nothing to do with her?

She continued on. The thickly clustered trees cut out most of the moonlight, letting in only eerie pockets. No streetlights here. On a clear night the sweep of stars would be spectacular.

"We should suggest Bonnie offer a stargazing night," Trinidad said to Noodles, who seemed to approve the idea. Silver starlight and the golden moon helped her stay on Frank's trail.

Finally, the runaway dog stopped his sniffing and sat. She leapt out and scooped him up. "You are so grounded, mister." As she tucked the shivering dog under her arm, something rustled in the bushes.

Frozen, she listened. So did Frank, triangle ears swiveling. After a moment, she pressed a hand to her heart. "Whew. Scared me too. A rat or a fox or something," she said. "Nothing to worry about." She put Frank in the back seat where he promptly curled up and fell asleep on her coat.

"Let's get you home, Frank, before the wild creatures come out again."

But the next thing that lurched onto the road was a different kind of animal altogether. She slammed on the brakes and screamed.

Chapter Eight

TRINIDAD'S HEART WHAMMED IN HER throat. In the glare of the Pontiac's headlamps, the man's skin shone an otherworldly white. He was tall, wearing a dark-colored track suit that made his face look detached, like a disembodied head, Ichabod Crane in reverse. His shoes were slip-ons, the kind that people kept by their front door so as not to track dirt on the carpet, pallid ankles revealed. He held up his hand to shade his eyes as he continued on, lurching almost.

Trembling fingers pressed to her lips, she watched as he crossed the road, one arm slightly out in front of his body as if he were trying to grab hold of something. A man…in the road. Part of her brain told her he looked familiar, but the rest of her neurons were firing too wildly to take notice. What should she do? Grabbing the phone, she put her finger on the emergency button. But what should she say?

The man did not seem to be hurt, and he had done nothing wrong. If he thought it was a good idea to traipse around the woods on foot at night, who was she to call the cops on him? But there was something so unnatural about his movement that the hairs on the back of her neck prickled. Something was definitely not right.

"What do you think, Noo?" she whispered.

The dog stood on the passenger seat, staring at the strange figure, growling low and deep. Not an angry growl, but a "what in the world" kind of growl. Frank contributed a snore.

She rolled down the window a few inches and eased the car forward alongside the man.

"Sir, are you okay?"

He didn't answer. Her hands went clammy on the phone.

Perhaps he was hearing-impaired. "Sir," she said louder. "Do you need some help?" She practically shouted out the window.

Now he turned to look at her full-on. Moonlight shone on his face.

Judge Torpine.

"Judge," she called over her surprise. "Is everything okay?"

He didn't answer, head cocked as if he was listening to something she couldn't hear. Was he drunk? High on something?

"Judge Torpine, please stop for a minute."

He was speaking, she realized, so she rolled down the window further and strained to hear.

"Gone," he said.

"Who's gone?"

He didn't answer. It hit her in a flash. The man was

sleepwalking. Her brother, Yolo, had been a sleepwalker as a young teen. On one occasion they'd found him miles away at a dock in the dead of night, which had deeply frightened her mother. They had been advised by the doctors to speak quietly and guide Yolo back to bed when it happened rather than try to awaken him. She'd never understood why, but doctors were doctors. She jerked the car into park and got out. Noodles scrambled after her and padded right over to the judge, who seemed not to notice. After a deep nostril flare, Noodles stopped growling and sat to see what developed.

"Uh, Judge Torpine? How about I take you back home?" The cold seemed more intense in this dark pocket of woods. With bare ankles and no jacket, the judge must be chilled through.

He bent near the shrubs, prying the branches apart, peering between them. Perhaps having had enough cold night air, Noodles bonked him on the leg with no result. Trinidad was starting to shiver, goose bumps rippling over her body.

"Okay, Judge" she said, a smidge louder than she'd meant. "I'm going to take care of you." Though her words were brave, her nerves were a bunch of startled birds, flitting in every direction. First a lost dog, then a wandering judge. She left him long enough to open the rear door of the Pontiac before returning and speaking quietly as she sidled close. Laying her hand lightly on his elbow caused him to stop his foraging. "Time to go home."

She grasped and tugged with subtle pressure until he was facing the car, and then it was a matter of propelling him inside with a palm on his back. It only took a few moments, but she felt as if they'd run a marathon along the dark and twisted road. He sat silently, staring. Frank woke up long enough to sniff him. She and Noodles resumed their positions, and she turned the car into a tight U-turn.

It was like having a benign zombie in the back seat. Noodles kept sneaking looks over his shoulder, probably wondering why their passenger had nothing to say.

"We're almost home, Judge," Trinidad said. The hairs went up on her forearms when he responded with a whisper.

"She's gone."

Trinidad looked at Noodles's twitching ears to confirm that he had heard the judge speak too. "Who's gone?" Maybe a beloved cat? Dog?

He leaned so his cheek touched the window. She thought maybe she and Noodles had imagined the comment when he answered in one word. "Cherry."

Trinidad was so taken aback she instinctively braked. Cherry? He could not be mumbling about Cherry Lighter. That would be a massive coincidence, wouldn't it?

Keep him talking, she thought, once again pressing the accelerator.

"Are you talking about Cherry Lighter?" Trinidad asked. "The woman who disappeared from Sprocket thirty years ago?"

Silence.

"Judge?"

The seconds ticked by almost painfully, but the judge didn't answer. Instead, he sighed so plaintively she thought it might be a precursor to a sob.

"Gone," he repeated in a sad whisper.

If she hadn't been staring with Noodles seated beside her, she might have thought she herself was sleepwalking. The cold seemed to permeate her blood, carrying a chill to every nerve and sinew. Though she asked him several times to explain, he lapsed back into a profound silence until she pulled up at the semicircular driveway of the log cabin. "Noodles, you stay with him a minute, okay? I'm going to go see if Gretchen will answer the door."

Ruing her decision to go on her night errand in her pajamas, she jogged as fast as her slippers would allow and rang the doorbell. The pealing bells sounded out of place in the quiet of the woods. What exactly was she going to do if no one was home? But, after a few moments, feet thudded in the entry and the door was yanked open. Gretchen stood there in a flannel robe tied at the waist.

"Why in the world are you knocking on our door at this hour?"

Trinidad stifled a feeling of annoyance. *Just figured I'd throw on some pajamas and pop in for a visit.* She should probably be more embarrassed that she was wearing her ice cream sleepwear, but at least Gretchen, too, was in dishabille.

"I found your brother in the woods." She could not suppress her shivers now.

The shock made Gretchen's mouth drop open so wide, Trinidad could see a silver filling on the bottom molar.

"What? Where? Is he hurt?"

"No. He's in the back seat." Gretchen didn't wait for any more answers but jetted around Trinidad and ran to the Pontiac. She moved swiftly for a stocky sixtysomething. Her sisterly tone must have been more convincing than Trinidad's, because it took her no more than a moment to grasp his hand and pull him out. Slamming the door shut, she led him into the house and directly up the spiraling staircase to the upper floor.

"Make yourself at home in the kitchen," Gretchen called. "I'll be right down."

Since Frank seemed content to snooze atop her jacket, Trinidad left him in the car while she and Noodles headed into the cabin, through an elegantly furnished sitting room, down a wood-floored hallway. She passed a photo framed in heavy silver, the judge receiving his gavel, Gretchen smiling proudly next to him. So young, she thought, no more than thirty-five, maybe.

And when exactly had thirty-five become "young" in her mind? Probably when she turned thirty-six last year. There was something about passing that halfway point to the next decade that changed a person's perspective. "It doesn't pay to 'round up,'" as Papa would say, though he meant the remark for accounting purposes.

The kitchen ceiling soared off into exposed beams, which blended nicely with the enormous stone chimney that flanked the hood over the oven. That hood, she couldn't help but notice, was a gorgeous hammered copper. A rustic tile floor circled a large island with a granite countertop, empty save for a knife block and a pot of rosemary. Everything was neat and tidy, expensive, a 180-degree change from her current residence. Even the kitty bowls in the corner nestled in a filigreed metal frame. Noodles followed the feline scent to the gleaming bowls. Trinidad sank down at the round table set into a nook that looked out into the forest. Probably a lovely view during the daylight hours but not much to see at night.

Trinidad was still taking it all in when Gretchen returned. Darned if the woman hadn't gone and thrown on jeans and a sweater. Now Trinidad felt even more out of place in her shabby pj's. Gretchen went right for the gas stove.

"Let me make you some tea. You must be freezing."

Trinidad didn't argue as Gretchen prepared her steaming cup of jasmine tea…in an actual white teacup with a silver rim. A far cry from her trusty, "What's your pint?" mug with a chip in the handle. Gretchen prepared her own cup, removed two cookies from the cupboard, and slid them onto a plate before she joined her at the table.

"What do you think of these? A recipe I've been working on."

Trinidad selected a cookie and took a bite of brown sugary cookie treat with the tang of fruit bits. "Heavenly. Currants?"

"Yes. I'm going to make them for the Station."

"How do you manage the Station and this place? I would think running this household would be a full-time job."

Gretchen quirked an eyebrow. Her hair was pulled from her face with a clip. "I like to earn my own money. I don't exist for the sole purpose of serving my brother, and my talents would be wasted as a housekeeper."

Trinidad gulped. "I'm sorry. I didn't mean…"

She waved the comment away. "Sometimes I think young women these days are clueless. They have so much opportunity. No one looks at them oddly if they want to become doctors or lawyers. That wasn't the case in my day." She ate the other cookie. "I've had early onset rheumatoid arthritis since I was fifteen, so I know what a struggle is. I'm going to publish a cookbook with Bonnie's help. *Cooking at the Station*."

"What a great idea. I'll buy a copy."

Gretchen smiled. "Thank you so much for bringing Alexander home. He's been a sleepwalker since he was a child. It used to infuriate our father; he was a judge too. 'Embarrassing to have your son wandering around like a lunatic,' he'd say. He would try to shake Alexander awake. Once he even slapped him. My mother was horrified, so, after that, we tried hard to deal with it ourselves. I used to hang a jingle bell on the doorknob of his room so I'd hear if he woke up."

"He's fortunate to have a good big sister."

Gretchen sipped. "Behind every great man is a strong woman."

Trinidad noticed that Noodles had found a stray bit of kitty chow and was delicately crunching it, as if sampling a new cuisine. From behind a potted ficus, a white cat appeared. He moved quickly but stealthily toward the unsuspecting Noodles.

"Noo," she started. "That's not for you."

But her warning came a moment too late. Lightning fast, the cat swiped at Noodles, hissing and spitting. Noodles yelped and scrambled to Trinidad, squeezing himself on her lap, his body squashed against the underside of the kitchen table.

"Sorry," Gretchen said. "Morris is the king of the cat castle. He isn't going to share anything with a dog, especially his food."

"Of course," Trinidad said, backing her chair slightly from under the table and trying to coax the dog from her lap. Noodles was an immovable mountain, so she gave up and patted him gently while he nursed the scratch on his paw. Morris retreated behind the plant again, but Trinidad was sure he was keeping his feline eyes peeled.

She figured this was the only time she would have a chance to indulge her nosiness in the judge's house. "Does your brother sleepwalk when he's agitated?"

Gretchen pursed her lips. "Yes, but it's not common anymore." She sniffed. "Probably it's that Hardwick woman. She's been smitten with my brother since we moved here, and lately, she's flat-out pursuing him."

"When did you move here?"

"Alex was barely twenty-one when Dad died, and Mom was already gone. We inherited the summer cabin here in Upper Sprocket, and it was close to the place where he was clerking to get experience. It's beautiful, so we stayed."

"And you think Mayor Hardwick upset your brother somehow?"

Gretchen huffed out a breath. "I dunno about him, but she upsets me plenty. I should be discreet, but that has never been my strong suit. Ramona is a crook. She coerces people into promoting her ridiculous *Betty the Beaver* book in exchange for political favors. My brother shouldn't be around that."

"Does she want political favors from the judge?"

"No, she wants *other* kinds of favors." Gretchen's face darkened.

"Oh, that kind." Trinidad felt her cheeks warm.

"I've told him until I'm blue in the face that she's a crook. One whiff of that kind of thing will sink a judge's career. He's worked too hard for that."

"Does he…er, I mean, find her attractive?" Had she really asked that aloud?

"For reasons I cannot fathom, yes, but at least he's prepared to listen to the truth, if anyone could actually pin her to any wrongdoing. She's slippery and can charm men like you wouldn't believe. She came over here today to talk to him about something. That's probably what upset him. Deep down, he knows she is dishonest, but he requires proof."

Trinidad screwed up her courage. "In the woods, he appeared to be searching for someone. He mentioned the name Cherry."

Gretchen's eyebrows zinged up. "Cherry?"

"I wondered if he was talking about Cherry Lighter, the girl who disappeared."

Anger tightened her mouth. "Oh for the love of tuna. Please don't tell me that whole legend is getting stirred up again. It was a nightmare the first time." She glared at Trinidad. "Are you spreading rumors about her?"

"No, not me. I heard it from someone else." She would

not disclose it was the twins in search of a sordid story to exploit. "But you know of the woman?"

Gretchen sighed and pushed her cup away. "Cherry lived in Scotch Corners. It's a town close to here where my brother was clerking. She met Alexander because he used to buy coffee at a shop there where she worked, after we settled in Sprocket. She became infatuated with him. She would come to town at every opportunity, babysitting, doing part-time cleaning jobs, anything to see him. Honestly, it was sad. She had nothing really to offer, no life goals, but he didn't want to hurt her feelings. They went out for a while, but he broke things off. She was angry at the brush-off and left town abruptly—left the area as a matter of fact. She didn't disappear, like the gossips would love for you to believe. Alexander got a letter from her about a month after her so-called disappearance, which he showed the police."

"The police opened a case?"

She nodded. "Absolutely. It was all thoroughly investigated. Cherry's mother insisted she'd gone missing and went so far as to accuse my brother of abducting her or something. It upset him so badly, he started to drink a touch too much until I stepped in."

Trinidad stroked her lapful of Labrador, thinking, until Gretchen pointedly removed the cookie plate.

"Thank you for the cookies and tea," she said, taking her cue and sliding Noodles off her lap as she stood.

"And thank you again for helping my brother." Gretchen walked her to the door. "The whole Cherry Lighter thing was very hard on him. He's a gentle, good-hearted man who has served his community unselfishly. He certainly doesn't deserve to have the whole slanderous soap opera dredged up again."

"I understand."

Gretchen nodded and closed the door.

The next stop was Ramona's house. There was no answer to her knock, or the doorbell, and Trinidad was cold and frazzled. She left a message for Ramona on a scrap of paper shoved under one corner of her doormat. "I found Frank wandering in the woods. I'm taking him home for the night."

Trinidad thought hard as she drove the rest of the way to the little house. The judge seemed like an honest man. But might he have been different as a young twentysomething? The learning curve from twenty-one to one's fifties was enormous, deeper than the famed Hells Canyon.

If the judge truly believed Cherry had simply walked out of his life, why was his subconscious mind leading him into dark forests to search for her in the dead of night?

Chapter Nine

THE TWINS WERE SWEEPING THE floor at the Shimmy, bickering about a musician Trinidad had never heard of. Frank and Noodles curled together on the cushion until Ramona bustled in. She swept Frank up and plastered him with kisses.

"You naughty thing. What am I going to do with you?" She flashed an apologetic smile to Trinidad. "So sorry I didn't hear you at the door. I sleep like the dead. Thanks so much for your help."

"No problem," she said, "I know you'd do the same if you found Noodles wandering."

Ramona shot a dubious look at Noodles. "I would call you, for sure."

Trinidad wondered what Ramona would say if she knew about the other wanderer in the woods.

Ramona smiled. "Things are looking up. Frank's been returned, and my campaign for reelection is back on track."

"Because Forge is dead?" Not tactful, she realized as she said it.

Ramona's chagrin was fleeting. "Why not call it what it is? Yes, Forge's death made my life easier. Running uncontested is a piece of cake. His death, my gain."

"Doesn't that, you know, give you a motive?"

"Motive and murder are two different things. You'd do well to remember that." Her eyes narrowed. "Besides, Quinn had motive, too, right? What if he decided he didn't want to sell his land after all, but Forge wouldn't let him out of the deal?"

Trinidad resisted the urge to squirm, but Ramona must have felt vindicated, since she smiled and hurried out with her dog.

His death, my gain. Could anyone have a clearer motive than that? Ramona had gone so far as to shove the man in public. She realized the twins were both regarding her with that familiar gleam.

"Motive," Carlos said.

"And plenty of it to go around," Diego chimed in.

"Work," she insisted. "There's plenty of that too." She continued to mull it over as she readied herself to depart for the fields adjoining the park at Messabout Creek. This time it was Juliette who agreed to accompany her. Juliette kept up an energizing chatter all the way to the wide grassy area where the scheduled Sprocket Alpenfest festivities were set to commence. A pageant, craft booths, food tables, and plenty of yodeling sprinkled in throughout the day until the final extravaganza, which had something to do with burning a giant tissue-paper hamburger after sunset.

Juliette yawned, lifting boxes of ice cream spoons and

cups into the back of the truck. "I wouldn't think any tourists would be hitting town at ten a.m."

"The early food truck gets the worm." At the few Alpenfest planning meetings she'd attended, Chairperson Lydia Apperton had explained the necessity of capitalizing on the early-morning hours so as not to interfere with the big events in Josef, which tended toward late afternoon. Good neighbors made good business partners. It seemed the Josefinians were not hosting a burger burning. That was a Sprocket exclusive.

Juliette squinted at the printed schedule, too vain to put on her reading glasses. "I can kinda figure out what a Princess Pageant is, but what in the world is the Burning of the Burger or the lampion-making challenge? Burgers and lampions? I thought a lampion was a fish."

"That's a lamprey. A lampion is easy. Bonnie explained that to me because she's volunteering at the table. It's a lantern made from tissue paper. The burger is a mystery to me, too, because I didn't get to all the meetings, but Lydia said something about a custom to incinerate your worries."

Juliette clucked. "Should have had something like that when I was put in jail. I had plenty of worries and no burgers to burn."

Trinidad laughed. "You and me both."

The sunlight hit Juliette's hair, gilding it. "Some people in this town still see me as some sort of criminal, even though I was cleared."

Trinidad gave Juliette's shoulder a squeeze before she closed the doors. "Most will not hold that against you."

The words were kind, but suspicions stuck around longer than Trinidad cared to admit. Would suspicion forever cling to Quinn? Ramona? Zap? Herself for meddling in the investigation and finding the body in Papa's trunk?

With Noodles curled at Juliette's feet, they took off. She filled Juliette in on the sleepwalking judge, Quinn's shovel, and the strange case of Cherry Lighter as they headed to their destination. South on Main, a turn on Messabout Lane, and a jaunt on the flyaway that bridged the creek brought them into the fields dotted with people and Porta-Potties. It took the entire journey for her to relay all the facts.

"Unbelievable. So you think Cherry might really be missing? How? Maybe the judge killed her?" Juliette shook her head. Her light-blond hair had changed to a darker hue, become more serious like the woman herself.

Trinidad considered. "I don't know, but there's plenty of strange things going on in Sprocket just now."

"I can't believe that the judge offed Cherry Lighter. He doesn't seem like the violent type, and he's certainly not smooth with the ladies, although Ramona can't seem to get enough of him." Juliette swiped a tube of tinted lip gloss over her mouth. "Maybe the mayor killed Forge. She had plenty of reasons. What do we need to find out to solve this mystery and figure out how Quinn's involved, if he is?"

Trinidad yanked a look at her before she guided the truck into a spot between the Bratwurst Mobile and a beverage truck. "We aren't going to do anything. I'm a scooper, not a sleuther."

She shrugged. "Well I run a storage place, but that doesn't

mean I can't ask questions. I like Quinn, even though I advise caution in the romance department." She aimed a meaningful glance at Trinidad. "You've got skin in this game, and that means I do too."

Trinidad felt the balloon of confusion billowing up again. "Yes, I do." She cleared her throat. "He's lying about something." There. She'd said it. "I don't know if I can open myself up to being lied to again."

Juliette touched Trinidad's shoulder. "When I was dating Kevin, I knew, deep down, that he was two-timing. I didn't know it with my brain, but I ignored the signals my heart was giving me because I didn't want to believe. Or maybe I just wanted so desperately to be in a loving relationship with someone who meant what they said, unlike Gabe."

Trinidad stayed quiet for a moment, fiddling with the keys. "Bonnie said Gabe has good in him."

Juliette quirked a brow. "So did King Kong, but he still wrecked the city."

Trinidad chuckled.

"I've heard people gossiping in town about Quinn and Forge. If Quinn's lying," Juliette said finally, "you're right to be cautious. Still, though, seems out of character for him. In spite of my cynicism, I have to ask. Could he have a good reason for keeping secrets that's got nothing to do with you?"

"Maybe. But he's under Bigley's cloud of suspicion until the Forge Emberly case is solved."

Juliette held up an index finger, the nail painted a fall gold. "If Forge's murder is somehow related to the Cherry Lighter thing, we should investigate."

"I don't see how the two things could possibly be connected."

"And I didn't think my storage business and my boyfriend's murder could have been related, but there you go." A flash of pain twitched her mouth, and Trinidad impulsively reached out to take her hand.

"That's all behind you now."

But it wasn't, of course. Juliette really had loved Kevin Heartly, the self-proclaimed Popcorn King, even though he'd betrayed her. It wasn't an easy thing to command the heart to feel what the brain ordered. She suspected it was in part what motivated Juliette to get involved in Forge's murder investigation, to distract herself from long, lonely hours and too many memories. She unbuckled, and they piled out of the truck.

Juliette erected an easel and fixed a smudge on the chalkboard menu she'd painstakingly written with the day's offerings. Her penmanship trumped Trinidad's and the twins'.

"We should get a chalkboard for Bonnie, and you could write out the menus. Gretchen's handwriting is terrible, and you could save her the trouble of typing everything."

Juliette rewrote a letter with ultimate care. "It took me an hour to do this. I'd never be able to keep up at the Station."

They prepped the toppings and stacked the waffle cones, setting out the chalkboard sign with the OPENING AT 11:30 note. The work was done in time for them to climb down from the truck to view the Alpenfest Princess Pageant preparations.

No exploitative female beauty contest in Sprocket. This

one was a pairing of owners and their dogs. The "princess," the animal most perfectly attired with the Alpenfest theme, would win a prize. Noodles looked in astonishment at the canine chaos, everything from fuzzy antlers on a retriever to a pair of beagles clad in snow suits and even a dachshund with fake mittened arms holding a stein.

"Wow," Trinidad said. "Clearly I need to update your costume wardrobe, Noo."

The dog sent her an arch look, which seemed to communicate that he was not on board with such avenues of humiliation.

Dogs and owners chatted and enthused, biding time before their prance in front of the judge's dais, a raised platform decorated with autumn garlands where Ramona Hardwick and Judge Torpine sat side by side. In honor of the occasion, the judge had even driven his snappy 1968 Mustang convertible.

He looked lively enough, not suffering any ill effects from his somnambulation the previous evening. Gretchen would frown at the easy way Ramona touched his arm after every few comments.

The Shimmy truck wouldn't be attracting much of a crowd until lunchtime, so Trinidad and Juliette took a stroll to enjoy the other preparations.

Bonnie greeted them from the craft table where she was attempting to fill in the cutouts of a cardboard lantern shape with orange and yellow tissue paper. Felice was wandering close by, her collecting jar peeking out of her pocket. Instead of taking in the Alpenfest fun, she was bent over, poking at a clump of miniscule flowering weeds. After a moment, she pried a bit of rock loose and carefully stowed it in her jar.

Bonnie smiled and gathered her own long mane of hair with one hand, tying it up one of the free Alpenfest bandanas being handed out. Unlike Juliette, her face was bare of makeup. "Is that normal?" Bonnie said, glancing at her daughter. "Shouldn't she be wanting to make a lantern or watch the dogs or something instead of filling up her collection jar?"

Juliette watched for a moment. "If the kid likes jars of rocks, that's a pretty cheap hobby. Much less expensive than princess clothes or horses or whatever. I say she's an original, and what's wrong with that?"

Bonnie looked to Trinidad as if, because she was the eldest of the sister exes, she might have some maternal insight. "I only have a dog, but I'm with Juliette on this one." Felice came trotting over. She squeezed Juliette around the knees and did the same to Trinidad. The gesture started up tears in Trinidad's eyes for some maddening reason.

"Did you find something good for your collection?" Trinidad asked, as Felice scrubbed Noodles in that place under his collar that made his back leg piston back and forth.

Felice nodded.

"How are things going at the inn?" Juliette asked Bonnie.

"Right as rain, I think. The yodelers weren't put off at all by the..." she lowered her voice. "Umm...situation in the woods. Gretchen is doing a great job keeping them distracted with amazing food. The police confiscated Forge's car from our lot, but they're gone now." She shivered.

A loose dog raced past, pink earmuffs askew, an owner in hot pursuit.

"All right, Felice," Bonnie said. "We have to make a prototype lampion to show everyone how it's done. Let's do this."

They left the two in deep concentration over which colors of tissue paper to choose. As if pulled by a gravitational force, Trinidad and Juliette approached what appeared to be a ten-foot-high burger made of paper and balsa wood. Flutters of green paper lettuce and red tissue tomatoes peeked from beneath a brown dome of bun. Lydia was on a ladder with a paintbrush, filling in the lettering that spelled out "Burning of the Burger."

Zap was using a small paper cutter to carefully slice a stack of white sheets into smaller squares. A box of tiny golf pencils sat at his elbow.

"Hey," he said, grinning at them. "Morning. Long time no see. Marco said to tell you your Pinto's ready."

"Thank you. I'll get over there as soon as I can."

His smile widened at Juliette, as most men's smiles did. "You come to write down your worry?"

"No," she said. "We came to find out why we are burning a burger in effigy."

"Well…" he started, then looked up the ladder at his wife. "Babe, what's the deal with this hamburger again?"

Lydia didn't start down the ladder but launched into her explanation while still painstakingly applying paint. "Don't you guys go to the meetings? It's a new event we created. We can't do the customary Swiss burning of the snowman

Böögg because that's a tradition to welcome spring, but we put our own twist on it. Had to do something to make our town stand out, right?" She didn't wait for confirmation. "You write down your worries, shove them inside the burger, and we light it on fire tomorrow night after sunset. Bammo. Your worries are gone, and we have a really cool bonfire to welcome in the cold season." Finished with her painting, she smiled and climbed down the ladder.

"Here," she said, handing them each a square of paper and a tiny pencil. "Write down whatever you're worrying about, okay? Then all you'll have left is the good stuff."

Zap grinned at Juliette. "Speaking of the good stuff, did you hear the news? I'm the new owner of Forge Railriders." He patted his skinny chest. "Ain't that something?"

Lydia laughed, throwing her braid over her shoulder. The sun teased sparkles from her deep-set eyes. "He's been saying that nonstop since he heard."

"I guess it doesn't feel real yet."

Lydia scanned the crowd. "We got some visitors to Sprocket now but wait until we have a route up to the Wallowas. This town's going to be officially on the map, and so are we."

Trinidad felt a lurch of dismay. "Oh. So you've decided to keep the railriders going and expand the route?"

Zap shrugged.

"Our business now," Lydia said. "Not Forge's anymore. We'll keep the name, though, because it's too expensive to reprint the marketing materials. I'm going to run it and close up Off the Rack."

Trinidad noted the pronoun. Lydia was not expecting Zap to be much help.

Lydia's look was calculating. "We'll start on the second route cut-through before the weather turns, then, hopefully, finish it in time for next summer." She frowned. "Why do you look so unenthusiastic? It's going to make us a tourist hot spot, which will help the Store Some More and the Shimmy and Bonnie's inn, not to mention all the other businesses in this town. Nothing but progress."

Zap looked uncertain. "Super, right?"

"Sure. Super." Except that Quinn had been pressured somehow to sell that land. "But I thought the mayor wasn't on board with the plan."

Smugness crept into Lydia's expression. "She'll come around. You'll see." She turned to Zap. "Help me steady the ladder around the back of the burger. I need to cut the hole to put the worries in."

Zap gave them a mock salute for a goodbye and followed his wife behind the bulging sculpture.

"They fared pretty well after Forge's murder," Juliette whispered.

Trinidad nodded. "The chief has Zap on her suspect list. I wonder if Lydia's on there too."

"Lydia?" Juliette grew thoughtful. "Oh. You're thinking maybe she learned that Zap would inherit and decided to speed that along by killing Forge? But she wasn't at the yodel fest, was she?"

"No, but that doesn't mean she couldn't have arrived there and left without being noticed."

"Aww man. This is getting convoluted." She looked at their scraps of paper. "Do you want to write down your worries?"

Trinidad was already returning her paper and pencil to the table. "Suddenly, all I want to do is scoop my troubles away. Shall we go prepare for launch?"

Juliette followed her past craft booths filled with jams and jellies, autumn wreaths, candles, dried apple dolls, wooden picture frames and handmade candles. The people of Sprocket were crafty, for sure. And it would be good for business to have a second railrider route.

Juliette startled her from her thoughts. "Did you get the feeling that Zap is not the mastermind behind running the railriders biz?"

"He's probably not the mastermind of anything," Trinidad agreed. "I think he would be more at home in his tow truck with his key chain collection than he would be running Forge's business."

"It'd be better if he left the wheeling and dealing to Lydia. She seems to have the killer business vision." She rolled her eyes. "Excuse that phrase."

"Wonder what she meant about Ramona coming around," Trinidad said.

"Me too." They rolled up the metal door and tied on their aprons, along with the Alpenfest kerchiefs they'd been given upon entry.

The day warmed nicely as the September sunlight bathed the distant mountains in their jagged glory. Visitors, aside from the local Sprocketerians, slowly filled the parking area as the lunch hour approached. What started with one or two sturdy souls looking for pre-lunch ice creams turned into an avalanche. The patrons were aglow, chatting about the princess pageant and the massive burger. Trinidad could make out Zap's silhouette as he trudged up and down the ladder, stuffing the burger full of worries.

Odd, she thought, how the outwardly cheerful people standing in line for ice cream could have so many secret burdens. Her gaze went to the dais where Ramona and the judge were perusing the costumed dogs to determine a winner. Was it her imagination, or did the judge keep looking toward the Shimmy truck, as if he was distracted by something?

Finally, wrists aching and feet complaining, they rolled down the doors at two o'clock.

"Shame, really," Juliette said. "There are more ice cream–hungry peeps out there, for sure."

"But we agreed not to compete with Josef, and, anyway, my arms are killing me."

"Mine too," she confessed. "I'm going to get a sausage before they close up. Want one?"

"No, thanks. I'm having an early dinner with Papa tonight before we return here for the burger burning. But Noodles might be persuaded to accompany you for a small fee."

Juliette laughed. "All right, Noodles. But you only get one bite, and I'm slicing it off for you. No offense, but I don't know where your lips have been."

The dog trotted happily after Juliette. Trinidad stripped off her apron and got out of the truck to await the completion of the sausage errand. She noticed Ramona chatting with several tourists, waving as they headed to their cars. Trinidad scurried over.

"Hi, Ramona."

The smile she cultivated for visitors dimmed a notch when she realized who had approached her. "Hello, Trinidad."

"Looks like today was a big success."

"Yes."

She gulped. "May I ask you a question?"

"This better not be about Forge." Wariness crept into the mayor's tone.

"Ummm, I heard from somewhere, I can't quite recall where, that you used to employ a woman named…"

"Cherry Lighter," Ramona snapped. "Why is that name suddenly popping up? I had some reporter grill me about it, and he was ostensibly writing an article about Alpenfest. Now you. What gives?"

"I…uh…"

"Never mind. I'll cut this short by telling you what I told him. Yes, I knew her. She did filing work for me when I first started my real estate office. No, I don't know where she took off to after I fired her, and I don't really care."

"You fired her? Why?"

"Because she was a terrible employee. Careless, more concerned with her manicure and lipstick than her work. Always skipping out of the office whenever she saw him drive by."

"Him?"

Ramona clicked her tongue, as if disciplining it for

talking out of turn. "Alexander. He didn't have much interest in Cherry, of course, except the usual interest a man gives a pretty girl. Anyway, he tried to brush her off after a while, but she wouldn't accept it." Ramona held up a hand. "And, to answer the other question you're undoubtedly going to ask, I don't believe there was any foul play involved in her leaving town. She left because she had no steady job and the man she wanted didn't want her. That's all. If there had been some indication of a crime, the police would surely have chased that down, right? That is what they get paid for."

Ramona's view matched Gretchen's. "I understood her mother didn't believe that she left of her own accord."

"Her mother was, and probably still is, a drunk. Cherry wasn't even living with her most of the time. She couch-surfed from one place to the next. Quinn's mom let her stay there for a weekend a time or two, I think. Once I even found Cherry sleeping on the couch in the break room at my realty office. Can you believe that? Like it was a hostel or something. I was glad when she left. That was thirty years ago. Shouldn't we let it go?"

Should they? "Could be you're right. I mean, I heard she'd sent a letter."

Ramona buttoned her sweater. "I heard that, too, but I never saw it. If Alexander is convinced she left town, then that's good enough for me."

But Alexander was out sleepwalking in the bushes in the wee hours, searching for Cherry by moonlight. What would Ramona think of that?

"Anyway, I've got to go type up some emails. There's a

recycling initiative being proposed I want to read over." She offered a serene smile. "Got to keep Sprocket green, don't we?"

"That's why you didn't want Forge to cut the access through Quinn's property? To keep Sprocket green?"

Ramona's eyes narrowed for a moment. "Of course." Her smile was grim. "But I didn't have him killed, if that's the next juicy story ready to be spun in Sprocket." Suddenly she let out a breath that took some of the starch out of her posture. "Believe it or not, I love this town, and I want to do the best I can for the people in it. I'm just a Realtor who writes kids' books who ran for mayor because hardly anyone else wanted to. Being the mayor isn't a moneymaker for me, you know. I earn a couple hundred bucks a month for endless hours of work. It's public service, a way to help people." Her old aplomb back in place, she fired off a parting shot. "By the way, has anyone ever told you you're way too nosy? Stick to your business, is my motto. That's what brings success, and you're going to need all the friends you can get to peddle ice cream over a very long winter." She marched away toward the parking area.

Trinidad watched her go. She'd earned the "nosy" remark, but it had stung to be reminded of her perilous business status. *All the friends you can get.* Was there an implied threat in there? Continue asking questions about Forge and Cherry and earn the animosity of the mayor?

Being the mayor wasn't a moneymaker, but was it true that Ramona's political connections helped her market her children's book...and kept people in check who disagreed with her?

Was the mayorship a public service…a way to help others? Or herself?

When the food truck hours were up, Juliette helped clean up and pack away the supplies.

"The sausage was excellent," Juliette pronounced upon her return. "I'm going to hitch a ride back to town with Bonnie, okay? I'm told I'm to learn how to be a waitress to help with the breakfast service at the inn when needed."

"You're going to be sorry business is slow at the Store Some More. Too much free time to help your sister exes. Or is it almost-in-laws? I get confused."

"I hired a manager, so I have plenty of time. And how about we drop the 'ex' thing? You're my sisters, especially after what's happened to my life in the past year."

Trinidad's heart swelled. Sisters.

Juliette shrugged a careless shoulder. "I'm bored at the storage place, and it holds only bad memories. Besides, I love being around Bonnie and Felice. It's like the family I never had."

Trinidad was stabbed by a sudden wave of wistfulness. Felice represented the child she'd always wanted with Gabe. Now as a thirty-six-year-old divorcée, she was wondering if her chances had dried up in that department.

She realized Juliette was watching her. "Why don't you come too? It will be fun to hang out at the inn."

"Oh, I've got to get to the shop for a little bit. I'll meet you back here tonight for the Burning of the Burger, okay?"

Juliette departed with a wave.

Trinidad let Noodles into his assigned spot and was

about to climb up into the driver's seat when she heard a throat being cleared. Whirling around, she found Judge Torpine, hands stuffed into the pockets of his trousers.

"Hello, Trinidad," he said, a dusky flush creeping up his neck. "I…uh…" He cleared his throat again. She had never known the self-assured judge to be at a loss for words. "My sister told me you brought me home last night. I wanted to thank you for doing that. I was very fortunate that you happened along just then before I took a fall or the like."

"No problem. I was happy to help. Gretchen said you sleepwalk sometimes when something is on your mind." Had Gretchen told him what he'd said about Cherry? She decided to indulge the nosiness of which she'd recently been accused. The twins would no doubt call it "investigating." "When I found you in the woods, you said you were looking for Cherry."

His gaze dropped to his loafers. "Gretchen mentioned that too. I suppose you're curious."

She waited. Silence was the ultimate encouragement to talk, she'd learned.

"It's simple really," he said, eyes still roving the ground. "Clichéd, I suppose. The short story is that I loved a girl and she dumped me."

"Cherry Lighter?"

He nodded. "I was young and inexperienced. She was my first crush. I built plans in my mind, elaborate plans, of our future together, and, when it all dried up and blew away, I couldn't accept that she took off. Leaving town without a word is a bad way to break up with a guy, isn't it?" There was a note of pleading in his voice.

Seemed like Gretchen and Ramona had both under-played the depth of the judge's affection for Cherry.

He sighed. "I really couldn't accept that. I guess that's why I still feel it's an unresolved issue."

"Not because something bad happened to her?"

He started. "No, no of course not. Believe me, no one worked harder to find her than I did. Imagining the tearful, romantic reunion, I suppose. When the police came around insinuating something might have happened to her, I became frantic. It was clear they thought I might have had a hand in whatever they believed happened, which hurt even more. I loved her intensely." His tone sounded as if he were dreaming. "Cherry was the most beautiful woman I'd ever seen, long black hair, eyes green like spring grass. She fascinated me, her laugh, the way she was so full of life, and completely reckless, and eager for adventure, legal or not, everything I wasn't. I know it sounds silly, but she truly broke my heart. And I don't think it ever healed correctly."

"I can understand that," Trinidad said softly. "Believe me."

He jingled the coins in his pocket. "Anyway, I wanted to explain, since you were so kind as to help me last night. I'll let you get to your packing up." He turned to go.

"Judge…"

She could not tell if he looked at her with reluctance, sorrow, worry, or a mixture thereof. Judges must spend hours cultivating their poker faces, she thought. "I heard from your sister that Cherry sent you a letter after she left town."

"Yes. The police examined it. They took it as proof, at

last, that I hadn't done anything to her, along with the fact that there was no physical evidence of foul play. Eventually they closed the case. I was glad when I got that letter back in my possession."

"So you're convinced she's fine...in spite of her mother's accusations."

His brows crimped slightly. "Yes. It took me years to accept, but she rejected me and left town. I don't know why she didn't return to her mother, but there was dysfunction there. Cherry often lamented that her mom loved the bottle more than her child. Addiction leaves lifelong scars, sometimes."

So does rejection, she thought.

"Would you...like to see it?"

Now it was her turn to be surprised. "See what?"

"The letter she wrote me."

"Why would you want me to see it, Judge?"

He looked embarrassed again. "It was examined thoroughly by police, and I've read it a thousand times, but I still don't understand. I thought maybe a woman's perspective might help me."

Help him understand why Cherry fell out of love with him.

He smiled. "And it might convince you that I'm not a murderer and I've got her body stashed under my cabin."

"I didn't think..."

He waved his hand elegantly. "No need. Rumors carry so much more weight than the truth, sometimes. Are you coming to the bonfire tonight? I'll bring it then."

"All right," she found herself saying. "See you tonight."

She climbed aboard the truck and cranked up the engine. The judge stood watching as she maneuvered clumsily out of the lot.

He'd actually offered to let her see Cherry's letter.

Was it simply to deflect the rumors his sister might have warned him about? A way to put to rest the gossip that might endanger his appellate court appointment? Or was he honestly still seeking to understand why his first love had fled?

As far as she knew, the judge had never married, and Juliette said he wasn't known to be involved with local women. Could Cherry have meant so much to him that he'd seek Trinidad's help in reading between the lines?

Love made people do uncharacteristic things.

Then again, maybe she was being manipulated by a smooth-talking, charming man.

Like Gabe had done so efficiently. And Quinn too?

As the truck bounced over the grassy field, her thoughts jounced along with it. She was no sleuth. So why did she feel like she was knee deep in a mystery again?

Chapter Ten

TRINIDAD HAD ENOUGH TIME AFTER she closed the Shimmy to pick up her Pinto and shoot by Off the Rack. The temperature was expected to drop into the thirties, and she didn't want Noodles to suffer at the burger burning.

Lydia looked up, a roll of packing tape in her hand. The dainty shop was a labyrinth with racks of clothing in the middle and floor-to-ceiling shelves filled with clear boxes of small items, intermingled with books, lamps, kids' toys, and kitchen utensils.

"Hi, Trinidad," Lydia called out. "Gotta squeeze in some work between all the Alpenfest events, right? Me too. Looking for something in particular?"

Right to business, this gal, the polar opposite of her chatty hubby. Trinidad told her the objective and without so much as an eyebrow quirk over the odd request, Lydia pointed her to a rack by the shelves. She cast a look at Noodles, who'd trotted right along into the shop as if he was welcomed everywhere. "Find a teen-sized snow jacket and cut the sleeves. That should fit him. Or maybe an adult size, since he's beefy around the belly."

Beefy? Trinidad showed her disdain for this remark, but Lydia didn't notice, nor did she much care about a dog inside her shop as long as she got a sale. Ignoring the "beefy" comment, Trinidad began to paw through the racks while Noodles sauntered to the shoe area to sniff the wares. The only coat she could find for herself was neon yellow, which would make her stand out like a traffic sign, but it was lined with some sort of stuffing that looked warm enough. She found one for Papa Luis too. The only choice for Noodles turned out to be a puffy red coat with stars printed on it. Noodles, bless his heart, merely wagged in excitement when she held it up to him.

"You're going to be the talk of the town," she said, hoping he would not think she was cramming him in a costume like the demoralized princess pageant participants. On the way to the counter to pay, she stopped to scan the open boxes on the floor. Lydia didn't miss her interest.

"That junk is all going to donation, so if you want anything, help yourself. I'm happy to lighten the boxes for Zap."

Trinidad could not resist the siren song of a freebie. She selected a spatula for Papa and a small dented colander perfect for rinsing delicate berries for the summer Freakshakes. Her eye caught a barrette, adorned with fake red jewels connected by twining green leaves. One jewel had fallen off, but Trinidad thought it would be the very thing for Felice. She would likely strip off all the sparkly bits for her collection, anyway, rather than wear it in her hair. Trinidad carried her prizes to the counter where Lydia rang her up and shoved her purchases into a used paper bag.

"How's the packing coming?" Trinidad asked.

Lydia grinned. "Great. I'm very motivated. I've got a rail-riders business to run, now, remember? I might even have someone lined up to take it over the shop, if I clean it up enough to be attractive."

"Zap was so shocked that Forge deeded him the business. Were you just as surprised?"

Lydia shrugged. "I guess so. They weren't close. Really, I thought Forge was a stingy old man not to offer Zap a job when we moved to town. Zap's really mechanical, and he could have helped out someway with the rails and such. But windfalls come to hard workers, and Zap and I have clawed and scraped to keep ourselves afloat. We deserve this."

Trinidad didn't object, but she'd known plenty of hard-working people who were still waiting for their windfalls. Had Lydia "deserved" the business more than Forge and decided not to wait for her husband's future inheritance?

"Enjoy your clothes," Lydia said. "See you at the burger burning?"

Trinidad nodded. "Wouldn't miss it."

Back at the tiny house, she passed the time until dark, snipping off the cuffs of the jacket until each sleeve ended just before Noodles's front paws, quickly hemming the ends. She also removed the hood because Noodles was already slightly hard of hearing.

"Sit, Noo." The dog complied, and she pulled it around his back and zipped up along the tummy, careful not to catch any fur. Noodles gave a shake, but otherwise did not appear to mind his new getup.

Papa watched with amusement. "With your yellow coat and his red one, you look like two beautiful peppers."

She kissed him. "Thank you for not saying we look like a McDonald's sign."

"Never," he said with a shudder. As far as she knew, Papa hadn't set foot inside a McDonalds.

He pulled on the winter coat she'd bought him, a plaid affair with a fuzzy lining and enormous pockets. He posed awkwardly. "How do I look? Lumberjack comes to mind."

"Like the perfect escort for two peppers. Are you ready?"

"My car is in pristine condition and at your service."

And it was. Papa had labored on it when he was not supervising the construction of the greenhouse. The car had been waxed and polished, the carpets vacuumed, and the seats buffed. She didn't want to think about him cleaning out the trunk.

"Too bad it's dark and people can't appreciate the triumphant return of the car," Trinidad said.

Papa beamed. "They will enjoy it tomorrow when I am driving around town with customers. I have some rides arranged for Bonnie's visitors." Papa, Sprocket's newly minted Uber driver.

She suppressed a shiver. "Whatever you do, don't leave your trunk open."

His smile vanished. "You can be sure I won't. Fort Knox will have nothing on my vehicle. There has been no further word from the police?"

"No, but I'm finding out Forge wasn't beloved in Sprocket." The list of people who disliked the man was growing: Ramona, Lydia to some degree, and then there was Quinn. "Why do you think Quinn sold the land to Forge? He said it was money, but I'm certain it's something deeper."

"The only thing that stokes passion as much as money is love."

Love…of whom? His brother? An insidious thought struck her like a gong. What if there was someone else Quinn loved enough to lie for? That made her sit up. And what did any of it have to do with Cherry Lighter? Or maybe it didn't.

This is why you own an ice cream shop, not a detective agency.

Rolling up once again to the open field area, they scanned the parking places marked off with luminous spray paint and deposited their two dollars in a cardboard "Parking Fee" box set on a stool festooned with a string of white lights. The judge's Mustang was there, earning a sniff from Papa.

"A nice car I suppose," he said, giving it a thorough once-over.

She estimated close to seventy vehicles parked on the field. Not bad given that Sprocket was a new entry into the Alpenfest event hosting. They parked in the second row, third slot, in an area Papa deemed to be the cleaner region of the field. Noodles hopped out in his DIY coat and took the end of his own leash between his teeth.

"Hang on to your leash, and be careful you don't lose yourself," she cautioned the dog.

He wagged his tail.

She grabbed the thermos and followed Papa, who toted two lawn chairs. They found Bonnie already sitting on a blanket with Felice, who wore a pom-pom hat. The blanket seating was a good idea, since Bonnie was so tall that, if she sat in a chair, no one would be able to see around her. Juliette opted for an old camp seat, and Stan and his sister Meg sat in fancier chairs with attached footrests and arms with cupholders.

If this hamburger burning thing caught on, she'd have to upgrade to comfier seats for next year. Maybe Lydia would be offloading some as the store changed hands. Papa eased into the simple chair without complaint. Would he be here for the next Fourth of July? She hoped the greenhouse plans would give him a reason to stay. She'd take her mother's wrath in exchange for Papa's permanent presence.

Juliette smiled. "That is some coat, Trin. It glows in the dark."

"The better to find her with, my dear," quipped Stan.

"And Noodles is in red?" Bonnie's smile was brilliant in the moonlight. "So you're ketchup and mustard."

"Papa said red and yellow peppers."

Papa pulled a dog biscuit from his pocket and handed it into Felice's tiny palm. "You can give it to Noodles. It's homemade with all the finest ingredients."

Made from Trinidad's recipe with promises from Papa that he would not add embellishments. He could not be convinced that garlic was bad for any living creature, but she'd persisted. Bad enough the dog was beefy; she wasn't about to let him get sick on garlic.

From there Papa moved to asking Felice, "Do you know the color of Napoleon's white horse?" That made Trinidad chuckle. It was his favorite joke, along with one about Grant's tomb.

Felice grinned, revealing a missing front tooth. "White?"

Papa roared with laughter. "She is a smart cookie, this one."

Trinidad greeted everyone as she squirmed on the uncomfortable seat. There was no order to the seating, merely random bunches of grouped chairs, and some families gathered on blankets. It felt as though everyone in Sprocket had turned out, but someone was missing—or two people, rather.

"Where are Doug and Quinn?"

Stan sipped from a metal camping cup, the smell of jasmine tea wafting through the air. "He's getting things in order on the farm." Stan sighed. "The contract was indeed fully executed at the time of Forge's death, so the rail route will go through Quinn's property, I'm afraid. I broke it to him this morning. He said he and Doug will come by later if they can."

No Quinn or Doug. Again. The knowledge depressed her, as did the thought of those glorious trees being chopped down.

The crowd chatter ebbed and flowed around her. She spotted the twins with their mother and a man with a ponytail sticking out from under his baseball cap. It took her a few moments to realize it was T. J. Orwell. He wasn't talking to anyone, leaning with his back against a tree, somewhat removed from the group.

Two empty chairs near the giant hamburger sported taped notes that read "Reserved for Judge Torpine and Mayor Hardwick." Presumably they would be the official witnesses as the ceremonial burger rid the town of worries. She tried to spot the judge, wondering if he would actually follow through and bring her the letter.

Papa shoved his glasses up his nose and laced his thick fingers across his plaid-covered belly. "At the library, I read about the snowman Böögg in Switzerland, but I still do not quite understand why we are burning a hamburger."

Juliette launched into another explanation of the symbolic incineration of summer to welcome fall and the reason people were milling about stuffing slips of paper into a hole immediately to the right of the tissue paper pickle.

Papa chuckled. "Silly, of course. If bad things could be burned away so easily, Hell would be a tropical vacation."

Juliette laughed heartily and reached up to pat Papa on the knee. "Papa, you are a one in a million. Honestly."

Again the slight pang of what had to be jealousy pricked Trinidad's gut. Uncharitable, she scolded herself. Juliette and Bonnie and Felice would grow to love Papa Luis, and that was right and proper. Everyone did, and he deserved it. Love was a thing that expanded the heart, not crowded it.

Trinidad noticed Lydia cutting more paper and rounding up the wandering pencils at the "deposit your worries here" table. The woman was a dynamo. There was no sign of Zap, but she didn't doubt he wasn't far from Lydia. Or maybe he'd been ordered to work on tidying the Off the Rack. Trinidad remembered her Off the Rack purchase and fished it from her pocket.

Bonnie held her phone light so Felice could see. The fake jewels glittered, reflected in Felice's wide eyes.

"Oohhhhhh," she breathed, delighted.

"Tell Auntie Trinidad thank you," Bonnie urged.

Felice climbed into Trinidad's lap and pressed a kiss to Trinidad's cheek. Her lips were featherlight and warm in spite of the dropping temperature.

"Thank you for the treasure," she said. "It's pretty."

"Just like you," Trinidad said. "I thought you could take the jewels off for your jar, if you didn't want to wear it."

Felice nodded soberly and resumed her spot next to Noodles, who was still licking every inch of his dog biscuit. Trinidad's gaze wandered again over the milling crowd.

Gretchen stood with a to-go cup, chatting with Mr. Mavis and his wife. This time her hair was neatly pinned back.

"You are going to have to try Gretchen's apple spice scones," Bonnie said, casting a look her way but speaking to Trinidad. Her smile was dreamy.

Juliette nodded. "Oh yes. Bonnie brought me one to taste just now. They are so moist they don't even need a glaze."

"Gretchen's unveiling them tomorrow morning," Bonnie said.

Juliette arched a mischievous brow. "The judge will be there," she said, "so that probably means Ramona too. Better set an extra table."

Bonnie nodded. "Seven a.m. breakfast service. I'll be suited up and ready."

Trinidad's fickle stomach grumbled at the mention of scones. Never mind that she'd eaten a small dinner of a tuna sandwich and sliced tomatoes with Papa to make time to alter Noodles's coat. Her body was clamoring for sweets. Marshmallows and hot cocoa would have to do. Groaning, she remembered she had left the cups in Papa's car.

"I'll be right back," she said. Noodles half-rose, tongue still extended in comical fashion toward his biscuit. "No, you stay with Felice, Noo. This will only take a minute."

The others were deep in various conversations as she slipped away. She stepped carefully past the chairs until she could accelerate the pace. The evening air was crisp, scented with the fall leaves that rustled and crackled in the trees bordering the empty field. Moonlight made the branches look like fingers reaching for something they could not quite attain.

Maybe it was Felice that made her wax poetic or the sadness she felt that Quinn and Doug were not present. She tipped her face to the moon, which gilded the peaks of the faraway Wallowas. What a place, she thought suddenly. What a home. The only thing missing was Quinn.

"Trinidad," said a voice from the darkness. Judge Torpine hurried up. "I saw you heading this way." He held up a manilla envelope with her name on it tucked inside a plastic bag. "Cherry's letter."

He was actually making good on his promise to share it with her. Startling.

"Thank you," she said, taking it from him. "I'll be certain to return it to you, safe and sound."

"I'd appreciate that, though I've read it so many times I'm sure I could recite it from memory. I figured, with the way you acted as amateur sleuth in that other nasty business, you might have some insight."

"I think the key word there is amateur, but I will give it a look."

"I, um, well I'd be grateful it if you didn't mention this to anyone. I didn't even tell my sister. She believes in letting sleeping dogs lie."

She could not read his expression in the dim light, but she saw the slump of his shoulders.

He'd loved Cherry Lighter. Whatever had happened to the woman, that much was true. But people hurt those they loved all the time, sometimes fatally. Was his decision to share with her some kind of ruse to cover up the truth? But the police hadn't found any sign of foul play, so what was she worried about? "Thank you, Judge. I will be discreet."

A horn blared through the darkness.

"Ah. That's my cue," he said, resuming his erect posture. "Shall we walk back together for the ceremonial torching?"

"I've got to grab something from the car, but thanks. I'll meet you there."

He said goodbye and strolled toward the crowd.

The letter in her hand called her name. Curiosity burned inside her like a marshmallow toasting from the inside out. A quick peek, she promised herself. And then she'd read it over carefully at home. She pulled the envelope from the bag and opened the clasp. The paper was petal-soft and worn at the edges from repeated folding and refolding. She was surprised to see the message was typed, the letters dark.

dear alex…

She squinted closer, picking out words and phrases.

 …too different
     …wont work between us.
     …dont want the same thing.

The page was missing capitals and periods. Either Cherry wasn't the greatest typist or, perhaps, she'd been in a great hurry. Was there a message behind the words? A deeper meaning caged by the sentences that would set the judge free if she could only unlock it? She leaned closer to squint. A cheer went up from the crowd, and a flame flickered to life. She watched for a moment as the fire reared golden against the sky.

The rest would have to wait until later. She hurried to Papa's Chevy. Squeals of delight echoed all around her as she edged her way between the cars.

Then a whooshing sound mingled with the cheering, someone moving close, fast.

She looked around to spot the arrival, but, instead, a hard smack sent her falling forward, the ground rushing up to meet her.

Chapter Eleven

THERE HAD BEEN NO TIME to react. Trinidad's shoulders were shoved hard from behind by two outstretched hands. Down she went, face-first in the grassy parking area, the breath driven out of her in a whoosh. For several seconds, her brain struggled with the act of breathing, but she finally rolled over and jumped to her feet, fists raised like some sort of mustard-clad warrior. Her senses swam. Blinking, she scanned wildly, but all around her was nothing but unoccupied cars.

Call the police.

She realized with a wave of sickness, that she'd left her phone back at the chair. Screaming might help, but she was not convinced she could force out a squeak, much less a holler.

Another sickening thought assailed her. Her attacker might still be there, hiding behind Papa's car where the moonlight didn't penetrate. She crept around the back bumper one terrified step at a time but saw nothing at all until someone rushed toward her.

"Stop or I'll punch," she shouted.

"Trinidad." Quinn skidded to a halt, eyes opened so wide the white shone all around the irises. "What happened? Are you all right?"

"Quinn," she breathed, shoving the mass of hair that covered her left eye with one fist. Doug stood slightly behind, an echo of his brother's startled expression on his own. "Sorry. I wasn't going to punch you, probably."

He moved closer. "Don't worry about that. What happened?"

She held a finger to her lips. "Someone knocked me over. They might still be hiding."

"Okay," he whispered back. "Stay here. I'll sneak around and look. Text me if anyone approaches." Doug and Quinn padded away into the maze of cars before she had a chance to tell him she didn't have her phone.

Her heart rate was slowing slightly, but her brain still buzzed with uncertainty. One look around confirmed what she'd already known. Cherry Lighter's letter was gone. Only the plastic bag remained on the grass under Papa's car. It made no sense at all. Who could have known she had possession of it? And why did they want it in the first place?

Quinn and Doug returned, and Quinn's chagrin was clear. "Uh, I only found one sneaky person."

Chief Bigley stepped into view. "Police chiefs are authorized to be sneaky. It's in our job description. I was merely walking from my car, though."

"Sorry," Quinn said.

"What's the problem?" Bigley swiveled to observe

Trinidad more closely. "You look like you're ready to punch someone."

Trinidad hadn't realized she was still holding up her fists. Embarrassed, she lowered them. "Um, no. Someone knocked me down and took a letter from me."

"Did you see who?"

"No. They got me from behind." She knew what question was coming next.

"What letter?"

"I promised I'd be discreet."

Bigley cocked her head. "Police chiefs are nothing if not discreet." She glanced at Quinn and Doug.

"You two up for some discretion, or should I ask you to leave?"

Quinn smiled. "Nut farmers are nothing if not discreet," he echoed. "Besides, I'm staying with Trinidad until I'm sure she's okay."

The last remark took some of Trinidad's chill away. Now was not the time for suspicion. She needed comfort. She blew out a long breath. "Well, Chief, you're probably not going to believe this."

Bigley might have rolled her eyes but it was hard to know for sure in the dark. Trinidad forged ahead, explaining.

"The letter from Cherry Lighter," the chief finally said after a long moment of ominous silence. "Well that's interesting. Did you read it before you lost possession of it?"

She wanted to object that she hadn't lost it, it had been snatched, but she figured it wasn't worth it. "Bits and pieces. I wish I could have read more."

"Snatching it didn't accomplish much. I have no doubt there's a copy of the letter in the police file. All the material is three decades old and in a secure file room, which looks like the wreck of the *Hesperus*, but I put Officer Chang on the task after you mentioned the Cherry Lighter angle to me. He's been plowing through piles for days, but I think he kind of enjoys the quiet. And I've heard crunching, so I'm pretty sure he's got corn chips in there. He's built himself a bunker."

Trinidad was pleased to know the chief really had taken the Cherry Lighter case seriously enough to look into it. How could someone so conscientious and stalwart be the sister of criminally inclined Gabe? "Can I read it when you do?"

"Cheeky of you to ask, Jones."

Trinidad offered a wobbly smile.

"I'll let you know," the chief finished. Her gaze returned to Quinn. "Your timing is good. You happened to be right here when Trinidad was being jumped."

Trinidad heard Quinn's teeth grind together. "Doug and I were working at the orchard. We arrived late." And then, before she said another word, he was yanking his coat zipper down, pulling it off, and upending all the pockets, finally tossing his jacket on the ground. "See? No letter," he snapped. "Doug, unzip your coat and turn out your pockets."

Doug did as he was told. Quinn's eyes flashed in the gloom. "I didn't take the letter. Even if it was the answer to all my problems, I wouldn't do anything that would hurt Trinidad."

Bigley's tone was calm as untroubled waters. "All right." She turned to Trinidad. "Are you okay to rejoin the festivities while I look around? We're probably not going to get footprints, but you never know."

"We'll walk her back," Quinn said. He still sounded mad, but, when he stooped to get his jacket, the action was more resigned than angry.

Without another word the chief disappeared into the maze of cars.

Quinn walked elbow to elbow with Trinidad, Doug following a few feet away.

"I'm sorry about…" She stopped. "I know you would never…"

"It's okay." He looped his arm through hers and squeezed her close. "I've been acting squirrelly, and the chief is only doing her job."

Squirrelly for sure. Trinidad tried not to read too much into the feel of his strong arm intertwined with hers. *Don't let yourself love a liar…not again.*

"I've been thinking about Cherry since you asked me about her. Figured it might help in some way if I could remember something about her. Now that someone swiped the letter, could be there's definitely something going on. Something connecting her with what happened to Forge? Who knew you had it?"

"That's the weird thing. The judge said he didn't tell anyone, even his sister. Someone could have seen me walking with it, but how would they have known what it was?"

"So back to Cherry," Quinn said. "She slept at our house

a few times, I remember, because I'd have to bunk with
Doug. She was kind of a slob. Left her scarf and bracelets
and stuff. She was the kind who wore rings on every finger.
Mom would put it all in a bag and give it to her when she
next came around."

"Was that often?"

He squinted. "I wish I could remember. Doug? How
often was Cherry at our house?"

Doug merely lifted a shoulder.

"Can't help you there. I also remembered one time she
came over to watch Doug and Mom sent her away. I didn't
understand why, at the time, because I was mad that Mom
couldn't give me a ride to practice. I remember thinking
Cherry looked funny, glassy-eyed, stumbling on the door
mat. I think she'd been drinking and Mom didn't want her
in the house. I remember Mom said, 'You're going to ruin
both of you.' I don't know why I remember that, except that
Mom was so intense, which wasn't like her."

"Who was your mother talking about?"

"I don't know."

Trinidad sighed. "I wish you could ask her."

Quinn went silent. They continued on without talking
until he approached the edge of the seating area.

"Back safe and sound," he said, giving her fingers a
squeeze before he let them go. In spite of her doubts, she
wished he'd pressed a kiss to her knuckle like he'd done in
the past.

"Aren't you and Doug going to come and sit with us?
We'll make space."

"No thanks." He looked suddenly downcast. "Looks like we missed most of the good stuff, and I didn't bother putting my worries into the burger. It's not big enough to hold them. Tell everyone hi for me."

"Okay. I'll see you soon. You know, when you come over to work on the greenhouse." Did she sound too eager? Desperate?

He nodded. "By the way, I like your coat. Makes you look like…"

She braced for a bottle of mustard, or a juicy pepper comparison.

"A daffodil," he said shyly, "one of the best things about spring." Then he hurriedly kissed her cheek and watched her wend her way back to her chair. When she arrived at her destination, he lifted his hand, and she did the same.

A daffodil, she thought, unable to prevent a smile creeping across her face. She was brought back to earth with a thud by Juliette.

"Where have you been?" Juliette demanded. "And is that a grass stain on your neon coat?"

"I…" she started, but there was a sudden whoosh of the bonfire as the top bun caught fire. The flames roared into the night. The judge and the mayor craned their necks upward, Ramona's arm resting on the judge's bicep. They were caught in an eerie glow, competing light and darkness.

In front of her were happy spectators, laughing and reveling in the moment.

But, behind her, someone had stolen the judge's precious letter and shoved her to the ground to accomplish it.

There was no tissue paper burger big enough to hold all of the worry that provoked for her either. And, to top that off, she hadn't even remembered the cups for the cocoa.

With a sigh, she sank down into her chair.

———

The alarm was shrill on Sunday morning as she dragged herself awake. She'd managed to complete her duties for the first weekend of Alpenfest. Now she'd get a breather until the next weekend's concluding events rolled around. *Let the birthday shenanigans commence.*

She didn't feel as refreshed as she should have. She knew that the chief would have already broken the news to the judge about the stolen letter, but she felt a strong urge to deliver an apology herself. His letter, his only connection to the woman he'd adored, had been lost on her watch. Whether or not it was her fault, an apology was in order, so she and Noodles hit the road to Bonnie's property at six thirty, figuring she would catch him there.

Noodles had blinked sleepily at her when she'd awakened him, but she'd packed a bowl of kibble and a boiled egg so he could breakfast at a more humane hour.

"Go back to sleep, sweetie," she said when they were in the car, and he did. She let out a breath and realized that she'd been nervous walking to the vehicle in the predawn gloom. It was as if she could feel the hands that shoved her to the ground all over again. The same hands that had struck down Forge and stuffed him into Papa's trunk?

Turning on Linger Longer Road reminded her of the bizarre meeting with the judge in the dead of night, a restless soul in search of answers. Restless or guilty?

She mulled over what Quinn had revealed of his memories. Cherry had been known to indulge in alcohol as a young woman. Gretchen admitted that her brother had, too, as a youth. But what did it all mean?

Quinn's mother's comment stuck in her mind. *You're going to ruin both of you.* She probably meant Cherry would ruin Alexander Torpine, unless Cherry had been dating multiple people. And, again, she could not imagine what Cherry's situation might have to do with Forge Emberly's death.

Tackling the precarious slope, they chugged their way to the inn. Trinidad found the parking lot full and the heavenly smell of coffee wafting from the dining car. She was glad the judge's car was parked there. No sign of the mayor's.

Gretchen and Bonnie emerged from the kitchen building striding rapidly across the distance to the dining car, each carrying trays laden with covered dishes. Noodles was still snoring softly, so she rolled the window down a few inches and left him napping under a blanket. Wrapped in her daffodil-yellow coat to fend off the morning cool, she hurried after Gretchen and Bonnie. The dining car was once again packed with yodelers and their friends and significant others. The diners were sipping coffee, and they all looked eagerly at Bonnie and Gretchen as they scooted in with the trays. For Bonnie, who had held on to her athletic physique, the job was easy. Gretchen struggled with her heavy platter.

When a side of it wobbled, Trinidad leapt in to steady it and set it on the antique sideboard that held the buffet.

"Thanks," Gretchen said. She flexed the fingers of one hand with the other but politely elbowed Trinidad out of the way to unveil the food herself. Trinidad understood the pride of the creator for the creation. She always wanted to be the one to personally deliver her Freakshakes to her expectant customers.

The smell of the apple spice scones danced over Trinidad's senses. And was that fresh nutmeg? A delicate veil of white glaze added the perfect amount of sheen. "Oh, my word. Those look incredible," she said, inhaling deeply.

"They are." Gretchen's grin was impish. Trinidad forgave the prideful remark when Gretchen slid a scone onto a napkin with a pair of tongs and handed it to her. "Here. I made plenty. Took me three batches to get the recipe right."

Trinidad scuttled with her prize to a corner as the onslaught of yodelers swarmed the buffet. Bonnie and Gretchen delivered piles of scones, bacon, scrambled eggs and fried apples onto their plates. The cloth-covered tables held rounds of butter, salt and pepper, pots of homemade jam, and tiny train vases that each contained a yellow carnation in the smokestack hole. Where had Bonnie found such adorable things? She should purchase some ice cream–themed vases for the Shimmy when the budget allowed.

Bonnie rushed around with extra napkins and a wide smile, doling out plenty of charm and warmth. She saw Trinidad standing with her scone and enveloped her in a massive hug. These types of embraces were slowly becoming less awkward and more comfortable for Trinidad.

"Good morning," Bonnie trilled. "I love the breakfast hour. Everyone is fueling up, stoked for the day." Someone waved at her for another napkin. She steered Trinidad toward the only table that had a single occupant, the judge. "Why don't you two sit together?" she said. "I'll fix you a plate, Judge."

"I..." the judge started, but Bonnie was already gone. He sighed. "I was going to say I only needed a scone to support my sister. I had to taste all the prototype batches. Also, I'm not too hungry this morning, in light of everything."

Trinidad heaved out a breath. "Judge, I am so very sorry the letter was taken."

He shook his head. "It wasn't your fault. Chief Bigley said you were knocked over from behind. I'm glad you weren't hurt. What I can't figure out is why."

"And who," Trinidad added. "You said you didn't tell anyone that you were going to loan me the letter."

"Correct. I did not. But why would anyone care, anyway? It's a thirty-year-old Dear John letter."

"The chief might uncover something we didn't think of."

His focus softened in thought. "You know I was watching this TV program about a woman who returns after leaving town for decades, only she hides her identity." His Adam's apple wobbled. "It made my imagination go a bit wild, I'm afraid."

"If Cherry did return, under a fake identity or not, I am sure she would have come to see you, right? Or contacted you in some way?"

He sagged. "You're right. That's what I get for watching those kind of programs." Bonnie delivered a plate heaped with food, which he thanked her for.

When she was gone, he sipped some coffee. She could no longer hold back from taking a bite of her scone. Luscious, as she'd thought it would be, with the perfect amount of sweet and spice. "Your sister is an amazing baker. Her cookbook will be a hot seller." Trinidad stopped, led to a thought. "Judge, can I ask you something? Has a reporter named T. J. Orwell come to see you?"

He toyed with his napkin. "Yes, as a matter of fact. He wanted to interview me about Alpenfest."

"Did he ask you anything about Cherry?"

The frown deepened. "No, but why would he?"

"He didn't bring her up at all?"

He shook his head, expression bland. "We chatted about Sprocket and the various elements of the events, how it will help the town, etc."

That made no sense. Why wouldn't Orwell have grilled the judge about Cherry, since that was the story he seemed eager to sniff out? And why wasn't he lapping up details about the Forge murder?

The judge took another sip of coffee. "I was going to meet Ramona here, but I guess she had a change in plans. If you see her, tell her I went back to my office, will you?"

"Yes," Trinidad said. When the judge left, Trinidad eyed the untouched scone on his plate. After all Gretchen's work, it would be a terrible shame to let that scone be discarded. Besides, Gretchen's feelings might be hurt.

Having justified the indulgence, she ate the judge's scone and helped herself to the eggs and bacon on his plate for good measure. Excellent. Bonnie's Sprocket Station would no doubt earn a reputation for the quality of the cooking for sure.

Leaving her empty plate as evidence of the food's quality, she went outside. A mellow sun was rising over the tree line behind the Station. Bonnie popped her head out of the dining car.

"Trin, can you check on Felice? Gretchen went back to the kitchen, so I can't leave right now. I told Fee she could go as far as the sphere rock but no farther, but she's a daydreamer. I don't like her being out of my sight for very long. Zap's across the bridge at the grove figuring out how to clear the trees so she's probably curious."

"I figured Lydia would hire that out. Those trees are enormous."

She shrugged. "I dunno."

"I'll check on her. Oh, and I've got an idea for the birthday party today. Can you bring two jelly or pickle jars when you come?"

"With or without the jelly and pickles?"

Trinidad laughed. "Empty and clean, please."

"Assignment accepted." A voice called from inside. "Gotta go. Thanks."

Trinidad walked along the trail, the grass knee-high around the edges of the path. In the distance, the pines kept their steadfast green, but the interspersed shrubbery was starting to show the colors of fall, brilliant yellows and flashes of rust, a fleck of scarlet here and there. *Winter will follow*, her gut whispered. *Still no plan?*

Trinidad saw Felice's pom-pom hat pop up, a few feet from the sphere rock.

"Hi, Felice," she said. The girl was adding something to her collection jar.

"Hi, Auntie. Where's Noodles?"

Trinidad explained. Felice wrinkled her button nose. "Wanna see my collection?"

Trinidad dutifully knelt. Inside the jar were small rocks, a pine cone, the glittery red stones Felice had indeed pried off the barrette, and a small rectangular white rock that shone like marble in the sun. "Is that a tooth?"

Felice grinned, her jack-o'-lantern smile making Trinidad laugh.

"I see you put the jewels in your jar."

"They're rubies," Felice said solemnly. "But I kept the other part too." She pulled the bare barrette out of her pocket, the sad green leaves all that remained of the pretty ornament. Trinidad felt a pang. It would have looked beautiful in Felice's blond hair, but what did it matter? Felice saw treasure differently than other people.

"Your mommy said to come back now."

"Okay," Felice screwed the top back on her jar. "Is he gonna chop the trees today?"

Trinidad looked where Felice had pointed. Zap stood at the other side of the footbridge; neck craned to take in the treetops. "I'll ask him. Why don't you go back to the dining car? There are yummy scones for breakfast."

"Can I play with Noodles after?"

"You sure can." Trinidad waited until Felice had trotted with her jar back along the path to the inn before she headed for the bridge. When she'd almost made it across, she heard talking and realized that Zap was on the phone, his cell pressed to his ear.

"I can handle it," he said.

His tone was frustrated.

"Like I said, I can handle it, and no one will know."

She paused, uncertain if she should turn around and walk away or stand there and wait for him to finish.

"Listen, you don't get to tell me what I can't do. It's my business now. I'll take care of it, and no one will be the wiser." He stabbed the phone off, grumbling, and caught sight of Trinidad. His mouth slackened in shock, before he scrubbed his fingers across his scalp.

"Man, you scared me."

"I'm sorry. I wanted to ask you a question. I didn't realize you were on the phone."

He rolled his eyes. "This business stuff. Makes me think I should stick to towing." His smile was back in place. "So what's the question?"

"Felice wondered if you would be taking down the trees today."

He looked again to the treetops where the branches brushed the blue sky. "I gotta round up some equipment first, so it might be a while."

"Those are really big trees," she said. "Are you sure you want to tackle it by yourself? It might be dangerous."

He shrugged. "Gotta keep the costs down, don't I? Key tenet of the business world, right? Expenditures vs. revenues?" When she didn't reply, he looked again at the trees. "I can do it. No problem." The dubious cast to his face made her wonder if he believed his own words.

They both looked at the trees, now, and Trinidad recalled that not very long ago they'd found the shovel that had likely killed Forge in this very spot.

She remembered an anonymous poem she'd read to Felice recently about trees and their secrets. "*We have a secret, just we three, the robin and I, and the sweet cherry tree.*" If only she could ask the towering pines what they knew about Forge's death. Would they know anything about Cherry Lighter too?

Who had Zap been talking to in such an irate tone?

Her thoughts twirled like a soft-serve ice cream. Someone killed Forge, that much she knew. It wasn't Quinn, her heart told her. He was not a killer, nor was Doug. But he was concealing something that had to do with Forge and the trees. What? Why? Who?

Those were questions for the police chief, not for her, she reminded herself as she left Zap to his trees.

Chapter Twelve

SHE MEANDERED BACK AND LET Noodles out to play with Felice in the grass by the firepit.

The breakfast service was concluded, and some of the visitors returned to their train cars while others found seats around the fire Bonnie had lit to fend off the chill. Trinidad followed Bonnie into the dining car and helped load up the trays with the leftover eggs and bacon and the dirty silverware, since Gretchen had gone to start on the dishes at Bonnie's request. Trinidad suspected the tenderhearted Bonnie would not allow her to heft any more heavy trays. Between the two of them, they cleared the room in fifteen minutes, leaving the dishware soaking in Gretchen's soapy water. "The scones were a hit, right?" Gretchen said.

"Were they ever," Bonnie said. "There wasn't a single one left."

Trinidad felt even better about her decision to eat the judge's scone.

"I'll work up my new menu ideas after the lunch service," she said, trying to hide a smile of pride.

They headed to the parking area. Gretchen stripped off her gloves to join them, fanning her face. "Warm in there," she said. "I need a minute."

They watched the tranquil scene by the firepit as Felice and Noodles laid in a sunny spot of ground, belly-up, noses to the sky. Bonnie took a picture with her phone. "Aren't they darling together?"

And they were, of course. "I'm looking forward to our birthday outing today," Trinidad said. "I think Felice will love it." A late-afternoon trip on the railriders with Quinn and Doug would be followed up by a party at the store.

"I really appreciate it. I've got inventory to deal with, and Felice is on her own too much." Her smile dimmed a moment. "I have to find more kids for her to play with."

"No school chums live close by?" That explained why there would not be a gaggle of kiddies at Felice's birthday party.

Bonnie shrugged. "I'm going to homeschool her."

Trinidad raised both eyebrows. "Really?"

"School wasn't working out," Bonnie said breezily. "That's another thing I need to organize while you're on the ride, the homeschool materials. She can't spend all her time finding things for her collection jar."

"She'll do fine with you teaching her," Gretchen said. "And I'm great at math and science, so I can help if you run into a snarl."

"That'd be super," Bonnie said.

Super. Trinidad's mind wandered back to the trees and Zap's puzzling statement. *I can handle it, and no one will know.* She'd never heard Zap speak with such intensity. "Zap said he's going to cut down the trees himself."

"Oh boy. He doesn't strike me as the axe-wielding type," Bonnie said.

"An idiot, through and through." Gretchen heaved a breath. "That boy is gonna lose a limb or worse. Our father had the bright idea of chopping down a tree in our backyard by himself. Never mind that the man had never even operated a chainsaw before. Of course he mishandled it and nearly cut his thumb off. I never heard my mother shriek so loud." She sniffed. "Why is it that men seem to think they're invincible and women are taught to question their confidence at every step? There has to be something in the middle, doesn't there?"

They watched Felice and Noodles in silence until Bonnie said, "I guess I'm guilty of your dad's way of thinking. To be a successful athlete, you always have to believe you're going to win, whether or not it's likely." She cocked her head, playing with her long blond braid. "I want Felice to have whatever is in the middle of those two extremes, a healthy level of confidence." She shot a look at the tree line. "And I sure hope Zap doesn't kill himself trying to prove he can cut those trees himself."

"Would teach him a lesson if he did," Gretchen said.

"Hard to learn a lesson when you're dead," Bonnie pointed out.

Gretchen shrugged. "He probably couldn't learn it if he was alive either."

A car pulled up, snagging their attention.

"The mayor approaches. I'd rather do dishes." Gretchen stopped a few steps away. "You know the person with the best motive to kill Forge is Ramona. I never saw her leave after the yodelfest. She could have easily stayed long enough to clobber someone. And she used to brag about being a high school softball champion, so her swing's probably pretty good still. Just my two cents." Gretchen marched back to the kitchen.

Bonnie blanched. "I wonder if the chief knows that."

Ramona hopped out, expression falling as she took in the postprandial chatterers. "I missed the judge." She blew out a breath. "I overslept. Restless night."

"I'll get you a cup of coffee," Bonnie said. "Be right back."

Trinidad relayed the judge's message as Zap returned down the trail. "All figured out," he said.

"Zap is going to cut the trees himself," Trinidad explained.

"Not gonna be a problem," he said, grin in place. "Gonna be super simple. Just a matter of planning."

Ramona nodded. Trinidad waited for her to start up her angry tirade against the clearing of the trees as she'd done with Forge, but she stayed quiet—preoccupied? Zap ambled away after a cheerful salute, climbed into a van with "Forge Railriders" stenciled on the side, and drove away. Trinidad could not keep her puzzlement under wraps.

"Something wrong, Trinidad?" Ramona said. "You're staring at me like I've grown a second head."

"You're not upset that Zap is going to cut the trees? You and Forge fought over it right here at the Station four days ago." *Right before he was murdered*, she refrained from adding.

Ramona took a mug of coffee from Bonnie and thanked her before taking a dainty swig. "That was different."

"Why? Aren't we talking about the same trees?"

"Because it was Forge's idea, probably," she said with a smirk.

Trinidad was startled. So her environmental views could shift so easily? Politics were a dirty business indeed.

"He took every chance he could to malign my character and integrity, so I'd have opposed whatever plan he cooked up. I'm all about ecology, but I've warmed to the second rail route idea since Forge died. Sure it's not optimal to cut trees, but Zap and Lydia assured me they intend to plant more in another spot to replace them. A tree's a tree, right?"

Bonnie's lip crimped in a way that indicated she wasn't convinced. Wisely, she held her tongue. She had a business to run, and the mayor could make things difficult.

There was more to the Forge and Ramona story, Trinidad's gut told her. "You've already met with Zap and Lydia?"

"Yes, and I don't appreciate your disapproving tone. Why wouldn't I reach out to the new owners of the railriders? Forge is dead and gone. There was no love lost between us, and a mourning period seems a touch insincere, doesn't it? Business is business." She paused, eyes narrowed as Papa's Chevy made the turn into the lot. "Who is that in the passenger seat?"

It took Trinidad a moment to identify the man. "It's T. J. Orwell."

"That clod of a reporter," she snapped. "All the charm of a root canal. He wants to 'chat' about Alpenfest, he says, but all he does is ask questions about Cherry Lighter, Forge, and my business dealings. He's a troublemaker with some sort of secret agenda. You all would be advised to give him the cold shoulder as well. He doesn't have the welfare of Sprocket at heart." She handed the coffee mug to Bonnie. "Thanks for the coffee. I'm out of here."

She hopped into her car and drove too fast out of the lot.

Bonnie's smile was savvy. "Sometimes I'm not so sure our illustrious mayor has the welfare of Sprocket at heart either." She chuckled. "She asked me if I wanted to offer copies of *Betty the Beaver* in our gift shop."

"I didn't know you had a gift shop."

"We don't, which is what I told her. She said we should work on that posthaste, but I'm just not feeling the vibe on that, you know? The experience here is the gift."

As Trinidad watched a bird skimming the treetops against a swirl of morning gold, she had to agree. Regardless of Forge's attack and Zap's chainsaws, the place was a jewel.

Orwell approached them, hands on his waist. "Aww man. Wasn't that the mayor? I've been trying to get a second interview with her, but she's dodging me. Her secretary at the realty office said I might catch her here."

"Sorry," Bonnie said. "You were sixty seconds too slow."

"Who'd think sixty seconds would make a difference?" he said.

"Depends on what game you're playing," Bonnie said over her shoulder as she moved away to add wood to the firepit.

Orwell did not seem to note her sardonic undertone.

Trinidad decided she was done trying to jolly this confusing reporter along. "You can interview me. We never really got around to the questions about the Shimmy or Alpenfest."

He chewed a thumbnail. "We didn't?"

"No. You were too busy with the Cherry Lighter idea the twins cooked up."

"Oh. I guess I got a lot of Alpenfest details from other people. I'll come by later, okay?" He turned to go.

"Mr. Orwell, before you take off, I was talking to the judge, and he said you never asked him a single question about Cherry."

His grin turned down at the corners. "So? I told you I'm getting paid to write about Alpenfest. The Cherry Lighter thing is just a sideline."

"Then why are you badgering the mayor about it?"

His pupils were so deeply black she could see herself mirrored in them. She'd guessed him to be in his mid-thirties when they'd first met, but she saw the beginning of crow's-feet bracketing his eyes.

"I wasn't badgering her," he said stiffly, as if she'd offended him. "It's my job to ask questions."

"Then why not ask those questions to the judge? He was Cherry's boyfriend."

He paused. The information about the judge's relationship with Cherry had not surprised him. "Police checked him out. No point in pursuing that. But Ramona had a real beef with Cherry. Did you know she assaulted another girl back at her private college?"

Trinidad's eyebrows zinged up. "She did?"

"Uh-huh. Took me forever to dig that one up, and I had to bribe a clerk at the college in the process. Notes say they were arguing over some guy and Ramona shoved her. Sound familiar?"

Trinidad remembered Ramona's well-manicured hands reaching out to knock over Forge Emberly. Forge was a sturdy man, and he'd gone over like a poorly pitched tent in a windstorm. *Over some guy…*

"What happened to the girl she pushed?"

"She fell down a flight of stairs and broke her arm in two places. Ramona's parents paid 'restitution' and covered the medical costs, but, basically, it was their way of keeping Ramona from getting booted out. She pushed Forge, too, right? Tendencies like that, violent ones, don't go away, you know. They eventually rise to the surface."

Trinidad frowned. Did they? Was Ramona a violent woman at the core? Or was the college incident a simple accident? A product of immaturity and bad timing? People grew and changed. Trinidad did not want to recall the awkward, insecure teen she herself had been back in the day. But he was right. Ramona had technically assaulted Forge as well.

Orwell pursed his lips as if he'd picked up on her doubts. "Anyway, it's proof that Ramona has a jealous streak and she's capable of violence." He shrugged. "Figured I'd beat the bushes and see what crawled out. Stuff like that can make a reporter's career, you know? Get me off the travel and leisure section. Everyone wants to show me sausages and picnic areas around here, but, deep down, Sprocket isn't the sleepy small town it appears to be. This place could be a jackpot."

"Mr. Orwell, I still don't understand why you seem to be going at Ramona hammer and tongs and treating the judge with kid gloves." The metaphor had gotten mixed, but she knew she'd made her point.

He laughed. "Purely self-preservation. I don't want a judge angry at me. That guy's headed for the appellate court, and I don't need any enemies. A crooked local mayor I can handle, but a guy's got to look out for himself, right? A paycheck's a paycheck, but it only goes so far." He was shouldering his backpack, as if ready to leave.

"All right," she said, giving up.

He shot her a look. "I heard Lydia at the coffee shop saying that Ramona's on board with removing the trees. Do you have any idea why she's suddenly reversing her position?" He pointed to the cluster of pines and oak in the distance.

Trinidad blinked. "I have to admit I was wondering that myself."

He considered, rocking back and forth on the heels of his sneakers. "It must be somehow working in her favor. Does she have any financial interest in the land?"

"I don't think so. Quinn owned the cut-through land, and the rest of the property is county-owned; Railriders pays a fee to use it. Ramona isn't a business partner with Railriders." That she knew of.

A sly gleam crept into his eyes. "But the business has

recently changed ownership after Forge was bumped off, hasn't it?"

The man did not miss a thing. She nodded.

He grinned. "Well, then, I'll be sure to look into it. Thanks for the tip."

Trinidad held in a groan. All she needed was the mayor thinking she was agitating the pain-in-the-neck reporter.

Orwell waved at Papa. "I don't need a ride back. I'm gonna do some hiking." He hitched up his pack and eyed the small coffee station Gretchen was refilling near the fire-pit. "After I snag some coffee. I never pass up anything free."

Trinidad went to Papa, who was warming his toes by the fire, eating a plate of scrambled eggs Bonnie had delivered.

"Sit, Trina. Gorgeous morning. I am getting used to the climate here." He was bundled in a hat and his plaid jacket, even though they'd likely hit the low seventies by lunchtime. His tropical blood had not yet thickened. Winter would be an adventure for both of them. It was as if she could already feel the chill.

She took a seat. "Busy today?"

"I have only to give a trip to Josef and two others a ride into town. I am free to help at the Shimmy before I go over the greenhouse plans again with Quinn. Then, I think, Noodles and I will visit Pastor Phil while you are off on your adventure with Felice."

"You're not exactly living the slow life here in Sprocket."

He shrugged a stocky shoulder. "If you can't keep mind and body active, there's nothing to be gained by a slow life."

She must have inherited his "busy" gene, because she'd

never been able to appreciate the restorative powers of idleness either. "Did you and Mr. Orwell chat much while you were driving him here?"

"Not very. Mostly I talked and he said yes or no or mmm-hmmm. He asked me only one question." Papa pursed his lips in thought. "And that is odd, don't you think, for a journalist?"

"That there was only one? What was the question?"

"He asked me if I knew the mayor. Once I told him I was a relative newcomer to town, he had nothing more to ask. A reporter, out of questions." Papa waved his fork. "It's like a farmer with no seeds. It seems to me he might be in the wrong line of work; don't you think?"

Her gaze wandered over the picturesque scene. An odd detail that she forgot prodded at her, something she'd learned here, right on Bonnie's property, something out of place that she should pay attention to, maybe gleaned while talking to Felice? Looking at the cheerful train cars and the gorgeous mountain landscape did not help bring it to her mind again.

She stared in the direction Orwell had taken. Both Ramona and Orwell were not completely forthcoming, she suspected. And what about the judge? Could one of them know what really happened to Forge? Or Cherry, for that matter?

Business was business, and trees were trees, Ramona had said.

And a paycheck was a paycheck, according to Orwell.

And murder was…well, murder. The clues seemed to

lead away into a million different directions rather than toward the solution. A murderer was still at large, disguised under the persona of an innocent local, perhaps someone they knew very well.

Papa's warm shoulder next to hers did not quite erase the cold shiver that ran up her spine. As she drove back to the Shimmy, something tugged at her again, something Felice had said. About what? Some out-of-place detail that floated just out of reach in Trinidad's mind, but she could not catch hold of it.

Some detective, she thought.

━━━━━━━━

Trinidad told Felice she would be back to pick her up for the birthday railride. It was the big "oh six," and, now that Trinidad had discovered the child was lacking in friends, that was cause to pull out the stops.

Alpenfest or no, Sundays were slow at the Shimmy, and the twins were happy to squeeze in some extra work hours. They were chatting animatedly as they rushed into the shop later that day. Noodles lifted an ear as if he was eager to hear what in the world they might have come up with this time.

She resisted grumbling. "Hello, boys. I've got the ice cream churning."

"Miss Jones," Carlos launched in, grabbing his apron with one hand and waving his phone at her with the other. "This is like the coolest thing ever. We went into surveillance mode with our drone."

"You did what?"

Chief Bigley hurried in next in street clothes. "Diego and Carlos have decided to be the eye in the sky, using their drone to scour the town for clues to Forge's murder and the Cherry Lighter mystery. That's why I'm here. They called me."

The confidence of youth was an astounding thing, Trinidad thought. Would she have had the chutzpah at their age to cavalierly summon the chief of police to a private meeting?

"Thank you for coming, ma'am." Diego gallantly gestured the chief into a chair, where he opened a laptop and centered it in front of her. "You're going to flip when you see this."

"First, I feel duty-bound to tell you there are laws about flying drones," the chief said as Trinidad joined them.

Carlos nodded with some impatience. "Yes, we know. We registered our drone and kept it within line of sight and below four hundred feet and all that."

"And that landowners can bring legal action against people flying drones over their property," she continued.

"Chief," Carlos said, exasperated. "What we found trumps all of those bogus rules."

The chief's expression made it clear she did not believe the rules to be bogus, but she sat back as Diego fiddled with his laptop, brought up a video, and clicked play. Trinidad felt her stomach go tight as the screen blinked to life.

"We flew our drone along the railrider tracks. While on foot, of course, 'cuz we couldn't pay the fee for the ride. Did you know it's like two hundred bucks per ride? And you have to pedal yourself. What a rip. And they've got a no drone rule, anyway. Lydia wouldn't let us on the property at the office, so we asked Bonnie. And she let us start our route at the inn. Bonnie's cool, and we showed Felice how the drone works. Mentoring the youth," he proclaimed grandly.

"Right, so after the mentoring was finished…" Bigley made a rolling motion for them to continue.

"Well, so like I said, we hiked alongside the rails and when someone came along, we ducked out of sight so we wouldn't get Lydia on our cases if a tourist complained. We should have brought a costume. It would have been super funny if they thought we were Bigfoot." He started to giggle, but his brother punched him on the shoulder. "Yeah, so we followed the river for like…four hours."

"Two hours and twenty minutes," Diego corrected. "Approximately four miles until our drone died. It runs on lithium polymer batteries, so you only get about twenty minutes before you have to switch them out. And we only have four sets," he explained. "We'd love to get a drone with solar-powered batteries but—"

"Yeah, what he said," Carlos interrupted. "But look what we recorded right when the rails come out of the woods and into the open field."

Trinidad bent over Chief Bigley, who pulled on a pair of reading glasses. Together they leaned in. The footage showed the splendid colors of a perfect autumn day in Sprocket. The darker olives and charcoals of the trees gave way to a lush expanse of green rippled hills where the tracks wound in picturesque fashion through it all.

"Lovely," Trinidad said. "This would be a good advertisement for Railriders."

Carlos frowned. "Hold on. We're coming to the spot." Poised, he tapped a finger at the precise moment, freezing the screen in place. A grassy field, the rails visible in the lower left corner, a swath of blue sky and a hint of trees.

"There," Carlos said. "Right there, see?"

They craned forward. Grass, rails, trees. She searched for something else.

"I'm looking at a crow," Bigley said finally. "Two crows, large robust specimens."

"Right." Carlos was almost dancing up and down.

Bigley gave him a look that might have scorched someone with less teenage confidence. "You brought me here to see crows?"

"Yes." His grin was pure Cheshire cat. Trinidad waited for the big reveal.

"But look what happens when I zoom in. We didn't notice until we reviewed the footage back home." With some further manipulation, he zoomed in on one of the big black birds. He used a spoon handle to point. This one was perched on a stout branch of a pine, the last tree between the forested area and the grassy hills.

"Uh-huh," Bigley said. "So you've captured a crow in its natural habitat. Nicely done, boys. You have a future in nature photography."

Carlos punched the button again and the crow filled the screen with glossy black. "Look. Look what it's got in its paw."

"Claw," Diego corrected.

Now Trinidad was squinting too. The chief swiveled her head up and down, peering through her reading glasses. Was there something white clutched in that bird's claw? About four inches long maybe? Slender. A branch, she thought, but she felt the chief stiffen next to her.

"What do you think this is, gentlemen?" she said, tone flat.

As if they'd practiced their announcement, they spoke at the same time. "A human bone."

Trinidad turned around and noticed that Orwell had come in, just then.

"Did you say a human bone?" he said. "Where?"

Bigley snapped the laptop shut with a withering glare at Orwell. "This is a private conversation. Boys, I'm going to take this for a bit. Can one of you techno whizzes download or upload or whatever to transfer the footage onto my computer?"

"Sure," Diego said. "I can do it."

"All right. We'll take a quick trip to the station. Can you spare him, Trinidad?"

"Yes, ma'am, if he comes back shortly."

Carlos looked crestfallen to be left out.

The chief turned to Orwell and included him in her sweeping gaze. "We don't have anything here we need to spread around town. Am I clear?"

Everyone nodded, even Orwell.

"Trinidad, can I speak to you outside for a moment?" the chief said.

Trinidad left the boys and Orwell and walked outside with her. Noodles got up from his cushion and joined them.

"This is most likely nothing," she said. "It's probably an animal bone, squirrel or deer."

"You seem rather urgent about it though, taking their computer."

"Mostly I'd like to make sure they transfer it to me and delete it. Rumors like this can ignite like the burning burger."

That was for sure. "At least we know it isn't related to Forge's murder. He, er, was in possession of all his bones when he was killed."

"I can't say it isn't related to other cases, but yes, it's not Forge's bone." Her pause lasted until she cleared her throat. "Officer Chang finally dug up the Cherry Lighter file. Not much to it, but there was an interview with the mom, no dad in the picture that we can tell. Mom was in and out of alcohol treatment programs and Cherry hadn't lived with her full-time since she was eighteen. Even then, Cherry would strike out on her own from time to time. Their relationship was contentious. Before she was of age, she'd run away occasionally. Cops returned her twice that I know of."

"Why did she think her daughter had disappeared instead of run away again?"

"The mom had scraped up some money for a birthday present—not much, a hundred bucks. She told Cherry about it, and Cherry was supposed to come and pick it up, but she never did. The mom said Cherry wouldn't have left town without picking up her money."

Trinidad felt a twinge of sadness that a mother-daughter

bond could be stripped away to the point where money was the only connection. It pained her to think of Cherry's mother saving up to give her daughter a present when she couldn't supply what she really needed, a stable parent. Addiction was a killer of everything it touched. She'd transcribed plenty of cases during her stenography days where drugs or alcohol were at the root of the problem.

"Cherry didn't have a car, so that's another reason Mom was suspicious, but there are other ways to get around." Bigley's brow was furrowed.

"Do you think her mom might have been right that Cherry was abducted or something?"

"I'd love to have a follow-up interview with her." Bigley sighed. "But she died six months ago of liver failure."

Trinidad felt like the breath had been knocked out of her. "Oh no."

Bigley drew a paper from her pocket. "It's a photocopy of the judge's letter from the file. I don't see anything helpful in it, but..." she shrugged. "You have a different way of looking at things."

Trinidad felt her mouth open in surprise. It felt almost as though the chief might think of her as an ally, if not a friend. Considering Bigley's loyalty to her baby brother, Trinidad would have never thought it possible they'd be anything but frosty strangers.

"Thank you," she said. "For trusting me with this." She saw the chief open her mouth, and she raised a hand. "I will not show it to the twins or Orwell, I promise."

She relaxed. "All right. I'll go see about this crow with a

bone video. Like I said, it's probably nothing, but something is keeping me awake at night."

"Instincts prickling?" Trinidad suggested.

"Could be indigestion from the late-night Alpenfest sausages, but, until I know for sure, I'd like to be thorough. We're still waiting on the lab about Forge, but his lawyer confirmed he changed his will last year to include Zap. He asked that it be kept confidential, so, outwardly, it would appear Zap didn't know he was going to inherit."

"Outwardly?"

"The lawyer's secretary retired and settled in Scotch Corners before she died. The lawyer said she was a bit of a gossip, and he'd had to have a chat with her to encourage her retirement. It's not impossible that she might have dropped some comment to someone who passed it to someone and on and on until it reached Zap or Lydia's ears." Bigley climbed into her car, an excited Diego joining her with his laptop.

Orwell waited inside the shop with Carlos, no doubt eager to know about her private conversation with the chief. She should go in and calm the waters, read the letter later. Then she recalled the last time it had been snatched from her grasp before she could peruse the contents.

Not again. Popping her head inside quickly she called for Noodles. "Taking Noo out for a quick minute. Be right back."

Before they could reply, she'd ushered Noodles from the shop and strode quickly to Full of Beans.

A nice quiet table and ten minutes was all she needed.

Chapter Thirteen

A BOW-TIED STAN GREETED HER in his usual formal fashion. "Good afternoon, Trinidad and Noodles. How lovely to see you. May I get you a coffee or a pastry, perhaps? Meg has made her fabulous Strawberry Pie Bars, which are known to reduce grown people to tears of joy."

She laughed. "How can I refuse that?"

He prepared her order and handed a dog biscuit from the jar on the counter to Noodles with a graceful bow. Noodles responded with a hearty ear flap.

She glanced around at the crowded tables. Ernst, Lydia, and several other folks she recognized as yodelers sipped and talked. "What I really need is a few minutes of peace and quiet."

He gave her a knowing nod. "Of course. Follow me. I have just the place." With her coffee and strawberry square in hand, Stan guided her into the back of the old shop. Noodles followed along, treat clutched firmly in his mouth. They arrived at a wee spot, an alcove cut into the old brick that had been painted a cheery shade of yellow. It was furnished with a comfortable padded armchair, an antique herb drying rack for a side table, and a hurricane glass lamp he switched on for her. On the floor was a neatly piled stack of books, *The Farmer's Almanac*, a pastry cookbook, and a crisply folded copy of the London *Times*.

"Meg's idea to furnish this spot," he said. "The building used to be an old general store, so it's got plenty of hidden nooks. Perfect place for tea or coffee and solitude."

"Thank you," she said. "You're so kind."

"Not at all. I will leave you to your pondering." But he hesitated, clearing his throat with delicacy, probably a remnant of his days as a butler.

"What is it, Stan?"

"I, ah, well, I am not one to gossip."

"No, you aren't."

"And you are such a good friend to Quinn." He frowned. "I find myself worried over a detail that maybe you could explain, since you know him better than I."

Until lately, she might have agreed. "Maybe."

"It's a matter of public record, so I am not betraying private information, you understand."

"Yes, I do." Stan had as much integrity as her Papa, she was sure of it. He would never share secrets unless there was good reason.

"I found it strange, is all. The sum for the land Forge paid Quinn."

"What about it?"

"It was below market value."

"How far below?"

He coughed. "Well below." His silvery brows quirked together. "Half, at least."

She tried not to outright gape. "Why would Quinn sell off those two acres for less than they were worth?"

"That is my question too. I asked him about it, but he did not give an answer—not really. Has he mentioned his rationale to you?"

She shook her head. "No."

"Ah, well, then. It's his own personal business. I found it…curious and worrying, I suppose, since I know he has a brother to care for and his life is farming." The chime of the bell attached to the front door echoed down the narrow corridor. "Best be getting back to the front of house." With another formal nod of the head, he left her there, deeper in consternation than she'd been when she arrived.

Quinn needed money. That was the reason he gave for selling his land to Forge. What possible motive could he have had to undercut the value? Forge had some sort of leverage over Quinn, that had to be. Blackmail? Her senses buzzed.

Noodles pawed gently at her knee. She reached to fondle his ears. "I'm okay, Noo." Reassured, he began to lick his treat, and she opened the photocopied letter the chief had given her. "One mystery at a time," she muttered to herself. At least casting her attention elsewhere allowed her to escape the tension that came with wondering about Quinn's secrets. A fortifying bite of the strawberry square was in order. The combination of streusel topping and sweet strawberry jam set her taste buds firing on all cylinders. Hoping her brain would follow suit, Trinidad began to read.

dear alex,

i am sorry for leaving like this, but i didnt want to speak to you in person because you would try to talk me out of it. youll be a good lawyer someday. i have decided to leave because its just not going to work out between us. we dont want the same things. i want to have fun, go to parties, and see the world…you are going to be a lawyer and a judge someday. youre too smart for me. im just starting out and youre already climbing the ladder to success. i hope you will not be too upset but i know youll move on. wishing you well with all my heart.

cherry

Trinidad sat back and took another bite of strawberry square and a sip of Stan's strong-brewed coffee. Her initial impression of Cherry? An immature girl looking to escape a relationship. She read it a second time, trying to see between the lines as Judge Torpine had wanted her to.

Perhaps it was insecurity rather than immaturity. Deep down, Cherry didn't actually believe she was good enough or smart enough for the judge. Certainly, she wasn't qualified to be a typist, without some serious training, but that meant nothing. Gabe had escaped typing class and eventually learned to produce entire accounting reports with only his index fingers. And his lack of proper keyboarding skills didn't dampen his career as an embezzler, she thought with some acid.

Maybe you're reading too much into this, Trinidad. Possibly Cherry's reason for dumping him was exactly what she said. She wanted to go to parties, have fun. The judge, at fifty-something, was, to all appearances, cerebral, intellectual, cautious, but that didn't mean he was like that in his early twenties. He'd been clerking at a law office, he'd said, so maybe that was enough evidence that he had a vision for his life that did not include a woman like Cherry. But…

More sugar helped her remember. He'd said he had built plans.

…elaborate plans for our future together.

And he'd known of her nature.

…completely reckless, eager for adventure, legal or not.

Perhaps Cherry did not feel worthy of a relationship, especially in light of her own family struggles, and she realized that no matter what the judge said he wanted, their desires were not compatible.

She burned to know more about Cherry Lighter. Such a shame Quinn's mom had passed away or she could have possibly asked for information.

And in a flash, the enigma of Quinn Logan jockeyed for position in her thoughts. On top of that, Forge's murder was still a puzzle, and there was always the crow with the bone in his claw and that strange detail that kept nagging at her— something to do with Felice. Something she'd mentioned to Trinidad during their chat at the Station that settled uneasily in Trinidad's memory, just out of reach. It was dizzying. Plus she wasn't sure she had the bandwidth to juggle all the mysteries and still figure out how to keep the Shimmy alive over the winter.

"You know what I need, Noo?" she asked.

Noodles cocked his head.

"A nice birthday adventure with Felice to clear my mind."

He ran a tongue over his nose.

"But first we have to go back to the shop and fend off a bunch of questions from a teen boy and a nosy reporter. Maybe Papa will take you with him to visit Pastor Phil."

Noodles gave her that head waggle that was surely a sign of approval.

———————

The last railriders excursion of the afternoon, dubbed the "sunset adventure," was slated to depart the depot at four o'clock. With Noodles and Papa off to the pastor's, and the shop closed up early, Trinidad picked up Felice from the Station.

"I'll meet you at the Shimmy for the ice cream party, okay?" Bonnie said, planting a kiss on Felice's forehead. "I've got to get the health inspection done while the troops are away at the Alpenfest talent show in Josef. Gretchen and I have been putting in overtime getting the kitchen and dining car up to snuff." She raised her arms in a gargantuan stretch. "All we need now is a signature on the dotted line."

"Good luck," Trinidad said.

Bonnie surprised her by reaching out and taking her

hand. "I am so happy. Not just that you're taking Felice out for her birthday, but that she has you for an auntie."

Trinidad's breath caught. "I always wanted to be an auntie, and Felice is an angel. The blessings go both ways." And they did, she realized. Three years before, when she'd heard about Bonnie and Felice, she'd felt the full range of anger, betrayal, sadness. Now here she was, a part of Felice's life. She gave Bonnie a squeeze as Felice hopped on one foot out to meet her.

"Ready?" Trinidad asked.

Felice responded with two thumbs up, her collection jar tucked under one arm.

"We'll see you for Freakshakes," Trinidad called to Bonnie. "Don't forget the jars." She drove them to the depot where Quinn and Doug were already waiting.

Quinn's smile made her heart thunk as she helped Felice unbuckle. Doug stood ready with a striped bicycle helmet.

"Can I bring my collecting jar?" Felice said.

"I'm afraid not, sweetie. It might fall and break, and we won't be getting out for treasure hunting." Felice's face fell. "But, when we go back to the Shimmy for ice cream after, we have a surprise for you that might be great for your jar."

With her smile back in place, they joined Quinn and Doug.

"Hello, birthday girl," Quinn said. "Thanks for letting us come along on your trip."

Bonnie had tried to purchase the tickets for the "party," but everyone had insisted on paying their own way. Had it been a hardship on Quinn to spend the money? She wondered, after Stan's revelation that he'd accepted a pittance for his land. The need to ask him about it burned like lemon juice on a paper cut, but she stuffed it down as they met Lydia inside the small log building for a safety briefing. The interior was cozy with pinewood chairs and a gift shop in the corner smelling of fresh paint. Boxes stacked against one wall and an unassembled office chair emphasized that the two were still settling into their new line of work. It made her feel uneasy, thinking of how very recently it had been owned and operated by a man who'd been murdered. The transition had occurred quickly…maybe because Lydia or Zap knew what was going to happen to Forge? Relax, she told herself. This is a birthday outing, and you're supposed to be cheerful.

Zap was on his cell phone behind the front counter, but he waved. There was a groove of concentration on his forehead, and he looked tired. Perhaps the stress of owning a business or the plans to remove the trees himself were weighing on him. Possibly Zap might have been happiest fixing cars or driving his tow truck. She suspected Lydia was the one with big plans for her hapless hubby.

She did not seem careworn by her new duties in the slightest. Snappily dressed in dark pants and a red windbreaker with "Forge Railriders" embroidered on the front pocket, she greeted them and set about her game plan. First, she took out a tape measure and used it to ensure that Felice met the height requirement. Thanks to Bonnie's genetics, Felice was tall enough and then some. She sat them down on benches and went over the protocols with the efficiency of a

Marine Corps drill instructor. Occasionally she referred to a small screen that was playing a video of the route. "There's an optional motorized assist to help you up grades or to keep you going if you need a break. Here's a liability release form." Out came a clipboard with an attached pen. "It gets chilly when in the forest this late in the day, so I hope you brought jackets."

Felice nodded, pointing to her feet. "And these kind of shoes. No toes showing, Mommy said."

That brought a slight smile to Lydia's face. "Right. Are you ready to go?"

They followed her out to a wooden boarding platform where a four-seater railbike was parked. They were nothing more than steel frames with two elevated seats in front and back and four sets of bicycle pedals. She handed them each a helmet.

Doug clutched the one he'd carried.

"He likes his own stuff," Quinn said.

She shrugged. "No skin off my nose."

Felice did not want to remove her pink knitted cap, so they crammed the helmet over it and strapped it under her chin. Her small face was dwarfed by the getup, and Quinn took a picture with his cell phone to send Bonnie.

"Can I sit with Mr. Doug?" Felice said. "He's good at finding animals."

Quinn shot a look at Doug, who shoved his glasses up his nose and nodded.

"All right, then," Quinn said. "I guess I'm your shotgun passenger, Trinidad."

That notion sent her stomach flipping. What secrets are you keeping from me? she wanted to holler. Wrong place. Wrong moment.

"Hop on in and buckle up. Enjoy your ride," Lydia said. "I'll email you the information on how to leave a stellar review."

Trinidad and Quinn exchanged a look. *Stellar, huh?*

Another bike was pulling up at the return, bearing four red-cheeked visitors. "We got it all on video," the woman squealed.

Lydia flashed them an enormous smile. "Gotta go."

Trinidad remembered what the boys had caught with their drone. But this was going to be purely a recreational ride where they could celebrate Felice and forget about it all: the murder, the crow with the bone, Cherry, and Quinn's shady land deal. Especially that.

As she looked ahead, the trees crept closer to the tracks, dark shadow fingers closing around them like a giant hand.

She swallowed down the surge of foreboding.

Just a birthday ride, she told herself. What could go wrong?

Buckled in, helmets on, they pedaled off. Felice's squeals of excitement made something dance inside Trinidad and helped the angst drop away. The railbike was easy to pedal, and she had Quinn's long legs to assist. When she took a quick look, Doug's smile echoed Felice's jack-o'-lantern grin. Felice put her arms up and shouted, "Whee!" at top volume, which made them all laugh. This auntie thing was a good gig, she told herself. All the fun of parenting but none of the worry.

They pedaled easily away from the station. The wind rushing at them was cold, and she reached behind to zip Felice's jacket all the way. But Doug got there first, pulling it carefully up but stopping short of potentially pinching her chin. "Thank you, Mr. Doug," Felice said.

He nodded, without answering.

Felice was holding on tight to her seat, face awash in wonder. They pedaled on, out of town in the direction of Linger Longer Road, which took them along grassy stretches of green.

Another half hour and they could see the slope that led up to the Station. "Way up there is where you live, Felice," Quinn explained.

"Hi, Mommy!" Felice shrilled.

Quinn's legs slowed a fraction as they passed. "This is where they'll probably lay the tracks that will go through my property," he said, gloomily. "Gonna take folks across an acre to meet the tracks on the eastern side. Then it's smooth sailing to the Wallowas. Real scenic. Postcard stuff, is how Forge put it."

She looked at his profile, chin set, and a muscle in his jaw jumping. Confrontation did not come naturally to Trinidad. That might explain why she loved her job making ice cream. As messy as people's lives could be, they were rarely upset or angry when they were ordering a fantastic frozen dessert. It was almost magical the way ice cream made people happy. Enduring Gabe's betrayal and sniffing out a murderer in the summer had shored up Trinidad's spine, however. She could not endure much longer the suspicion that was growing like a persistent weed in her soul. *Best to know*, she thought. *You can survive the truth, you've done it before.* "Quinn," she said, after a breath. "I've heard you sold your land to Forge for a fraction of what it's worth." Her stomach clenched.

He jerked a look at her, almost as if he was in pain. Then he huffed out a breath. "Yeah. I did."

Why, why, why? They stopped to watch a rabbit nosing greens on the edge of the tracks. Quinn mechanically took a picture, but Trinidad did not think his heart was in it. She clenched her teeth together to keep from smoothing over the painful quiet.

When his silence told her he was not going to explain, she tried to conceal her hurt. "I guess it's not my business. I apologize for bringing it up."

"You don't have anything to apologize for." Then suddenly he snatched up her hand and squeezed hard. "I need to tell you something. This…" He shook his head and lowered his voice. "This hiding stuff isn't good." He shot an anxious glance toward his brother. Doug was tracking a red-feathered bird that had caught Felice's attention. She knew that he had almost superhuman powers of hearing, though. Now Quinn leaned closer. "I can't tell you right now, okay?" he breathed in her ear, sending shivers along her side. "But I will. I want to."

She realized he was keeping a secret from his brother too. It made her feel both better and more worried that he'd seemingly decided to unburden himself at an appropriate time. What would he say? And how might their relationship change because of it? Whatever it was, it was going to be a bombshell.

The bitter memory resurfaced, the moment Gabe had sat across from her at the antique table in their Portland apartment on a rainy weekday morning surrounded by half-packed moving boxes and said, "Honey, I need to tell you something else."

Something else? Aside from the fact that he was unfaithful? She'd learned he was cheating on her. It was the reason they'd split and were packing up their lives into separate piles in as amicable a fashion as possible after the divorce. The truth had come out that he'd been married previously, to Bonnie and had married Juliette before the ink was dry on their marriage dissolution, but the last revelation landed like a nuclear blast. Gabe had been busily helping himself to the proceeds from the various businesses for which he was an accountant. His bosses' accusations were true. Gabe wasn't merely a philanderer but a criminal as well. She must have been a fool not to know something was up, but Juliette and Bonnie hadn't known about the other marriages or criminal activity either.

Bonnie and Juliette were smart women, even if she doubted her own mental prowess. And they'd all been duped. But this was different. Quinn hadn't tricked her.

Had he? Was his secret going to change the way she saw him?

A shiver seized her body. What if he was married? That thought made her feel ill.

He'd dropped her hand, or maybe she'd edged her fingers from his. Either way, he was now staring out into the woods as they pedaled, wheels squeaking along the rails in a musical rhythm. Overhead, branches filtered the waning light. Her phone tickled as it buzzed in her pocket, but she ignored it.

Keep pedaling, she told herself. If it was the twins, Juliette could help them. Whatever happened later between her and Quinn, this was Felice's moment, and she was determined to be as mentally present as she could be. Crows flitted from branch to branch. Felice chortled as a shining black feather drifted down from the treetops. Doug flung out a long arm and caught it for her.

"Oh, thank you, Mr. Doug," Felice said. "I'm gonna put it in my jar."

Trinidad wasn't sure who looked more pleased, Felice or Doug for having obtained the treasure. They pedaled some more and used the fancy assisted motor to coast for a while.

"Look at the squirrel chomping that pine cone," Quinn said.

But Trinidad's eyes had fastened on something else. A man in uniform. Officer Chang, prowling along in a stretch of trees. He was peering at the ground, walking in a slow and methodical route that took him in and out of their vision.

"Is that…?" Quinn asked.

"Yes," she confirmed.

Quinn didn't ask the question. What was Officer Chang looking for?

The open fields were coming into view. A crow cawed as it launched its heavy body from one branch to another. Upset at Chang's presence? At the rail bike passing through its domain?

The knowledge coalesced in one sickening rush. It could not be a coincidence that Chang had been dispatched to search the very spot the twins had videoed the crow with the bone. If it had been only an animal bone, the police would have no reason to be searching the woods.

"What is it?" Quinn whispered. "You went pale."

She swallowed as they wheeled smoothly along. Chang planted a colored flag next to a small sparkling white stone.

Not a stone.

A bone. Another one.

Chang bent to photograph the spot as a second officer came into view leading a K-9, a bloodhound straining against the leash.

A tracking dog, sent in for one reason.

To find a body.

Fighting panic, she tried to keep her voice calm. "I'll tell you when we get back."

He nodded in understanding. "I think I have the general idea after seeing that dog. It's not good, is it?"

She shook her head.

Felice and Doug were counting crows as they rolled into the grassy clearing that was captured in the twins' video.

The clearing where a crow perched in a tree with a bone it its claw.

And now there were more.

Chapter Fourteen

THE RIDE BACK TOWARD THE station passed in a blur. Trinidad tried to keep up with Felice's lively comments, as did Quinn, but she couldn't focus after seeing Officer Chang and the dog. She could be wrong, but her gut told her differently.

The twins had been right, and the bone was human. And now there were more. Who did they belong to? Her mind leapt to Cherry Lighter. But there was nothing but her twin-fueled suspicions to suggest that. The temperature had dropped into the forties range, and Trinidad's skin was all goose-bumpy, or maybe that was more a reflection of her mental climate. They completed the agonizingly slow trip back to the railriders depot.

Lydia was on the phone when they derailed and entered. "So, what if they are human bones, Chief?"

Trinidad and Quinn exchanged a look. He cleared his throat, and Lydia darted a look at them. "You poke around the woods all you want," she snarled into the phone, "but the railroad tracks are on our property, so that's private and you'd better have a properly executed search warrant."

Bigley's reply must have been frosty. "Fine, then. Do what you have to do, but don't discourage my riders. Haven't we had enough bad news floating around with Forge's murder?" A murder, Trinidad noted, that had resulted in a new business venture for Lydia and Zap. "I can't talk now." Lydia slammed down her cell phone so hard Trinidad wouldn't have been surprised if it cracked in half.

Lydia's smile was forced, reminiscent of a grinning skull as she collected their helmets. "How did you enjoy your ride?"

Felice gave her a thumbs-up, and so did Doug. Trinidad and Quinn added their praise.

"Great," she said without looking directly at them. "So I've gotta lock up in a minute. Stand in front of that poster, and I'll take your picture for the birthday wall." It did not seem to be a request, so they gathered dutifully in front of a floor-to-ceiling poster with the Forge Railriders emblem and a photo of a rail bike against a luxurious wooded landscape. On the count of three they "cheesed" appropriately, and Lydia pushed an orange goody bag at Felice. "Happy birthday from Forge Railriders. There's a present and a coupon inside for 20 percent off if you bring a friend. You have lots of friends, right?"

Trinidad jumped in before Lydia demanded the names and emails of Felice's playmates. "Will do, Lydia. Thank you very much." Doug and Felice walked toward the door, far enough away that Trinidad could make her comment without being overheard.

"We saw the police searching along the tracks," she said.

Lydia glowered. "I know. Some rigamarole about bones. The coroner concluded the first one they found was human. But it's from a long time ago, right? And the crow could have carried it here from who knows where? Those birds built a nest in that grove of trees behind the depot. Nothing to do with me or Zap or this business." She jingled her keys meaningfully. Trinidad took the hint and walked out with Quinn.

"Cold," Quinn said when they were outside. She was not sure if he was talking about Lydia or the weather.

Felice was smiling, and that was a win, anyway. The child was not as skilled as Noodles at picking up on emotions.

"Meet you back at the Shimmy," Quinn said. He and Doug got in their truck.

In the Pinto, Felice carefully slid the feather into her treasure jar. They chatted about the ride, which Felice had enjoyed tremendously, oblivious to the police activity. She listed the animals she'd seen as they tootled along. Pulling up at the Shimmy, they found the CLOSED sign displayed and Bonnie and Juliette inside, along with Papa Luis and Noodles. They'd covered the tables with cheerful place mats, and a small pile of presents adorned the counter. There were no balloons, as Bonnie maintained they were dangerous to animals and damaging to the environment. Quinn and Doug strolled in a minute afterward.

Felice hugged her mother and rambled on about all the sights, including the crow feather that Doug had obtained. "See?" She thrust the jar up at her mother.

"More treasure?" Bonnie said. "I am going to have to find another jar for you."

Felice pulled a stuffed animal out of the bag Lydia had given her and held it up for them to see.

Juliette frowned. "Is it a hamster?"

"That needs an orthodontist?" Quinn added.

"Beaver," Doug corrected.

"Ah," Quinn said. "That explains the front teeth."

On the stuffed animal's chest was a gold sticker badge printed with "Forge Railriders." Around its neck was a beaded necklace with a charm that read "Betty."

"You're kidding," Juliette said. "Betty the Beaver is the face of Railriders? Ramona Hardwick's Betty the Beaver?"

Felice handed over the small flyer that had accompanied the toy.

Juliette frowned over it. "It's information about beavers in their natural habitat." She shot them a look of pure disdain. "And an order form for a certain *Betty the Beaver Brushes Her Teeth* book."

"That explains why Ramona has reversed her stance on clearing the trees," Trinidad said. "She's found herself a new partner to peddle her books."

Quinn groaned. "I was half-hoping she might find a way to stop Zap from cutting the trees, some sort of legal loophole."

Juliette shook her head. "Sorry to disappoint, but Ramona is on the side of Betty the Beaver, not environmental causes." She hesitated. "I hate to break it to you, but I saw Zap in town buying a chainsaw. Chet at the hardware store was explaining to him how to use it, but Zap looked sort of glazed-over. After he left, I heard Chet telling a buddy that the only thing more dangerous than a chainsaw is an idiot who thinks he knows how to use one."

Out of the corner of her eye, Trinidad spotted Noodles sidling up to the table to sniff at the beaver.

It gave her a pang. When she'd adopted Noodles from the shelter, he'd come with a "lovey" that happened to be a stuffed rattlesnake. Unfortunately, it had gotten lost in the move to Sprocket. Trinidad suspected Noodles had been unrequitedly grieving for that rattlesnake ever since. She picked up the beaver. "How about I put Betty up here near the cash register, okay?"

Felice nodded and stood on tiptoe to scope out the ice cream shop counter. It was time to focus on the soon-to-be six-year-old.

"All right, birthday girl," Trinidad said. "Guess what? We are going to make my special Pickle Jar Ice Cream." She laughed at Felice's surprise. "Don't worry. It's not made of pickles. Everyone got your jars?"

The group collectively held up their containers to which Trinidad added heavy cream, vanilla, sugar, and a pinch of salt—and maraschino cherry juice to Felice's, which turned it a cheerful pink. Caps screwed firmly back in place, she commanded, "All right! Shake, everyone."

Five minutes later, she stowed the jars into her blast chiller.

"Let's have presents while the ice cream is ripening."

Felice crooned over her new nature coloring book and pencils from Quinn and Doug and the sparkly scarf and mittens from Juliette.

Trinidad offered a tiny bag to Felice with a stab of worry. Would she be disappointed in the odd gift? Papa had pronounced it the perfect present for a brilliant child, but Trinidad wasn't sure. What did she really know about young girls? And this unique young girl in particular? Felice poured the collection of polished rocks, rose quartz, obsidian, and agate out of the velvet bag.

She went round eyed with pleasure and Papa beamed. "You see?" he said to Trinidad. "For her jar. Perfect."

Trinidad beamed. "Perfect," she agreed. She wondered exactly what age the pleasure transitioned from receiving a gift to bestowing one.

While Felice was fingering the lustrous stones, Juliette drew Trinidad to the corner and other guests followed, except for Doug, who sat and watched Felice curiously as she sorted and resorted the stones.

"When you called, you said something was going on," Juliette said. "Time to spill it."

Trinidad told them in hushed tones about Officer Chang's presence in the forest and Lydia's information about what the coroner had said.

Bonnie hugged herself. "Human bones?" she murmured. "That's horrifying."

"And it's going to be all over town by morning," Juliette said. "And guess what else I heard today."

Trinidad tensed.

"That Mayor Ramona approached Forge with an offer the week before he was murdered."

Bonnie frowned. "What kind of offer?"

"I don't know, only that he laughed in her face and told her he didn't need her to get what he wanted."

Quinn glowered. "Probably because he'd already gotten an agreement from me to sell him the land for the cut-through."

"Who told you about the conversation?" Trinidad asked.

"The gas station guy, Mr. Mavis. He remembered he'd overheard them arguing about it outside the coffee shop, and he was marching off to report it to Chief Bigley. But he stopped me to ask if he had to make an appointment at the police station or if I thought it was okay to pop in."

"You advised the popping in, I take it?" Bonnie said.

"Yep. If murder and mayhem isn't a good enough reason to arrive at the police station unannounced, I don't know what is."

Papa frowned. "The question is if there is a relationship between the bones and Forge's murder. Perhaps one is entirely unrelated to the other."

"At least we know they don't belong to Forge," Juliette said. "We should look into missing persons cases, people who have vanished in the region over the past few years." She raised a meaningful eyebrow. "Or people like Cherry Lighter, who supposedly moved away never to be heard from again."

Trinidad thought of the letter. She sighed. "This is overwhelming. I don't think I'm cut out for criminal research, especially cold cases."

"Well, I am," Juliette said firmly.

"Have at it," Trinidad said. "But keep it quiet, okay? We don't want to aggravate any local killers, right?"

She shivered. "Right. Been there. Done that."

The ice cream was sufficiently cooled, and everyone spooned out their miraculous concoctions into bowls or shake glasses. "All right, Felice. You just made your ice cream, but you get to pick anything you want for your very own Freakshake. Are you ready to start choosing?"

Felice nodded. Trinidad relished the look of awe and delight on Felice's face. What child did not dream of walking into an ice cream parlor and picking out whatever their heart desired? Bonnie took dozens of pictures with her phone as Quinn hoisted Felice up so she could get a good look at the offerings. When the serious business was concluded, Felice had commissioned a Freakshake slathered in a marshmallow sauce with pink wafer cookies stuck all around the brim, dusted with pink and white sprinkles.

Not one, but two pink lollipops stuck out of the top like antennas, and there were gummy cherries sprinkled all around the plate.

"You should make that a regular item," Bonnie said. "We can call it the Railriders Rager or something."

"No, thanks," Trinidad said. "I don't want anyone to think I'm marketing for them. Betty the Beaver can have that job."

The other party guests were content to enjoy their homemade vanilla flavor with Trinidad's made-from-scratch caramel sauce and a browned butter apple bar on the side.

Juliette's eyes rolled back in her head. "Oh man. This is like all the best things about fall in one dessert."

"We aim to please," Trinidad said modestly, but she was thrilled at the compliment.

Bonnie yawned. "This was a fabulous day for my girl, but I'd better get her back."

Quinn offered to drop Bonnie and Felice at the Station while Trinidad finished the last few cleanup items. He met her gaze, his own strained. Whatever his revelation was, it would have to wait until they were alone. Anticipation and dread circled her stomach.

"I'll talk to you soon," he said.

Felice was pulling on her windbreaker when she noticed the theft. "Betty's gone."

Sure enough, Betty the Beaver was missing from her spot next to the register.

Trinidad immediately approached Noodles, who was sitting on his cushion. Tucked next to his chest was Betty the Beaver, big white felt teeth grinning away. Noodles rested his chin on the toy and wagged his tail.

"Oh dear, Noo. I know you miss your rattlesnake, but that's not yours. It belongs to Felice."

Felice came over and bent to give Noodles a scratch. "It's okay. I have a treasure jar. Noodles can keep Betty."

"Are you sure, sweetie?"

"Uh-huh."

Trinidad kissed Felice. "Thank you very much. I know Noodles thanks you too."

"You are a very kind young lady," Papa added.

Noodles swabbed her hand in thanks as well, or perhaps, it was to collect a taste of ice cream. The bell clamored as the party guest departed.

When Papa and Trinidad were alone in the shop,

Trinidad cleaned the counter and started on the next day's supply of caramel and chocolate sauces. Papa chopped piles of walnuts and restocked the vat of maraschino cherries before he began to sweep the tile floor. She could tell his active mind was mulling over the evening's revelations. Hers was churning like a blender, and she kept returning to the subject of bones. Tucked neatly inside a person's body, they were hardly given a thought, but finding them outside their human container was a game changer. She tried to clean away her nonsensical notions.

"I was thinking about Forge Emberly, the unfortunate dead man," Papa said, as he plied the broom. "He was at the Station when he was deposited in my trunk."

Trinidad's mouth went dry at the recollection. "Yes."

"And now these human bones…"

"Alleged human bones," Trinidad felt compelled to add.

"Alleged," he allowed. "Turn up in the woods a few miles from the spot where Forge was struck down. Does that seem coincidental that both events are geographically close? Might the deaths be related in other ways?"

She tossed a towel into the laundry hamper. "But how could they be? I mean…well…the bones, that first one, anyway, appears to have been there for a while, and Forge's murder was recent. His bones haven't gone missing." No doubt about it: she would be a terrible forensic specialist.

He paused. "What is that quote about the sins of the father? It's from Exodus: 'visiting the iniquity of the fathers upon the children unto the third and fourth generation.'" Papa's Bible was well-worn with use, a tattered old thing.

He cupped the broom handle and leaned his chin on his hand. "Maybe there's a sin in Sprocket that won't stay buried."

The chill that swept through her was so unnerving that she had to shake herself away from it to finish her tasks. She recited to herself while she worked. *Cream not crime—sugar, chocolate, strawberries, marshmallow… Stick with what you know.* Noodles was content to watch with Betty from his cushion as the time ticked away until it was almost ten p.m.

"Another treasure," Papa said, bending to pick up an object from under the edge of Noodles's bed. He handed it to Trinidad.

"Oh, it's the barrette I gave Felice. Must have fallen out of her pocket." She laughed. "It's not very pretty now that she's stripped away all the jewels for her jar." Trinidad stuck it in her own back pocket. "I'll return it later."

A palm whapping on the door made them both jump.

Trinidad figured it was someone craving ice cream and ignoring the CLOSED sign. They must be in a bad way to approach the store so late, especially in a town like Sprocket that rolled up the sidewalks before the sun went down. She was on her way to redirect the stricken individual when Papa exclaimed, "It's the mayor," he said. And then, a moment later, "And I don't think she's here for ice cream."

Trinidad pulled off her apron as the banging on the door continued. Mayor or no mayor, she wasn't about to let anyone abuse her expensive glass door. There was no money in the budget to replace it…again.

Quickly she threw the bolt and yanked it open. "Mayor

Hardwick…" she began, until she recognized the man standing hollow-eyed and staring next to her.

In shock, Trinidad ushered Ramona inside. Ramona lead Judge Torpine by the hand. The mayor was dressed for the weather, in long pants and a jacket over her turtleneck. The judge wore pajamas with no robe, moccasin slippers on his feet. His face was pale save for two high spots of color on his cheeks. His gaze was unfocused, fixed on something she could not discern.

"I found him walking along the sidewalk as I was returning from a weenie roast in Josef." Ramona said. "Something's wrong with him. He's like a zombie."

"He's a sleepwalker," Trinidad said. "Gretchen told me about it."

Ramona frowned, waving a palm in front of his face. "He's asleep? His home is four miles from here. He walked all that way? No wonder he's about frozen."

Papa took his plaid coat from the hook and draped it around the judge's shoulders. Ramona nodded gratefully.

Noodles approached and began to paw at the judge's knee to rouse him, but Trinidad eased the dog away.

Ramona chewed her lip. "Your light was on, and I figured I could get him warmed up, you know, rather than call the police or an ambulance that might embarrass him." She reached a hand to brush the hair from his brow. It was such a tender gesture, and it carried so much affection that it caught Trinidad off guard.

"I'm sure he's okay," she said. "It's best not to wake him. I'll call Gretchen and ask her to come and pick him up."

Ramona did not seem to hear. She was staring at the judge. The years fell away from her face, and Trinidad thought she might be getting a glimpse of what Ramona had looked like as a young woman, infatuated. No, deeper than that. A woman in love, no doubt about it. Was she in love enough to kill her rival Cherry? Or dispatch her political adversary Forge some three decades later?

"I'll call Gretchen now," Trinidad said. She texted Bonnie and got the number. The phone rang only twice before Gretchen answered. Trinidad quickly explained.

"I was typing up recipes," Gretchen said. "He hasn't been sleeping well, so he retired early. I didn't hear him let himself out. I'll be there in fifteen minutes." She disconnected.

The judge began to blink and rock slightly from side to side. "Where…?" he started.

"You're at the Shimmy and Shake Shop," Ramona said, taking his hand and chafing it between both of hers. "It's okay. You're safe."

He clutched her hand between both of his. "Where is she?" he whispered.

Ramona stiffened. "Where is who?"

Trinidad wondered if she should share about her previous encounter with the somnambulating judge, but she figured that was private information.

"Cherry," he whispered. "Where are you?" Tears gathered in the corner of his eyes and rolled down his cheeks. "You never should have done it."

Ramona looked as if she'd been slapped. She stared from the judge to Trinidad. "He's talking about Cherry Lighter?"

"I think so," Trinidad said, burning with curiosity. *Cherry never should have done what?*

And then the animation seemed to drain away from Ramona. She sat back in her chair, mouth sagging. "Thirty years later, and it's still all about Cherry. I know I said he wasn't that much into her, but the truth is he was hooked on her like a drug," Ramona said. "Nothing could separate them."

But something had, Trinidad thought. She glanced at Papa Luis, who had moistened a dish towel and began to dab it on Judge Torpine's forehead. The judge was still in a fog, looking around in confusion.

"You loved him too?" Trinidad said softly to Ramona.

Ramona twitched and chewed her lip until Trinidad saw a hint of blood. "No secret, I guess. I did, but he never had time for me, not while she was around. I was smart, ambitious. Cherry was a party girl, but she had this magnetic power over him. I never could understand it. When I looked at her, I saw a selfish person who only cared about having fun. Why do men worship women like that?" Her gaze drifted to the floor. "I'm embarrassed to admit I tried to dress more like Cherry, do up my hair in clips like she did. Pretty pathetic. I might as well have been invisible for all the good it did." She turned pained eyes to Trinidad, carefully concealed wrinkles beginning to peep through the makeup. The young girl was gone, and a bitter woman had taken her place. "I used to ask myself what was wrong with me—what did I lack, you know?"

Trinidad sighed. "Yes, I do know." The "why wasn't I

enough" question was insidious and unanswerable. She felt pity because she knew, for Ramona, the torch was still very much aflame for Judge Torpine.

As Papa patted the wet cloth on his head, the judge sighed as if he was awakening from a troubling dream. Ramona pushed her chair back, straightened her jacket, and got to her feet. The judge shook his head and the focus returned to his eyes. He looked around.

"Hello, Judge," Trinidad said. "You were sleepwalking again."

His mouth dropped open. "I was? I walked all the way here?"

"Not exactly. Ramona brought you because you were wandering along the street."

He gaped at Ramona and clutched the tabletop. "I am terribly embarrassed."

Ramona shrugged, her self-assured smile back in place. "No problem. Better me finding you than a tourist out for a drive. Your sister is coming to get you now."

He exhaled and waved a thank-you at Papa Luis as he withdrew the damp cloth. "It's so inexplicable, the way I do that. Just humiliating. Doctors have never been able to explain it."

"Perhaps your subconscious is upset about something," Ramona said evenly. "You were talking in your sleep about Cherry."

He jerked. "I was? I don't know what brought her back to my mind at this moment."

Ramona paused. "Maybe you heard about the bones."

Trinidad jerked this time. There was something sly and hard in Ramona's dark eyes, now. She turned to look at the judge to see if the information had surprised him. His expression read confusion, shock, perhaps a frisson of fear? The front door opened, and Gretchen marched in. Ignoring Ramona and Trinidad, she went right to her brother.

"Oh, Alexander. The trouble you get into," she said with an exasperated eye roll. She must have dressed in a rush, white hair frizzed around her cheeks, baggy T-shirt wrinkled along with the sweatpants.

He didn't look at his sister but straight at Ramona. "What bones? What are you talking about?"

"You haven't heard?" Ramona said, almost purring.

Gretchen frowned. "Bones? Did I miss something?"

"There was a bone found in the clearing outside the woods, and more nearer the railriders station just this afternoon," Ramona said. "I pressured the chief into telling me, basically. The perks of politics. They're human bones, but it will take months to get any DNA tests to prove who it was... or what gender, even."

The judge and Ramona were staring at each other as if there was no one else in the room.

"Why are you bringing this up?" Gretchen demanded. "Are you insinuating something about my brother? Or trying to upset him?"

Ramona shrugged innocently. "Neither. It's merely that he's always been so perplexed all these years about what happened to his girlfriend. Now, with these old bones turning up…" She brushed something from her jacket. "Maybe Cherry never really left him after all…of her own accord, anyhow."

The judge's face drained of color as Gretchen's took on a scarlet hue. "Ramona, I don't care if you're the King of Siam, you keep your nasty troublemaking nose away from my brother," she snapped. "The bones have nothing to do with him or Cherry. She left years ago of her own choosing, and, if you don't believe me, you can ask the police. They investigated the whole business." The judge shrugged off Papa's coat and lurched to his feet as if he was going to say something, but Gretchen grabbed his sleeve and guided him to the door. Noodles stood up, ears pricked.

"It doesn't suit you," Gretchen said to Ramona over her shoulder, "to be jealous of a woman who left thirty years ago. Why don't you grow up?" She almost spat out the last two words before she pulled the still-silent judge out the door.

Papa Luis discreetly retired to the kitchen. Noodles sank back down onto his cushion.

Ramona stared after them.

Trinidad had no idea what to say. Even her elegant, never-at-a-loss-for-words mother would have been struggling over this situation.

"Gretchen's right, actually," Ramona said quietly. "I shouldn't have said those things to hurt him. I have a vindictive streak. I inherited it from my mother." Her mouth wobbled just for a moment before her tone turned light again. "Oh, well. The milk can't be unspilt, can it? Or maybe I should say the bone can't be unfound."

"I guess not," Trinidad said. And some scars couldn't be erased, no matter how much time had elapsed.

Ramona focused on Noodles. "Is your dog chewing on my Betty the Beaver?"

Noodles was mouthing the stuffed toy. "Uh…not chewing—loving. Betty will never have a more devoted fan than Noodles."

Ramona shook her head. "Figures." Without another word, the mayor left the store, the bells jangling after her.

Chapter Fifteen

TRINIDAD OVERSLEPT HER MONDAY-MORNING 4:30 a.m. alarm. Awakening with a start, she raced through her morning routine, yanking a jacket over her sweatshirt, and bustled into the empty kitchen to pour coffee and fix an English muffin. Whole wheat, topped with cream cheese and some fresh blueberries. The epitome of good health on a plate.

Papa was outside when she plowed through the predawn chill toward her car. They'd talked late into the night about the uncomfortable exchange at the ice cream shop. Ramona had definitely been baiting the judge, or perhaps Gretchen, or both.

Did she know something about what had happened to Cherry? Or was it simply an overlooked woman exercising her "vindictive streak?" Ramona wouldn't be the first woman to act out in anger against a man who had wronged her. Trinidad herself had used one of Gabe's prized stamps from his collection to mail one of the unexpected bills that had appeared after his departure.

Papa looked up from the plans he was reading by the faint porch light. "Shall I come along?"

"No need. I enjoy the quiet time in the wee hours." Alone in her shop, a feeling of peace invaded her soul, a deep sense of satisfaction that she was doing what she was meant to. Old failures fell away, and everything felt better when she could smell a whiff of vanilla and hear the whirr of the ice cream machines in action.

"But…" He stopped.

She shot him a questioning look.

He shoved up his glasses. "Bodies and bones and…"

"Beavers, oh my," she finished with a chuckle. "Don't worry. I'll be fine. Mr. Mavis and Stan are right across the street, and the intrepid Noodles will be at his post."

"Still…"

"You go ahead and meet with Quinn. He's coming today, right?"

"Yes, and we intend to work the full day. I will cook a pork roast for supper."

A full day meant Quinn would still be there when Trinidad returned from the shop. No more delays. Confession time. She brushed away the trepidation. "I'll meet up with you later."

He allowed her to buss his cheek before she took off. Fumbling for her keys in her pocket, her fingers found a piece of metal, and she pulled out the denuded hair clip Felice had dropped at the Shimmy. She'd return it on her way, she decided, and maybe it would give her an excuse to prod Gretchen more about Ramona's accusation.

The thought occurred to her that Gretchen should be higher on the suspect list. Maybe she knew exactly what had happened to Cherry. If the truth was that her brother had somehow caused Cherry harm, Gretchen would be covering it up for all she was worth. A few probing questions might shake something loose.

When did you get so darn nosy? she asked herself. Right about the time a body showed up in Papa's trunk, was the answer. At least Papa hadn't been branded a suspect. Not for long, anyway.

She drove to the Station. Climbing the steep grade, she felt that same doubt that always crept into her mind about the effectiveness of the brakes on her elderly car. Marco at the garage had suggested she have them replaced, but money being what it was, she'd declined. Perhaps Alpenfest profits would stretch far enough to accommodate new brakes. Then again, whatever surplus she gained needed to be put aside for the lean winter months.

"Brakes, you'll just have to wait," she muttered. Relieved when she reached the Station lot, she was soon disappointed to find that Gretchen was not in a visiting mood.

"She just scolded me for being underfoot," Bonnie said, customary grin in place as she opened the door of the dining car. "I told her I'm six foot eight. There's no physical way I could be under her tiny foot."

"Cranky," Juliette confirmed in the dining car, tying an apron around her trim waist and arranging platters of bacon and eggs while Bonnie started the coffee pot.

"She said she was awake all night after the judge's

gadabout town. He's been sleepwalking again, I take it?" Juliette said.

Trinidad nodded. "Something is definitely preying on his mind for him to be roaming around at night."

Juliette grinned. "Good thing he wears pajamas to bed."

They all laughed over that one.

Through the window, she caught sight of Felice tiptoeing along a moss-covered log. Trinidad excused herself, walked over, and greeted her. "Papa found this on the floor of the Shimmy." She handed over the barrette. "Maybe we could find you some more jewels to stick on. It's, um, not too spiffy-looking without the sparkle."

Felice nodded. "They don't look like strawberries anymore." Puzzled by the remark, she watched Felice trace her fingertip over the green patterned lines on the barrette. Was she feeling sad? Neutral? Thoughtful? Children were a mysterious breed. If only they had tails like dogs, easily readable mood barometers.

"So…" she started when engine noise drowned her out.

Zap's tow truck rumbled to life. He spotted them and rolled down his window. "Hey, Felice. Hi, Trinidad. How's the Pinto performing?"

"Firing on all cylinders," she said, "as near as I can tell."

"You got a dent there in the front fender. I could pop that out easy for you, any time." She thought he looked wistful, as if he missed his previous life before he became a tow truck driver and then a business owner. The man loved dings and dents, and he'd found himself in a world of chainsaws and cash registers.

"What are you doing at the Station so early? Someone need a tow?" she asked.

He yawned and waved an open thermos in her direction before taking a swig. In his other hand was a peanut butter and jelly sandwich, heavy on the jelly. Never too early for carbs. "Nah. I was scoping out the tree project again. I'm thinking maybe I need a better chainsaw. The one I left here overnight is busted or something. Won't start no matter how many times I try, and I even broke down and read the directions that came with it."

A man reading directions? He must have been desperate. Score one for the tree. Felice became absorbed again in her moss, so Trinidad stepped closer to the truck and lowered her voice. "Has there been any word about the police search?" She avoided the use of the word "bone."

"No, but they wanted to come to the depot to search, even though it's a good mile away from where the first bone was found as the crow flies. Oh, man. Bad taste, right?" He laughed, almost spilling his coffee. "Guess they're figuring the crow might have carried that bone from our place and we got ourselves a body buried behind the depot or something. Lydia said no way unless they showed her a warrant." He grinned and drank more coffee. "You don't wanna mess with Lyds. She's a tiger when she's riled. An angry tiger."

An angry tiger that had benefited from Forge's death. She remembered Zap's phone comment. "*I can handle it and no one will know.*" She wondered who he had been talking to. Lydia, maybe? Try as she might, she couldn't think of a casual way to bring the conversation around so she could ask. Giving up, she left him to finish his coffee, kissed Felice goodbye, and got back into the Pinto with Noodles. They passed Ramona driving in on their way out. She offered a curt wave.

Was she hoping to run into the judge at his favorite table? Perhaps try and make amends for the way she'd baited him the night before? Trinidad did not have any more time for nosing around. She eased the Pinto out onto the steep road, once again considering her brakes until the morning distracted her. The sky was infused with color as soft and satiny as freshly churned custard. Swirls of gold and pink shimmered together, and she could not help but slow to savor the view as the light painted the steep green hills and the mountains beyond.

"Sprocket is one beautiful town, no question."

Noodles wagged congenially and pulled Betty the Beaver from under his chest.

"Oh, you brought your beaver? It's a match made in heaven."

Noodles began to groom Betty with his long tongue, giving particular attention to the sparkly felt teeth. She laughed, distracted by a glint in her rear-view mirror. Zap in his tow truck was coming down the steep road behind her.

With one chain saw down and a second about to be purchased, she considered how much money it might require before Zap actually completed his task of removing the trees for the cut-through. Probably cheaper to go with a tree removal service in the first place—certainly safer. She wondered again who he'd been speaking to.

I can handle it and no one will know.

Know what?

Zap's truck came closer. The daytime-running head-lights created an uncomfortable glare in her rearview mirror. Shielding her eyes with her palm, she looked for a place to ease over and let him pass, but the grassy hills that bumped up against the road were irregular and festooned with piles of rocks. Rolling over such uneven ground could wreck her newly repaired axle, no doubt, and might even cause her to flip. She accelerated. The tow truck did not drop back.

"What is the matter with you, Zap?" she grumbled. "Not like the store is going to run out of chainsaws before you get there."

Her acceleration increased the distance between vehi-cles, but only for a moment or two. The tow truck rumbled closer, picking up speed downhill.

"Stop," she muttered uselessly.

Noodles sat up and dropped Betty, offering a bark as he tried to pinpoint the source of her angst. The noise was making his sensitive ears twitch.

"Back off, why don't you?"

Now the truck was close enough that her mirror was filled with Zap's yellow-and-blue front chassis. She flicked her brake lights, hoping it would cause him to slow. It didn't. What was the matter with him? When she was safely down, she intended to give him the biggest piece of her mind that she could spare.

At the bottom of the slope was a bend to the left that would lead back toward town, noted by the SLOW FOR SHARP TURN sign. Zap would have to hit the brakes or he'd shoot right off the road and down the rugged hillside. But it was another hundred feet until the turn, and the tow truck was practically kissing the Pinto's bumper. Zap was driving like a lunatic.

Nerves flashed all over her body. Driving had never been her favorite pastime, perhaps because it had taken her four tries to pass the driving test and earn her license. Parallel parking eluded her, and busy city driving caused her to break out in a cold sweat. The last thing she needed was to be rear ended…in a Pinto which could very well burst into flames.

She tried to speed up a touch more when she felt the truck tap her back bumper. She screamed and goosed the accelerator, causing Noodles to lurch forward. Throat tight, she struggled to keep the wheels on the road. Was Zap trying to kill them? The goofy guy who had moments before cheerfully offered to bump out a dent in her fender? Was that all an act to cover a murderous plan? The turn was coming up, and fast. She was not sure she could make it at her current rate of speed but slowing was not an option with the metal marauder threatening to smash into them again.

The turn came closer and closer. The landscape flashed by. Three, two, one, she counted. At the last second, she cranked the wheel. Half skidding, with a screech of tires, the Pinto squealed around the turn. Gravity yanked them toward the edge. The passenger wheels slid on the loose gravel, and she scraped across a pile of rocks before she was able to force the car back onto the road at the last heart-stopping second. She'd taken her foot off the gas in her panic.

Her lungs screamed for air. And then she heard something else, something terrifying. Pulse pounding, brain spinning, she winced at a terrible squeal of rubber. The tow truck continued on its trajectory. Her relief turned to horror.

She'd done it; she'd made the turn, but Zap had not.

The truck careened off the road down the hillside, disappearing. She jammed the car in park, grabbed her phone, and ran to the edge to look over. Noodles opened his own car door and raced after her.

The tow truck was still plowing onward, picking up speed as it sped down the slope, faster and faster.

Trinidad sucked in a breath. A cluster of enormous trees, their trunks as big around as tractor wheels, nestled at the bottom of the slope. He had to slow, had to stop, but he didn't. Horrified, she watched as the truck traveled the remaining distance.

"Zap," she screamed. For a moment, the world went silent.

Then the ground shook with the impact as the vehicle slammed into the trees, branches crunching with a sound like breaking bones.

She froze, petrified, until her brain finally overrode her body. Since she could not run and call at the same time, she forced her shaking hands to dial the emergency services and then the Station.

"Bonnie..." she gasped. "Zap's had an accident, at the turn."

"I'm on my way," she said. "Stay put."

Though staying put sounded like the best choice, she couldn't. Terrified as she was to consider what she would find, she had to get to Zap and see if he could be helped.

Before she could talk herself out of it, she ran gracelessly down the slope, falling and skidding on her bottom from time to time, sinking ankle-deep into a muddy hole at one point. Noodles galloped along.

What happened? Why hadn't Zap slowed? Stopped? She'd assumed he was up to no good, but there could have been another cause. He must have had some sort of medical issue—a stroke or heart attack or maybe he'd blacked out. That was a much better explanation about his erratic driving than a bungled attempt on her life.

Smoke, or maybe steam, burbled out of the mangled engine compartment. Glass shards were strewn everywhere, the ground reflecting the sunrise in sparkling facets. She stopped Noodles outside the crash zone and insisted he sit so he would not cut his paws. Reluctantly, he obeyed.

She drew closer, crunching along. "Zap?" she called. "Zap, are you all right?" It was a monster of a vehicle. It would have afforded him some protection from the impact. He might be fine. The truck had tipped on its passenger side, front end crushed into the trees.

Why couldn't she hear sirens? Surely they should be close, shouldn't they? She worked her way around to the wheels and climbed up onto the frame. Noodles was barking now, uncomfortable with her actions.

"I'm not comfortable with them either, Noo," she muttered. She made it to the driver's door, which was tipped up to the sky. At first, she could not get the handle to move. But, finally, it cooperated and she was able to shove it open.

Deep breath. Trembling, she hauled herself over the door frame. The inside was dark, shaded by the trees. "Zap?" she said again, but her voice was only a faint murmur.

"You can do this," she whispered to herself. In spite of the terror at what she might find, she forced herself to peer into the cab. There he was, not suspended from a seat belt as she'd been hoping, but crumpled against the passenger door, eyes closed. The wad of key chains he'd kept clipped to his rearview mirror had detached and come to rest on his chest, so it looked as if he was wearing a wild collection of beads and baubles.

Please, don't let him be dead. "Zap?"

He did not answer or stir. Gulping, she climbed in and shimmied her way along to him. "It's gonna be okay," she squeaked as she felt for a pulse with her own trembling fingers. Was there a little beat? And wasn't that his chest rising and falling despite the blood that was trickling down his temple?

"You're alive, Zap," she told him firmly. "Good boy." Then she found his hand and gripped it. "I'm going to stay here with you. Help is coming."

The tiniest sliver of white appeared as Zap's left eyelid lifted ever so slightly. She directed her brightest smile at him. "Hey, there. It's me, Trinidad Jones. You had an accident."

His pupil rolled upward, taking in the smashed cab, and then rotating back to her. "Crashed?"

She nodded.

"Bad?"

"Uh, possibly."

"I'm sorry, Trinidad. So sorry."

Sorry because he'd tried to kill her? Or sorry because he hadn't succeeded? Or neither? "Don't move, okay?" she said as he wriggled.

He winced as if something hurt him deep inside. "Am I going to die?" he croaked.

"Die?" She felt the words fountaining out. "No, no dying. Not any of that dying stuff. No way. Maybe you'll need some stitches. Or bandages and splints and things, but there will definitely be no dying." She realized she was babbling and made a concerted effort to stop. This man might have tried to murder her, but, for some reason, she was desperate to offer comfort. "You're not dying."

"Dying," he murmured again. "Aww man."

"No, I said…" She was about to launch into more babbling when he opened his mouth to speak. She leaned close to hear.

"They…" he whispered, groaning in pain.

"Don't try and talk, Zap," she said, tears filling her eyes. "You're going to be okay."

"They…" He looked at her again, the oddest expression twisting his mouth. Whatever it was, it was obviously important. A loving message for his wife, perhaps? A confession that someone had hired him to drive her off the road? Trinidad's heart whammed. This might be her chance to find out if Zap was a killer or not.

Bending close, shaking, she put her ear to his mouth. "I'm listening." She felt his warm breath tickle her cheek.

"They were already dead," he whispered.

A chill enveloped her. She jerked back, banging her head on a twisted bit of metal. "What...what do you mean?"

But his eyes were fully closed, now, his face serene almost. *They were already dead.*

What had she just heard? An admission? A confession?

"Zap?" she asked again, but he still did not move. It was possible he never would again.

Struggling to keep from screaming, she crouched there nestled between a half-empty pizza box and a musty sweatshirt and waited for help to arrive.

Chapter Sixteen

TRINIDAD WAS WRAPPED IN A blanket and still shivering. Bonnie'd picked her and Noodles up from the crash site and brought them back to the inn. Noodles was right by her knee, comforting, as always. They sat by the firepit. Since two visitors were playing a game of cards in the dining car, they'd opted to debrief outside.

"He said they were already dead? They, like plural?" Chief Bigley said, pencil poised over her notebook.

Trinidad nodded.

"Any idea what he meant by that?"

"No," she said miserably. The fire snapped and crackled with a warmth she could not feel. Noodles rested his head on her lap, dark eyes fixed on her face. Bonnie bustled around with Gretchen, pouring cups of coffee for Chief Bigley and Trinidad. The chief nodded her thanks and drank with gusto, apparently inured to things like mangled bodies. Trinidad could not manage a sip.

"Did you think he was intentionally targeting you?"

"I did at first, but he apologized. Maybe his brakes went out."

Bigley did not look convinced by Trinidad's theory. Her skepticism became even more apparent when she heard about Zap's sinister admission.

"I have to go refill the coffeepot," Bonnie said. "Be right back."

Juliette was keeping Felice busy, walking with her on the log by the trees. This was certainly not what a child should hear.

"All right," Bigley said, setting the empty mug down with thanks. "Time for me to have a talk with Lydia. Chang says she's at the hospital with Zap."

"Is he...I mean..." Trinidad felt hot and then cold.

Bigley touched Trinidad's shoulder, a casual gesture, but there was empathy in it, Trinidad thought. "He made it to the hospital and went right into surgery to alleviate pressure on his brain from a fractured skull. I don't have a further update. He's alive, and that's the best we can hope for right now."

Trinidad had to look away to blink back tears. Zap was alive, and that was such a relief it made her dizzy, but she was also awash in confusion. She still could hardly make herself believe what she'd just experienced. The fear of his tow truck smacking her bumper. The sickening crash as it hit the tree.

And that eerie confession. Was that what it had been?

"Chief, do you think Zap stole Forge's body from Papa's car?"

She hesitated, as if she would not share her thoughts. "He's high on the list, especially now. He's strong, could have easily done the job. He had everything to gain, though there is no proof he knew of Forge's will."

"And he has a headstrong wife who might have helped him," Trinidad said.

"I wasn't going to say that, but yes, he does. And Lydia has been pleased as punch to take charge of the railriders."

Trinidad nodded, her mind wandering back to the depot. "That might explain Forge's murder, but not the extra bones. Lydia seems reluctant to let you on her property to investigate that situation."

"Yep, that's the part that's stymieing me. What does one have to do with the other? It's easy to jump to the conclusion that the bones are Cherry's, but Forge wasn't even a resident of Sprocket when Cherry went missing."

"Were Zap and Lydia?"

"Zap was. Lydia's only been here for five years."

"Could the bones be from someone else who crossed Zap in the past, and Lydia is covering?"

The chief shrugged. "Speculating isn't getting us anywhere. Wish we could get an ID faster, but forensics is a slow business. We'll have a search warrant soon enough for the Railriders property."

Felice was balancing on the log with Juliette cheering her on. Trinidad watched hungrily, eager for a vignette so full of life after what she'd just seen. Felice's white-blond hair trailed in the breeze, peeking out from underneath her knitted hat, this one a red color constructed to look like a strawberry.

Strawberry.

Trinidad stood up so fast, Noodles yelped in consternation at her sudden movement. "They were cherries, not strawberries."

The chief raised a hand. "Did we just segue to fruit? Are you feeling all right? Shock sometimes—"

"No, it's not that. Hold on." She cupped her hands around her mouth and called to Juliette and Felice. They came over.

Trinidad tried to smile and hoped it didn't look like a grimace. "Felice, hon, can I see that barrette? The one I returned to you this morning?" This morning, only an hour before, but it seemed like months with all that had happened. *Focus, Trinidad. This is important.*

Felice extracted the barrette from her pocket.

"Thanks, sweetie." She held it up to the chief. "I got this at Off the Rack in a box of junk that Lydia was giving away."

The chief examined it. "Looks like it used to be pretty."

"It had red jewels that Felice took off for her collection jar." She pointed to the scrawls on the white painted metal. "These green marks, Felice thought they were strawberry leaves, but they aren't." She swallowed. "They're cherries. It occurred to me when I saw Felice's hat."

Bigley stilled as she turned the barrette every which way. "Cherries, huh? Looks old."

"Uh-huh. I remember Ramona said something about Cherry always wearing clips in her hair. The judge mentioned it, too, and Quinn said she loved jewelry and accessories…a ring on each finger, he said."

The chief was silent for a moment. "I'm going to add it to the list of things I need to ask Lydia about."

"Could be an innocent reason why it was at the shop, or a coincidence," Juliette said.

Bigley frowned. "I'd possibly have bought into that explanation a few weeks ago, but with someone stealing the original letter from Cherry, and the bones in the woods…"

"Felice," Juliette interrupted. "How about you go to the kitchen and get a plastic bag so the chief can borrow the barrette for a while?"

"You want to wear it?" Felice's brow puckered in confusion.

Bigley smiled. "I just want to look at it closer. Is that okay?"

"I'll go help you find a bag," Gretchen said.

Felice nodded and skipped off with Gretchen.

"The bones in the woods," Juliette asked. "Is it Cherry?"

"Too soon to tell, but the coroner believes it's female," Bigley said.

Trinidad's spirit shrank. If it had been from a man, then the Cherry rumors could have faded quietly away. A woman's bone, snatched up by a crow from who knew where? Maybe the bird had even snagged it in another town. She thought it unlikely that the crow would have flown any great distance with such a thing, but what did she know about crows?

Juliette cocked her chin at the chief. "Do you think Zap had something to do with Cherry's disappearance?"

"That would be conjecture at this point."

"He said 'they'…" Trinidad said, circling back to the point. "They…as if there were two bodies to consider, or more."

Bigley frowned. "Maybe there are."

Gretchen and Felice returned, and the chief accepted the bag with a thank you.

"I looked into missing persons in the area," Juliette said, earning her a sharp look from the chief. Juliette spread her hands. "Hey, after my time in the slammer, I have developed an interest in justice." There was a slight challenge in Juliette's voice.

Bigley looked a shade nonplussed. She had, after all, been the one to erroneously arrest Juliette for murder.

Juliette flipped her hair off her shoulder and continued. "I found nothing except a hiker who fell at Hells Canyon. He was missing for a few months, but they found him during the spring thaw."

Gretchen clucked her tongue. "That's a dangerous area. Who knows how many skeletons are down there?"

Trinidad's stomach heaved, and she sat down suddenly. Noodles climbed into her lap, warm head tucked comfortingly under her chin.

"Sorry, Trinidad," Gretchen said.

Bonnie returned with a stack of towels under one arm. "What did I miss?"

"Um, it's possible," Juliette said, "that the barrette Trinidad gave Felice might have been Cherry Lighter's. She's taking it for a while."

Bonnie goggled. "Cherry's? But how...?" She shut her mouth abruptly. "Forget I asked. Do you need the jewels too?"

"Possibly later. For now, this will do." The chief said a polite goodbye, got into her squad car, and drove away. Trinidad made a move to go, too, but Bonnie waved her back into the chair. Gretchen gathered the coffee cups and returned them to the kitchen.

Bonnie squeezed her shoulder. "Stay here, long as you like. You've been through a terrible mess today. One of the cops drove your Pinto back up here after they photographed it, but there's no need to rush."

Trinidad sighed. "I need to get going pretty soon." Still, the thought of driving back down the steep slope made her stomach churn.

Gretchen came back with a crate of blueberries and handed them to Trinidad. "While you're here, might as well pick these up and save Papa Luis a trip. I figure the show must go on, even with the bodies piling up."

Bonnie winced, eyeing her daughter who'd gone to scour the grass for flowers.

"Oh sorry, again," Gretchen said. "Was that indelicate?"

Juliette rolled her eyes. "You could say that."

Gretchen huffed. "Well a guy who can't work a chainsaw probably shouldn't be racing a tow truck down a mountain."

If only that was all it was, Trinidad thought. A simple accident. But his behavior had been so erratic. She had to assume he wasn't in his right mind.

They were already dead.

She could not get the horrifying whisper out of her mind. But Gretchen was right in one sense. The Shimmy show did, indeed, need to go on, so she climbed to her feet, collected her berries, and seated herself in the Pinto alongside her faithful companion.

Bonnie and Juliette hovered outside the open driver's

window. "Are you sure you don't want to stay here a while?" Bonnie said.

"Or let me drive you back to town?" Juliette put in. "We can get your car later."

Their concern lit a flame inside her, the warmth easing away some of the chill. "Thank you both, but I have to do this sooner or later, so it might as well be now."

"All right." Juliette fisted her hands on her hips. "But I'm going to call you in twenty minutes. If you're not at the shop, I'm sending a search party, which will be Bonnie and me."

"Make it thirty. I'm going to drive very slowly." They watched her go, Juliette's arm around Bonnie's waist, one woman's head and shoulders above the other. An unlikely pair, an unexpected blessing.

It took all her will and fortitude to inch back down the mountain without reliving the whole experience of the crash. She determinedly kept her eyes on the road and away from the police, who were examining and deciding what to do with the crashed tow truck.

Back at the Shimmy, the twins were blissfully unaware of what had recently transpired as she breezed in. Since they had one more day off from school, they'd offered to spend their Monday at the Shimmy, and she was grateful. They were in the middle of an argument about which athlete was the greatest of all time. Happy for their distraction, she took a quick call from Juliette to let her know no search party was required.

"I still haven't gotten my laptop back from the chief," Diego grumped. "So I can't even put together a spreadsheet to analyze the sports numbers. Then you'd see that I'm right, Carlos."

"In your dreams, pencil neck."

The feuding brothers set to work, and Trinidad did the same. The Alpenfest crowd had thinned in town, but it would hopefully build again for the culminating weekend. Sprocket would finish in style, with their very own 10K Sprocket Sprint race and an honest-to-goodness cash prize for the winner. The runners would terminate at the end of Main Street, and Trinidad hoped each and every one of the participants would celebrate with a visit to the Shimmy. The events would finish up with an Alpenfeast at Bonnie's inn.

She'd invented an ice cream extravaganza specially for the racers, called the Finish Line Freakshake. It was a take on one of their favorite classic milkshakes utilizing freshly churned French vanilla, blobs of eggless cookie dough, and a plethora of goodies decorating the glass and plate. She'd even found white chocolate running shoes tinted a fetching shade of blue that added the right splash of color. It took her almost a half hour to assemble one in order to photograph it and hype it on her Shimmy and Shake social media sites. Orwell arrived when she was adding the final touch, a strip of yellow candy with "Finish line" written on it, an addition that received kudos from her teenage helpers.

"Out of this world," Orwell said as he snapped a picture with his cell phone. "It will run with the article," he said. "Are you ready for the interview?"

She was, and she did her best to paint Sprocket and the shop in the best light possible. She even offered Orwell the prototype sundae, on the house. Okay, so maybe it was a bribe, but she needed all the promo help she could get.

Orwell polished off every last sip and slurp and pronounced it excellent. "I stopped in at the Railriders," he said, rubbing a hand over his stomach.

She stiffened, fearing his next comment might reveal the whole Zap disaster in front of the twins. "Uh-huh."

"Lydia gave me an interview. I took some pictures. She's got a gift shop with a whole collection of Betty the Beavers. That's the mayor's book's mascot, right?"

"Yes."

He licked a dot of fudge from his finger. "Weird partnership, don't you think?"

"I don't know. Is it?"

"What's a railride got to do with beavers and dental health? Lydia didn't want to talk about the details."

"But I'm sure she was thrilled to chat about her business...for your article."

"Yeah, but sometimes the most interesting material is the stuff people don't want to discuss." He was still watching out the window. "All right. I've gotta go. Thanks for the ice cream." With a snappy salute, he headed for the door.

"When will it come out?" she called.

He frowned. "What?"

"The Alpenfest article."

"Oh that. Uh, probably next week."

Next week? "But that will be too late to promote Alpenfest. It ends this Sunday."

"Did I say next week? I meant Wednesday."

"Oh," she said. "Okay."

He left.

Diego shook his head. "Either that guy is the world's worst reporter…"

Or he's not a reporter at all, Trinidad thought. But why else would he come to town asking so many questions about the Sprocketerian skeletons that seemed to be popping out of closets at every turn? And why his fixation on the mayor?

A family of visitors entered, along with Ernst the yodeler. He spotted Noodles and whipped off a peal of "yodelahhee-hoos" that sent Noodles into canine accompaniment, which elicited howls of laughter from everyone. She might just have to book the two as a permanent act.

Her thoughts turned away from Orwell and back to all things ice cream.

After the crowd thinned out, she released the twins for their lunch break. They returned after a half hour, practically running through the shop door, their earlier feud forgotten. "Hey, there's a police search going on at Off the Rack. No one would tell us anything, but Mr. Mavis rode his bike by while we were checking it out, and he says they're looking for Cherry Lighter's stuff. Plus he said Zap was in an accident and he's in the hospital on death's door."

Trinidad marveled afresh at the speed of information flow in Upper Sprocket. Fortunately, her part in Zap's rescue had not been made common knowledge.

Carlos steepled his fingers and pursed his lips. "Maybe the bone we found really was from that missing lady."

"Too early to tell," Trinidad said.

Carlos snapped. "I've got it. Suppose Zap was responsible for her death, so he tried to take his life in a fit of guilty despair by crashing his truck?"

"That's a pretty dramatic scenario," Trinidad said, though she did not want to get into the details of the accident. Her knees still went rubbery when she allowed the thoughts in.

"I wish I could do some cybersleuthing," Diego griped. "I think the chief's keeping my laptop because it's better than the one she's got. That thing practically still uses floppy disks."

"From the Fred Flintstone era?" Trinidad said, wiping down the tables.

They stared at her. "Who's Fred Flintstone?"

"Never mind," she said with a sigh. "We've got work to do."

It was a decent afternoon, as far as patrons went, and she was happily distracted from her dark musings. Papa would be planting his greenhouse soon, and she'd have a ready supply of fresh mint for the winter offerings. Winter meant rich treats, peppermint, chocolate, eggnog, etc. Sprocketerians would host winter festivities, parties, and the like, and they'd want dessert. But how could she make sure her product got to all the holiday festivities? Her food truck would be the key.

Ice cream would be the core offering, but she'd add some warm element…maybe a reverse Freakshake with a freshly baked slab of cake or pie smothered in an upside-down frozen delight. The notions were so exciting she jotted them down on the nearest paper napkin, which was full by the time five o'clock rolled around.

She said goodbye to the boys and closed up. On her way out of town, she saw the yellow police tape across the door of Lydia's shop, as the twins had mentioned. She was surprised that Lydia stood outside on the sidewalk, arms crossed, watching through the plate glass windows. Trinidad had thought she would be at the hospital with her husband. Talk about awkward. What did one say to a woman with an injured spouse who was a person of interest for the police? But she'd been there with Zap, at his worst moment, and she owed his wife a kind word, at least.

She parked across the street and got out with Noodles.

Lydia's eyes were red-rimmed, her mouth pinched tight as she stared through the front window. Inside the store, Chief Bigley and Officer Chang were digging through boxes, their hands in blue rubber gloves.

Lydia flicked a glance as Trinidad approached, then continued her thousand-yard stare.

Trinidad hesitated, second-guessing her earlier impulse. "Lydia, I wanted to tell you how sorry I am about the accident. Is…I mean…how is Zap?"

She shrugged, lips twitching. "Unconscious, comatose, to be precise. He's got a skull fracture, broken ribs, and a ruptured spleen. The cranial surgery saved his life." Her mouth trembled. "And you did, I guess, by calling for help. Thank you." Her tone was hard and flat, and she still wasn't looking at Trinidad.

"Nothing to thank me for."

"No," she said, now turning toward her. "I suppose there isn't, really, is there? You took advantage of an injured man."

Her mouth fell open. "Huh?"

"He was in shock, bleeding, and you didn't have to blab whatever it was he said to you to the chief. He was obviously confused from the accident…or you misheard."

"I didn't mishear," she said gently. "I…"

"Yeah, well, Zap didn't do anything to anyone. And I don't know how that stupid barrette got into my shop. A lot of junk passes through it. People drop off bags for donation, etc. We're not hiding any murders, and I don't appreciate you spreading gossip about my husband."

"I told the police what I heard. That's all."

"And then you concocted some old barrette story. As if it wasn't enough to have Zap hurt and the truck wrecked and a business to run. Things were finally starting to go our way." Her lips trembled. "Thanks a whole lot, Trinidad."

Trinidad's face was molten. Her heart pounded. "I sincerely hope Zap will be all right."

Lydia glared. "Yeah, right. You want to see him sent to prison for something he didn't do. Why don't you just get out of here now and stop inflicting your amateur sleuthing skills on innocent people? You've done enough."

Trinidad had to stop herself from running back to her car. Sleuthing skills? She had been minding her own business, that was all, and Zap had almost killed her with his truck. And how could she keep the barrette to herself when she knew in her gut that it had belonged to a missing woman?

What had caused the accident, anyway? She didn't believe the twins' theory that it was a suicide attempt gone awry, but maybe the idea wasn't out of left field.

Zap's question rang in her ears. *Am I going to die?* But certainly he'd seemed more scared about that possibility than hopeful. Would he wake up and be able to explain everything?

She had no answers, only a twisted sensation in her nerves that there were secrets in Sprocket, both new and old.

Though her ears rang with Lydia's condemnation, she was pleased to see the wooden frame of the greenhouse as she parked. Hunger, fatigue, and emotional distress all fought for dominance, but her relief at being home topped them all with an added swirl of pleasure that Quinn's truck was parked there too. Papa Luis was in the kitchen, and the aroma of roasted potatoes and garlic-studded pork roast made her mouth water.

Noodles greeted Papa, Doug, and Quinn in turn.

Quinn looked nervous, she thought. He smiled at her, but it didn't exactly reach his eyes.

"Hungry, Trina?" Papa asked.

"Famished. You wouldn't believe the day I've had." She gave them a brief rundown. Papa was horrified. He wrapped her in a hug. "You could have been injured, killed."

"I'm fine, Papa, and so is Noodles," she said, when he finally freed her.

Quinn grimaced. "What is going on in this town? Does everyone have something to hide?"

It was a good question, and he must have realized the statement applied to himself, because he flushed before he dropped his gaze. Papa said grace. They were settling in when Officer Chang knocked. Noodles scurried to open the door before Trinidad could even get up from the table. The officer bustled in, nostrils twitching.

"Uh, the chief wanted me to make sure you were all right, Miss Jones. She saw you having the run-in with Lydia outside Off the Rack."

Trinidad was touched. "I'm okay. That was kind of her to send you to check."

Chang inhaled deeply.

"Can you have something to eat, Officer?" Papa said. "I always cook extra in case of visitors."

He did too. There was no one more welcoming than her grandfather.

Chang smiled widely. "Hold on," he said, staring at his watch. Ten seconds later, he announced, "I am now officially off duty, and since I'm here and everything, I would be happy to partake." His brows zinged. "Is that pork roast?"

She laid out a plateful, and they squeezed him in at the table. He began to shovel in his food at such a rate she figured he would probably develop a killer case of indigestion.

"Is Zap still holding his own?" Quinn asked.

"So far." Chang washed down a mouthful with a chug of water. "Guy had a lot to deal with on top of his skull fracture. Preliminary only, but it looks as though he was drugged."

"Drugged?" Trinidad gaped. "How did you figure that out so fast?"

Chang shrugged. "Didn't take a Sherlock. I mean, you could see the pill residue in the bottom of the thermos."

Trinidad abandoned her fork. "Well that explains his

terrible driving." It made her feel better to know he hadn't set out trying to kill her.

"Uh-huh." Chang accepted a golden-brown roll Papa handed over, which he slathered with butter.

"Incredible." Papa eased his own food apart with his knife so the meat was not touching the potatoes or the peas. Never would entrees commingle with side dishes on his plate. Doug was a kindred spirit. His grilled cheese squares were neatly separated from the precisely arranged apple slices, and he ate everything with his fork. Compartmentalized eating at its finest.

"How would that have happened?" Papa asked. "Drugs put into the man's own thermos. Right here in Sprocket."

Chang raised an eyebrow. "You know what Holmes said, 'The lowest and vilest alleys in London do not present a more dreadful record of sin than does the smiling and beautiful countryside,'" he intoned in a terrible British accent. The man was obviously still devouring Sherlock's stories on audio.

"But someone had to have a chance to doctor the coffee," Quinn persisted. "When?"

Chang waved a knife between bites. "That's the problem. Plenty of opportunities. Zap filled his thermos at home, but he made several stops. One at Railriders, where he left it in his truck while he replaced some light bulbs in the visitor area. After that, he swung by Full of Beans and bought a bag of scones. Stan said he didn't have a thermos with him then, so it was likely also sitting in the truck all that time. Zap never locked it."

No one in Sprocket locked their cars. Maybe it was time to change that practice. Look what had happened with trunks left open.

Chang speared the last piece of meat, and Trinidad filled his plate again, for which he thanked her heartily and continued both eating and talking.

"Then there was the hardware stop for leather gloves and one at the Station right before the wreck. Like I said, plenty of opportunity. Whoever put the sedatives in the coffee didn't leave prints on the thermos, of course. They might have been trying to kill him outright with the pills rather than force an accident. He didn't ingest enough for a lethal dosage before he wrecked."

Trinidad's nerves prickled. Who? Why? Chang's words snapped her from her reverie.

"And then there's the weirdest thing: the key chain hanging from Zap's rearview mirror...the one with the A on it. It's one of those things that's split in half between two sweethearts and stuff. I remember getting one for Olivia when we were dating. We noticed it in the tow truck because it's in the shape of a—"

"Cherry," Trinidad finished, resisting the urge to smack her forehead. "Why didn't I figure that out when I was staring at it while he drove me back to the garage? It was Cherry's?"

"Possibly."

"But it had the letter A..." She broke off. "Oh. For Alex Torpine, right?"

"Yep. The chief spoke with the judge over the phone. He has the other half, a keepsake they presented each other. The judge was rattled by the information, but, as I told him, this is a connection. At this point, not proof of anything. Cherry Lighter might have been in Zap's tow truck or somehow he got ahold of her possessions." Chang finished the meal and crossed his fork over his knife. "Man that was fantastic. Best meal I've had in ages." As he leaned back in his chair, he glanced around at his audience as if noticing them fully for the first time. A flicker of worry crossed his face. "Uh, now that I think of it, I probably shouldn't have told you all that stuff." He sighed. "Something happens to me when I eat. I lose all my self-control. Maybe that's why the chief tells me I should bring a bagged lunch and eat in my car." He grimaced. "Unprofessional. Sorry."

"It's okay," Trinidad told him. "We won't leak any information, I promise."

He sighed. "I'd appreciate that." He scanned the kitchen counter, landing on the plate of leftover browned butter apple bars Trinidad had brought home. He eyed their plates, only half-finished.

"I'd better go," he said regretfully. "Olivia will be waiting. Three of the four have colds, and my shift is coming up." He sighed.

Trinidad slid a family-sized supply of the bars onto a paper plate and sealed it with foil. "Here you go. Take it home." The glint in his eye made Trinidad suspect a few of the bars would disappear before he reached his destination.

"That's really kind of you, Miss Jones." He bid them goodbye, whistling, as Noodles let him out the front door.

Quinn sat back in his chair. "So much for the quiet town life, huh?"

They talked over the information as they finished their meal.

"This keeps coming back to Cherry," Trinidad said. "The barrette, the key chain." And, perhaps, that other elusive detail from her visit with Felice that kept dancing just out of reach. It had been bugging her since Felice showed off her treasure jar, but Trinidad could not bring it to the forefront. "The twins have been doing some sleuthing, but no one seems to know much about her—except Mr. Mavis remembers that she bought Raisinets on a regular basis when he stocked them at the gas station. She didn't have many social connections here. It's too bad there is no one in town who remembers her besides Ramona."

Quinn shifted, toying with his fork. "Yeah, that's too bad."

Her trouble antenna began to quiver.

They finished their dinner, and Doug pulled on a pair of long yellow rubber gloves and set to work on the dishes with Papa after Trinidad and Quinn cleared the table.

"That was a great dinner, sir. Thank you." Quinn shoved his hands in his pockets. " Uh, Trinidad, can I talk to you for a minute on the porch?"

His forehead was shiny with sweat. Throat tight, she followed him outside. It was a very long walk, as if she was marching to the guillotine instead of the front porch.

In life there were moments, she thought, tiny ticks of the clock, that changed everything. A sliver of a clue noticed...

or overlooked. A lie spoken that led to disaster. A wandering eye that lit a spark of temptation which would later explode a relationship.

She lowered herself onto the tiny porch swing, clammy fingers laced together. He stood, gazing out at the greenhouse frame. Moonlight gilded the beams, and an occasional moth flickered in and out of sight. Seconds ticked by.

He cleared his throat. "I've been meaning to talk to you, to tell you something. With all this going on, the accident and everything, it's getting dangerous around here. For you. I don't like it." He skimmed his sleeve cross his brow. "You could have been killed by that tow truck, and now Zap..." He huffed. "Drugged? Cherry's stuff at the shop and in his vehicle? That can't be coincidence."

She wasn't sure if she should say anything but decided not to interrupt the long-awaited revelation. Whatever the result, she had to know.

"There's someone else," his gaze wandered over the wood frame.

Someone else. Her heart plummeted to her shoes. He was about to sever whatever her silly dream had been, the frothy fancy that there could be an "us" with Quinn. Again, her heart chided. *Once more you weren't as worthy of love as the "someone else."* Maybe she never would be. She blinked hard against tears.

Quinn seemed to grow shorter, shoulders hunched. "I've been lying about it, or maybe not telling, which I'm pretty sure is the same as lying."

She forced herself to sit there, though her instincts were

urging her to run away, leave him alone, to escape the words he was going to speak. Noodles let himself outside and laid his head on her knee. Gratefully, she stroked his fur, her steadfast friend who had been there before Quinn and would be there after. She would survive it, like she'd survived Gabe.

"There's someone else I could ask about Cherry," he said. "I don't want to, since I don't have a good relationship with her, but, with everything happening, I know I can't keep quiet."

Trinidad frowned in confusion. This wasn't about another woman? Quinn knew someone who'd lived in town back then who'd known Cherry? Her body was still prickled with goose bumps as she caressed Noodles, hardly daring to look at Quinn. "Who are you talking about, Quinn?"

He pulled in a breath as if he were about to run the Alpenfest 10K.

"My mother," he said. "I could ask my mother."

Chapter Seventeen

"YOUR MOTHER?" TRINIDAD FIGURED SHE'D misheard. "But I thought she passed away."

Quinn's face was haggard, shirt improperly buttoned.

"That's what everyone thinks...even Doug."

She was struggling to process. "You...lied to Doug? About your mother being dead?"

He winced as if he was being run through. "Yes."

It took a moment for her to process. "Why would you do that?"

"It's a long story, and, to be honest, I don't know if I would have ever told it to anyone if this whole situation with Forge and Cherry hadn't come up."

Confusion danced through her senses like an errant moth searching for light. "You're going to have to spell it out for me, Quinn. I don't follow."

He began to pace in slow, labored steps. "I didn't want to sell the land to Forge, and I didn't need the money. Well, I mean, we could always use money, but I would rather peddle hazelnuts on the street corner than give up my land, especially to Forge." He almost spat the name. "Those beautiful trees have been there for hundreds of years. How could he possibly decide to chop them down just so people could get a better view on their tourist excursions?"

Yet, he'd sold to Forge, his enemy. Why? With extreme effort, she remained quiet, stroking the dog.

He rounded on her. "I didn't want to tell you the truth, but I can't stand this anymore. It's one thing to keep a secret from the locals…" And here he reached for her hand.

Their fingers met, and she felt the tension in his touch, and the earnestness. The knot of despair loosened inside her. Whatever he'd done, it wasn't about her. The "other woman" she'd suspected was his very own mother. The relief she felt shamed her.

Noodles sat curiously, watching them. Trinidad looked at the roughened hands that clutched hers. His palms were tense, his grip almost painful. "I'm sorry I didn't tell you sooner. I didn't know how. But it doesn't feel right to keep secrets from you. You're not like everyone else. You're special to me."

Special to me. It was as if she was sleepwalking through the conversation. "I…I appreciate your honesty, Quinn."

"I figured you, above all people, deserve it, especially after what you went through with Gabe." He cleared his throat. "And now if there's a chance I can help solve the Cherry mystery and end the danger you're facing, I've got to do it."

She heard him gulp, felt the spasm in his strong fingers. She braced herself.

"I sold the land to Forge because he knew the truth about my mother and threatened to make it public."

Now her fingers went cold. "How did he find out?"

Quinn rocked their palms back and forth, mouth working to put the confession together. "I told you that Doug lived in a group home, right? While I was in the service? It was too much for Mom to deal with after Dad died, and she needed help with his care."

"I remember."

"And I told you when I got out I came home and Mom died, so I became Doug's legal guardian and brought him to live with me on the farm."

"Yes."

He heaved out a deep breath and abruptly got up, resuming his pacing. "Most of it was true, except for the part about Mom being dead."

Trinidad looked at him, his face hangdog and defeated. She realized at that moment, whatever the reason for the lie, it had not been a selfish one. He was worthy of her trust, and she was right to have given it to him. The knowledge made her stronger, steadier. "Tell me about it, Quinn."

He sighed. "Doug had a real hard time as an adolescent. He was difficult. Sometimes he'd get into these meltdowns where he'd hurt himself or smash things. Dad's death kind of put the cap on things, from what I figured out, and my mother couldn't cope. That's why she put him in a group home. I don't fault her for making the decision, I mean, I certainly wasn't around to help, and it might have been great for him, except it wasn't. Doug wasn't designed to live in close proximity to a lot of other people. It's just the way God made him."

He stopped talking. After a long silence, he started up again, voice hardening. "But the part I can't forgive is how she did it. Mom left, plain and simple. I was in Afghanistan, and I got these messages from the home about paperwork and questions about payments and such. I finally got ahold of my mom, and she said she couldn't do it anymore. She said she had to leave Sprocket." Pain rippled across his face. "So she did. Packed up and left Doug where he was. Her child." He snapped out the words like rubber bands. "She ran away from her son and her responsibilities. Doug was alone then. He had no one, and I was half a world away."

Tears blurred her vision as she imagined how Doug must have wondered why his mother had disappeared from his life.

"I managed to get a hardship discharge, and I came home and got Doug out of there. He was a wreck. Fits and rages, whacking his head into things until I thought he would get a concussion. It was really rough the first few months, but, deep down, Doug is a very gentle man. He doesn't have the same processing tools other people have, is all." Quinn paused. "He's also very smart, and I knew he would find out that Mom had abandoned him." He turned desperate eyes on Trinidad. "I couldn't do it. I couldn't tell him Mom left him there because she didn't want to be around him anymore."

"So you told him she died," Trinidad finished.

He nodded miserably. "I told Doug and everyone else that she'd gone to visit a relative and passed away while there. The last time I talked to her she said that she was sorry but she was never coming back so I didn't fully consider the consequences of that lie down the road."

"But Forge found out, didn't he?"

"Yeah. Ironically, it was when he was planning out his railriders idea. He was traveling up and down the state, checking out abandoned railways and figuring which ones might be best to expand his business. Mom lives on a farm about two hours from here and, wouldn't you know, there's a defunct railway across the property. He recognized Mom, of course, but he never said anything until he needed my land. Forge was like that, a person who'd file away bits of information to leverage for his own personal gain."

Trinidad nodded. "When he decided to push for a second railrider route across your property, he looked you up."

"He slithered on over and told me he wanted to buy a section of my property. I said no way on earth, and then he played his trump card. Give him the land, or he'd make it public that my mother hadn't died but run away."

Trinidad groaned quietly, watching the hurt and anger play across Quinn's features.

"I'm tough, I could handle folks thinking I was a liar, but I knew Forge would make sure Doug would know that Mom left him—left us." Now he circled back around to her and scrubbed his head with his fists. "To be honest, I was so angry I'd probably have brained him with a shovel if I had the chance, but I didn't. I'm a liar, but I'm not a murderer." He riveted her with a look of naked tenderness. "Do you believe me?"

She didn't hesitate. "One hundred percent."

Moisture gleamed in his eyes. "Trinidad," his voice broke. "I'm sorry I lied to you. Will you forgive me?"

Forgive him? This tenderhearted man who tried so desperately to protect his brother? She thought how Bonnie'd said the only statistic that mattered was the final score. Fear had led her to doubt Quinn's deeply ingrained integrity. The shadow of Gabe's betrayal had nearly cost her a relationship with Quinn, whatever that might turn out to be, but she hadn't lost him, the final buzzer had not yet sounded.

She got up and wrapped him in a hug. He pressed a soft kiss on her lips that told her how much he'd been suffering and what her belief in him had meant. That kiss electrified every cell and synapse, leaving her breathless. She'd been right. Quinn was a good, honest, decent man and, what's more, he cared for her like she did for him. The notion was sweeter than any ice cream flavor she'd ever dreamed up.

"I'm a coward," he murmured. "I should have told Doug. I should have told you."

"You did the wrong thing for the right reason. Cowardice has nothing to do with it."

"I'm sorry," he said again, staring at his feet.

Reaching out a finger, she tipped his chin up until their eyes met. "There's nothing to forgive where I'm concerned," she said.

She heard the hitch in his breathing.

"Thank you." He kissed her neck and then her lips again. "I was scared that you'd leave me too."

It came to her in a rush that he'd experienced his own

kind of abandonment. When his mother had walked away from Doug's special needs, she'd walked away from Quinn also. They held each other until he was once again quiet. Then they crooked arms together and looked up into the moonlight sky.

"Has your mother been in contact at all over the years?"

"Yes. She writes letters I pitch before Doug sees. She called once or twice in the first few months until I told her flat out what I'd said, that she was basically dead to both of us." He squinched his eyes closed for a moment. "It wasn't a proud moment for me, but I couldn't get past what she'd done."

"What are you going to do now?"

"Talk to the chief. Put her in contact with my mother and hope it doesn't get back to Doug or anyone else in town." He sighed, a deep exhalation that came from a place of profound grief. "I don't know if what I did was right or wrong, Trinidad. And I'm not sure if I should try and undo the damage. Is it better to tell the truth that will hurt him? Or keep on lying?"

Trinidad had no answer.

Selfishly, her heart was lighter because he had trusted her with his deepest secret shame.

I'll stand by you, no matter what you decide, her soul whispered, though she lacked the courage to say it aloud.

Instead she nestled into his side. "We'll figure it out somehow."

Another Saturday rolled around, ushering in the last two days of Alpenfest. Zap remained in a coma, according to Mr. Mavis after his Saturday-morning bicycle ride. The doctors did not expect him to awaken immediately, if at all.

True to his word, Quinn had asked Chief Bigley to stop by the greenhouse construction project when Doug was helping Papa make jam from the blueberries. He'd taken her aside and delivered the information about his mother, Glenda.

"She said she'd contact her and try to keep things quiet," he'd reported to Trinidad. "I really think she means it. The chief's all right, deep down."

Trinidad agreed, but she understood the frown of worry that darkened Quinn's brow. If word did get to Doug that his mother was alive, what then? The final Alpenfest to-do list kept her from seeing much of Quinn or Doug, so she had to shelve the worry in between constructing Freakshakes and scooping ice cream.

She'd been at the store since early morning, determined to be as prepared as possible for the aftermath of the Sprocket Sprint race. The photos of the Finish Line Freakshake were on proud display in the shop windows, alongside a box of handy flyers describing all the sugary pleasures that would be available starting promptly at eleven o'clock. Noodles wedged Betty the Beaver under his cushion and settled in for a nap while the ice cream makers purred and whirred.

Outside and one block down, the race organizers were already bustling to chalk the starting line and lug bottles of water to strategic points. The route was meant to funnel participants in a circuitous path that would deposit them back at the place they'd started, conveniently near the Shimmy and Shake Shop. The massive finish line was neatly rolled up, waiting to be unfurled by the committee as soon as the racers departed.

Trinidad's cell phone rang with an unfamiliar number.

"It's Alex Torpine," he said, when she answered.

The judge was calling her cell phone? When had they attained that level of familiarity? "Hello, Judge. What can I do for you?"

"I wanted to thank you again for dealing with me during yet another sleepwalking episode. You didn't deserve to go through that twice."

"No need to thank me, and it was really Ramona who came to your aid."

"Yes," he said. "She's always watched out for me, whether I wanted her to or not."

What was that in his voice? Something wistful? Resentful?

"The police came to ask me about the key chain and other things," he said.

"That must have been painful."

"The implication is that Cherry is dead, killed somewhere close, perhaps." His tone was level, calm. "Maybe even involving Zap Apperton. And I've heard rumblings that Zap had a motive to kill Forge, since he's inherited the business. Could he be a serial killer, living right here in our town? Or maybe he was an accomplice and now someone tried to silence him. I can't even take it all in."

She walked through her neat pink tables, checking for

any water spots or stains. "It's too early to know much. Maybe when Zap wakes up..." *If* he did.

"It's the letter," he interrupted. "I've always thought there was something strange about it...something subtle, like a note missing from a chord. That's why I asked you to read it. It just didn't sound like it came from her."

She could hear his fingers drumming on a desktop.

"I read a copy from the police file," she admitted, hoping she was not going to get Chief Bigley in hot water.

He didn't ask how that came about.

"And what did you think?" His eagerness communicated clearly. "Did it sound authentic to you?"

"Nothing stood out to me, Judge, except the typing was terrible. But I never met Cherry, so I wouldn't be able to detect anything off-tone."

"Yes," he said, "of course, you're right. Foolish of me to ask you, probably." He paused. "I can see how Cherry's barrette would have gotten to Lydia's store. She was always leaving them places. But the key chain in Zap's truck. That was a special memento." He cleared his throat. "I'd like to think she would not have willingly parted with it."

"But, if it was foul play," Trinidad said, "and we certainly don't know that for sure, who would have reason to harm Cherry? There doesn't seem to be a connection between her and Zap."

"It's the very question, isn't it? I know they always look to the boyfriend, but I loved her. I never would have harmed a hair on her head. She didn't have friends in town that I know of. When she worked for Ramona, she would catch the bus from wherever she was staying to get to work and then leave again for her mom's at Scotch Corners or whichever friend's place she was sleeping that night. I don't think she felt especially comfortable in Sprocket. She only came because I was living here, at least that's what I thought." He paused. "Could be I was wrong and she was seeing someone else. She gave away the key chain, left it somewhere, because it didn't matter to her anymore." He sighed. "I know it would be best to leave the investigation to the police and put her out of my mind. It was such a long time ago, wasn't it?"

So long ago…but it might as well have been yesterday. The ache in his words made it clear that, no matter how many years had passed, the judge hadn't gotten over Cherry Lighter and likely never would. Trinidad didn't think he could have harmed her. "We'll hope the police can figure out what happened."

"Right. Well, thank you for your time," he said, disconnecting.

Trinidad donned a pristine "Shimmy and Shake Shop" apron and strolled with Noodles into the gathering crowd outside, handing flyers to whomever would take one. Her own boldness impressed her. How far she'd come from the shy, wallflower type of woman she once was. Considering the wild events of the past few weeks, the background didn't sound like a bad place to be. Still, the profound relief she felt at learning that Quinn had not betrayed her gave her cheer that belied the murder investigation. Relief and…well… gosh if she wasn't filled with the warm fuzzies in every nook and cranny.

She caught up to Juliette, who was a picture of fitness in her running leggings and tank top pinned with the number 12. Bonnie, with Felice on her shoulders, was also representing her business with a "Join Me at the Station" T-shirt and glossy brochures. The woman was so tall her shirt logo was as obvious as a billboard sign above the shoulders of the crowd.

Trinidad greeted her sisters and Felice.

"Go, Auntie Juliette," Felice said, pumping a little fist. "You're gonna win."

Juliette laughed. "I appreciate the confidence. Who's running the inn while you two are slacking off at race headquarters?"

"Most of the guests have come to town after we stuffed them full of banana French toast," Bonnie said, "but Gretchen is keeping an eye on things while she finalizes the new menu for next week. I'm working with Stan to buy some of his beans so we can offer coffee that lives up to the food."

"I'll be sure to come by," Juliette said, "especially if Gretchen's making more scones. And that clotted cream… and that lemon curd stuff." She shivered. "No wonder I have to run so much. Hey, there's Doug and Quinn. Let's go say hello."

They wound their way through the crowd to the two men. Doug was swathed in a blue jogging suit with a headband around his forehead. His number was taped on his shirt, since he did not like pins near his person. He stood a careful distance from the crowd.

"Go, Doug, go," Felice said with another fist pump. "You're gonna win."

Doug smiled and pumped his fist in return.

"Hey," Juliette said to Felice. "I thought you said I was going to win."

"You can win together," Felice said, with a smile that spotlighted her missing front tooth. That darling grin melted Trinidad's heart like a scoop of Rocky Road on a summer day.

"I have to get a picture," Trinidad said. "Stand together."

She clicked the button and captured the moment. Doug and Quinn, Juliette, Bonnie with Felice on her shoulders, fist clenched in victory and gap toothed, and Noodles, tail erect with Betty the Beaver in his mouth. What a perfect gathering of preciously imperfect people.

When it was time for the race to begin, the crowd congregated along the sidewalks. Ramona held the starting gun aloft. Doug put his hands over his ears. He was still a distance apart from the runners.

"He actually doesn't care much about winning," Quinn said, observing his brother. "He's wearing earplugs so he doesn't get startled by the gun. He just wants a finisher's medal. I'm proud of him." His eyes were damp.

She squeezed Quinn's hand. "Me too."

He kissed her quickly, before anyone else saw. It was not the same as the first kiss. There was something more assertive about it, as if he was making it clear to both of them that he wanted more than friendship. Her heart bumpity-bumped along as he released her.

When the racers were assembled behind the starting tape, there was a bang and a collective cheer as they sprinted away. Some seemed very serious in shiny spandex running gear, and others were more casual, laughing and talking with their counterparts as they jogged away from the starting line. Doug's dark head stayed visible to the side of the racers as he ran with a slightly awkward gait into the distance. Steady, moving at a pace that was comfortable for him, navigating the world with wondrous courage, Trinidad thought. That was winning.

The fastest runners, she'd heard the twins say, would complete the distance in about an hour. "I wouldn't be able to complete a 10K even if I was driving the Pinto."

Quinn laughed. "Me neither. Doug trains by running the perimeter of our property faithfully twice a day. I don't know how he…" He stopped abruptly. His mouth opened, eyes almost bugging out.

She turned to see a heavyset lady with graying hair and cornflower-blue eyes standing a few feet away, staring straight at Quinn.

She looked from the lady to Quinn, and the truth became obvious.

Quinn confirmed her suspicions a moment later.

"Hello, Mom," he said.

Chapter Eighteen

WITH AN HOUR TO GO before opening, Trinidad invited Quinn and his mother into her shop and locked the door behind them. Noodles spent time between the two, nosing Quinn's hand and then his mother's as they sat at the table. He no doubt picked up on the mood. Awkward didn't begin to cover it. Concluding it was too early to ply them with ice cream, she decided she would busy herself in the back room to allow them privacy, but Quinn called to her.

"I suppose introductions are in order. This is my mother, Glenda," Quinn said stiffly. "Mom, this is Trinidad Jones. She's an important part of my life and Doug's, and this is her shop. I share everything with her, so she knows the situation."

Important part...share everything with her... Trinidad pinked with pleasure. He slid out a chair for her, and she perched uncertainly next to him.

Glenda nodded. "I'm pleased to meet you." She had a slight southern lilt.

"Why did you come here, Mom?" Quinn asked.

No small talk. The edge in his tone made both Glenda and Trinidad wince.

"I told Chief Bigley when she called what I knew about Cherry Lighter. I thought you might want to hear it too."

"You could have phoned."

"Would you have taken my call?"

Quinn ignored the comment and sat back, arms folded. "All right. You're here. Tell me, then."

Glenda looked at the table and then took a breath. "Cherry was smitten with Judge Torpine. She told me once they were going to get married, someday."

"Uh-huh. We figured that."

Trinidad was desperate to try and smooth the turbulent conversational flow. "That describes how the judge felt about her, too, from what he's told me," Trinidad said. "But it certainly was not the sentiment in the letter he got which was supposedly from her."

"Things change; people change," Quinn said. "Maybe she met someone else and didn't have the courage to tell him, so she just ran away."

The last two words held a sharp message, and the slight flinch told her that Glenda hadn't missed it.

Glenda turned her gaze slightly to the side, as if she was admiring the sparkling window and the view of Main Street. "The last day I saw her, she was looking especially pretty, her hair was in a nice updo, and she wore a skirt and blouse when she showed up to babysit Doug. When I paid her, she was very cheerful, upbeat. I asked about it, and she said it was the year anniversary of when she started dating Alex Torpine. She didn't exactly spell it out, but I believe she might have been expecting a proposal. I remember thinking she was so young, naive about all the things in life that come rushing at a married couple, especially a very young couple."

Trinidad swallowed. The more she heard, the more she had a sick feeling that Cherry had not left town of her own accord. "Did you happen to see her key chain? The one that was like a half cherry?"

"The chief asked me that too."

Trinidad realized she was sitting at the extreme edge of her chair.

Glenda continued. "She did have it. I know because she accidentally dropped her purse, and everything came tumbling out. I helped her pick up the contents. According to the chief, no one ever saw her again after that day."

An invisible chill chased up Trinidad's spine. The last time anyone saw Cherry Lighter she'd been in possession of that key chain...the one that had ended up in Zap's tow truck. The silence stretched between them until Glenda broke it. "And one other thing."

Trinidad leaned forward.

"One time, only once that I can recall anyway, a month or so before she disappeared, Cherry said that she and Alex had gotten into a fight because she wanted him to leave town with her."

Trinidad raised her eyebrows. She certainty hadn't heard that before. "And he declined?"

"Yes. Said she was behaving like a silly girl. Cherry was

shaken up. She said he'd never talked to her that way before. Gretchen even stepped in and told him to calm down."

Mild-mannered Alex Torpine?

"Anyway, that's all I know."

"All right. Thanks for the info. You could have called and left a voicemail," Quinn said.

"I wanted to see you…and him." Her slight smile was dreamlike as she looked out the window to the place where the finish line had been erected. "He likes to run. Always, since he was a boy. Doug's always been a runner."

Quinn shook his head. "Yeah. He does."

She lifted her chin. "You shouldn't have told him I died."

Quinn's mouth tightened. "Would it have been better to tell him you no longer loved him and didn't want to be his mother anymore?" Each syllable dripped with betrayal and pain.

Glenda looked away at first, but then her gaze swiveled back. "I messed up, but I never stopped loving him—or you. You can believe it or not, but it's the truth."

Quinn started to talk and then heaved out an exhausted breath. "I don't understand your choice, Mom. I never have."

"I know," she said, voice soft as down. "Sometimes I don't either."

He pressed his knuckles to the tabletop. "You know how many times I've felt like a failure? Like I had no idea what to do when he was having one of his meltdowns? When I first brought him home, he didn't sleep, and neither did I. I felt like I was living with a time bomb, but you know what?" His eyes blazed. "We got through it. Some days were ugly, but we did it, and we're still doing it, every single day."

"I'm sorry," she whispered.

"Sorry doesn't cut it. Maybe I shouldn't have told him you were dead, but I didn't know I was going to be his brother, mother, and father, all rolled into one. I'm not smart enough for that, and I was dealing with my own stuff after deployment. I did the best I could."

"You did well, Quinn," Glenda said. "Doug seems content. I couldn't understand how to give him that."

Quinn did not look at her.

Tears started down Glenda's cheeks, leaving wet trails. "I can't fix it. I wish I could."

His voice caught and he blew out a breath. "I guess it does mean something to hear you say that."

Now she sat up straighter, expression imperceptibly altering. "I thought I could...maybe...find a way to connect with my boys again."

Quinn's eyes flew wide. "He thinks you're dead, Mom. I don't know how to undo that."

"All I am asking is that you'll think about it. Doug has always been resilient. You...we...can maybe find a way." Trinidad saw her throat constrict as she swallowed. "Please."

Trinidad heard the love there, the desperation, the regret. She held her breath.

He stared at his clenched hands, a vein jumping in his jaw. Without looking at her, he answered. "I'll try to think about what's best for Doug."

Glenda blinked and nodded. She had no doubt been afraid of total rejection. "All right." She got to her feet. "That is good enough for me. You have my number. I hope we can talk again soon." She hesitated, as if she wanted to reach out and touch his shoulder.

Trinidad launched to her feet and offered a handshake in an awkward goodbye. "Er, nice to meet you."

She held Trinidad's hands for a moment. "It might be hard to believe, after how I've behaved, but I love both my sons," she said quietly. "And I'm glad Quinn has someone to share with."

Quinn did not speak as his mother turned to leave. Trinidad let her out onto the sunlit sidewalk. When she returned, Quinn was pacing. "She's got nerve, right? Walking away from us and then expecting to waltz on in again." But she caught his hesitation, and she knew he was wrestling with the possibility. His expression turned to one of stark terror. "I don't know what to do, Trinidad. What if I hurt Doug worse by telling him the truth?"

She thought of her own brother. Yolo was a free spirit, impetuous and creative, always zipping from one endeavor into the next. His last business venture had something to do with aquariums, and it had been a bust. His romances trended the same way. Yolo dove wholeheartedly into relationships. At the age of ten, he'd developed a massive crush on their twenty-eight-year-old piano teacher, Miss Marsha, never minding that she was married with twin babies at home. Before every lesson, he would bake her cookies or draw elaborate pictures, everything but practicing the piano.

"I'm sorry," Miss Marsha had said to their mortified mother, "but all he wants to do is stare at me. He couldn't care less about the piano lessons. It's weird." And she'd promptly quit.

Unwilling to see her son shattered, her mother had told him that Miss Marsha had closed her piano shop. Yolo had pined for two weeks until his passion fixed on something else...snorkeling. To this day, she was not sure Yolo knew that he'd been lied to about the reason for Miss Marsha's departure. But this lie with Doug was so much more weighty.

"How do you think Doug would take it?"

Quinn rolled his eyes. "Which thing? Knowing I'd lied or that Mom abandoned him?"

"Both."

"I don't know, and that's what scares me."

She paused. "I was thinking what Papa would say."

"What's that?"

"No blessing is free." Love, she knew, cost most of all.

Quinn hunched his shoulders. "Your Papa is a wise man, and a good one too."

"And so are you," she said, wrapping her arms around him. "Whatever you decide to do, I'll help any way I can."

Quinn embraced her, resting his cheek on the crown of her head.

She felt the soft thud of his heart.

Doug would forgive Quinn for his lie.

He had to, or Quinn's heart would never beat right again.

A few hours later, Ernst the yodeler celebrated his crushing Sprocket Sprint victory with a Finish Line Freakshake, as did a multitude of people who hadn't even come close to the front of the pack.

"It's the yodeling," he said, holding his trophy aloft. "Helps with the lungs."

Trinidad and the twins welcomed the customers one and all. Doug celebrated with a bowl of vanilla ice cream, wearing his finisher's medal with pride, his chair squeezed in the corner on the other side of the counter next to Noodles rather than in the seating area.

"We're gonna have to build you a display shelf for your medal," Quinn said to Doug. "If you ever take it off, that is." She could tell by the way Quinn looked at his brother, that his mother's request remained heavily on his heart and mind.

Juliette virtuously enjoyed a small caramel crunch ice cream cone, her cheeks flushed.

"You won, Auntie," Felice squealed.

"Yes, I did, and it doesn't matter a bit that a hundred people 'won' before me, right?" She finished her ice cream. "I'm going home to a hot shower and a couple of hours of trash television. See you all later."

By late afternoon, Trinidad figured she'd probably sold ice cream to about half of the racers or bystanders as the crowd thinned. A successful day in her book. Maybe she could propose a snowshoe race for the winter. Would she be able to peddle Freakshakes to snowshoers? No, the food truck dessert catering was probably still the best idea.

The twins hung up their aprons and scooped up unsold waffle cups full of their favorites before they left. The best perk of working at an ice cream shop.

"See you tomorrow, Miss Jones," Diego sang out. "Bye, Noodles."

She watched them walk down the street, eating ice cream, Diego gesturing with his spoon to make a point. Antagonists sometimes, but always brothers. She hoped whatever Quinn decided to do did not disturb the deep bond he'd created with Doug. It reminded her it had been a long time since she'd chatted with her own mercurial brother. She made a mental note to call him when Alpenfest was over.

Ignoring the ache in her back, she picked up a handful of fallen napkins and swept the floor clean. She was about to put the broom away when she noticed a bit of white sparkly stuff sticking to the bristles. She plucked it off.

"Oh, it's Betty's front teeth," she said to Noodles. "I think you groomed her a tad too excessively. Now she's tooth-less." Something tugged at the tired recesses of her brain. What was it? That same niggling item that had escaped her for days, now. Staring at the bit of felt, she tried to relax her mind and let the detail flow in. Nothing.

Papa took a bag of trash and disappeared out the back door for the dumpster.

With a sigh, she refilled the napkin dispenser and dried the glass jar that had contained the walnuts she'd shelled herself and used to bake the browned butter apple bars. With Felice's treasure jar almost full, Trinidad figured she could use another.

Screwing on the lid, she went to get her keys, and it hit her like a blast of frigid air from the walk-in freezer.

Felice.

Jar.

Tooth.

Diving for her phone, she quickly brought up the prerace photos she'd taken. There was the lovely shot with Felice on her mother's shoulders, gap-toothed grin on display, the tiny dark space indicating a previous occupant.

A lost tooth, but something off about it. That miniscule tooth couldn't have been more than a quarter-inch long. What did she know about a six-year-old's teeth? Maybe she was wrong.

But what if she wasn't?

The ice cream wall clock ticked mercilessly away. It was closing in on eight thirty, and the town was dark, the visitors gone home.

It could wait until tomorrow.

With a stab of dismay, she knew it couldn't. If she was right in her suspicions, it would change everything.

She pictured the road to the Station, long and dark and twisted. With her eyes closed, she could still hear the sounds of the crash ringing in her memory, Zap's broken body and horrifying whisper. Cold sweat prickled her back.

She should be one of those intrepid women who threw caution to the wind, followed their steely nerves into scary situations, the kind that trusted their intuitions and sailed on, fueled by their own confidence. *I am woman, hear me roar*. But the truth was she was more of a Piglet than a Tigger.

When Papa came back, he noted her standing there, phone in one hand and empty jar in the other.

"You look as though you'd had a revelation, Trina. Another Freakshake idea?"

"Not exactly. Papa are you in the mood for a quick ride to the Station?"

He cocked his head. "At this hour?"

"It's important. I promise I'll explain on the way."

He fished in his baggy trouser pocket and removed his keys, twirling them jauntily around his forefinger. "Your chariot awaits, my dear."

Grateful that she would not be alone in a dilapidated Pinto to face the frightening memories, and more grateful still to have someone believe in her, she squeezed him in a hug. Whistling to Noodles, who carried Betty in his mouth, they hurried to the Chevy.

He smiled with satisfaction as the motor purred to life. "Now, then, does your old grandpa get a hint about our mysterious mission?"

"It's too wild to even believe," she said.

"Not for this town," he said.

Chapter Nineteen

PAPA LUIS HAD THE GOOD grace not to outright hoot when she explained her theory about the tooth, but she saw behind the glint of his glasses that he was trying to take it all in, his logical, engineering mind struggling to make the same leap she had. "I see why you were reluctant to call the chief," he said finally.

Trinidad nodded. "If I'm wrong, I'd look like a nut, a bigger nut than usual, I mean."

He patted her knee. "Nothing wrong with thinking outside the box."

Noodles thumped his tail from the back seat where Papa had placed a mat, ostensibly for the dog's comfort, but more likely to keep canine particles off his pristine car seats. She'd called ahead, and, as they crested the steep slope, she saw the lights of Bonnie's small cabin glowing in the darkness. The firepit was a pile of embers and the parking lot was still.

Bonnie ushered them into the dining car, where Felice was waiting, wearing a pajama top and pants with pink unicorns on them. Bonnie was dressed in jeans and a "play like a champion" sweatshirt.

"I didn't really grasp what you were talking about on the phone, to be honest," Bonnie said. "Something about Felice's jar?"

Felice kicked one slippered foot, and stroked Noodles between the ears.

"Yes," Trinidad said. "Felice, would it be okay if I looked at the treasures in your jar again for a minute?"

"Uh-huh," she said.

"That would be great."

Bonnie took her hand. "We'll go get it. Be right back."

While they were gone, Trinidad wandered the dining car area noting the new curtains Bonnie had installed and the antique light fixtures. When Bonnie was finished, the place would be a showpiece for the whole community. She felt a swell of pride. Bonnie was still an enigma in so many ways, but she was growing to be an integral part of Trinidad's life, as was Felice. Trinidad couldn't say exactly how it had happened, but she was mighty glad it had.

A piece of paper, neatly typed in all caps, was taped to an easel-mounted chalkboard. Trinidad scanned it eagerly. Bacon, country potatoes, eggs, and caramel apple scones with an assortment of jellies, jams, and clotted cream. Her stomach gurgled at the thought of all that amazing food. Maybe she'd have to close the shop one day when the snow piled up and stay at the inn.

Bonnie returned, sheepish, holding a bulging pillowcase. Felice clutched a glass jar, empty save for one small pine cone. Empty? Trinidad's heart skipped a beat. "What happened to all the treasures?"

"There's been a slight complication," Bonnie said.

"It was full, so I put all the things in the pillowcase so I could fill it up again." Felice slid the empty glass jar on the tabletop.

Bonnie heaved up the pillowcase. It thunked solidly on the wood.

"Those are all the things you've collected?" Trinidad said, trying not to sound as tired as she suddenly felt.

"Uh-huh. I've filled up my jar six times since we moved here." Felice nodded. "I have a big collection," she said proudly.

Trinidad sighed. Papa pushed up his glasses. Noodles settled under a table with Betty.

"All right," Papa said, rolling up his sleeves. "Seems we have some sorting to do. Just like those scientists who dig through the rubble for dinosaur bones."

Felice was smiling now. "Paleontologists."

"Exactly," he said, grinning at her. "Let's get started, shall we?"

Bonnie laughed and dumped out the mountain of treasures. The contents filled nearly the entire surface. Beads and buttons, pennies and petals, fragments of stone and shell, Felice had amassed an impressive horde. There was even a mini stapler in her collection.

"Tell me again what we're looking for," Bonnie said, bending over the hodgepodge.

Trinidad tried to sound matter-of-fact. "A tooth."

Bonnie cocked her head as if she'd heard wrong. "Come again?"

"When Felice showed me her jar with the tooth in it, I assumed it was hers, since she'd obviously lost one, but then I realized it couldn't have been her tooth in that jar."

A frown crimped Bonnie's ever-present smile. "Well of course you didn't see Felice's tooth in the jar," she said. "The tooth fairy takes all of them and leaves her a dollar for each one."

"A dollar? This tooth fairy is a generous character," Papa said.

Bonnie shrugged. "Maybe whatever you saw wasn't actually a tooth."

"That's why I didn't invite the chief to join in," Trinidad said. "Possibly I saw a rock or shell, in which case I'm keeping you all up late for nothing."

"This is fun," Felice piped up. "I am going to make a button tower."

"An excellent idea," Papa said. "The best way to categorize buttons."

They began to paw through the stash, looking for any bit of white material that caught their eye. White shells, pumpkin seeds, even a sugar cube materialized in Trinidad's section. Papa discovered a white Lego brick and a bottle cap.

Nothing toothlike presented itself. Fifteen minutes passed, and Trinidad was feeling the first flush of discouragement.

Lydia had been right. Her sleuthing efforts only caused inconvenience. This time she'd rustled a little girl out of bed. *Go back to your ice cream, Trin.*

With a whoop of triumph, Bonnie called out. "Ah ha!" She held up an oblong object between her thumb and forefinger. "Yep," she said. "It's definitely a tooth, but it's not Felice's, for sure." Then it dawned on her what she was holding and she quickly dropped it on the table. "Oh man. It's a stranger's tooth," she said, wiping her hands on her jeans. "Who knows what mouth that came from?"

Trinidad got out her phone and used the zoom function to magnify the tooth. "It finally dawned on me when I saw Betty the Beaver's felt teeth that what I'd seen in the jar couldn't possibly be a child-sized tooth."

They all stared. An incisor, by the look of it, a spot of gleaming ivory in the messy spangle. She remembered hearing that dental enamel was harder than gold, silver, iron, or steel. In fact, teeth were the hardest substance in the human body. When other things would pass into the proverbial dust, the teeth remained behind, meager remnants of a life. A wave of dizziness swept over her.

"So, if it's not your tooth, Felice," Bonnie said, "where did you find it, honey?"

Felice wasn't listening. She was attempting to stack ten buttons one upon another. Where in the world had she discovered so many buttons? Trinidad figured there were plenty of guests wondering where their lost buttons could have possibly gotten to, their pants held together with safety pins.

"Felice," Bonnie said again, kneeling next to her and laying a big hand on her shoulder. "Do you remember where you found this...um...tooth?"

Felice glanced up now and gave the tooth a long look. "Yes," she said, returning her attention to the button stack. "I remember where I found all my treasures."

"Was it...?" Bonnie swallowed and wiggled hopeful eyebrows. "At the park? Or maybe when we went to play in Messabout Creek?"

"No," she shook her head, tongue poking through the empty space in her mouth. "Not those places."

"Where then, honey?"

Papa, Trinidad, and Bonnie all hung on Felice's next words.

"I found it here, Mommy."

Bonnie bit her bottom lip. "Here...at the Station, you mean?"

She nodded. "Want me to show you where?"

"Oh, uh, sure," Bonnie said weakly. "Let's go get a flashlight and put some clothes on you."

When they left, Trinidad tried to wrestle her unruly thoughts into submission. The tooth had been found here, right on the property. She battled down another swell of nausea. "But...it doesn't necessarily mean..." She couldn't bring herself to say the word "murder" aloud in this cozy dining car built on Bonnie's hard work and dreams. The land was Gabe's gift, and, although he earned himself a bunk in jail, and the scorn of three ex-wives, good had come out of the morass. Bonnie's inn was supposed to be a place of refreshment and memory-making, not...this. Bad enough Forge had been clobbered here.

Still, she couldn't ignore the fact that finding a tooth

separated from its human container was ominous. An unattended incisor lying around had to be a harbinger of other grisly finds, didn't it? Like the bones the crow had found.

"Wait," she said suddenly, "Maybe Forge lost a tooth when he was clubbed over the head with the shovel. The police wouldn't have told us that detail." If it was Forge's missing tooth, then Felice had simply found a grisly reminder of his murder. Horrible, yes, but not as bad as where her imagination had been leading.

Papa had started in on returning the remaining treasures back to the pillowcase. "Possible, yes," he said, "depending on the timing."

Felice returned wearing a warm coat and boots into which she'd tucked her pajama pants. Bonnie handed them each a flashlight and Felice a small battery-powered lantern.

As they headed along the grassy path, Trinidad quietly mentioned her idea to Bonnie.

"Did she find the tooth before or after Forge turned up in Papa's trunk?" Trinidad whispered.

"I have no idea," Bonnie whispered back. "I didn't even know Felice had a stash in her pillowcase. I guess I'm not the world's most observant mother." She huffed out a breath. "When we left our apartment and started working full-time on the inn, I was extremely busy. In the summer, when the creek was dry, I let her cross the footbridge and play in the trees because I could still see her from the Station." Trinidad heard her gulp. "I don't think I'm going to let her explore too far anymore. My mother never worried about where I'd wandered since I towered over everyone for most of my life, Gulliver in the land of the Lilliputians. It was one of two advantages I can think of for being an absurdly tall woman."

"And the other is basketball?"

She grinned. "I could clean up on any court, even with the boys. Still can."

Felice walked a few steps ahead of them, her lantern piercing the blackness with pools of golden light. As they approached nearer and nearer the footbridge, Trinidad felt her stomach fold in on itself.

A bat zinged across the path and into the woods, startling everyone but Felice. She stopped at the sphere rock. Trinidad braced herself.

"You found the tooth here, Fee?" Bonnie asked.

Felice shook her head. "Nuh-uh, but you made the stopping rule, so I stopped." She held up her pointer finger in a solemn imitation of her mother. "Stop at the sphere rock."

Bonnie chuckled. "And you are so awesome about doing that. I am proud of you, but, in this case, I give you permission to break the rule."

"Are you sure, Mommy?"

"Sure as sugar. Show us the spot right where it was, okay?"

They continued on.

"When did you teach her about the sphere rock?" Papa asked, as Noodles stopped to sniff the scent of the river that now permeated the air.

"The beginning of September. We had workers finishing up on the property and that weird storm filled up the creek so I didn't want her alone out here."

The beginning of September, approximately four weeks

earlier. Trinidad sighed inwardly. Her wild theory that maybe it had been Forge's knocked-out tooth no longer held water, since Felice had found the tooth before the stopping rule was enacted. The tension in her stomach cinched up another notch as they crossed the bridge, the railing still broken from where she'd plunged in.

Noodles whined, the sound muffled by the beaver in his mouth.

She patted his back. "I know this is odd." Noodles never relaxed fully until they were tucked in for the night. Then he could hang the OFF DUTY sign and put his paws up, so to speak. This nighttime patrol was taxing the old dog's energy levels.

They passed over the water like some spooky parade, Felice leading the way with her lantern held aloft. The air was damp and cold. Trinidad longed for her daffodil jacket.

Felice took them to the three trees, the same trees that Forge had marked with an "x" for removal. Zap's chainsaw sat on a rock, gleaming in the lantern light.

Poor Zap. Would he ever wield a chainsaw again?

"I found it in the needles and leaves," Felice said.

They scanned the ground, trailing their lights across the chips of rocks and tree debris. Of course, they saw nothing. What had she expected? That there would be a complete set of teeth lying around? Or maybe an orderly but toothless skeleton waiting to be discovered?

She thought about the crow with the bone in its claw. Perhaps there were human remains buried deep in the forest somewhere and the tooth had been washed along by the river. She whispered her idea to Papa, so as not to upset Felice.

He shook his head. "Wrong direction. The water would have taken it away from here, not brought it."

Another theory melted away.

Felice was flashing her lantern around, watching the spiraling arcs of light. At least she was enjoying the strange outing. Cold seeped through the soles of Trinidad's shoes. Noodles shook himself, collar chiming.

"I guess I'll have to call Chief Bigley," Trinidad started. "Hopefully she won't…" The words froze in her throat.

Noodles's body language had changed. The hair on the scruff of his neck bristled, his ears flat. With Betty still in his mouth, he trembled.

Bonnie and Papa looked at him. "What's wrong with Noodles?" Bonnie said.

They watched as he crept forward toward the trees. Bonnie called to Felice and gathered her up as Noodles continued on, inch by inch, until he was immediately underneath the sprawling oak. She saw now that the roots of the tree snaked all the way to the creek, like grasping claws. Between some of the roots, the earth had given away, revealing a pocket of oily darkness. Noodles sat directly in front of the concavity, shivering. Then he promptly dropped Betty and issued one hair-raising howl that lasted only for a few seconds. Before the sound had died away, he grabbed Betty in his mouth and bolted back across the bridge as if his tail was on fire.

Bonnie's eyes were round with fear, arms tightening

around her daughter. "Hey, Fee. Can you go wait on the other side of the bridge with Noodles? I think he's not feeling well."

"He got sick?" Felice asked. "Did he eat too many treats?"

"That's probably it," Trinidad managed.

After Bonnie released her, Felice trotted back across the wooden slats, her lantern bobbing. When she'd safely reached the other side, Bonnie let out a deep breath. "This isn't going to be good, is it?"

Trinidad didn't answer, grateful when Papa took her elbow. Without a word, they edged closer to the empty place where Noodles had let loose his keening. Bonnie followed a pace behind. The tree screened all the starlight. It was as though they were stepping into a bottomless pool, silent, save for the scuffling of dry leaves overhead.

One flitted down and landed on her head. If she hadn't clapped a hand over her mouth to avoid scaring Felice, she felt sure her scream would have been audible to Sprocketerians far and wide.

"We…we should look there, under the tree," Bonnie whispered.

"Yes," Papa said calmly, though his touch on Trinidad's shoulder was dead cold. "That is what we should do."

Together they beamed their flashlights into the hole.

At first, she thought they'd found nothing more than the remnants of camping gear, some old tent fragment. But, as she leaned closer, she saw the object was a tattered shred of rubberized tarp. Why would that have upset Noodles?

Gripping the flashlight harder, she crouched, focusing

the beam deeper into the hole. The light played over what nestled there, reflecting an object back at them.

It was beautiful, really, smooth as untroubled water, luminous as stardust. A skull, tipped away from her coyly, avoiding the beam of her flashlight.

Never before had she realized that a human skull could be so elegant and perfect. And never before had she fought so hard to keep from screaming.

Chapter Twenty

IN A FOG, TRINIDAD FOLLOWED Papa and Bonnie back over the bridge where they met a quivering Noodles. If dogs did actually express human emotion, Noodles was giving off waves of mortification at having abandoned his post at Trinidad's side. He'd even dropped Betty again in his agitation.

She patted and stroked him as they waited for the police. "It's okay, baby. You weren't designed to be a cadaver dog." The word sent an arrow of fresh horror through her as they walked back. Yes, there was no denying what they'd seen under that tree. A skeleton peered out at them from its place of concealment. Clearly it had been there for a long time. Thirty years, perhaps? Trinidad struggled to keep her breathing in check.

Thank goodness Bonnie was there to deflect Felice's questions.

"Can I have my treasures?" Felice wanted to know.

"Oh, yes. I'll bring your pillowcase to you after I tuck you in." She stopped. "Unless Chief Bigley wants to see anything else."

"She can see my treasures if she wants," Felice said, as she dispensed good night kisses to Papa, Trinidad, and Noodles. "She liked my barrette too."

Trinidad's throat clogged as she thought of how Cherry's mom must have felt all those years, sensing deep down something had happened to her daughter yet never knowing the truth. She wondered if it was better for a mother's heart to always wonder or to be broken by the answer. Somehow, she managed to hold it together in front of Felice before Bonnie guided her away for tucking in.

They convened in the dining car again and waited for Bonnie with Officer Chang, who disappeared into the darkness with a snappily dressed Chief Bigley. She returned first, without her officer. She wore a short skirt and heels, a soft-green blouse setting off her tanned skin and brown eyes. Some sparkly drop earrings completed the look. Trinidad tried not to stare, but she must have, anyway. In civilian clothes, she bore an unnerving resemblance to Gabe.

"I was on a date in Josef," she said, by way of explanation. "Believe it or not, police chiefs do have dates. We'll see if we ever have a second since I left him at the table with two uneaten orders of crème brûlées and the bill." She laid a sleek clutch on the table and brought out a small tape recorder. "I took a quick look. Chang is taping up the scene. I'll need to talk to you one at a time. I can wait until tomorrow for Felice, if there's anything I need to ask her."

Bonnie nodded gratefully. "It's way past her bedtime."

Papa and Trinidad sat at another table while the chief spoke with Bonnie. When she finished her part, she turned to Trinidad and Papa. "Before the debriefing starts, I want to say you are both staying here tonight. We had a cancellation, so we have an empty train car, all set up, with two double beds. Plenty big enough for you both and Noodles. It's too late and too dark for you to be driving down Linger Longer."

Trinidad started to protest, but Bonnie cut her off with a smile. "Really. I want you to stay, and so will Felice. Tomorrow, you can sample Gretchen's brunch. I'll ask her to make extra since..." she swallowed. "Since the police will have a team on the premises at sunrise. Besides," she said softly. "It would be nice to have my friends here, just for tonight."

Guests aside, Bonnie was lonely. Loneliness was an emotion Trinidad knew all too well. Loneliness mixed with long-buried bodies was close to intolerable. "All right. We'll stay. Thank you for the kind offer."

The chief sat down and kicked off her pumps. "You first, Mr. Jones."

"Only if you will call me Luis or Papa. I answer to either."

"I'll try," she said, with a mischievous smile. "Jones sounds like an alias, you know."

He fired back an equally mischievous look. "It is, a product of a long-ago feud between my great grandpa and his brother."

"Noted." She dropped the playfulness. "Tell me what happened here tonight."

During Papa's thorough detailing of the events, Trinidad

tried not to let her thoughts wander out into the dark woods to the girl with the bubbly personality who loved pretty things in her hair and imagined Alexander Torpine was going to marry her. But it might not be her after all. Would that be any better to discover a different person buried underneath a tree for all those years? In her restlessness, she found a clean towel and began to wipe the spotless buffet table. Wasted effort, but the inactivity was unbearable.

When it was her turn, she explained her jumbled impressions as best she could. "I keep thinking about Zap. Did he know Cherry was buried there? Could he have been referring to her when he said 'they were already dead'?"

Bigley considered. "Zap's under investigation. We've got another angle to tackle now that a body's turned up. Here's what we know. Zap was living here when Cherry disappeared. Lydia claims she'd never met Cherry, and that holds water since she didn't move here until five years ago. Zap owned a car restoration business and did towing on the side. I haven't found any outward connection between Cherry and Zap, nor Cherry and Lydia. But maybe one of them killed her accidentally and covered it up. Fast-forward thirty years and Forge was going to uproot the trees and expose the body so they killed him too." She paused. "Tell me again about the judge and his sleepwalking episodes."

"The judge?" Trinidad said. "But he's pined for her for years. The sleepwalking shows…"

"That something is lying heavy on his conscience," she finished. "Don't you think a fifty-something-year-old man would have gotten over being jilted by now? Maybe the pining thing is an act. Could be he wrote the letter to himself, pretending it was from Cherry. Or maybe his sister helped him."

"I thought of that too. Gretchen would cover for him, I'm pretty sure. But, if he killed Cherry, why would he ask me to look at the letter? If he knew it was a fake?"

"He wouldn't be the first murderer to try the smoke screen tactic."

Trinidad frowned. "But someone stole the letter from me."

"Judge could have done it to make it look like there was another party in play, or he had his big sister do it. He's smart, you know, extremely smart."

Smart, yes, but a brilliant actor?

You were fooled by a man who conducted an affair right under your nose and had a family with another woman that he hid from you. So what do you know about brilliant acting?

"I did hear from…er…someone…that Cherry and Alex had a fight a month before she disappeared. He called her a silly girl."

"Yes," the chief said carefully. "I heard that from the same someone." Trinidad was grateful that the chief was doing her part to keep Quinn's family business private. "We're reviewing all the judge's statements from the police file."

Trinidad wondered how the judge and his sister felt about the new attention on that painful chapter.

The chief stretched her arms, sending her bracelets jingling. "Okay. I've gotta stay here to make sure everything is secure. We'll post someone overnight and start digging in the morning."

Digging. Trinidad gulped. "Oh, Diego would never forgive me if I didn't pass along that he needs his laptop back."

She grinned. "I'll return it, but man is his laptop fast. You wouldn't believe how quickly I found out all that stuff about Zap. My computer takes a day and a half to warm up."

Trinidad remembered that Gabe had told her his little sis had been sent to juvenile hall for stealing cars before she reformed. Possibly there was a touch of the rogue left in her. Could be that was an asset in a job like hers.

Bigley's phone buzzed, and she answered. After a moment she clicked it off. "Not official," she said and hesitated for a moment. "But Chang noticed a necklace near the skull, a gold heart, inscribed."

Trinidad braced herself.

"Cherry." She sighed. "It's not proof, but it's looking more certain that it's her." The chief shook her head. "The mom was right, and no one believed her."

Trinidad knew it would be a long time before she could get what she'd seen in that dark wooded tomb out of her mind. Part of the mystery was solved, Cherry's whereabouts discovered.

But two important questions remained: Who killed her? Zap? The judge? Trinidad gulped. Both working together?

And did it have anything to do with Forge's murder?

"Chief, the judge suggested to me during a phone conversation that maybe Zap was involved in…"

"Forge's murder and possibly Cherry's?"

Trinidad nodded, relieved that it wasn't such a ridiculous thought.

"Another bunny trail to follow."

Would it lead to one criminal or two?

─────────

Trinidad awoke disoriented. Somewhere a gaggle of birds was warbling, and it blended with the nightmare she'd just escaped about a crow plucking out her tooth. Oddly the bird had not flown away with the purloined teeth but driven her food truck and crashed it into a tree. Facts assembled themselves slowly in her consciousness as pale-yellow walls swam into view. She was in Bonnie's Sprocket Station, Papa Luis's bed next to hers, already empty at the lazy hour of seven a.m. She was about ready to throw back the covers and begin the morning scramble when she remembered that Sunday was an easy day. The only remaining Alpenfest event didn't start until evening at Bonnie's. The Shimmy wouldn't fling wide the doors until noon. How luxurious it would be to retreat under those soft sheets for another hour of shut-eye.

But Bonnie might need her help, and, with the police starting their grisly work, Trinidad intended to be as busy as possible. Busy was always better.

Noodles got up from the blanket bed Bonnie had provided for him and greeted her for a morning ear rub. Betty was gripped between his jaws, minus her front teeth.

Teeth.

A shudder seized her limbs. Now it was back, all the horror of the discovery in that dark hole, cradled by roots. Not merely teeth, but the rest of Cherry Lighter, too, folded under the tree. She'd talked it over with Papa long into the night. It was obvious, even to their untrained eyes, that Cherry had been buried under the oak when it was a much younger tree—thirty years younger, she surmised. Bonnie explained that her side of the land had been unused before she'd inherited it from Gabe, and, before him, it had belonged to some distant relative who'd never cultivated the property. Quinn said as much about his family use of the fringe area, which hadn't even had a bridge until Quinn built one when he moved onto the farm with Doug.

Cherry had likely remained there, undiscovered, until, gradually…Trinidad's throat seized again…the tree roots grew and shifted, causing tiny clues to leak out: the tooth Felice had found, perhaps the bone carried by the crow the boys had spotted, and the rest of the bones that had been carried by water, wind, animals, or all three to the area alongside the railride.

Who could have buried Cherry under that tree?

Zap? Lydia?

The judge? Gretchen?

Ramona?

Someone else in town she hadn't even thought of?

And there were two murders to consider. Forge had been killed right near Cherry's secret tomb. His murder was beginning to make more sense. He'd been going to have the trees removed, unaware that there was a body underneath that someone did not want disturbed. They'd stopped him before he enacted his plan.

A more sinister thought intruded. Or had Forge actually

known there was a body under that oak tree? Blackmail might have been on his mind. He wasn't above using that technique, as they'd learned from his treatment of Quinn.

Blackmailing whom? The killer who'd put her there?

Forge wanted the railriders route to go through, and he'd gotten that accomplished. What else might he have tried to use his blackmail evidence for? A legal trouble he needed the judge to excuse? A favor he wanted from Ramona? Perhaps the killer had tired of being blackmailed.

Trinidad rubbed her forehead. How did the police manage to find answers when human beings were a jumbled mess of lies and contradictions? She was glad her job was scooping, not sleuthing. Even so, she could not stop herself from wondering.

It was a luxury to enjoy a shower in the railcar bathroom, which was surprisingly spacious, but, then again, most everything seemed that way when one lived in a tiny home. As she towel-dried her hair, she detected the succulent aroma of bacon, so she threw on her clothes and led Noodles out into the crisp Sunday morning. Papa was installed by the firepit, talking to Ernst and rolling a cup of hot coffee between his palms. In the distance she was relieved to see that the police had erected a tent, underneath which they were going about their grisly work. At least Bonnie and Felice and the guests would be spared that view.

"Good morning," Papa said. "Ernst here was admiring my car." He beamed.

Ernst slugged some coffee. "The only car I've seen in this town sweeter than your Chevy is the judge's Mustang. Saw it at the burger burning. That one's a beauty. Says he's had it since he first got his license."

Papa was gracious, though Trinidad knew him well enough to recognize that inside he was mumbling about how anyone could possibly compare the two. "It is a fine automobile," Papa said. "I spoke to the judge about it." He waved a dismissive hand. "He does not do the work himself on the car. Engines, I believe, are not his thing. Clearly the bodywork is not well supervised either."

"Bodywork?" Trinidad said.

"A slightly different shade of paint on the passenger side. Almost undetectable to anyone without a discerning eye."

And Papa's eye was the ultimate in discernment where cars were concerned. He only rode in her Pinto when there was no other option, though he kept her engine running with his mechanical prowess. *A slightly different shade…*

Her heart began to beat a faster tempo. The judge could have had his car patch-painted to cover up damage sustained from hitting something…or someone. But there could be lots of ways for a car to sustain dings and dents besides running into a human being.

Ernst inhaled. "That bacon is calling my name."

They headed into the dining car, which only had two tables occupied, one with a visiting couple and the other with the judge and Ramona. The judge looked pale and dazed, Ramona stroking his forearm. Trinidad was surprised to note Bigley was there, too, frowning as she stood at their table. Her low tones carried well in the confines of the train car.

"Excuse me, Mayor," Bigley said. "I need a private word with the judge."

"It can wait a few moments, can't it?" Ramona said loftily. "In the spirit of compassion and consideration?"

Trinidad saw the chief's shoulders stiffen. "I will be back in five," she said, and Trinidad thought it sounded like she was speaking through clenched teeth. Ramona bent toward the judge, touching his wrist and speaking in a hushed volume.

Bigley walked to the table Trinidad shared with Papa, as Bonnie and Gretchen added tongs to the bacon platter and fancy glass bowls of condiments for the scones. Ernst beelined for the buffet table, as did the other couple. The cheerful clatter of cutlery chimed along with the soft music Bonnie activated through a tiny speaker.

"Papa noticed something interesting," Trinidad said to the chief as quietly as she could, "about the judge's car."

Bigley slid into a chair. "I've been thinking about cars. Zap ran his bodywork business right around the time Cherry disappeared and since he turned up with her key chain, I figured there might be a connection between him and Cherry via his shop. We got a search warrant to go through his personal belongings, but he didn't keep the paperwork from back then." She glanced at Papa. "What did you notice?"

He polished his glasses with a paper napkin. "I was merely pointing out that the Mustang judge owns..."

"The '68," she nodded. "He bought it when he was fresh out of high school. It's his baby."

Papa shrugged. "Perhaps the baby needs a bit more fussing."

"How so?"

"I am not one to criticize a man's relationship with his car, mind you, but a classic requires the *mejor esfuerzo*..." He waved a hand. "The best effort."

"Point taken. So what did you notice?"

"Tell her what you said to Ernst, Papa," Trinidad urged.

Papa told her about the slight mismatch on the paint. "Hardly noticeable, I am sure. Only detectable in the right sunlight. A small thing."

Trinidad hid a smile.

Bigley's gaze drifted in thought. "And this would indicate repair work, perhaps hastily done."

He nodded. "Far too hastily. A perfect paint match is almost impossible, which is why..." He stopped, his eyes rounding as he realized what the paint patch might indicate. "I should have mentioned it sooner, but I did not think it important."

"I appreciate it," Bigley said, standing abruptly. "Time for me to have a word with the judge."

As the chief returned to the judge's table, sending her a "your five minutes are up" message, Ramona stood, gathered her purse and walked out.

Trinidad caught up with her outside. "Ramona," she said.

Ramona stopped. Trinidad saw the smudges of fatigue and the fine lines that her carefully applied makeup could not conceal.

"Yes?" her tone was cold.

Trinidad suddenly wished she had not stopped her. "Um, I was, uh, just wanting to see how you're doing. Uh, with the rumors going around."

"That Cherry's been found at long last?"

"Uh, yes. Those rumors."

She started to shrug and then stopped. "I don't know what to think. If it's true…then she's been right here the whole darn time. And someone in town wrote that letter to trick the judge into thinking she was alive. It's beyond cruel."

Unless he wrote it himself, she thought. Or Gretchen did. Or the jealous woman standing before her. Ramona glowered, as if she read the thought.

"Whatever happened to that girl, he had nothing to do with it." Her mouth softened as she looked toward the dining car. "This might be for the best, though, right? The poor man finally has a chance to grieve properly, and then he can move on with his life."

Was that the slight lift of hope she heard in Ramona's voice? Did she believe the judge would consider moving on with her?

Trinidad watched her go and went back inside. Bigley was standing, now, the judge staring up at her, aghast. "You can't possibly think…" he whispered. "But I never even had an accident. Not so much as a fender bender."

"People don't patch paint cars unless there's been damage," Bigley said. "Cherry wanted you to run away with her. You had an argument. Called her a silly girl."

His mouth fell open. "We were kids. I was working on a career. I…"

Gretchen looked up from her table arrangements and headed right for her brother.

"What's going on?" she said. "Are you okay, Alexander?"

His mouth opened and closed a few times before he could speak. "The police are impounding my Mustang."

Gretchen fisted her hands on her hips. "Why? Why on earth?"

Her brother's skin was waxy, the sheen of perspiration on his brow. "They think I killed Cherry. That I had the car repainted to hide the damage. I never even noticed that paint patch."

Gretchen jerked as if she'd been electrified. She rounded on the chief. "What reason could you possibly have for that wild notion? If that is Cherry out there under the tree, my brother had nothing to do with it."

Bigley remained stoic. "We'll be in touch. Thank you for your time, Judge."

Gretchen closed her mouth and wrapped her brother in a hug. He swayed until he dropped back down into the chair, head in his hands. "This is a nightmare. She's been buried there, all these years."

"This is all theories, the police grasping at straws. Justice will come out." Gretchen shot a desperate look at Bonnie; the first time Trinidad had ever seen her uncertain.

Bonnie hurried over. "Take all the time you need, Gretchen," she said. "I can handle the kitchen work, and I'll call Juliette to help with the finale tonight."

"And I'm in too," Trinidad called.

"And me," Papa said. "I am unbelievably efficient at doing dishes."

Now it was Bonnie who looked as though she might cry as she eyed her helpers. "Thank you," she mouthed.

Gretchen let out a long slow breath. "I won't abandon my post, especially for the Alpenfeast," she said. "But right now I need to get him home, make sure he's settled."

"Of course," Bonnie said. "As long as it takes."

He followed his sister by the hand, but when he drew even with Trinidad he stopped.

"I did not kill Cherry," he said. "Evidence lies sometimes, I know that for a fact."

Trinidad was not sure how to respond, so she settled for a nod.

"Someone is trying to frame my brother," Gretchen added, "and I won't have it." Her chin wobbled before she set her jaw.

"I…" Trinidad started, but she was saved from coming up with a reply as they'd passed out of the train car.

If the judge was innocent, then, perhaps, someone really was trying to frame him. It was possible that both the judge and his sister were telling the truth. Then again, they both could be lying.

It's not your job to figure it out, she told herself, but the disconnected puzzle pieces continued to tumble in untidy circles.

The white police tent flapped in the breeze, the side bulging outward as if it struggled to contain a secret. Shivering, she returned to the dining car.

Chapter Twenty-One

QUINN HELPED TRINIDAD PACK THE coolers into his truck later that afternoon for the finale, which would officially mark the end of Alpenfest. Doug was in the shop with Diego and Carlos bundling napkins and the Shimmy's adorable-yet-compostable wooden spoons into boxes. There was no way she could drive her behemoth Shimmy truck up the steep road to Bonnie's, especially after what she'd recently experienced on that same precarious grade. The assortment of frozen goodies (already pre-scooped into compostable cartons) would have to suffice, along with a coupon to reward those who might be tempted to visit the store again before their departure. Between Quinn's truck and the Pinto, they'd crammed in all the supplies.

Quinn stacked the coolers and fastened them securely, moving in that athletic way that made her heart thunkity thunk.

"The chief won't be revealing the cause of death or a formal ID anytime soon," he said, "but, I mean, it has to be Cherry, right? I feel sick thinking about her underneath that tree all those years. We didn't ever use that acreage when my dad operated the orchard. It all ran wild. Whoever buried her knew she wouldn't be found for a long while." He grimaced. "She probably never would have been, except for Forge and his railriders, and your tooth deduction, of course." He smiled at her. "That really was some amazing detective work."

She shrugged off the compliment, but her pride thrilled with it. "I've actually got another idea too."

"Let's hear it, Detective Jones." She reveled in the renewed easiness between them.

"Forge might have been getting too close to the truth when he decided to disturb the trees, but it could also be that Forge was blackmailing someone to keep the remains a secret. He was going to divert around that particular tree, maybe, if he got his payment?"

Quinn considered. "Or maybe the reverse; he'd agreed to get rid of the evidence in exchange for a hefty payment when he took the trees out. Forge might have gotten greedy and asked for more to keep the secret."

Trinidad groaned. "I can hardly stand to think about it."

"Me neither." He wrapped her in a tight hug. "The truth will all come out soon. Too late for Cherry, but, hopefully, some-one will be punished for what they did to her and to Forge."

She allowed the embrace to momentarily soothe her worries away. He released her and looped an arm around her shoulders while they walked back to the Shimmy.

"What have you decided about...the other matter?" she

whispered. Doug was deep in concentration as he tallied the supplies in the back of the shop, but she didn't want to risk him overhearing.

His brows knitted. "I'm still mulling it over. I don't want to make a bad choice."

"You won't," she reassured him with a squeeze.

Diego looked up from Doug's notepad exasperated. "If I had my laptop back, I could whip this data into a spreadsheet in a hot minute. We might as well be scratching information onto stone tablets. How is that an efficient way of keeping inventory?"

Trinidad grabbed an apron from the peg. "I passed along your request to the chief. She said she'll be at the Station today. Maybe she'll have it for you then."

He fumed. "I think she's gonna keep it. A police chief who steals from innocent young high schoolers. There oughta be a law."

Despite his bad mood, Diego helped Doug finish the packing. Trinidad drove the Pinto with Noodles and the twins, following Quinn and Doug.

When they arrived, they set up their supplies on a table decorated with a harvest-themed tablecloth on the far side of the firepit.

Diego was still lost in inventory land. The young man was definitely one for sticking to a topic. "We prepared two hundred cups of ice cream, allowing for three different flavors. Is that going to be enough? Or too much? Can't exactly reuse whatever isn't sold."

"Thus is the constant tension of food providers, Diego.

Too much inventory and you've thrown away supply money. Too little inventory and you lose potential buyers."

Diego frowned. "No offense, Miss Jones, but I'm going to find a job that's way more lucrative than this."

She laughed. "No offense taken, but, when you come to town in your fancy car and clothes, you're going to want to stop at the Shimmy for a Freakshake, I hope."

He grinned. "You know it."

The firepit was already blazing, surrounded by clustered chairs and tables. Another long table would provide the dinner for the big finale, an all-you-can-eat sausage and kraut spread for which people paid ten dollars to attend. They would be entertained by another yodeling concert and it would all be topped off with a final marshmallow roast and cups of her ice cream. Thankfully no burgers would be torched this evening. Visions of that burning tissue paper reminded her of Zap and the crash, thoughts best put away when there was work to be done.

Papa Luis arrived. After kissing her, he immediately dove into amiable conversation with the people gathered around the glowing firepit. He'd been there earlier to set up the tables while Bonnie took over Gretchen's cooking duties. The sun was slanting across the treetops, and, fortunately, though police tape still kept the footbridge and beyond off-limits, the tent and the sad remains had been removed.

She heard a few of the people discussing the matter as they checked in with Bonnie to purchase their tickets.

"They found her right over there," she heard Mr. Mavis

say to his wife, pointing past the bridge. "No wonder that tree grew so well."

Trinidad kept her disgust to herself as she waited for a break in the action to approach Bonnie's ticket table. "Hey, Bonnie. How did the cooking go?"

Bonnie rolled her eyes. "Turns out sauerkraut only requires a can opener, and Gretchen told me how to steam the sausages in the oven to keep them warm. Juliette looked up whatever we needed to know about making the rest of the stuff. You've got the dessert handled. I handwrote the menu and posted it. Not as nice as Gretchen's typing but better than her handwriting, which is atrocious. We're all set. Way easier than breakfast."

Trinidad noticed a stack of Forge Railriders brochures at Bonnie's elbow.

"Lydia drove up this afternoon and asked me to lay them out," Bonnie said. "I figured it was the least I could do after what she's been through. Zap is still unconscious, and he's showing no signs of rousing."

"I'm sorry to hear that." Also sorry that he wasn't able to answer a whole lot of questions. Despite what his wife claimed, Zap was involved in whatever had happened to Cherry, Trinidad felt sure of it. And his accomplice had drugged him with the intent to kill. It seemed more and more likely that it might be the same person who'd murdered Forge and Cherry.

The next in line behind Trinidad for tickets was Ernst. He leaned forward. "They figure out who did it?" he whispered.

"Not yet," Bonnie said brightly. "But I'm so glad you

could attend tonight. We're going to have a wonderful Alpenfeast." Her unspoken rejoinder was, "And we're not talking about a murder tonight."

Bonnie was right. Alpenfest should finish with a bang, not a whimper. Trinidad tried to keep her own smile as bright as Bonnie's as she approached their assigned table. She said hello to Felice, who clutched an empty jar.

"Looking for more treasures, sweetie?"

"Yes, but Mommy said no more teeth."

"I agree," she said weakly. *Or any other body parts.* "Come find me after your dinner. I made a special ice cream cup for you. Cake batter with pink sprinkles."

Felice lit up. There were some perks to being the auntie who ran an ice cream shop. No cooler job in the world in the eyes of a kid. Others might cure cancer and negotiate world peace, but she dispensed joy in every scoop. Priceless.

Diego stayed with her at their table while Carlos helped Quinn and Doug unload the last of the coolers. As the sun peeked lower behind the pines, Trinidad saw Gretchen arrive, head down, hurrying toward the kitchen. Trinidad hoped she approved of Bonnie's culinary efforts.

Ernst got the crowd warmed up with a yodeling number that sent Noodles into ecstatic accompaniment. At least the yowls were muted now by the stuffed beaver in his mouth. The concert was great, or perhaps it wasn't. Trinidad still had no idea what were markers of success for a quality yodel. The chairs were almost filled by the end, which meant Bonnie would make a profit. Fantastic, Trinidad thought, considering recent events. There was a cold lump in the pit of her stomach as she considered that it was just such a jolly gathering where Ramona and Forge had fought and Forge had later been killed. Was the killer in attendance again? Hiding behind a smile and idle chitchat?

Quinn set out more chairs and gestured Trinidad over. "I saved these for us." Doug was already sitting in his, hands folded neatly in his lap. Noodles snuggled next to him within easy scratching distance.

The scent of meat and kraut filled the air as the kitchen door opened. Gretchen emerged carrying a platter full of plump sausages in her precarious grip.

"Whoa, she's about to lose the load." Quinn strode over to take it from her.

Gretchen ignored his offer to help. "I'm arthritic, not incapable," she snapped.

Quinn apologized and returned to Trinidad. "Guess I hurt her pride."

"I don't think this is her finest hour, with her brother being under suspicion for murder. I'm sure she feels like everyone is gossiping about her."

Trinidad knew the feeling.

Juliette emerged next from the kitchen and set out bowls of sauerkraut, mashed potatoes, rolls, and butter. Her cheeks were rosy with the effort, hair pulled into a tight ponytail high on her head. A massive bowl of tossed salad and a beverage table with coffee and lemonade completed the offerings. Bonnie rattled a dinner bell, which ended the yodeling and sent the gathering lining up at the food tables.

The visitors took their place in the queue and began to

progress through the buffet. Gretchen doled out meat while Juliette and Bonnie handled the condiments. Felice was tasked with delivering each guest a napkin-wrapped set of utensils. Carlos strolled over with a plate piled-high with everything but sauerkraut. "How'd you get your food so fast?" she asked.

He spoke around a bulging cheek. "I can get to the front of any line. It's a life skill I've been honing for years."

She laughed.

The chief, in uniform this time, greeted Trinidad and the scowling Diego. She pulled a laptop from her bag and handed it to the teen.

"Here you go," she said. "Sorry it took me so long to return. I've been really busy with important police business and everything."

"Thought you were going to keep it," Diego said.

Her brows shot up. "Who me? Taking advantage of defenseless teens? Never."

Diego glowered. "Thanks," he said, sitting down immediately at the table, fingers flying over his keyboard.

Trinidad marveled. "I got pretty good as a stenographer, but I never had anywhere near that speed typing," she said, watching him construct a spreadsheet in a matter of moments.

"I do finger exercises," Diego said without looking up.

"You would," his brother teased, spearing his second sausage.

Bigley waited with Trinidad while Diego, Quinn, and Doug went to fetch their dinners, promising to snag her a plate. She hoped the sausage delivery would be soon. Noodles's nose was quivering big-time. Trinidad figured he was probably thinking the same thing.

"How's the case…?" Trinidad started. She didn't get to finish her question as Ramona approached.

"You learn anything from impounding the judge's car?" she asked the chief.

Bigley's expression remained blandly polite. "Not able to say at this time, Mayor Hardwick."

She rolled her eyes. "If he killed Cherry, he would have come clean about it. He has integrity."

Bigley didn't react. "Thank you for your insight. We're trying to be thorough. Cherry Lighter didn't have many enemies that I can find, except possibly you. Interesting that you disliked both Forge and Cherry and both of them are dead."

Trinidad tried to conceal her interest, which sizzled like a sausage in a cast-iron pan. Ramona did hate Cherry, that much was fact. Perhaps she'd lost her temper and the result was Cherry's murder? And she'd despised Forge too. Interesting, indeed.

Ramona sniffed in a breath. "No secret. I didn't like her. She would have ruined him, eventually. More likely she was killed by another guy, a boyfriend she jilted like she did to Alex."

"But she was buried right here on this property," Bigley said, "probably by a local, maybe the same local who killed Forge and sunk his body in the lake."

Ramona stared daggers. "Well, it wasn't me. Keep on investigating and you'll discover the real killer. Forge wasn't worth my time to kill, and he never would have been elected mayor. Incumbents win nine times out of ten. And why aren't you protecting the citizens of this town, anyway? I've put in two calls to your office about this stalker I've got."

"Mr. Orwell? Yes, I got the calls, but we've been busy around here lately and it didn't sound as though Orwell had threatened you in any way."

"He's pestering me with questions. That's harassment."

Bigley raised a hand. "As soon as we're finished with preliminaries on the body, I will have a talk with Mr. Orwell."

"You might as well stop pursuing the judge. Save yourself some time. Though it wouldn't hurt to look at Gretchen. She certainly wasn't a Cherry fan."

The remark had been loud enough to carry to Gretchen, who was walking by.

Gretchen marched up. "No, I wasn't a fan of the girl, but fortunately it's not against the law to dislike people," she snapped at Ramona. "Thanks for the support, Mayor."

Ramona shrugged. "Blood is thicker than water. You'd do anything to protect your brother."

"I probably would lie to protect him, but in this case, I don't have to. He's innocent. On that much we agree." She turned to Bigley. "Chief, may I have a word?"

"Of course."

Ramona left as the two women moved away from the noise of the yodeling but snatches of their conversation carried to Trinidad anyway.

"Not fair," Gretchen said. "This is a plot to ruin my brother, and I won't have it. He's worked hard all his life for justice."

"He's not been accused of anything yet," Bigley said.

"You know rumors can wreck a person's career," she said. "It doesn't matter what the truth is. With a tarnished reputation, he won't ever reach the appellate court level."

"Like I told the mayor, we're casting a wide net, but obviously the judge had a connection to Cherry. And we can't ignore that, no matter how illustrious his career."

Gretchen's postured stiffened. "Remember, while you're casting your nets, that my brother is a lawyer, and he knows all about defamation of character lawsuits." She whirled on her heel and marched to the kitchen.

The chief sighed and retook her chair near Trinidad.

Trinidad caught the shadow of fatigue on her face. "It's not easy being a chief, is it?"

Bigley laughed. "Somebody has to do it." She shot a glance at Trinidad. "Speaking of lawyers, I talked to Gabe."

Trinidad jerked. Well why wouldn't she have had a jail conversation with her cherished baby brother? Nothing odd there, except maybe the chief's mentioning of it. "Really?" she said.

"Yeah. He's hopeful about parole."

Parole? Startling thought. Trinidad had never really considered Gabe's post-prison plans. "Ah," she said. And what was the correct response? *That's great? He deserves it? Where does he plan on settling afterward?*

An alarming thought hit her. Surely, he would not return to his hometown of Upper Sprocket. Would he?

It was dark, now. Light shone from the dining room, the firepit, and the outdoor lamps Bonnie had purchased, wrapping the place in a soothing glow. Sprocket was her home now, her sanctuary, but how would she feel if her slithery ex returned? She filled her lungs with a deep breath of pine-scented air, mingled with the aromas of campfire, well-cooked meat, the distant fragrance of an approaching autumn. Right now, right here, she would not let thoughts of Gabe intrude. As the silence spooled out between them, the chief was distracted by a text on her phone.

Trinidad's nerves twanged. Try as she might to enjoy the small-town moment, something inside was still poking with insistent jabs. It was the same feeling she'd gotten over that tooth in the jar thing. Was it thoughts of Gabe? The case against the judge? Memories of what they had found in this idyllic spot?

There was a detail out of reach, fluttering on the edges of her mind. *Think, think.* But the crowds began to toss their food remains in the trash and recycling bins, a sure sign they were ready for dessert. Still nothing had materialized in her brain. Mechanically, she served up the ice cream cups to the milling crowd.

Cups of caramel crunch.

Two apple pie flavors.

Felice's cake batter and sprinkles.

Happy chatter and laughter infused the cozy scene. Yet, still, there was the tug of something out of her reach, strong now, insistent. Scoop, scoop, scoop. Nothing. It was maddening.

When it began to approach nine o'clock, the air grew cold, and most people headed for their cars. Only a few die-hards, including Papa in his plaid jacket, remained around the firepit. Ramona sat there, too, talking to Ernst, and the chief stood in the shadows looking at her phone. Carlos and Doug wiped down the table as Trinidad closed the coolers and Quinn hauled them back to his truck.

Diego was once again typing at a furious pace. "That's one hundred sixty-two paid ice creams and one freebie for Felice, a total of two hundred fifty napkins, and two hundred ten spoons, which means some cheapskates must have split a dessert."

"Look on the bright side, maybe they enjoyed it so much they'll visit the Shimmy."

"Moguls don't look on the bright side," Diego said. "Don't you want to be rich?"

"I'd settle for solvent."

Bonnie, Juliette, and Gretchen began to carry leftovers back to the kitchen. Trinidad watched Diego enter a few more items into his spreadsheet. The document reflected in his glasses as he typed information into tiny cells.

The way he arched his fingers over the clacking keys…

Something stirred in her brain.

The judge's letter materialized in her memory. No capitals, no apostrophes. She looked closer at Diego, the easy tapping as he entered data. She stood behind him watching each finger hit certain prescribed keys.

A bomb exploded in her mind. She went breathless.

She knew.

She knew who'd concocted the letter, murdered Cherry Lighter, killed Forge Emberly. The revelation rooted her to the spot.

Quinn laid a hand on her shoulder and she screamed.

"What?" he said, wide-eyed.

"I think," she said slowly, "I think I just solved a murder... or two."

He searched her face for a moment, and then he took her hand and led her to find Chief Bigley.

Chapter Twenty-Two

THE CHIEF LISTENED. THEN SHE made a call. "All right," she said when she clicked off the phone. "Let's go find out if you're right. Your conclusion lines up with all of our evidence so far." She arched a brow. "Amateur sleuths are a pain in the neck, but if you got this right I'll treat you and Papa to the best Cuban restaurant I can find."

Papa shrugged. "No offense, but my cooking is better than anything you could pay for."

The chief didn't comment on Papa's hubris. She might not have even been listening. She had on her game face.

Trinidad followed the chief, reluctant to let go of Quinn's hand. Elephants were stampeding through her stomach. The smell of sausage in the air made her queasy. It was always so neat and tidy in mystery novels, the accusation part. None of the heroines she'd ever read about had ever been close to upchucking.

"I'll be right here," Quinn said, stopping outside the kitchen when the chief gestured for them not to enter. "With Papa."

Papa nodded. They looked good together, standing

shoulder to shoulder, she thought. But shivers had started up her spine. It was all she could do to force herself to follow the chief into the kitchen.

Bonnie was wrapping the leftover sausages in foil, handing the empty platters to Gretchen who dunked them into the soapy sink. A typed menu for the next day lay on the table, all caps, almost like shouting, Trinidad thought. And now the clues were shouting for sure.

Bonnie's remark replayed in her memory. *Atrocious handwriting.*

"Oh, hi, Trinidad, Chief," Bonnie said. "Did you want more to eat? I wrapped a plate for Officer Chang. He called to see if there were leftovers."

"No, thank you on the food," Bigley said. "We need to talk to Gretchen."

Gretchen turned and stood motionless, rubber gloves funneling water down her arthritic pinkies onto the floor.

"I have dishes to do," she said. "And I want to get home to Alexander."

The chief didn't answer. Gretchen took in her stony expression.

Juliette clutched a box of tinfoil, staring between Gretchen and the chief. Slowly, she sidled closer to Bonnie and put an arm around her waist. Everyone seemed to be holding their breath.

Gretchen stripped off the gloves, gathering them both in one hand. Her eyes burned, defiant. "Ask your question."

"All right," Bigley said. "Gretchen, did you kill Cherry Lighter?"

Bonnie dropped her panful of sauerkraut. "Oh gosh. Sorry…" She scurried to get a roll of paper towels to scoop up the ruined food. Juliette just stood there as if transfixed. Trinidad, too, was rooted to the spot.

"Isn't it enough that you're trying to ruin my brother's life?" Gretchen said. "Now you have to go after me too?"

"The question stands. Did you kill her?"

"Why would you think so?"

"I didn't. Trinidad did. The typed note to the judge, the one that was supposedly from Cherry. It was missing capitals and periods." The chief picked up one of the old typed menus piled in the recycling bin. "I notice you use all caps now. Easier, huh? When you typed Cherry's letter you hadn't yet developed that habit."

Gretchen looked from the chief to Trinidad. "I didn't type that letter."

"I think you did," the chief said.

"Wild theories, nothing in the way of proof."

"I'll know more after Officer Chang confiscates the type-writer at your cabin. I'm sure you destroyed the original letter by now, but we've got a copy. And I have a dinner out riding on the fact that you were driving the judge's car and you arranged to have it repaired without his knowledge after you ran Cherry over." She cocked her head. "Or, maybe, your brother killed Cherry and you're covering for him."

Gretchen lifted her chin and moved ever so slightly as if she might try to run for the door. Her eyes flicked to the set of chef's knives in the block on the counter.

Trinidad felt frozen with panic, but the chief must have

noticed the tell, too, because she eased closer and laid a hand casually on her holster. "Nowhere to run, Gretchen."

Gretchen flicked another panicked glance around the room and then she sagged. "Okay. You want to know so badly. I'll tell you. This has nothing to do with my brother, so you can leave him out of it. I killed her."

Trinidad felt as if her legs would give out. She'd been right. Gretchen. The woman with the killer scones was an actual killer.

"And I buried her under the tree thirty years ago," Gretchen added. "My brother doesn't know a thing. He thinks she really did run off."

The chief remained impassive. Trinidad was not sure how. She was certain her own eyeballs were popping out like a Kermit the Frog puppet.

"Why and how?" the chief said.

"It was an accident. I was driving Alexander's Mustang, coming home late one night. I didn't see Cherry walking in the dark, and I ran into her and killed her. I knew it would devastate him. I panicked and called Zap. He'd done some bodywork for my car in the past. I offered him five thousand dollars to fix Alexander's car and help me bury Cherry. He agreed. He said she was already dead, so what was the harm?"

Smiling, easygoing Zap.

"He took her purse and belongings and disposed of them," Gretchen said.

Except for the key chain and maybe the barrette. The barrette might have fallen to the floor of Zap's tow truck until he'd cleaned out the junk, and from there, it had landed in Lydia's shop. But the key chain...Zap had a collection, and he'd added Cherry's right in. Evidence hanging in his rear-view mirror the whole time. How could he live with himself?

His justification was simple. He hadn't killed her. She was already dead.

Trinidad remembered his phone conversation. "That's why Zap was trying to cut the trees himself. He figured he could do it without unearthing her remains."

Gretchen's mouth tightened. "Not out of the goodness of his heart. I've been paying him for his silence for thirty years. He is an idiot. I knew he couldn't take those trees down without someone finding Cherry's body."

"So you drugged him," Bigley said. "Figuring he would crash on the steep part of Linger Longer Road."

Trinidad could hardly keep up with the widening scope. Cherry's murder, now Zap's attempted murder...

"Yes," she said simply. "Alex has sleep problems, so the doctor gave him pills. I added them to the thermos in Zap's tow truck."

Juliette was standing now, the paper towel dangling from her fingertips, mouth open.

"Gretchen..." Bonnie whispered.

Gretchen ignored Bonnie. "How did you figure it out?"

Bigley arched an eyebrow at Trinidad.

"Your fingers," Trinidad managed. "The pinkies are very arthritic and have been for a long time, you told me. When you typed the note that was supposed to be from Cherry, you didn't use the shift or apostrophes because your pinkies were stiff. I imagined that's worsened over the years, which is why you used all cap on the Station menus. No shift key and such required. Easier on the pinkies."

Gretchen stared at her, steely and unyielding.

"Incredible," Juliette said, eyes wide as quarters.

The chief's tone was still measured and calm. "All right. Let's back up some more. What about Forge? He was going to cut those trees and unearth Cherry, so you had to stop him."

"Greedy fool. After the yodel fest he set off to explore the trees. I saw him carving into them, lost in thought. There was no way he could run his tracks without exposing Cherry's remains. I hit him with a shovel and wiped off the prints with a cloth in my pocket. I didn't want to bring police attention to the spot, but he was so heavy. I saw Felice's wagon, so I hauled him in, covered him with my apron, and rolled him back."

Bonnie turned a faint shade of green. Trinidad knew Felice would be getting a new wagon in the near future.

"I was going to put him in my car to dispose of," Gretchen said, "but someone was coming, and I panicked and tumbled him in an open trunk."

"Papa's," Trinidad said.

"I almost gave up, he was so heavy, but I knew what would happen if he was found on the property."

"Then you called Zap?" the chief asked.

"He's guilty. He knew what happened to Cherry, and he covered it up all these years. If I went down for Cherry's murder, he would go to jail as an accomplice. He had to help me."

The chief nodded. "So you sent him to Trinidad's place to retrieve Forge from the trunk."

She stripped off her apron. "I've said enough. Let's get this over with."

"All right," Bigley said. "We'll walk out to my car." She snapped handcuffs on Gretchen's wrists.

As Gretchen passed, she looked at Trinidad. Another piece fell into place. "You shoved me to take the letter because you didn't want the Cherry thing to get stirred up again."

"I heard him on the phone talking to you. I'm not sorry. Cherry was going to ruin him. I was protecting my brother's reputation, and I'd do it again."

"Well he's going to have the reputation of being a murderer's brother now," the chief said, leading Gretchen out.

And then they were gone.

Trinidad, Bonnie, and Juliette stared at each other.

Bonnie wrapped her arms around herself. "I employed a murderer."

Trinidad nodded. "But you didn't know. None of us did."

Bonnie bit her lip. "At least it's over."

Juliette looked at Trinidad, who was suddenly covered in goose bumps. "Isn't it?"

"I don't know." Trinidad bit her lip. "I have this weird feeling we didn't get the whole story."

Bonnie was silent a moment. "My cook killed two people and tried to murder a third," Bonnie said, tears starting to leak from her eyes. "That's all the story I can stand."

"But you did it again, Trinidad," Juliette said. "You solved two murders."

"So why do I feel like crying?"

The three women embraced, absorbing the shock together.

Another murderer in Sprocket.

Another criminal on their way to jail.

But plenty of wreckage left in their wake.

———

The following evening Trinidad, Doug and Quinn, and Papa were sitting at a table, chatting about the next phase of the greenhouse construction. There was a forced quality to the chatter, as if they were all trying desperately to keep the conversation away from Gretchen's confession. The arrest rocked the town, and everyone coming to the Shimmy had wanted to talk about it.

At one point she'd felt close to tears until Diego announced loudly, "Hey, Ms. Jones doesn't want to talk about it. Are you here to order ice cream or not?"

His statement wasn't tactful, but she loved him for it, anyway. There had been no judge sightings by anyone, it seemed. She couldn't imagine how he must be coping with the twin tragedies: Cherry's murder and learning that his sister was the killer who'd deceived him for three decades.

There was a knock on the door.

"I got it, Noodles." Quinn opened it for Chief Bigley before the dog could.

"Evening all," she said. "Got time for a chat?"

"Of course, please come in," Trinidad said, but there was something about the chief's presence that made her nerves tighten. They'd put away a murderer. What else could possibly be left?

"I wanted to thank you for your help," Bigley said, "And tell you the rest of the story about Gretchen's confession."

Trinidad sat up. "What rest of the story?"

"There's more?" Papa asked.

Bigley drummed her fingers on the tabletop. "There sure is. I kept thinking something was missing. Gretchen spooled out the story a little too easily, as if she was eager to do it, yet she couldn't explain why she was driving her brother's car the night she supposedly killed Cherry. A piece didn't ring true about it."

"That's what I thought," Trinidad said.

"Well, we caught a break because Zap woke up," the chief announced.

Trinidad's heart jumped. "Is he going to be okay?"

"He'll get good medical treatment in jail, so I imagine he'll recover well enough. He told us a few important details that Gretchen left out."

"Such as?" Quinn said.

"Such as Gretchen wasn't driving the car when Cherry died. The judge was."

Trinidad jerked as if she'd been electrocuted. "Wait a minute. The *judge* was driving?"

Quinn looked just as baffled as she felt. "And he lied? All this time?"

"I can't believe it." Trinidad had been so sure his confusion about what had happened was real. The pain of betrayal, the unrequited love, all fake. *Some judge of character, Trin.*

"That's the bizarre part," Bigley said. "The judge was driving, but he doesn't remember it."

Now they were all open-mouthed.

"Zap's information filled in the blanks. The judge and Cherry were celebrating their one-year anniversary of dating, and they'd been drinking heavily. They hit a tree. Cherry was ejected and likely died on impact. Alex passed out. When her brother didn't come home, Gretchen went looking and found them, took her inebriated brother back to his room, and tucked him in to sleep off the alcohol. The rest of the story holds true about contacting Zap and burying Cherry. Gretchen slipped her dear brother a tranquilizer the next day to give Zap time to complete the repairs on the Mustang and return it. By the time he awoke from his "hangover" the car was fixed, and Cherry was buried. All Gretchen had to do was type up the letter and convince the judge she took off."

A crush of sadness overtook Trinidad. "The judge actually was responsible for Cherry's death and all these years he never knew it."

Bigley nodded. "Gretchen was protecting him and his career."

Trinidad thought back to her conversation with Gretchen the night she returned the judge home. *Behind every successful man is a strong woman.* Strong, but not every woman was so ruthless. Gretchen killed Forge and almost caused Zap's death too. How could she have watched her brother suffer for decades, wondering why Cherry left him? But perhaps that was kinder than him finding out that he was guilty of her death.

"What will happen now? To the judge?" Papa asked.

"He'll face manslaughter charges, but my guess is nothing will stick due to the circumstances. I would think having a sister commit murder for you is not going to help his chances at that appellate court appointment, though."

Trinidad was swallowed up by a wave of sadness. Justice was satisfying, but it came with a consequence of so much pain for so many. She let out a long slow breath before she got up and put on her apron. The urge to concoct something sweet to drive away the bitter truths was overwhelming.

"What are you doing?" Papa asked.

"Suddenly I feel like consoling myself with a giant bowl of ice cream with a puddle of chocolate sauce and maybe a cherry or two."

"An excellent idea," Papa said. "Will you stay to join us, Chief?"

"You know, since I missed my crème brûlée this week, I think I will."

"Sounds like a good way to put things to rest to me," Quinn said. "I'm in."

But things would never be at rest for Alexander Torpine, she thought. And he wouldn't have his sister to help him through it.

Pushing the thought aside, she headed for the ice cream.

———

Orwell pushed open the door of the Shimmy, shortly before four o'clock the next day. His backpack appeared heavier than usual, stuffed to plumpness and sagging on his hip. "Big doings at the sausage roast, huh? I heard Gretchen Torpine was arrested for murder."

"Yeah, and we were there when it happened," Carlos said with zeal. "We saw the chief put her in the car and everything."

"Too bad we weren't in on the final confrontation," Diego said, shooting a disgruntled look in Trinidad's direction. "But at least I got my computer back. I'm going to write an article about it for the school newspaper."

Orwell gave him a thumbs-up. "Right on, kid. I'm leaving town, but I figured I'd stop in for one more of those Freakshakes." A look of hope bloomed on his face. "Any chance I can get one on the house?"

"Sure," Trinidad snapped, "as soon as I see a copy of the article you've been promising."

He squirmed. "Uh, about that."

"Yes, about that." She waited, but he seemed to have run out of words. "You're not really a reporter, are you?"

"Uh, no, actually. How did you figure it out?"

Diego eyed him with a hostile stare. "Because I got my computer back from the chief and we did a search. I wanted to be prepared when the article came out to snag it for the Shimmy's website, but what do you know? There is no *Go West* magazine, and there's only one reporter named Orwell; and she's a hot, twenty-eight-year-old weather forecaster."

"Yeah," he sighed dreamily. "She is hot. You should see her talk about low pressure systems." He lifted a shoulder. "Her name popped into my head, so I used it."

Carlos joined his brother in the hostile staring. "You

certainly had us going for a while there. The truth, dude. Who are you?"

"My name is Tom Jefferson."

Carlos snorted. "You gotta be kidding me. That's the dumbest alias ever."

"It's not an alias. My father was a history professor. That's why I go by T. J. The Orwell I got from the hot weather girl."

Diego elbowed Carlos. "That's too ridiculous to make up. I think he's telling the truth."

Carlos snorted. "Seriously? Well, anyway, why are you pretending to be a reporter? Grilling Miss Jones and Mayor Hardwick and everyone?"

"Grilling them but soft pedaling the judge," Trinidad added, "and don't tell me it's because you're afraid you'll be hauled in front of him someday. The truth. Out with it."

He rubbed a hand over the back of his neck. "Actually, I worked for the judge...until it came out he was guilty of man-slaughter and didn't know it, that is. Probably never going to get my paycheck, now, with the mess he's got to sort out."

Trinidad didn't bother to hide her surprise. After all that had happened recently, the effort to put up a facade was just too much. "Worked for the judge how?"

"Private detective."

"Cool," both boys enthused.

"Who were you investigating?" Trinidad asked.

"Ramona Hardwick. The judge was considering dating her, but he got a bunch of angry earfuls from his sister about her alleged misuse of office, so he figured he'd find out for sure before he dove into the relationship waters."

A careful man. Had he become that way since, deep down, he knew with some part of his soul that carelessness had cost him the love of his life? Or perhaps he was reluctant to give his heart away again because he believed Cherry had abandoned him.

"And is she dirty?" Carlos said, eyes snapping with excitement. "Is she a crooked mayor?"

"Don't say another word," Trinidad said, smacking her towel on the counter. "If you've got proof, take it to the chief. Otherwise, zip it and go play detective somewhere else."

All three looked at her.

She would not explain her passionate remark. The turbulence from Cherry's death would sweep through many lives. Ramona was going to watch the man she loved come to grips with the fact that he'd killed his girlfriend. She would likely never have a real shot at the judge's heart because it belonged to a dead woman. And Zap, if he recovered, would go to prison for helping Gretchen hide Cherry's body, for depriving the judge of the truth and Cherry's mother of her child, and for disposing of Forge's body. Gretchen would know that she'd ruined her brother's chance at appellate court, the reason she'd buried Cherry and murdered Forge in the first place.

There were no winners. And it was not the time to drag a political scandal into the mix. That would have to wait.

"So what are you going to do now?" Diego was still eyeing Orwell with unabashed curiosity.

He shrugged. "Go back to the office and wait for the phone to ring." He winked. "Maybe I'll tip off a reporter buddy of mine to come to Upper Sprocket. This place is a hotbed of intrigue."

Trinidad resisted the urge to throw a towel at him as he left, without any freebies this time.

"Aww man," Carlos said. "I thought we were gonna get the Shimmy in a magazine."

She handed him a broom. "We're going to have to get our publicity the old-fashioned way."

Diego laughed until she thrust the dustpan at him. He sighed. "At least I got my computer back. Maybe I can write an article about the Shimmy."

The Alpenfest visitors had mostly left town, but Mr. Mavis came by for his scoop of banana ice cream and several high schoolers arrived after their cross-country competition. Noodles greeted everyone with a tail wag in between grooming sessions with Betty.

Quinn came in after the high schoolers amid their ice cream and chatter. He was edgy and tense. Doug sat at a table on the side porch, catching the afternoon sunshine. Quinn asked for a triple chocolate chunk scoop and a bowl of vanilla ice cream.

"Good news," he said, as she scooped up his order. "Lydia isn't going to complete the cut-through for the second rail-riders route. With Zap going to jail, she said it will be all she can do to keep one route in service. I returned the money, and the land is mine again."

"That's amazing," she said.

He didn't answer, sneaking nervous glances at Doug on the patio.

Trinidad wanted to grab his hand and squeeze, to reassure him that the meeting would go well, but it might just as easily be completely disastrous. "How did Doug take it when you told him the truth about your mother?"

Quinn gripped the cup of ice cream like it was the last flotation device on the sinking *Titanic*. "He listened while I talked—babbled, really. And he only asked one question... 'Why?'"

Her heart squeezed.

"I'm not sure if he wants to know why I lied or why she left, but..." He stopped, his spoon falling to the floor. Out the window, she followed his gaze and saw Glenda approach, dressed in worn jeans, a bulky sweater wrapped around her. Her hair was neatly combed this time, a soft cloud around her face.

She heard Quinn's panicked gulp.

"I'll be right here if you need me," she said softly, supplying him with a clean spoon.

He leaned over and kissed her. Then he straightened his shoulders and marched outside. Heart in her throat, she watched out the window. Quinn slid into the seat next to Doug who was staring at his ice cream.

Trinidad could not hear a word, but she watched the body language with bated breath.

Doug remained staring at his ice cream. Glenda stood a few feet from the table, arms hugging her sweater close.

Quinn pushed out a chair for her, and she sat, not exactly at the table, more like a bystander who'd stopped in to inquire about the weather, slightly apart but worlds away.

Doug flicked a quick glance at her over the top of his glasses and then back to his ice cream.

After they'd sat a while, Glenda reached a hand out and laid it on the tabletop. Trinidad's heart pounded. Doug stared at his ice cream, but he could not miss his mother's hand there, a tremulous invitation.

So quickly she almost missed it, Doug reached out a fingertip to the back of her hand. The touch lingered for no more than two seconds, then he pulled away and started to spoon up his ice cream as if she wasn't there.

She could see in Quinn's posture and Glenda's that a wall had been penetrated, a tiny hole maybe, but enough for a small ray of light to shine through.

It was a start, she thought, eyes misty. When Quinn looked at her through the plate glass window, she thought his eyes were damp too.

Murders aside, things in Sprocket might finally be turning in the right direction.

She heaved a deep breath. Sprocket had started out as Gabe's hometown, but it was hers now. She could feel herself beginning to take root in this odd place, both in the bright sunny spots and the darker ones. Light and dark, bitter and sweet. She'd had the sunny summer months, and now it was time to experience the cold.

Bring it on, winter, she thought. *I'm ready for you.*

Trinidad's Browned Butter Apple Bar Recipe

1½ cups butter

2 cups flour

1 teaspoon baking powder

1 teaspoon cinnamon

¼ teaspoon salt

1 cup granulated sugar

1 cup packed dark brown sugar

2 eggs

¼ teaspoon vanilla

3 medium apples (Pink Ladies or Gala work well), peeled, cored, and diced

Melt the butter in a skillet over medium heat until light brown, then pour into a large bowl and let cool for 30 minutes.

Preheat oven to 350°F. Grease a 9- x 13-inch baking dish.

Whisk the flour, baking powder, cinnamon, and salt in a bowl.

In the other bowl, with the cooled melted butter, add the sugars, eggs, and vanilla and beat until smooth.

Beat in the flour mixture until well combined. Fold in the apples and spread into the baking dish.

Bake for 45 minutes or until cooked through.

Cheery Cherry "Do-it-Yourself" Pickle Jar Ice Cream

This works best in a clean, 16-ounce-or-larger pickle or jelly jar. It's a fun activity for kids and adults alike!

> 1 cup whipping cream
> 3 tablespoons maraschino cherry juice
> 2 tablespoons sugar
> ½ teaspoon vanilla
> 1 pinch salt
> *Optional add-ins: ¼ cup of finely chopped maraschino cherries, 2 tablespoons chocolate sprinkles

Pour all of the ingredients into the jar except the optional add-ins. Close the lid tightly and shake for five minutes. (Recruit help if your arms get tired!)

Put the jar into the freezer and let sit for two hours.

Add your mix-ins to the jar, if you'd like. Stir the mixture around if it has gotten too solid.

Freeze for another hour until you've reached the desired consistency.

Check out Trinidad's first sweet mystery in
PINT OF NO RETURN

Chapter One

IT WAS AN ABSOLUTE MONSTER.

Trinidad Jones rubbed at a sticky splotch on her apron and slid her offering across the pink, flecked Formica counter. The decadent milkshake glittered under the Shimmy and Shake Shop's fluorescent bulbs, from the glorious crown of brûléed marshmallow down to the candy-splattered ganache coating the outer rim and the frosted glass through which peeked the red and white striped milkshake itself. Her own reflection stared back at her, hair frizzed, round cheeks flushed. Something this decadent just had to be a crime. "What should I call it?"

Trinidad's freshly minted employees, twins Carlos and Diego Martin, were transfixed, eyes lit with the enthusiasm only fifteen-year-old boys with bottomless appetites could attain. They might have been staring at a newly landed spaceship for all the wonder in their long-lashed brown gazes. She still wasn't entirely sure which twin was which, but they were doing a bang-up job helping her ready the shop for its launch in a scant seven days' time.

Noodles, her faithful Labrador, cocked his graying head from his cushion near the front door and swiped a fleshy tongue over his lips, which she took as approval. He had already been consulted on a pup-friendly shake she'd dubbed the Chilly Dog, determining it to be more than passable.

Noodles was an encouraging sort, which made Trinidad doubly glad she'd decided to adopt a senior citizen companion six months earlier instead of a younger pup. Besides, he had a wealth of skills she was still discovering.

Carlos whistled, running a hand through his spiky hair, sending it into further disarray. "It's like a Fourth of July Freakshake." He gripped the pink-coated paint roller he was holding as if it was a Roman spear. "Like, an eighth wonder of the world or something. You should put a sparkler on the top, you know, for the holiday. People would dig that."

Diego shook his head. "Bad move. Those things can burn at two thousand degrees Fahrenheit, depending on the fuel and oxidizer. Of course, temperature is not the same as thermal energy, which is going to relate to the mass, so…"

"Dude," Carlos said, punching his brother's arm. "You're such a dweeb. I mean, turn off your bloated brain and just admire it, wouldja?"

Diego ceased his impromptu physics lecture to join his brother in their mutual appreciation fest. He pulled a clunky video camera from his backpack, and his twin immediately grabbed a spoon and began speaking into it as if it was a microphone.

"This is Carlos Martin reporting live from the Shimmy and Shake Shop where an ice cream phenomenon is about to be revealed to the world," he pronounced in a booming baritone.

Trinidad laughed. "I didn't think people used video cameras anymore."

Carlos grinned. "They don't. We saw it at the flea market

for two bucks along with a bunch of old history stuff and home videos no one will ever watch. We just thought it'd be fun to mess around with it since Diego wants to be a news reporter someday."

"And a physicist," his brother added.

"It's good to have goals," Trinidad said. "So, the shake gets a thumbs-up from the news crew, then? We'll skip the sparklers and call it the Fourth of July Freakshake. What do you think about adding a hunk of a red, white, and blue nutty brownie star in the marshmallow?"

Diego smirked at her. "Is adding brownies a bad thing, like…ever?"

All three of them considered.

"Point taken," Trinidad said. "I'll bake them when I get back from my errands and freeze them for the opening. I have to run to the storage unit and pick up a few final things. Go ahead and lock up the shop if I'm not back when you finish for today, okay?" She knew Carlos had afternoon football practice, and they'd chatted about doing some additional odd jobs around town in their effort to bankroll a used Plymouth while they were both studying up for their driving permits. She eyed the fresh coat of pink paint the boys had been applying to the walls. "Looks like you're almost done."

Diego pointed to the longest wall. "We calculated the volume of paint just right, considering we had to apply a third coat. Weird how your husband's name keeps showing through. Reminds me of a horror movie I watched, like he's rematerializing in town again since all his ex-wives are living here now…" Carlos broke off as his brother elbowed him in the ribs.

"Ex-husband," she said, "and that would be a good trick for him to rematerialize himself out of jail." She swallowed down a lick of something that was part shame, part anger, as she considered the spot where "Gabe's Hot Dogs" was once emblazoned in blocky letters. Moving to the tiny eastern Oregon town of Upper Sprocket, hometown of her cheating ex-husband Gabe Bigley and his two other ex-wives, was her most mortifying life decision to date. At age thirty-six, she should have been settled, married, and raising a family, not jumping into a highly risky entrepreneurial endeavor in her ex-husband's hometown, no less. Funny how pride took a back seat to survival. The faster her money ran out, the more palatable the notion of taking over the building Gabe had deeded her on his way to jail became.

Her grandfather, Papa Luis, used every derogatory word in his Cuban Spanish arsenal to convince her that Gabe "The Hooligan" Bigley should be obliterated from her mind and that moving back to Miami with him and her mother was the prudent choice. He was probably correct, but here she was in Sprocket anyway.

Now "Gabe's Hot Dogs," a store Gabe had never actually helped run, was being reborn as the Shimmy and Shake Shop, and it was going to be the most successful establishment in the entire Pacific Northwest if it killed her. Upon arrival in Sprocket, she knew the small town tucked in the mountainous corner of eastern Oregon would be the perfect home for her shop. A gorgeous alpine backdrop, sweeping acres of fields, a constant stream of tourists arriving to witness the wonder of Hells Canyon and participate in various festivals... It could not fail. Especially since it wasn't a paltry run-of-the-mill ice cream parlor. Shimmy's would specialize in extravagant, over-the-top shakes that would take Sprocket and the dessert-loving world by storm. Unless it had all been a massive mental misfire on her part. She swallowed a surge of terror.

Noodles shook himself, his collar jingling in what had to be a show of support. He gingerly pulled a tissue from the box on the counter and presented it to her, a throwback to his service dog training. "It's okay," she said, giving the dog a pat. "No tears right now." She realized both boys were staring at her.

"That's an awesome dog," Diego said.

She nodded her agreement.

"Um, sorry, Miss Jones," Carlos said. "Mom said we weren't supposed to mention anything about, I mean, you know, your ex or the other exes or…uh…" His face squinched in embarrassment.

"No worries. I know the situation is a bit unorthodox." And delicious fodder for the local gossips. Somehow, she'd managed to be in town for six weeks and had not yet run into Juliette or Bonnie, Gabe's two other ex-wives, the ones she'd had no clue about until her life fell apart, but it was only a matter of time before their inevitable meeting; her own rented residence was only a short distance from Bonnie's property. She put Carlos out of his misery with a bright smile. "You didn't do anything wrong. It's a weird situation."

"Downright freaky," Carlos said, earning another elbow from his twin.

"Right. Well, I'll just go see to those errands." On the way to the door, Noodles stretched his stiff rear legs in the ultimate downward dog yoga pose and trotted after her.

"By the way, boys," Trinidad called over her shoulder. "I left two spoons on the counter. Someone has to taste test the Fourth of July Freakshake, right?" The door closed on the boys' enthusiastic whoops. She chuckled. There should be some perks to a job that only paid minimum wage and took up plenty of precious hours of summer vacation. If only she could pay them entirely in ice cream.

On the way to her car, she admired the whimsical pink and pearl gray striping on the front of her squat, one-story shop. The awning the three of them had painstakingly put up would keep off the summer sun, and some artfully arranged potted shrubs enclosed a makeshift patio with a half dozen small tables. Noodles had already staked out a location in the coolest corner as a designated napping area. She plodded down the block to spot where she'd parked the Pinto beneath the shade of a sprawling elm. What she wouldn't give to rest her aching feet. The doctor reminded her with ruthless regularity that losing thirty or so pounds would help her complaining metatarsals. Probably a nice vacation to Tahiti would do the same, but it was just as unlikely to happen. Her metatarsals would have to buck up and quit their bellyaching.

Trinidad regarded the shady main drag. Working from sunup to well past dark on a daily basis, she hadn't had nearly enough time to explore the charms of Upper Sprocket.

Somehow the quirky name suited the town settled firmly in the shadow of the mountains, with old trees lining the streets and people who still waved hello as they drove by. Five hours east of Portland, surrounded on three sides by the Wallowa Mountains, Sprocket was plopped at the edge of a sparkling green valley, with soaring peaks as a backdrop and air so clean it almost hurt to breathe it. The mountains were considered the "Swiss Alps of Oregon," and the nearest neighbor, Josef, hosted numerous events like the popular Alpenfest fall bash. Visitors had opportunities to take the Wallowa Lake Tramway to the top of Mount Howard—3,700 feet of eye-popping splendor. The multitude of outdoorsy activities and sheer loveliness brought plenty of visitors to the larger towns, and Sprocket, though more out of the way and shabbier than chic, pulled in its share of tourists too. Enough to keep Trinidad scooping ice cream in the warm weather months. Winter would be another challenge.

"One season at a time," she told herself. She passed a trailer and exchanged a friendly smile with the driver. The RV was one of many in town to enjoy the upcoming celebration. There would be plenty to do before the Fourth of July. Sprocket featured its very own lake, an annual apple festival, and even a third-generation popcorn stand that was a favorite of snackers far and wide. She'd also heard tell of hot springs in the area, though she'd not yet clapped eyes on them. It amazed her how much sunnier this little town was compared to her previous home in Portland with Gabe.

Her spirits edged up a notch. Sunshine, a fresh start, and a darling shop all her own. Rolling down the window, she let the air billow in, bringing with it the scent of dry grass and sunbaked road. On the way, she ticked off the items she needed to retrieve from her storage unit—something she hadn't yet had the time to tackle. There were three more plastic patio chairs she'd have the twins spray-paint a subtle shade of gray to offset the pink theme and her prized antique cookie cutter collection, passed down from her mother who had never so much as laid a finger on them.

Cruising away from the town's main street, she waved to the gas station owner who'd erected a card table on the sidewalk with a cooler on top and a scrawled sign that read Bait worms, five dollars/pint. As she drove along, she wondered exactly how many worms one got in a pint. The turn onto Little Bit Road took her to what passed for Sprocket's industrial center. It was comprised of an aged feed and grain store, a weedy property that used to be an air strip, and the Store Some More facility, a set of tidy white buildings with shiny metal corrugated doors. One lone tree in the lot next to the structure offered a paltry speck of shade and, nestled underneath, was a bird bath where a small brown wren was splashing with gusto. Parking the Pinto by the closest unit, she pulled out her key and unlatched the padlock that secured her space. The same young man who'd helped her sign the rental papers when she moved in was sweeping the walkway in front of the empty unit next to hers.

She waved. "Hi, Vince. Just back for a few supplies."

He nodded, hiking up the jeans that hung loose on his skinny frame. He was probably in his early twenties, by the look of him, a cell phone poking from his back pocket.

A woman with long blond hair stepped out of the office

and pulled his attention. She held a bucket. "Call for you, Vince. Your mom needs you to deliver a half dozen pepperonis and two veggie combos."

Trinidad felt her pulse thump. Everything about the woman was long and lean, including the delicate gold earrings that gleamed against the backdrop of her hair. She appeared to do a double take as she spotted Trinidad. After a pause, she walked over. "I'm Juliette Carpenter. Formerly..."

"Juliette Bigley," Trinidad filled in. She'd known that Juliette owned the storage place, but she didn't imagine the woman was engaged in the day-to-day running of it. She'd only ever dealt with Vince. The hour had arrived. She could practically hear the bells tolling as she cleared her throat. "And it seems like you recognize me, too."

Juliette's face was seared into her memory even though she'd only spoken with her briefly at the trial where Gabe was found guilty of embezzling money from various companies as their accountant. It had been a tense conversation. After all, Gabe had still been married to Trinidad when he'd started the relationship with Juliette, and neither of them had suspected a thing. When Trinidad had discovered Gabe's cheating, and their divorce became official, it was followed quickly by Juliette's whirlwind marriage and divorce. Juliette had not even known of Trinidad and their defunct marriage until a few weeks after Gabe was arrested. He was an accomplished liar. The final shoe had dropped at the trial, when they had not only met each other but also learned of another wife, Bonnie, Gabe's first.

The turbulent storm of memories resurfaced as Trinidad stared at Juliette. She tried not to notice the generous five or ten years between their ages. *You're the older model. Gabe traded you in for one right off the assembly line.* How was it possible to feel old at the age of thirty-six? Trinidad cleared her throat.

"I rented one of your storage spaces. I'm…uh…opening a store in town."

"I heard. I meant to come by and reintroduce myself, but…"

But the whole situation was just *too* ridiculously awkward.

Juliette stared at the bucket, then continued. "I was, um, just filling the bird bath. It's been so dry this year. You wouldn't believe the animals that drink out of it: birds, deer, raccoons." Her stream of conversation dried up.

Trinidad was desperate to fill the silence. Noodles, perhaps picking up on her tension, nosed her thigh, leaving a wet circle on her jeans. "This is Noodles. He's very easygoing. His real name is Reginald, but the shelter workers named him Noodles since he has a thing for them. The noodles, I mean, not the shelter workers."

Noodles offered a hospitable tail wag. Juliette put down the bucket, crouched next to the old Lab and rubbed his ears. "Bet you would be a great watchdog. We could use one around here. More effective than the new padlocks I had installed, and way cuter, too."

The conversation sputtered again. Trinidad tried to think of something to say, but Juliette rose to her feet.

"Let's just clear the air here. This is strange, running into each other, but it shouldn't be. It's just…I thought you said during our talk at the trial that you didn't want anything to do with Sprocket."

Trinidad went cold with shame. "The truth is I had to swallow my pride and take what Gabe deeded me." She didn't add more humiliating details, that her stenographer work had all but dried up and she could no longer make the rent for the Portland apartment she'd shared with Gabe. "It was move to Gabe's hometown or return to my family home in Miami, and I really wanted to prove to myself that I could make it on my own." It was more than she'd meant to say.

Juliette's expression softened, and she surprised Trinidad by gently touching her shoulder. "Hey, I get it, believe me. Same reason I moved here last year. I figured Gabe owed me something, and he had signed over his storage unit business to me, the rat." She shrugged. "It was doing better than my hotel manager gig, so here I am. New life, fresh start, just like you."

Trinidad nodded. "And, besides, who wouldn't want to move to a charming town called Sprocket?"

Acknowledgments

In my imagination, the little town of Upper Sprocket is wonderfully vivid, every street and business colorfully etched in my mind. Unfortunately, you won't find it on any real world map. While Sprocket is purely fictional, there is actually a town called Joseph in Eastern Oregon, and they do host a wonderful Alpenfest event. What's more, this lovely place boasts the Joseph Branch Railriders, a business that allows visitors to ride the rails and experience amazing pedal-powered adventures. I owe Joseph Branch Railriders a hearty thank-you for patiently answering my questions. Further, in my quest to learn everything there is to know about monster milkshakes (Freakshakes), I was able to use a few mouthwatering ice cream photos in my YouTube video entitled Freakshakes Explained, with the permission of several restaurants across the country. These included Big D's Burgers (Whittier, California), Kuchie's on the Water (Creve Coeur, Illinois), and The Scoop Ice Cream Shop (Six Mile, South Carolina). I can only imagine how much courage and tenacity is required to keep an eatery running through these very trying times. Thank you for allowing me to use the photos, and many thanks for keeping all those good eats coming! As for my personal circle of supporters, you know who you are. Sisters; hubby; parents; in-laws; super agent, Jessica; amazing publicist, Mandy; faboo editor, MJ…you all help make those sticky words into a tantalizing package.

With hugs and gratitude, Dana

About the Author

Dana Mentink is a national, *Publishers Weekly,* and *USA Today* bestselling author. She has written more than forty mystery and suspense novels for various publishers and is the recipient of the HOLT Medallion and Romantic Times Reviewers' Choice Award. A Northern California native, Dana is married to Papa Bear and mother of two young-adult bear cubs, affection- ately nicknamed Yogi and Boo Boo.